Dale Mayer

SIMON SAYS...
WALK

A KATE MORGAN NOVEL

SIMON SAYS… WALK (KATE MORGAN, BOOK 6)
Beverly Dale Mayer
Valley Publishing Ltd.

ISBN-13: 978-1-773367-86-6
Print Edition

Books in This Series

The Kate Morgan Series

Simon Says… Hide, Book 1

Simon Says… Jump, Book 2

Simon Says… Ride, Book 3

Simon Says… Scream, Book 4

Simon Says… Run, Book 5

Simon Says… Walk, Book 6

Simon Says… Forgive, Book 7

About This Book

Detective Kate Morgan isn't impressed with her latest case. A terrorized woman walks into the police station, with a message for Kate. Actually a message that drags Simon into the middle of it—no, make that front and center. A challenge has been issued, one that Kate is determined to solve, hopefully keeping Simon on the sidelines.

Blindsided, Simon doesn't understand the message or the hate being directed his way. And the last thing he wants to do is revisit his past. Yet being in the middle of one of Kate's cases doesn't give him an option. If he can't get to the bottom of this, his life will be, once again, torn apart—all to appease a madman's new game.

But the answer, … when it comes, is closer to home than anyone realizes.

Sign up to be notified of all Dale's releases here!
https://geni.us/DaleNews

PROLOGUE

Last Week in September

WHEN KATE MORGAN walked into the station Monday morning, the sergeant looked at her and frowned.

"Thought you were taking a couple days off."

"I didn't ask ahead of time," she noted, "and I did take yesterday off, which I needed badly, but I wasn't sure about scheduling more."

"You've got a lot of hours piled up," Sergeant Colby told her. "So why don't you take a few days?"

"Maybe." She shrugged. "I could finish off a few things that I didn't quite get done on Saturday, then maybe work this week and plan on taking a long weekend—if that's okay with you?"

"It's fine by me," he said. "You're doing a great job, you know?"

She looked at him in surprise because words of praise were very scarce from him. "Thank you, sir," she replied.

She walked into the bullpen to the others standing up and cheering. "What's that for?" she asked, embarrassed by the attention.

"Well, we couldn't decide if we should say something, like *Good job* or *Cheers* or whatever," Lilliana explained. "But you know? You seem to have accepted some of Simon's work. Rodney told us all about it. He heard it from Simon apparently, about his visions that connected to you."

Kate winced at that. "I'm still not really comfortable with that whole thing."

"Another thing," Owen added, as he walked toward her and gave her a hug. "You took a hell of a beating on that hill, but you held your own. So, *Yay for still being alive*. Not to mention the fact that you closed the case on four murders, and you got it all done within eight days."

She smiled. "Thanks, guys. I have to admit it was pretty nice to have it come to an end, without anybody else dying. I mean, obviously Charlie died, and, for that, I'm sorry. However, if there had to be an ending, that's a good one to have, I guess. So, please tell me there are no new cases and that it'll be an easy week, and then I can take a long weekend."

They all burst out laughing. "We caught one last night," Lilliana said. "If you're up for it, we got a couple gang fights out in lower Hastings again."

She winced. "What is with that area?"

"Hey, it's just one of those tough areas of town."

"Knives, I suppose?"

"Yep, two sliced out, one dead."

She asked, "Open-and-shut?"

"Yep, sounds like it."

"Okay, perfect," she replied. "That sounds like the case I could use right now."

"Right," Rodney agreed, "and don't worry. There'll be another crazy one coming your way pretty damn soon. There's always somebody in the department who catches the weird and wild and wonderful."

She looked at him and asked, "Am I it then?"

"You so are." Rodney laughed.

Just then, the woman staffing the front reception desk walked in. Audrey, who was still here on a maternity leave coverage, announced, "We've got a woman in the front here who's looking to talk to Detective Kate Morgan."

Kate looked at her. "Why me?"

She shrugged. "She read your name in the paper."

"Oh God, no." Kate moaned. "The last thing I need is notoriety."

"Too late." Audrey gave her a bright, winning smile. "That horse has already left the gate, and you're not getting it back in again." She pointed behind her. "I put her into the first interview room. Don't take too long though. Looks like she might bolt." And, with that, Audrey left.

Kate turned and looked at the others, then saw the grins on their faces. "Did you guys set me up or something?"

"Hell no," Rodney stated, "but I'll come with you and talk to her, if you want."

"Yeah, sure, come on, partner. Let's go talk to her." She grabbed a pad of paper and a pen, then turned to look at the others. "I guess you'll have to handle that open-and-shut on your own."

"Yeah, I think we can manage that, if we need to," Owen teased. "Besides, this witness could be about nothing."

"We'll see." She walked toward the interview room and stepped inside to see a woman, her face and hands covered with scratches, looking like she'd been completely traumatized. Kate looked at Rodney with a shrug, then stepped farther inside, introduced herself. "Look. First of all, do you need a doctor?"

The woman gave her a haunted look. "No, I've just checked out of the hospital," she noted quietly.

"Okay then." Kate sat down and waited for the woman

to speak. As the woman nervously fidgeted, clenching and unclenching her scratched up hands, Kate finally spoke. "What can I do for you?"

"I'd like to report a kidnapping," she said.

"Okay, of whom?"

The woman looked up at her. "Me."

Kate leaned forward, so she was sure of what she heard. "You were kidnapped?"

She nodded.

"Do you know who kidnapped you?"

She shook her head. "No, but it was for a game."

At that, Kate froze. "What do you mean?"

"He kidnapped me, took away my shoes and socks, my pants and my shirt, and then said we would go outside, and he would have me walk—only to start and to stop whenever he would say so."

"What?"

She nodded. "I know. It doesn't sound normal. But I was blindfolded, and he would tell me to walk ten paces. So I'd walk ten paces, but I wouldn't know what I was walking into. Sometimes it would be into a thicket of berry brambles. Sometimes into a river. And one time"—she stopped, and her breath hitched and hiccupped—"one time, it was into a rocky riverbed." She started to cry. "And then, whenever I would fall or get hurt, he would laugh and laugh and laugh. Sometimes he'd make me do it again and again."

"And how did he force you?"

"He had guns, lots and lots of guns," she said. "At least what I first saw. Then I had the blindfold on, and I never saw anything else again."

"Okay, did you tell anybody this at the hospital?"

She shook her head. "No, he dropped me off there and

gave me a message."

"A message? So what was in this message?"

The woman held up a piece of paper for her. "I don't know what it means, but he told me to give it to you."

Kate carefully took the paper from her hand and read the message out loud, so Rodney heard. "*Kate, see if Simon can do this.*" She flipped the paper forward and backward and then looked over at the woman. "Does this message mean anything to you?"

The other woman shook her head, with tears in her eyes. "No, I don't know anything about it. I don't know who Simon is, and I don't know what he's supposed to do," she murmured. "But I think it has to do with the game because he used to laugh all the time. He said something about *Simon thinks he's so fucking good, but I don't think he's got answers for this.*"

"And do you know who this Simon guy is?" Kate asked, her heart sinking, as she shot a look at Rodney, who now sat beside her, studying the note in her hand.

"No, but he made it sound like it was an old friend. Yet I got the feeling that maybe it wasn't so much of a friend as an old enemy."

"An enemy might sound better," Kate noted, "or at least a frenemy, a friend that became an enemy."

"Maybe," the young woman agreed, as she wrapped her arms around her chest.

Kate looked at her and frowned. "Are you sure you shouldn't be in the hospital?"

"He didn't hurt me," she whispered. "At least not this time. He said, if I didn't deliver the message, he'd show up, standing at the end of my bed, and I would know it's time to start the game all over again."

Kate winced. "Well, I sure as hell hope not. I think you've been through enough."

She nodded. "He did say," she added, then stopped for a moment and took a deep breath, which caught in her throat, before she exhaled noisily. "He did say that he likes to keep his pets."

Kate stared at her in shock. "What pets?"

The young woman looked up and stared at her, tears in her eyes, then replied, "I think he meant *human* pets. You have to stop him. Before he comes after me, please, please stop him."

Kate looked over at the young woman, now sobbing quietly, then got up, wrapped her arms around her, and whispered, "I will, sweetie. I will." And she sure as hell hoped that she wasn't lying.

I'll need Simon on this one in a big way, she thought to herself. Unfortunately he didn't yet know that he would play an integral part in this investigation because it could be all about his life. She knew that wasn't something Simon would be okay with, but he had to be, this time, because lives were at stake.

CHAPTER 1

DETECTIVE KATE MORGAN dropped into the seat behind her desk.

Colby marched over and glowered at her. "Why is one of my detectives, plus my confidential psychic source, linked to a kidnapping?"

Kate shook her head. "We just got this dropped in our laps minutes ago, sir."

"Well, find out, damn it. You got twenty-four hours, before we turn this over to Missing Persons." Then Colby stormed off.

Kate sighed and stared at the note. Her mind raced to what lay ahead. *Simon will not be impressed.*

Almost as if reading her thoughts, Rodney said, "Simon will so not like this."

She winced and nodded. "We'll have to tear apart his private life."

"Yet ... we have no choice," Rodney noted.

She frowned at him, her lips twitching in a wry look. "Yeah, you want to be the one who tells Simon that?"

Rodney's grin flashed brightly, and, with a booming laugh, he gave her a snarky reply. "Hell no. That's your department."

The others on her team walked in then—minus Andy, who was off duty on medical leave—and all focused on Kate.

"How bad was it?" Lilliana asked, as she walked to her desk and picked up her empty coffee cup, as if intent on refilling it.

"It was bad," Rodney stated.

Owen shifted in his chair to look at both of them. "When you say *bad*, what does that look like?"

By way of explanation, Rodney handed him the note that the woman brought with her.

Owen read it out loud and then whistled, his gaze immediately jumping to Kate. "Good God, is this for real?"

Kate nodded. "You should have seen her. She was scratched up, bruised, in tears, … terrified. She looked as if she'd been to hell and back. And, Rodney, did you see how she limped out of here, seemingly on both feet? She could have more injuries that we just didn't see in the interview."

Rodney nodded, with a grimace.

Kate added, "I don't think she faked any of it."

"No, I don't think so either," Rodney murmured, as he sat nearby. "Whoever did this to her, either he did this with the full intention of Simon being brought into it …"

"Or hoping," Kate interrupted immediately, "that Simon would get brought into it."

"Probably more to the point," Owen cut in the two of them, "the kidnapper did this so that *he* would get brought into it."

She nodded. "Yeah, that sounds about right."

"Which also means that we have no choice but to bring Simon into it as well," Rodney stated, his gaze steady on Kate.

She groaned. "Which is the point that we were discussing. He … won't like this."

Rodney snorted. "None of us like it, and that woman

who just walked out of here, looking like a ghost, liked it even less."

Kate couldn't say a whole lot to that. She stared down at the note. "He gave the message to her so it'll have prints, but that doesn't mean that he didn't wear gloves or something else. He made it fairly clear to that woman—should she *not* deliver this message—she would wake up one night to find him standing at the end of her bed, ready to start the game all over again."

Lilliana slowly sank into her chair, glaring at Kate intently. "Maybe you should tell us what that game was."

Kate explained what the woman had told them.

Eyes wide, Lilliana whispered, "Seriously?"

"Yeah, she is," Kate confirmed carefully. "Relatively she's unhurt, in that it could have been so much worse physically."

"Of course." Lilliana seemed dazed, as she looked around. "What kind of insanity is this?"

"I'm thinking," Rodney suggested, "it's whatever insanity her kidnapper thought would bring Simon into his orbit."

"Meaning, the kidnapper can't bring Simon into his orbit, won't bring him into his orbit, or, no matter what he does, it doesn't end up with Simon in his orbit, so he's doing something drastic, somehow knowing," Kate theorized, "that Simon's in my world and has been helping out on some of these cases."

The note was passed around from person to person on the team, as each studied it carefully, already in a plastic bag, knowing that any forensic evidence needed to be preserved.

"Remember what I just said about another psycho coming out of the woodwork?" Lilliana murmured. "Because it does seem as if we do get a regular run of people who have a weird idea of what proper and normal behavior is," she explained, looking over at the others. "In this case, somebody's … determined to involve Simon."

"And you also know that there is no way we *cannot* involve him," Owen acknowledged from the side. "He's got to be involved."

She stared down at her phone, as if it would reach out and bite her.

Rodney watched her hesitate and offered, "You want me to call him?"

Startled, she looked up and shook her head. "That won't help much," she pointed out. "He'll want to know why I didn't do the phoning."

Rodney grinned at her. "Hey, I would have said the same thing." He now chuckled. "I'm just telling you that you're not alone."

She smiled, for the first time in a long time realizing that she really wasn't alone anymore. Somehow as the newcomer, she had managed to fit into this craziness and become one of the team. The team itself had started to jell and had become something important. "I'm glad to hear that," she finally said, "because I'm not sure what'll be involved in this, but I highly suspect it won't have a quick and easy solution."

"Ooh, don't say that," Owen replied. "You're tempting fate with that one."

She again stared at her cell phone, as if it would bite her, and just then it rang. An eerie silence fell around the room almost immediately. Rodney eyed her, one of his eyebrows quirked. Her shoulders sagged, and she nodded. "Yes, it's Simon."

He and everybody else would be listening in, at least somewhat. She answered the call in a quiet tone of voice.

Simon immediately asked, "What's the matter?"

She winced. "Why does something always have to be *the matter?*" she muttered.

"Well, today it is," he snapped, his tone impatient, yet she sensed the worry in it.

She asked, "Why did you call?"

"Because I could *sense* something was wrong," he growled, "and nothing you tell me will change that."

"No, it won't change it." She pinched the bridge of her nose. "I need to talk to you," she stated abruptly. Rodney mouthed something at her. She nodded. "I need to talk to you down here."

Simon abruptly asked, "What's going on?"

"It's better if you come down." Then, in a soft voice, she added, "*Please.*"

"You think I will come down there because you added the word *please?*" he asked in a taunting tone. Not hearing anything back, he groaned. "Fine, but I'm also busy, you know?"

And just enough crossness had been added to his tone for her to realize that he'd already made time in his day to call her because he was worried, so this was probably beyond a break in his day. "I'm sorry, but it's important."

She heard him mumble something in the background, and then he declared, "I'll be there in about twenty minutes." After some shuffling in the background, he added, "I can give you maybe thirty more, but then I have another meeting."

"Fine," she said, "hopefully we can get it done within your schedule."

At that wording, he froze for a moment. "Get what done?"

She hesitated, then replied, "It's better if you are here. I'll see you in twenty." She quickly disconnected. She stared down at the phone and then swore. "No other way to handle it. But damn ..."

Lilliana spoke up. "You did the right thing. It needs to be here."

"I know. I know, but it feels ... not exactly as a betrayal—because he didn't do anything—but still he'll be so upset when he finds out."

"And again, not half as upset as the next person will be, if this guy decides to repeat his game."

"Speaking of which," Lilliana said, "give us the report as you have it right now, and we'll start running down the victim. Plus we can take a look at anything and everything in terms of forensic information."

Kate nodded. "She went to the hospital, but she didn't tell them about the kidnapper and his game, so that's a problem." Kate turned to face Lilliana. "She didn't think anybody would believe her. She told one of the nurses, but she'd already showered and been cleaned up at the hospital, never telling them about her kidnapping event, ... so probably no forensic evidence is on her."

Lilliana swore at that. "Why do people do that shit?" she asked, staring at Kate in frustration. "Without forensic data, ... it's hard to get a case to hold up in court."

Kate agreed with her but no point in arguing now. The woman had done what she'd done, and, to a certain extent, Kate understood. "I can talk to her again, once we collect a bit more evidence."

"Or lack thereof," Lilliana grumbled.

"We have a few more questions to ask her, but essentially the gist of the interview was, she doesn't know who her kidnapper was. He grabbed her while she was getting out of her vehicle at her own residential parking lot, heading home from work. He held her captive for a couple days. He did give her food and water, but he stripped her down to her underwear to keep her from taking off and kept her blindfolded."

"How was she released?" Owen asked, writing down notes.

"According to her, the kidnapper dropped her off at the hospital, via a side trip to point out her apartment to her."

"That's not good."

"Nope, it really is not. So, of course, he knows where she lives, so she's terrified that he is coming back, as he threatened to already."

"I don't think she would have come to us if he hadn't threatened her, if she didn't deliver the message," Rodney muttered.

"She was terrified of him," Kate shared.

"With good reason," Lilliana noted. "Christ, a psycho like this? … That's the last thing the city needs right now." She looked over at Kate intently this time. "The last thing *you* need either."

"Oh, I won't argue with you there," she declared, as she stared over at the woman who maybe wasn't a friend yet but at least had become a coworker Kate could respect. "I really don't need any Simon involvement either."

"And yet it's not Simon involvement per se. This seems to be *because* of Simon."

"I know that," Kate admitted. "He won't be happy when he finds out what's happened." Nobody wanted to imagine that happening because of them, or for them, or in any way a thing even remotely related to them. Kate grabbed her pen and paper and announced, "It's almost time. I'll let Sergeant Colby know what's happening."

"Good idea," Rodney agreed. "Do you want me to come in with you, when you talk to Simon?"

She swore. "I guess I need to make it official and on the books, so then, yes."

"Still, you can have a few minutes to explain to him what's going on first," Rodney offered. "If I come in, then you have a witness to everything that's being said, and that should help, or at least temper some of this."

"Sure," she noted, with a wry look in his direction. "We know how Simon doesn't love police stations."

"And yet he spends an awful lot of time here," Owen stated in a teasing tone.

She flushed at that. "Maybe. I suspect this will all completely shift things now though."

"It's not your fault," Rodney claimed, turning to look at her. "He won't blame you."

She nodded. "Yet somehow it feels as if I'm to blame."

Lilliana stepped forward. "I will say it once, and you better hear me. … Just because your name is on that envelope, you are not responsible for this. When you get a psycho, you get a psycho. They have their means. They have their motivations. They have everything under the sun, and usually common sense and any sanity aren't part of it." Lilliana shrugged. "You are a means to an end in this case. You are a tool to be used to hurt Simon." Lilliana was nothing if not blunt, and she was never shy about digging in and digging deep. "Remember that. It'll make it easier on you."

Lilliana was right, but there was no better way to handle this. It would be Kate's words hurting Simon that really struck home because this note was what it was all about. This asshole was doing this because he wanted something from Simon. What he wanted was a whole different story and that, as she checked the clock, she'd find out. *Hopefully soon too.*

***

SIMON ST. LAURENT pocketed his phone, turned to his foreman, barked off a few orders, and then added, "Unfortunately I've got a change of plans. I'll be back …" He checked his watch and frowned. "I won't be back until later this afternoon." He mentally calculated it—a sense of shifting his appointments around, clocking if he could still meet his other responsibilities for the day. He looked over at his foreman, but then thought better of it because this sense of lateness had settled in. "Maybe not even then."

At that, his foreman nodded. "We'll be fine," he shared comfortably. "You know that."

And he did know that. Simon was the one who liked to stay on top of things. Always that sense of not wanting to hand over complete control because that's when people took advantage of you, and that was hard for him—relinquishing control. He'd never had a problem with this guy before, and he'd worked with him for years, but that didn't change the worry that *this time* would be when something could go wrong. Simon nodded. "Anyway, I'll see you when I can get back."

"Good enough."

And, with that, Simon picked up his pace and headed to the police station. He contemplated his travel options as he got outside. He was a little too far away to walk there and make it in time, and maybe he could catch a cab—but, given the location, the cab itself would likely get snarled up in traffic. Simon quickly hopped the little ferry and ended up on the far side of the station and still had about a mile to go. With that, he flagged a cab and arrived at the station almost perfectly on time. He smiled as he got out.

It was one of the things that he did pride himself on. He often felt the people who were deliberately late could be because they cared about themselves more than they cared about the deadline or about anybody else. It didn't matter to them about making other people wait, and Simon was not that kind of person. He wasn't late in business matters, and he wasn't late in his personal life either.

At that, his thoughts immediately turned to the odd tone in Kate's voice when he'd talked to her. Something was definitely up. That it involved him wasn't a surprise, given the amount of police cases he'd become involved in recently. He frowned, as he walked up the front steps to the station. Simon had noted not just worry in her voice but fear.

For whatever reason she was afraid for him. Although that should make him feel better, not knowing what the circumstances were and wondering how he could possibly be sideways of the law, he headed to the front reception and was immediately told to take a seat. Kate would be with him in a minute.

Instead of sitting, he stood here and studied the small confined area, refraining from picking up his phone—which had almost became an instinctive habit—to check his messages and the weather and anything else to keep his mind off what was ahead of him.

Instead he calmed his mind in order to evaluate some of the crazy energy going on around him. But being in a police station made that hard to do. It was already difficult at any time, especially when fear, anger, and frustration all rolled into a maelstrom of energy. However, being here was harder on him, as a psychic, so he quickly built a few walls to keep some of the sensations back and away.

Jesus, the fury centering in the waiting room was something else. But that energy came from multiple cases, involving multiple people—fathers waiting for sons, mothers waiting for husbands, girlfriends bailing out boyfriends. He shook his head at the remnants of society all here for him to see and to read as he wanted to. Except he didn't want to. Some things should be left private. Yet everybody's emotions were wide open here.

For some, it was a natural state, but, for him, it was the opposite.

"Simon?"

He turned to see Kate staring at him. He smiled at her, caught her genuine smile in return, and settled back somewhat. He walked toward her as she held open the door.

"Come on this way."

He clocked the direction as—instead of heading to her desk that he had seen a couple times—going to an interview room. He stood at the entranceway and stared.

"Please come in." Her tone was casual, but her anguish underneath was hard to mistake.

Frowning, he stepped inside and sat down, sensing again an energy disturbance that he didn't want to deal with and quickly built up a few more walls to shoo it all away. "What's going on?" he asked.

She groaned. "I don't know how to explain this to you, so I'll lay it out. Then Rodney will come in, and we'll ask you a few questions *officially.*"

He stared at her and waited. None of this made any

sense. She held up a note but not so he could see it.

"I was called to interview a woman who came to the station this morning. She was hurt, scratched up. She had survived a kidnapping and was given a note to bring to the station. She was told, if she didn't bring the note to me, this guy promised to come back, and this game that he had inveigled her into would continue."

She explained a little bit of the game, and Simon felt the sickness in his stomach as he realized they had yet another crazy person out there. He nodded. "I'm sure you'll get to the point as to why I'm here sooner rather than later, right?"

She sighed and then placed the note before him. "This is the note that she was instructed to bring to the police station."

He picked it up and read it, the few short lines, his eyebrows shooting straight up when he saw both his name and hers. "What the hell?" he muttered out loud.

She nodded. "Yeah, *the hell* is why you're here." She carefully studied him. "I'm sorry because, if there was any way to keep you out of it, believe me. I would have. More so if … there was any way to keep me out of it," she added, with an eye roll, "I would have. But we have both been drawn into this because of this woman, who's already been victimized once. She's absolutely terrified to go home and have this asshole victimize her a second time."

"Has she moved?"

"I don't know if she's even capable of moving. She was released from the hospital, probably too early, but our medical system hospitals are pretty overwhelmed these days. Therefore, if she's capable of going home, then that's where she goes," Kate relayed abruptly. "Under these circumstances, I don't know. I'm not sure that staying home for her is a good idea, but, if he found her once, … there's a good chance that he would find her again. Plus, if she deliberately tried to leave, there is another good chance that he would punish her for it."

Simon nodded absentmindedly, as he studied the note. "So now you want to know who would do this, who do I know who would do this, and did I have anything to do with it?"

She stared at him, and her lips cracked in a parody of a smile. Then the door opened. He looked up to see Rodney move in. Simon nodded a greeting. "Fun times."

"No, not really," Kate disagreed. "I was in the interview with this woman when she came in, and she was terrified."

Simon nodded. "And, having seen the note, I have to tell you …" He shook his head. "Absolutely nobody comes to mind. It's not as if I live in the world of psychos." And then he laughed. "Although I'm pretty sure you would say that you don't either."

"Well, it's not where we would choose to live," Rodney admitted, with a half smile, as he took a chair. He quickly held out the recorder and put it on the table. "We'll make this official, so that we all have something to listen to afterward."

Simon nodded and waited, and, when they did their official disclaimer bit, Simon waved his hand. "Okay, so how long was she held? Do we know where she was held, and …" He picked up the note again, closed his eyes, but absolutely nothing came through. When he opened his eyes, both watched him expectantly. He shook his head. "Nothing is left on this note," he shared in a confused tone. "Whether he ever held it himself, … I don't know. Whether he ever held it with his own hands or with, say, gloves, I don't know." He shook his head. "I'm not getting anything off it."

"Of course not," she muttered. "That would be way too easy. So, given the fact that you don't have a clue who would have done this, do you happen to know the victim?"

He asked, "What was her name again?"

"Patricia Blinker," she stated.

Simon frowned and shook his head. "I've never heard of her."

"I do have a photo. Matter of fact, we took several photos while she was here. Unfortunately forensically there isn't anything on her because she spent several days in the hospital, showered several times, and at no point in time saw her attacker. However, we do have these photos." And, with that, she held up her phone and showed them to Simon.

He winced when he saw the abrasions on the poor woman's hands and face. "Wow, this asshole really did try to hurt her."

"And yet," Kate added, "he could have hurt her so much worse."

He nodded, a lot of truth to that. "The damage will be psychological in the long term," he replied, his voice quiet.

Rodney immediately nodded. "I suspect that was his purpose, psychological damage being so much harder for a victim to get over."

Simon knew all about that. He felt that slow burn inside, even after all these years, and then swore heavily and fluently for several minutes.

When he looked up, Kate grinned at him and said, "I hope that made you feel as good as it made me feel."

His eyebrows raised, he studied the woman who both fascinated, intrigued, and warmed his heart at the same time. "Now how the hell would my swearing make you feel better?"

She burst out laughing. "Because you swear in French, and it sounds so very different. Kinda hot, and I know that sounds so cheesy."

She looked over to see a grinning Rodney, who was nodding his head. "Yep, definitely doesn't sound the same," he noted. "Very poetic, very musical."

Simon shook his head. "BS, I can swear in English just as well, but, for whatever reason, this one triggered my French version."

"And yet," she asked him, "you don't use French very much, do you?"

He shrugged. "No, but it is something that I have worked hard to maintain for business." He tapped the note. "So what will we do about this?"

"That's the next challenge," she admitted. "In order to do something with this, we have to understand who is behind this, and that's a bit challenging. ... That's why you're here. We need a list of people who hate you, a list of people who would want to do this to *you*, a list of people who would play a sick game such as this."

"I think the game is what's important," Rodney shared.

"For some reason, whatever you have said or done to somebody, potentially in business," Kate pointed out, "where somebody didn't get what he wanted, it may have led to this. So maybe you stopped a deal from going through, and it caused somebody else financial hardship," she suggested, tiptoeing around him. "I'm throwing ideas out there because I really have no way of knowing any relation you might have to this psycho."

Simon nodded, as he again stared down at the note. "It's not a game I would have ever played," he admitted.

"And yet as a child?" Rodney poked.

"As a child possibly, but who can remember a childhood game?" He stared at the note again, his mind scrambling to make sense of this. "I don't particularly like being somebody in a position of power, somebody who has the ability to hurt and to damage somebody else's life," he told them, with a shrug. "Would I have squashed a deal if it was unfair or if somebody was lying, cheating, something along that line? … Absolutely." He took a moment to add, "I refuse to do shady deals, and I prefer to stay on the straight-and-narrow."

She nodded. "Of course. That was an element of your grandmother too, wasn't it?"

He nodded. "It's an element of my gift. If I lie, cheat, steal, anything along that line, it'll come back and haunt me. You might laugh about Karma, … but, when it comes to something in my world, Karma can be quite a bitch. So I cannot ignore that aspect in my business or my personal life." He shrugged. "Now, if somebody *were* cheating someone or being a rank asshole and hurting someone, and I could do something to stop it, then I would."

"So, more likely you would be obliged to act?" Rodney asked Simon.

Simon nodded. "Would that be the case here? I have no idea." He frowned. "I can't remember any time where that may have happened, but …" Then he kicked back his chair and stared at the note, his mind tumbling with ideas, and yet nothing really to lock on. Shaking his head, he looked over at the two of them. "I'm sorry, but I've got nothing."

Rodney's shoulders sagged, and he nodded. "We half expected that, but, of course, … we had to bring you in and ask."

"Of course," he agreed, "and because my name is right

there in black-and-white, along with Kate's, that will make me an integral part of this."

"So maybe that's what he wanted. Attention," Kate said suddenly. "Maybe it's not so much about hating something you did but hating *you*, hating your success, hating that you have a good name." She hesitated. "Because, if this becomes public, that could certainly affect your life, wouldn't it?"

He stared at her and down at the note, thought about the implications, and shrugged. "Maybe, but my world isn't built on public opinion, and it's not built on any of these assholes. So I'm not sure that that theory applies, but it is something to consider." He frowned again at the note. "I just, ... that whole bit, *Simon can do this*," he muttered out loud. "That's got a competitive edge, as if this guy's lost beside me in some way. That other part, *Simon thinks he's so fucking good, but I don't think he's got answers for this*," he read out loud. "I can't imagine the mentality of somebody who would be setting me up to fail."

"That's exactly what he is doing. Setting you up to fail," Kate interrupted, "and this is the only way he knows to bring you down."

Hearing the analysis in her words, he agreed and then slowly nodded. "I can see that aspect to this mess." Simon sighed. "Yet that would mean that this is somebody who has either lost against me multiple times or knows somebody who lost against me. However, I'm not competitive." He shrugged, shaking his head. "The only game I play is poker, as you well know, and I don't do that lightly."

"Yes, you do play," she confirmed instantly. "For you, it's ... fun. It's a release, and you do it to help, as all the money ends up going to charities—only most people don't know that about you. I think if they did know that, it would piss this guy right off even more."

Simon's lips twitched, as he looked over at Rodney. "Rodney didn't even know that," he pointed out, "so thanks for letting that out."

She flushed and looked over at Rodney. "But Rodney doesn't care that you are somebody who makes money at poker and then turns around and donates it because you can't live with yourself for having made it that way."

Simon burst out laughing. "I can live with myself all right," he countered, with a chuckle. "I don't donate all of it, but I do certainly donate a very hefty portion of it," he shared agreeably.

"So does somebody know that you do that? Because that whole philanthropic attitude might piss somebody off who's literally trying to make ends meet. And here, with you in the kidnapper's *game*, you could beat them not only at the game but at whatever it is that they're attempting to do, which could be to simply survive," she suggested. "Your world is so very different, for example, from what Rodney and I live, that I can understand a certain amount of—I don't know that *frustration*'s the right word—but *resentment* maybe."

Her words rang in his ears, and she was right; there had to be something more to this.

THE REST OF his afternoon had been a whirlwind of business and trying to keep his head organized, and Simon had been caught up in meetings right through the day and until late in the night. He'd really wanted to spend the evening with Kate but couldn't get his head wrapped around everything that he needed to get done. So, when she'd suggested they spend the evening apart, he hadn't been terribly impressed but understood it perfectly. Work was work.

At least it kept him busy throughout the day, and his mind was off Kate—mostly.

❧

YOU LOSE WHISPERED through his mind.

Simon bolted out of the bed, stark naked, spinning around in his bedroom, his heart slamming against his chest, realizing that he was once again caught up in a vision that had seemed so real that actual sweat poured off his body in buckets.

In a panic, Simon roared out loud, "Who are you, and what the fuck do you want with me?"

Of course only silence came, but Simon swore an almost mocking laughter could be heard in the distance. He shuddered, his skin now clammy, even though it was a decently warm day outside. It was late September, and time was marching on. However, here in Vancouver, it didn't march too cold. Even if it did get cold, it didn't ever stay too long. Yet his body was now chilled, chilled enough that he should remain in bed. Yet, as he checked his clock and noted it was almost 5:30 a.m., he admitted more sleep was now a thing of the past.

He headed for the shower and turned the heat on max, while he tried to get his body back to a normal awareness, until the threat, whatever that was, had passed. When he got out of the shower, still dripping with water, he felt warmer and marginally better. His heart had already calmed down, and he was busy analyzing whatever the hell the meaning of that strange message was.

It was easy to understand the message on the surface, but his psyche wasn't given to nightmares, and that's what this seemed to be more than anything. Frowning at that, he made coffee. While the sun still rose over the harbor, he sat down and sipped from his mug. He needed his world to get back to normal, sooner than later, given the fact that he still had to get through a lot of hours and a lot of business today.

It's not as if whatever this gift was—and he used the term *gift* with a note of sarcasm—gave a crap about the work he did or the projects he was involved in or the people who he helped. His *gift* was all about telling him that it needed answers now.

Not so easy for him. Hell, not so easy for any psychic, probably. His grandmother had been tormented by all of this; *Visions from afar-land,* she called it, and yet she'd felt compelled to continue in it, even though it had given her nothing but a lot of pain. Hell, his own birth mother, Meggie No-Last-Name, had more or less directed herself out of the family scene in order to avoid all the craziness it brought. Last Simon knew, Meggie was a junkie barmaid.

Despite her total lack of mothering skills and instincts, Simon couldn't really blame her sometimes, and yet he wanted more out of life than to hide from his gift. As long as he could do something good with it, then maybe there was a chance it was the right thing for him to be a psychic. And, when he thought of *good,* of course his mind immediately shifted to the enigmatic Kate, the woman who had somehow gotten under his skin, banged at his heart, and even, when he wasn't looking apparently, let herself in.

Of course that was foolishness right there because she would say that she hadn't let herself in, that he'd practically kidnapped her. He had, and he would have a lot earlier, if she'd given him any indication that she was open for any relationship, much less a relationship with a psychic, which

Kate was only just able to accept as possibly useful. Yet it had taken this long to get her to even communicate on that level with him.

He knew that they were still on a touchy relationship level that he wasn't terribly comfortable with, because he wanted to have a whole lot more permanency with her. Yet pushing her would give him absolutely the opposite reaction to what he wanted. That much he knew. So going slow and steady was about all he could do, while meanwhile helping her on her cases. The fact that she even wanted to talk with him now about her cases? That was a milestone.

Maybe a good milestone. He wasn't sure because, of course, it left him in the crossroads. He waited until it was 7:30 a.m., and then he quickly dressed and headed out, loving these early morning walks while he still could, before winter in Vancouver set in. A crispness to the air added a certain level of speed to his motion. A couple food carts were up ahead, and one hopefully would have fresh pretzels, and he would sign up for that in a heartbeat, providing they were coming out right now. As he walked closer, he smiled. Seemed he had perfect timing today.

The vendor looked up. "Hey, look at you. How's that for timing, *huh*?" He greeted Simon with a big grin.

"I keep thinking I'll miss you one of these days."

"*Naw.*" The vendor shook his head, still all smiles. "Besides, you're one of my regulars. If I don't cater to you, ... I won't have a business."

"Ooh, ouch," Simon replied. "I hope things aren't that bad ..."

The guy shrugged. "You know me. I always make a way out of the worst."

"I do know," he replied, "and it's much appreciated."

With a fresh cup of coffee and a pretzel, Simon took several deep breaths of the fresh air and inhaled the scent of the hot pretzel—and the coffee of course. Some things one needed to really love if one did a lot of walking in the city, and that was the love of all the smells and the hints of the world that so many people never even saw.

But Simon was up early almost every day. This was the world that he lived in, the world that he excelled in, and, no matter how many times he might want to try and leave it, it's not the world that he would ever leave behind. Now in a good mood, pretzel gone, still sipping his coffee, he quickly texted Kate. **Good morning.** When she responded with a **Good morning** back, he smiled.

She might not be the quickest to jump into a relation-ship, but he figured that, once he got her where he wanted her, she'd be the most steadfast. The challenge was getting her there. She was like a young fawn, scared, skittish, yet curious. And, so far, he was winning that whole curiosity vote. Besides, they blended on so many other levels, and it was rare for him to find anybody who could even tolerate his psychic abilities.

Some people were seriously fascinated, and others were seriously repulsed, but, in his world, the loyalty that she'd already exhibited? That went a long way. The fact that he'd saved her didn't hurt either.

CHAPTER 2

K ATE WOKE THE next morning, alone in her own bed. She had decided to get a good night's sleep and had stayed in her own place, particularly when Simon had had a late day, full of meetings. She got up, quickly showered, decided to forego breakfast and coffee, and headed into the office. She kept hoping that she'd wake up with some idea of who had done this to Patricia, but nothing came to mind. As Kate walked in the station, Owen was already there. She stared at him.

He shrugged. "We requested the camera surveillance from Patricia's apartment building and some in the adjacent area," he explained, "but the cameras don't cover that corner."

"Of course they don't," she muttered. "However, the kidnapper was looking for a response from Simon somehow, and I wouldn't be at all surprised if he is watching the police station to see if Simon showed up."

"Oh, that's a good thought too," Rodney noted behind her. "If that were the case, our kidnapper would have seen Simon show up yesterday, probably expecting something, or is quite happy to sit and chortle in his own little world, thinking that we were spinning on our heels and didn't have a clue what we were doing because he's so clever."

Owen offered to take a look at those cams too.

"Thanks, Owen." She nodded, as she walked over to her desk. "And that fits too, doesn't it? I kept thinking that there had to be more. It is likely Patricia doesn't know what she knows. Like possibly the kidnapper's voice."

She took time to consider her own words. "I'll have to keep on her and keep talking to her to see what else this guy may have slipped up on, even if she didn't recognize it at the time."

"She's also delicate," Owen added, "and we don't want her to run or to do anything that puts her life in danger or makes her clam up because she doesn't want anything more to do with this."

"Right, that's also a possibility." Kate frowned, her fingers tapping her desktop, as she picked up a pen and now started tapping the desk with it. "Rodney, while we were interviewing Patricia, did you ever get the feeling at any time that she was lying or holding anything back?"

He turned to face Kate and then slowly nodded. "Yes, but nothing that I could ask her about." Kate nodded. He asked her, "What are you thinking?"

"I wonder. … This guy held a woman captive for days, in her underwear, but he didn't rape her," she noted.

"Right." Rodney nodded. "Maybe she was withholding that info. Many women hide a rape."

Kate picked up her notes and then read through them. "She's not married."

"But she does have … or had a boyfriend," Rodney shared, thinking back to the info they had. "Maybe she thinks he won't stick around, if that's the case."

Kate frowned, as she continued to review her notes.

"How is that even a thing, bailing on a sick loved one?" Owen asked from the sidelines. "When women get breast cancer, apparently they're told during one of their first oncology visits to get prepared for a divorce because most men bail." Owen shook his head. "I just … don't understand. Why does some guy bail because a woman's been raped? Why does some guy bail because his partner has breast cancer?" He raised his palms, frowning. "I don't understand that psychology."

"That's because they're not there for a *long* time," Kate replied. "They're there for a *good* time. They didn't sign up for this kind of support, and they're out." She sighed. "However, you could be right, Rodney. She could be trying to hide this from her partner."

"Or," Rodney added, "Patricia could be trying to hide this from the world, if she feels that the world would look at her differently because of this."

"Good point," Kate muttered. "So I definitely need to talk to her again." She found Patricia's home address in her notes and tapped the entry. "I think I'll drive over there and talk to her in person. She might be more comfortable at home. Open up a little more."

"What? You drove this morning?"

She glared at him. "I do drive sometimes, you know." She reached for her cell phone to look up the address. "I want to see her parking lot."

"Oh? What'll the parking lot tell you?" Rodney asked curiously.

"Maybe nothing, maybe nothing that Google won't show me on my monitor." She shrugged. "On the other hand, it will give me a feel for the area, where her kidnapper could be sitting and watching for her. So I want to see the lay of the land."

"I'll come with you." Rodney stood, gathering his jacket.

She looked over and frowned. "You don't have to. I can go alone."

"No, in this case, I'm coming," Rodney stated with finality.

Immediately Owen nodded. "Yeah, let's not play Lone Ranger on this one."

Startled, she looked back at him. "That wasn't my intention at all. I just didn't figure that you guys would see any point in it."

Rodney laughed. "We're not stupid," he replied, with a grin. "We all think differently, and there's something unique about your processes—which I think we'd all like to understand because, let's face it, that is closing cases, and that is a good thing. Anyway," he said, "I'll pull as much information as I can before we go."

"I thought Lilliana was on it yesterday."

"She was, until she had to leave the office early for an appointment," he told Kate, with a pointed look. "I took over at that point in time, but some of Patricia's history is hard to get a hold of."

"In what way?" Kate asked. "And did it have anything to do with why the kidnapper chose her? We need to know about the victim, what brought our kidnapper to Patricia."

Rodney tilted his head, with a knowing look. "I think she used to work the streets."

"Oh, interesting," Kate noted, as she walked closer to look at the information on his monitor. "She's in our system, isn't she? She had to be."

He nodded. "And that'll be another reason why she wouldn't want to mention any rape. Nobody, ... in her mind, would believe her because of the work she does or did do." He shook his head. "Absolutely nothing here on her record recently. The last entry was from a couple years ago."

"Right," Kate acknowledged. "But if her kidnapper knew Patricia, had used her services from a few years ago," she pointed out, "he might see her as nothing less than disposable because of the work she was into. Definitely need to go over and talk to her myself."

Rodney immediately joined her. "Any chance we can stop and pick up food on our way over?"

"Good idea." She nodded. "I haven't eaten either."

At that, Owen told the two of them, "Definitely get food. You know what this job's like. It'll burn you up and spit you out. Therefore, keep strong and keep everything flowing, meaning, eat regularly and get a good night's sleep."

They grinned at him and walked outside, with Rodney offering to drive.

"What's the matter? You don't trust my driving?" Kate asked in a joking manner.

"Nope, nothing like that, and yet maybe I should be," he quipped, "but this way I get to choose where we go for breakfast."

That startled a laugh out of her. Now in a surprisingly good mood—that she hadn't really felt since she woke up— she got into his brown hybrid vehicle. "That's fine by me. Are you buying too?"

He snorted at that. "Hell no. Neither one of us makes enough money to start that." He looked over at her, as they settled in. "What's it like to date somebody who's got megamoney?"

She shrugged. "I don't really see it at all 'cause he's not the kind to throw it around," she shared. "So I can't really answer that question."

He laughed. "Of course you're not one to spend it, are

you?"

"No, sure not," she confirmed, with a smile. "I don't need more than what I've got anyway," she murmured.

"Nobody needs a lot of what they've got," Rodney declared, as he pulled out of the police parking lot. "The thing of it is, people still want it though."

"Right. Of course that *want* is enough to mess up all kinds of things," she stated, nodding. "If people would just not want quite so much, they'd probably get a whole lot more of it faster."

He shrugged. "I hope you don't go too philosophical on us," he pointed out. "We're still adjusting to the Kate we've known in the last few short months. You start giving us words of wisdom," he said, with a chuckle, "we'll really have trouble keeping up."

She stared at him, not exactly sure what he meant by that, and she didn't really have a chance to figure it out now, as he pulled into a restaurant almost immediately. "Wow, we could have even walked here and picked it up."

"Ha, I knew you would say that, and I wasn't up for the walk."

Instead of entering the restaurant, he moved to the drive-through. She added her order to it. They paid separately, and, by the time they were back on the road, she was digging into her food. "The problem with this is, we have to eat while we drive."

"Well," he replied, glancing at her, "in spite of all the jokes otherwise, I am quite capable, as an adult male, of multitasking."

"Sure, and, if we have an accident," she countered, "hopefully you're also capable of multitasking your way out of that one."

He laughed. "Haven't had an accident yet," he declared, with a bright smile in her direction, as he bit into his egg sandwich at the stoplight. She nodded and really hoped that his good driving streak stayed that way; they often took her car for all intents and purposes, sometimes with him driving, and she liked her car very much. It was paid for, and no amount of insurance doled out would replace that vehicle for her.

By the time they reached the address that Kate had on file for Patricia, they had both finished their fast-food breakfast and sipped away on coffee now.

Rodney looked over at her. "You want to talk to her first?"

"No, I want to get a lay of the land, take a look at the neighborhood."

"Well, this is a pretty average family-centered neighbor-hood," he noted, as he pulled up front into a visitor parking spot. "This apartment building is geared to, I would say, the working-class, so not exactly a ton of money."

"But," she pointed out, "also not likely to be streetwalk-ers."

"That's also possible," he agreed, with a nod. "Although some of them do well enough that maybe, while they might not work here, this neighborhood is where they retire."

"And I would hope that," Kate replied, "if they do that work, at least it'd be nice if they had a safe place to do it."

"Still not work I would want my sister doing," he point-ed out.

"No, me neither," she acknowledged, "but sometimes people are happy doing this. Also people can be so en-trenched in a way of life that they can't see another way out of it. Regardless, let's keep them safe, while they sort themselves out and hopefully find another way to move forward in life."

"You say so because you're a softy," Rodney said, "but you need to be prepared for anything. That way, you would stay on the job a little longer."

"Yeah, well," she murmured, "I've been on the job for a while and have seen quite a bit. Yet I still want to believe in people."

"You might want to believe in people," Rodney replied, "because you do believe in the law, and that is one of your saving graces."

And, with that, she veered off from him and headed for the residents' parking lot.

"Hey, wait," Rodney said behind her. "Where are you going?"

"Here." She pointed out the nearby covered parking garage, marked for the residents of Patricia's apartment building. "We need a good look around here first." Kate walked around the concrete lot. "A wide-open parking lot. Unmanned. Doesn't have very good up-to-date security, but locks are on the doors, plus a few cameras." She pointed them out as they went by.

"So this guy, Patricia's kidnapper, cased the place, knew about the cameras, and still managed to snag her."

She frowned at that. "I don't think Patricia's still in the business anymore."

He frowned at Kate. "What would give rise to that big supposition?"

"If she was in that business, I would think that she had cultivated a better sense of self-preservation," Kate offered, with a shrug.

"Potentially you're correct, but with a kidnapping ..."

"Did she say when she was snatched?"

He frowned at Kate, before speaking. "She told us early evening, but I don't know what that means. Another question to ask her because *early evening*, depending on the work you do," he pointed out, "could mean very different things to different people."

The parking lot had two entrances and two exits. Kate pointed to each of them. "Her kidnapper could have sat outside any one of these entrances or exits, out of sight, out of view from anybody, and nobody would have cared. He could have walked over, forced her into his car, and that would have been it." She looked around the garage once more. "It's a depressing place."

"It is now that you've pointed out all that." Rodney sent her a smirk. "I was thinking it was a pretty-darn decent place for people trying to better themselves in life."

"That's a nicer description. It does look kind of like that."

As they left the garage and walked toward the main entrance to the apartment building, a man stepped out and glared at them. She smiled. "You the manager here?"

Immediately he froze, frowning. "Why the hell would you even ask me that?"

"You're acting as if we don't belong here."

"Well, you don't belong." He gave them a clipped nod. "I know everybody who lives in this place, been here twenty-two years," he stated proudly. "You don't belong here."

"What if we're friends with someone who lives here?" she asked curiously.

He stared at her and then shrugged, as if he had smelled something foul. "You're coppers."

She flashed a smile. "That we are." She pulled out her

badge.

"Doesn't take much to see that," he muttered. "You guys stand out like a sore thumb, no matter where you are."

"I won't argue with you," she said, "because you're probably right. But a young woman was kidnapped from the parking lot for a few days. So given that you say that you know everybody at this place, did you happen to see that event?"

He stared at her and then slowly shook his head. "No, and I didn't hear nothing about it either," he replied suspiciously.

"I don't imagine that the woman in question has been too interested in letting the public know," Kate stated. "So I'm not surprised that you haven't heard."

He considered that for a second. "Most of the people here stick to themselves," he shared, his attitude tempered somewhat. "It's the way we like it."

"So you are the manager then?"

He nodded. "Twenty-two years, as I mentioned before. We ain't had a lick of trouble." And then he glared at her. "So don't you be bringing none now."

"Wasn't planning on it," she stated, "but I'm certain you would prefer that everybody who lives here is safe and happy, wouldn't you?"

"I don't give a crap about whether they're happy," he denied bluntly. "But safety? Now that's a different issue." He pondered it, looking at the parking lot, and nodded. "I've told the owners that they need to put in more cameras, but nobody ever listens. The minute money is involved ..." He glared around the parking lot again. "The woman should have come to me."

Kate asked him, "Why is that?"

He stared at her. "'Cause any problem regarding this place, people come to me about. That's what I'm here for. And, if they don't come to me, then I can't solve their problems."

"Maybe she wasn't looking for you to solve her problem," Kate suggested, "but maybe... needed medical attention."

"I don't know anybody who needed medical attention." He swore loudly. "I'll get back onto the management's case about cameras. This might give us enough ammunition to make that happen." And, sure enough, he almost seemed to be rubbing his hands in delight at having something to push management in the direction he wanted them to go.

As Kate and Rodney walked into the front of the building, she looked back at the manager, already on his cell phone, arguing with somebody. She turned to Rodney. "He seems a little too happy."

He nodded. "I gather cameras have been an issue for a while."

"Of course nobody ever wants to do what's right and safe for people."

"And that's probably what he's after now." Rodney chuckled. "Either that or giving them shit because he might get blamed for something that's not his fault, particularly if management wouldn't okay the extra security. You know how they feel when that happens."

"True, and he's standing up for himself, which is also an interesting twist," she noted. "He's not seemingly worried about losing his job."

"Ah, good point." With a thoughtful expression on his face, he asked her, "And remind me, how does that work?"

"Twenty-two years," she said. "If you ask me, that is a

long time. Maybe he figures he's in the clear. Or his family owns this property. Either way, let's check him out," she stated, with a careless gesture. "The tag on his shirt ID'd him as Dean McAllister."

"Right." He was already texting Owen on that. "Of course we don't know for sure that's who he is. But he'll run it and let us know if it's pertinent."

"Easy enough to check," she murmured, and together they stepped inside the apartment building. She had her phone to confirm the address. "Fourth floor." They took the elevator up. "I want to take the stairs back down again."

"Right, more of your fitness kick?" Rodney asked her.

"No, more about what easy surveillance access did this asshole have to track Patricia's movements," she explained.

As they reached the apartment, Kate hesitated and then gave a clipped rap on the door. There was no answer. She did it again and again, still no answer. She looked over at Rodney, one of her eyebrows raised. And then pulled out her phone and proceeded to phone the number she had for Patricia. Standing in the hallway, Kate heard a phone ringing inside the apartment. "Either Patricia's sound asleep or maybe left her phone behind …"

"Or something's wrong," Rodney added, frowning.

She nodded. "Then there's that, and, in the state she was in, … she wouldn't be sleeping like a log. I'm not prepared to leave until I know for sure that she's okay." She let the phone ring until it stopped. Then she turned at hearing footsteps to see the manager, walking toward them.

He stared at the apartment number intently. "What's the matter?"

"I need you to open up this apartment," Kate stated.

He shook his head, his face flushed. "I can't do that, …

not without some official document," he said, waving around his hand.

"This woman could be in danger." Kate glared at him. "As this is an official police investigation, I can charge you with obstruction." She gave him a challenging look. "Open the damn door."

He glared at her, then reluctantly stepped forward and pulled out his keys and unlocked the apartment. "If she sues you …"

As he was about to open the door, she cut him off. "You can leave now."

"Oh no, no. You forced me to do this. I have to make sure you don't steal anything."

She snorted at that and looked back at Rodney. "Keep him here."

And, with that, she quickly stepped inside and froze.

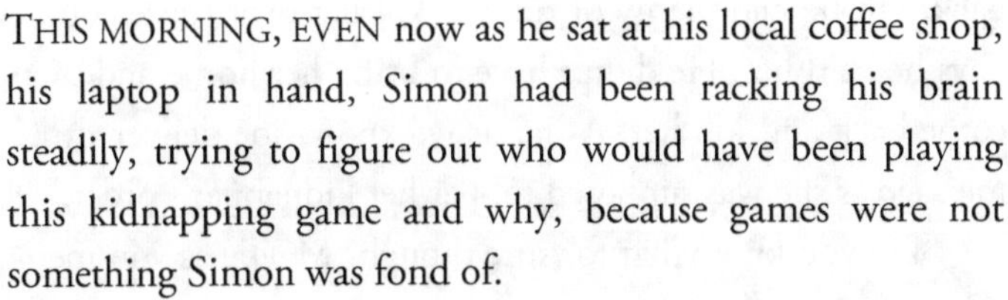

THIS MORNING, EVEN now as he sat at his local coffee shop, his laptop in hand, Simon had been racking his brain steadily, trying to figure out who would have been playing this kidnapping game and why, because games were not something Simon was fond of.

Yet obviously somebody wanted to inveigle him into this nightmare, and it seemed as if Simon could do very little about that—considering the kidnapper's *game* had started, and he'd been dragged into it, and yet nobody had told him the rules. Even if there were rules, it's not as if anybody was doing anything to clarify what Simon's role was in this supposed game.

When his phone rang, he looked down to see Kate's number. He smiled immediately and picked up. "Hey, how was your night?"

"A whole lot better than my morning," she declared, her tone crisp. Then she lowered her voice and whispered, "I came to check out Patricia's apartment building and garage, but I found her body instead. ... She's been murdered."

"Ah hell no." Simon groaned. "That's not fair, not after everything she survived. Her kidnapper shouldn't have come back for her so soon."

"And that's one of my questions for you. Did you pick up anything, think anything, have any insights," she muttered, "because I'm not sure that her killer was her kidnapper."

Simon froze. "What are you talking about?"

"The apartment wasn't broken into. I had the manager open up the door." She spoke in a hushed tone still. "Forensics is on their way now, and then we'll go through everything in her life, but I don't have any proof that the same guy did this. The kidnapper did state he would come back, but he had plenty of time to kill her over those couple days he held her. He didn't have to bring her home and then come back and kill her. As far as we know, she delivered the message as she was supposed to, per her kidnapper's order."

"Do you know that for sure though? Maybe as you mentioned before, she left something out, and maybe that pissed him right off." He heard her suck in her breath at that thought. "Any idea if she withheld anything from that original message?"

"I don't know," Kate admitted in frustration. "We did wonder if she had been raped and had not told us."

Simon pondered that, wondering what it would take for a woman to withhold that information, yet knowing what she had gone through already and what the repercussions would be if she didn't deliver the message. "Would her kidnapper/rapist tell Patricia specifically to divulge any rape? Sounds odd to me, but the rape detail does add more fear to his message and more psychological torture for Patricia, in my opinion. And, if he did rape her, why wouldn't she relay the message as he directed her to?"

"I don't know. I don't have a grasp on his or her mind-set," Kate admitted. "But, if it was him, the same guy, then he's escalated from kidnapping to murder. At least now it is clearly our case, and I don't have to pass it off to Missing Persons."

Simon hesitated and asked, "Is there any chance she committed suicide?"

"I wouldn't think so, not from what I'm looking at in front of me. It looks as if she was killed with a knife. It was there beside her but the handle is covered in blood."

"Which could still be suicide."

"Right, I know. I know. I'll wait for forensics on that one, but I'm going with murder. I have to get back to this, but, if you do pick up on anything"—she was stern and unyielding—"we need it, and we need it fast." And, with that, she disconnected.

It was hardly the kind of phone call that Simon wanted to have with his plus-one in life, but they had a habit of these kinds of conversations. As much as it made him happy to know that she was willing to look at any information he had to offer, it didn't make him happy to think that she might have been hoping he had information because she had nothing. And nothing was bad news for everyone.

He stared down at the coffee cup he slowly rotated in his hand. Unfortunately he hadn't picked up the original kidnapping; he hadn't picked up on the murder either. But then that note said so. *Simon thinks he's so damn good, but he doesn't have answers to this.* Of course he didn't have answers to this. He didn't have any answers, which meant that, so far, this asshole was winning whatever game this was.

As far as Simon was concerned, he hadn't even gotten into the game. At this point he didn't even look to be at the table.

CHAPTER 3

KATE STAYED AT Patricia's apartment for hours, while forensics worked away. Not a whole lot to go on here. The windows were untouched. The lock on the door hadn't been jimmied, and yet Patricia was dead inside a locked room on the fourth floor. That meant that she must have let somebody in, or they had entered her apartment earlier, while she was unaware, and she hadn't been in a position to fight them off.

Kate had already talked to the nearest neighbors, and the local cops were canvassing the rest of the people in the apartment building.

She wasn't hopeful; this guy had already been way too diligent in attacking Patricia and taking her captive, but the thought of what her last few moments would have been was heartbreaking. There hadn't been enough time for anybody to have a foothold in the investigation and to have stopped this from happening.

And had the kidnapper planned on killing Patricia right from the beginning? That brought Kate right back around full circle to where she questioned if that message for Kate had been completely delivered or where she questioned whether that message for her had been completely delivered or Patricia had withheld something If she had, how would the kidnapper know that's what Patricia had done?

Kate's mind immediately considered if a cop were involved, only to discard that thought immediately. That thought was possible, but not likely. Maybe the kidnapper had planned on killing Patricia right from the beginning, regardless of her handling of his message. That thought felt right. How could he leave somebody alive after what he'd done to Patricia?

When a disturbance came from the doorway, she turned to see the guard wrestling a large man out of the apartment. Whoever he was, he was strong.

She immediately walked over and held up her ID, motioning the man to calm the hell down. "Sir, take it easy. Who are you? Why are you here?" Kate could tell the shock in his gaze was genuine.

He moistened his lips several times and then finally spoke. "My name is Terry. I'm Patricia's brother." He turned toward the bedroom, but his view was now blocked.

Kate quickly pushed him farther out into the hallway. "Terry, I'm so sorry for your loss."

"What happened?" he muttered, looking at her in shock. "Please tell me that wasn't her."

"It *was* her." She eyed him carefully, noting his reaction to her words. "It appears she's been murdered. I do not, however, have any details as yet for you."

He blinked at her several times, tears immediately filling his eyes, and he whispered, "Why? ... Why? She was doing everything right."

At that, Kate's ears picked up. "What do you mean by that?"

He kept shaking his head, as if unable to answer, and finally managed to say, "She'd been working hard at putting that lifestyle behind her. ... I was helping, trying to get her back off the streets again. And she was off." He turned to face Kate to ensure that she understood. "She wasn't doing that work anymore."

Kate nodded reassuringly at him. "I'm really glad for her then. If that was what she wanted, it's nice that she made it."

His eyes filled with tears all over again. "But what's the point if some asshole comes after her and kills her anyway?" he cried out. "She had worked so hard. We worked so hard, getting her into a safe lifestyle, a safe neighborhood." His gaze roamed the hallway, as if looking for answers, answers that may never be found.

"You see anything unusual lately?" she asked him.

"I can't imagine who would want to hurt her. Everybody loved her."

She winced at that because it was almost a trite answer— *Everybody loved her*—and yet people, when they took a moment and stopped and went deeper and thought about it, they realized there were always issues. There were always people who didn't show love in quite the way that we thought about it, regarding that word *love*.

She faced him to ask some questions. "We don't know anything about what happened, but did she have an argument with anybody, any disputes, any fights, something that would have set off this? Anything unusual at all?"

He shook his head immediately. "She was not confrontational. If anything, … she was terrified of her own shadow." Terry sobbed quietly now. "I don't know anybody in her old world anymore, and I tried hard not to know anybody back then either. If anybody hurt her, … I would imagine it was from her world back then."

He took several deep breaths, as if trying to regain his composure, and then added in a curt tone, "She was hurt several times by several johns. That's one of the reasons that we struggled so hard to get her away from that business. Her pimp was no good either."

At that, Kate commiserated with him. "I can't say I know a pimp who is any good for anybody."

He nodded in understanding. "Right? And yet Patricia wasn't the easiest person to talk out of it. She felt so worthless, as if she had absolutely nothing to offer anybody, and I kept telling Patricia that her pimp was setting up that programming and how Patricia had to remember how she had a lot to offer, she was good people." He grimaced. "But, once you get into that destructive mind-set, ... it's damn hard to get anybody to switch out of it. Patricia had very little self-worth, and sometimes I think that when you're a victim ..."

He took a deep breath, as the tears once again threatened. "It's almost as if you're always a victim, even after we got her off the streets and into a regular job." He shook his head. "Even into this apartment and after we got her cleaned up, she was always afraid. She kept looking over her shoulder, afraid that somebody would see her, somebody would recognize her. She used to be in a rough area, so we moved her here, which was definitely a big step up. Plus, by moving farther away, we were hoping that she wouldn't meet any of the people who she may have seen on the streets."

He sighed. "And, in all the time she was here—it's been two years now—she never told me about seeing someone from her past, so we thought that we were good. Yet, I guess, it's quite possible that somebody from her old life had seen her."

"How did things end with the pimp?" Kate asked. "They don't often take it well to lose a girl."

He feigned not hearing her, but then nodded. "If I hadn't paid him a stupid sum of money to get my sister out of there"—he shook his head—"I might have thought the exact same thing." Terry gazed around the hallway, as if searching for something to latch on to. "The pimp smirked at me the whole time. Thought I'd made a fool's deal, told me that she'd be back voluntarily in no time and that he wouldn't even talk to me when she returned to him."

"Did she ever try to contact him again?"

He frowned at Kate and shook his head. "No, hell no." His tone was full of denial and hurt, but then he winced as his voice broke. "I don't know. I guess it's possible, but she was off the drugs. She wasn't on the streets. She could sleep at night. It seemed as if we really had managed to turn the corner for her, and now this." His tears appeared once again. "God, the pain," he murmured. "To think of all she's been through and that all she wanted was to have a half-decent life. She wasn't looking for millions. She was looking for a piece of her soul. She was looking for a chance to get up in the morning and to be normal, to have a normal job, working from nine to five, to work in the world that she had so wanted to be a part of."

"What set her on the streets in the first place?" Kate asked.

He hesitated. "You might as well know all of it. My father abused her, ... my stepfather," he corrected. "My father took me to live with him and left Patricia with my mother. Patricia, at that time, was very close with our mother, and then our mother remarried." He stared at Kate for a moment, these painful memories hurting him.

"My sister in her prime was an absolute beauty. She was the sweetest, cutest thing. It was really hard on me, when I was taken away from her. It was hard on her too. We were close. We did still see each other. Our parents couldn't do that much to us. They allowed us to go back and forth, but it wasn't ever quite the same. And then Patricia flipped at about fourteen, maybe fifteen." He shook his head.

"I don't remember exactly how old I was or how old she was when it started, but I found out she was doing tricks, and I couldn't believe it. I was absolutely stunned because that was so not her. And when I did finally get a chance to ask her what the hell was going on, she had this dead look in her eyes, and she shrugged. She told me, *What difference does it make? This is what men do to women.* Of course it broke my heart to even hear her say that, but I knew that she believed it, and I told her emphatically that that's not what true men did. That's what bastards did," he declared forcefully.

"She finally told me what had happened between her and our stepfather—and it took a few meetings. It took quite a lot of meetings actually." He stared down the hallway, as if reviewing the years of pain. "When she finally told me, I went straight to my mother and my father, and the three of us confronted my stepfather and brought in the cops. He admitted it, how he hadn't been able to resist Patricia. She was so beautiful that he couldn't keep his hands off her. Once he realized where it had sent her, I think, in some way, he was sorry," he added bitterly, "but I don't think he was ever sorry enough."

"What happened to him?"

"He did time, seven years," Terry replied bitterly. "Her life's completely ruined and that bastard? … He served seven lousy years. And look where she ended up," he said, once again struggling for control.

It was a familiar story, and one that Kate had absolutely

no satisfaction in hearing of again. Especially now when she considered Simon's own abuse by his foster father. Kate shook her head. Often abusers got off so much easier than their accusers thought they should, considering the damage that the abusers created for those poor people, the poor victims.

The law often kept these abusers on the streets, out on bail, presumed innocent until found guilty. And it made Kate's job that much harder. These victims never got over that abuse. Sometimes it stayed alive in their mind until they saw the person who had abused them so badly, and they often lost it and took them out. She understood killing an abuser because it was a delayed reaction of self-defense, but she didn't understand how Patricia's own stepfather could be a part of this, abusing a teenage girl he should have protected as his own daughter.

Terry studied Kate, as if realizing the way her thoughts were running. "This isn't his style." Terry pointed at Patricia's apartment. "He's a mouse of a man. He's pretty broken up about what happened to her and that he caused it." Terry dropped his head in his hands. "But he's not anywhere near broken up enough," he stated bitterly. "Believe me. I'll be having another go at him for what he did that brought her to this end." He stared at the apartment. "Do I ... do I have to stay?"

Kate shook her head. "No, you're probably fine. We can take it from here." She got his contact information and then, having a cop lead him outside to his car, she watched in the hallway when Rodney showed up after having to step out on some errand earlier.

He looked back to where the big man was being led away and then at her. "What was that all about?" Rodney asked her. Kate quickly explained, and he winced. "Terry's right in a way. It seems as if a victim who's been abused in life takes a series of really ugly turns, and they never quite get free of it."

"And yet we don't want to think of it that way," she countered. "That's the worst thing that you ever want to think about, how a victim is a victim is a victim."

"And yet," Rodney replied, "you yourself know victim-mentality is a hard one to kick."

She glared at him and then shrugged, nodding. "Very true," she muttered. "And yet how much of all this is connected, and how much of it has nothing to do with anything yet?" She shrugged. "None of this murder seems to fit together with her history."

"Meaning, you don't think it was her pimp or an old client?"

"I don't think so," Kate said. "I could be wrong, of course, but it doesn't feel that way."

He nodded. "I'll go with your feelings on this one. So far you've been right on the money."

She snorted at that. "You sure as hell can't count on that. I could be wrong on the next ten murders."

"In which case"—he grinned broadly—"we'll use that all against you, every time we decide which theory we'll go with."

She laughed. "Theory should be based on evidence and following the history of the victims and seeing what fits together. Theory should be puzzle-solving. Feelings? Now those are an entirely different thing."

"Especially gut feelings," he pointed out.

"True enough," she agreed. "This is definitely a gut feel-ing, but I don't think it's connected to the stepfather. I am not so sure about Patricia's history, but I doubt this murder is connected to her pimp. I did, however, forget to ask the brother what he paid to get his sister free from the pimp. I also didn't ask him if he knew about the kidnapping."

"You could be right about her pimp. He also knows he could turn around and pick up another girl off the streets, keep her locked up for a few days and strung out on drugs—which he gets her hooked on in the first place—and, before you know it, absolutely no defense is there, no fight is left in her."

"I know. That is unfortunately so often the way of it."

He smiled. "Remember. We can't solve everybody's problems."

"You sure?" she quipped. "We could give it a try."

"Ah, that would be one of those pointless attempts. Can't really say that I'm feeling that one."

She shook her head. "Oh, I don't know," she muttered. "This just feels so very wrong."

"In what way?"

Kate sighed. "Why would the kidnapper tell Patricia that, if she delivered the message, she's off the hook? Yet, if she doesn't deliver the message, he'd find out. And she'd wake up one morning to find him at the edge of her bed, and the game would start again. This isn't a game," she declared, throwing her arms out at the apartment. "This is a slaughter. This is ..." She stopped, winced, looked over at Rodney and added, "This is a you-lose kind of shit."

WITH A TEXT response from Kate, Simon tucked his phone in his back pocket and headed to his first building. He was rehabbing three buildings downtown at this point. Some of these projects seemed to go on forever, and a couple he had more or less dove into with his heart rather than his brain, and he was still paying the piper for those.

On the other hand, he'd never lost money on a project yet, and he wasn't about to start. It was just a matter of appealing to the correct audience and letting people know what was available and why something was special. As soon as people saw what made a building unique, they often bought into the whole emotional side of the property, and it wasn't then just concrete, wood, and marble.

He walked up to the first project on his route today, and his foreman paced on the front steps, arguing on his phone.

Simon stopped and winced. That was not a good start. He approached slowly. His foreman, now seeing Simon, quickly ended the call. "Problems?" Simon asked cautiously.

He snorted. "Nothing more than usual." He waved his cell phone around. "Things are stuck at the docks. Supplies can't come on time. Two men are down sick." He added an eye roll.

"And yet *sick* could be a euphemism for *It's a sunny day*," Simon noted, with a questioning look.

"It probably is. But they do good work, *when they work*, and it's damn hard to get them to work if their heart is not into it."

"Right. We've got way too many of those sometimes, don't we?"

"We're also spread thin. Lots of people are struggling right now, and they don't want to work."

"Right."

Since the pandemic had washed through the world, everything had shifted, causing supply chain issues, staffing issues, constant issues, and more issues atop that. There were always issues in this industry. Meanwhile, Simon wanted to take something old and turn it into a renewed beauty, but he also wanted function over form. He wanted both if he could get it, preferably at a price that was doable—and that was where the challenge often came in.

Still, turning his mind back to his foreman, Simon said, "Let's see where the problems are and see if we can find a way around them."

"You have to be a miracle worker to find ways around these headaches," his foreman muttered. But he turned and sent him a hard smile. "Come on. Let's go take a look."

***

GREAT, SIMON WAS up ahead.

To a casual passerby, when they saw a nondescript man, most won't interact. He smiled, tugged up his collar against his neck, being that nondescript man. Even though it was a warm day for late September in Vancouver, it helped to hide him, kept him feeling a little bit more secure. Besides, he didn't know whether Simon could tell who he was or not, and so, keeping quiet, keeping hidden, was even more paramount.

Simon's stalker shifted to the other side of the road and watched his prey, kept it up for several hours, picking up a few groceries as he went, even picked up a coffee, knowing that it was foolish to do this, but many people were in Simon's life and yet, in many ways, not enough.

He now watched the foreman and then another employee join the foreman, as soon as Simon left. A harsh interaction ensued between the man and the foreman.

He listened for tidbits. Seemed the employee was reaming out the foreman pretty good, called him a waste of space, stating that he, the employee, was so much better than everyone.

The stalker sneered. *The asshole.* He was hardly better than anyone. That's not fair, but guys like that were everywhere, and he knew lots of them. Instead of following Simon, his stalker eyed the verbal altercation, felt that familiar instinct, that killer instinct, rise again, and chose one of the two men, still arguing before him.

He continued watching the abuser, who'd been yelling at the foreman, now take a left turn and head down a separate street. The stalker quickly followed him. If he was lucky, maybe this asshole wouldn't be quite so bright. Watching him head into a pool hall, the stalker smiled with quiet joy. This would be almost too easy.

CHAPTER 4

ANSWERS WERE VERY slow in coming. As it was, Kate would have to wait days, if not weeks, for forensics. Multiple sets of fingerprints were in Patricia's apartment, and they needed to bring Terry back in, her brother, for fingerprint testing to exclude him. Kate did, however, have a printout of their victim's history. The stepfather had sexually abused Patricia at a young age, soon after he'd moved into the family home.

He'd done his time and was living in Toronto, a hell of a long way away from Vancouver. Kate would have to hunt down the pimp no matter what, just to ask some questions about Patricia and Terry. And, with that thought in mind, she phoned the brother. When he answered, she identified herself.

As soon as he heard the name, he sighed, and his tone was weary when he spoke again. "Do have any news for me?"

"No, not yet. I'm sorry," she said, although knowing that she had no reason to apologize when his sister was barely in the morgue. "I do need the name of the pimp you bought her from. Then I'll go talk to him to see if he's had anything to do with this."

Terry seemed surprised. "You'll really go talk to him?"

"Absolutely. Chances are he's well-known to our department already, and that'll make it a little easier for me to go there."

"If you say so," Terry replied, his tone curt. "I'd just as soon never see that asshole's face again. The only name I know him by is *Stone*."

"As in *stoner*?" she asked.

"I don't know. When I saw him, he wasn't drugged out. I never heard anybody call him by that name. However, Patricia only called him *Stone* anytime I ever talked to her about him."

"Did she say much?"

"Only that he was an asshole and that he beat her whenever she didn't bring in enough money."

"Unfortunately that's pretty common in the industry."

"Yet, if you beat your goods, how the hell are you supposed to make them create more money?"

Kate privately agreed, but there was no logic when you talked to these abusers. They knew perfectly well what they were doing. Usually the evidence that they beat the women was hidden, so that nobody had any idea. The pimps were careful enough to not leave any marks. Although if she was beaten, and often, it could be that Stone was renting Patricia out to johns who liked that little bit of extra *fun*. "Did she ever say she had rough johns or got beaten up by johns?"

"Sure, a couple of them," Terry confirmed. "She never really talked about them though, just that a lot of shitty men were out in the world."

"Right. I won't argue with you on that point," Kate noted. "I'm trying to figure out who all might have had something to do with this."

"Right. And I presume that I still need to come in, don't I?"

"Yes, they found multiple fingerprints in her apartment,

so we need to exclude yours from them."

"Right," he replied, but his tone was dead weary. "I also want to see her."

"I can arrange for that too," Kate agreed, "after the autopsy."

Another sigh came from Terry, or maybe it was almost a held-back sob. Finally he spoke. "Fine, I can wait for that." He was choking on his words. "Who would have thought that that's how my day would go?"

"Were you expecting to meet Patricia when you showed up at her apartment?"

"Sure, I was taking her out to lunch. And then I called to say I would be late, and she didn't answer my call. So, when I tried calling her again, seeing if we could postpone lunch for another day, I got no answer, By then I was so worried that I came over."

"Had she been dealing with depression, anything like that?"

"Why? You think she killed herself?" he asked, his tone turning harsh.

"No," Kate stated. "However, I do need to know if there's any chance that maybe she went back to her pimp, looking for drugs to numb the pain."

He sucked in his breath, as if the thought hadn't occurred to him.

Kate heard the faintest of sobs coming through the phone. She really hated to talk to the families because their pain was something that she took on herself. "I know it happened in the past to other people, but is there any chance? … And I know it is upsetting to even consider this, but sometimes pimps trade and sell their girls between them. So did Patricia have another pimp at all outside of this

Stone?"

"No, not that I know of." Terry was audibly sobbing now, yet a buzz filled the air, as if he were thinking about Kate's question still. "I don't think she ever mentioned that. God, … it doesn't even bear thinking about, does it? Jesus, my poor sister."

"Yes, it's not an easy thing to contemplate, but she is at peace now."

"Is she now?" he asked bitterly. "How would you know if she is? I want you to find that asshole and make him pay."

"That's what I plan to do."

She was writing down her notes from this conversation, when Terry asked, "Anything else?"

"Yes. Do you know what happened to her these last few days?" she asked bluntly.

A few moments of a dead silence came on the other end. "No, what are you talking about?"

"So you don't know that she came to the police station yesterday?"

"No, I don't. Why?" he asked, his voice rising. "Did you guys know something? What happened? Could you have stopped this?"

"No," she said gently. "We didn't know anything about this. She apparently … When was the last time you talked to your sister?"

He pondered that and then replied, "At least a few days ago. Maybe four or five. Once we had planned lunch for today, then we didn't confirm beyond that. I go to work, and she goes to work. I assume that, if she had any problem, she'd call me."

"Does she regularly do that?"

"Sure. We talk, I would say, a decent amount of the

time." But his tone turned wary. "What happened, Detective? What don't I know?"

She hesitated again, knowing that telling Terry would make him feel even shittier, but this revelation was inevitable. "She was kidnapped and held captive for a few days by somebody she couldn't identify."

"What?" his voice was low and lethal. "Are you serious?"

"I am. There's a little bit more to it than that. ... He released her outside a hospital, after driving by her apartment and pointing it out to her. Patricia couldn't tell us anything about him, couldn't tell us anything about the vehicle or even where she had been held, just that he wanted her to deliver a message to us. Which she did. And then, if she didn't deliver the message, he would come back for her."

She almost heard the heartbreak in Terry's voice when he said, "My God. I didn't know anything about it."

"She was in the hospital immediately afterward. However, as soon as she could, she checked herself out," Kate explained. "So I guess that's why I'm asking how close you are. Would she have told you something about this?"

"I don't know," he admitted. "I would have thought so. We've been through so much together," he cried out. "Jesus, Jesus, Jesus." He kept repeating that litany.

"I know. It's a lot to take in."

"You think that's who killed her?"

"I don't know that," she stated. "It could be a completely separate issue. Her kidnapper did tell her that, if Patricia delivered the message, then he would leave her alone. And she did deliver the message, but that means that we would have to believe this asshole."

"I don't believe any assholes," Terry declared bluntly. "Particularly assholes who kidnap vulnerable women and make them do this shit." He swore over and over again. "Christ, I wish she'd told me."

"Maybe she was ashamed. It seemed she was holding something back, so I went to her apartment to ask her. Instead I found her there, dead."

"So you came to ask her questions about the kidnapping?"

"Yes."

"Christ," he lamented. "I don't even know what to think anymore. I would have sworn that she'd have told me anything."

"Okay, so let's reverse that. What would she never tell you?"

First came a dead silence on the other end, and then he exploded. "If, for whatever reason, she was seeing her stepfather, our stepfather, again. I would never allow that to happen, but ... I also know that it's not something I have to worry about because it's never something that she would ever do."

"Right. Did she really hate him?'

"She absolutely hated him," he confirmed, his tone belligerent. "But I could see him doing this maybe."

"And yet you were just saying that you didn't think so."

"No, I don't see Patricia going to him, but I do see our stepfather seeking her out. Now I can't stop thinking about it," he snapped into the phone.

"I will talk to him, and you need to *not* talk to him, do you hear me?" she ordered, her voice hard—to try and get it through Terry's head that she couldn't have any interference in this.

He hemmed and hawed.

"I mean it, Terry. If you do anything to him, talk, yell, it could impinge on the case, giving him a good chance of getting away with this, if he had anything to do with it. We don't know that he did, so we need you to back off and to let me talk to him."

"Fine. You can talk to him, but, if he doesn't give you any answers that make you happy, you let me know. I know which buttons to push." And, with that, he disconnected.

She stared down at the phone, frowning, because, of course, if ever anybody could push buttons, it was definitely family, as she well knew. She sat eyeing the phone for a little bit longer, as she contemplated her options. When Rodney poked his head around and approached her, he asked, "What's next, boss?"

She snorted at that moniker. "I talked to the brother. I think I'll talk to the stepfather. Plus I need to roust up this one guy, Stone."

"Stone?" Owen repeated from his corner of the office, as he twisted in his seat to face her. "You mean, the pimp?"

She asked him, "Do you know him?"

"I don't *know* him," he clarified, with an eye roll, "but I know *of* him, most of us do. He has a long history here."

"A decent history or is he one of the biggest assholes on the earth?" Kate asked Owen.

"Decent history, as far as pimps go," he relayed. "If we tell him that he has to lay off, get rid of or take girls in for medical care, et cetera and more, he usually complies fairly quickly."

"Do we ever stop him from being a pimp?" she asked.

"We did, and then he turns around and does it again. He's still a pimp. You can't expect perfection, but he is one who tends to look after his girls, more so than others. On the other hand, he beats them if they're in trouble or if they don't bring in enough money." Owen shrugged. "So a pimp is always a pimp."

"Jesus, so apparently the brother bought his sister off this guy."

"And that's possible. I've heard a couple other cases like that. Sometimes I wondered if Stone was kidnapping young girls and holding them ransom, but he says that he never kidnaps them, and we've never had anybody charge him with that or even imply that. Usually he finds junkies on the street, and he tries to get them before other guys do because, of course, pretty young girls don't stay pretty on the streets for long. So you need a constant stream of them."

"Why would Stone have allowed this guy Terry to buy his sister?"

"I hate to say it, but chances are, she looked less than pretty, and much-less-than-pretty costs him because he can't command as high a price."

"Jesus, so what then?" Kate asked him. "They dispose of the not-so-pretty girls when the pimps turn them into this in the first place?"

Owen held up his hands in surrender. "Absolutely. Don't shoot the messenger."

She groaned at that. "Fine, I'll go down and have a talk with him." At that, Owen eyed her with slight alarm. She narrowed her gaze. "What? Is that a problem?'

He shrugged. "Just so you know, he doesn't like women much."

"Just so you know, I don't like pimps much," she snapped right back.

He flashed a grin at her. "Would you mind if I come with you? I almost want to see the fireworks."

"Too bad." Rodney rose from his desk. "I'll go with

her."

"You guys, is there any way to check the history on pimps, so I can find out if she was with another pimp beforehand?" Kate asked her team. "I've asked the brother, but he doesn't know anything about it. I need to track down the stepfather and see where he is. If there's any chance he's local, I want his ass in here for questioning. Supposedly he lives back east, but where was he when Patricia was killed?"

"Oh, we can get right on that." Owen smiled.

"And what about … you've got other cases too, don't you?" she asked him.

"Yep, sure do," Owen confirmed, "but we're getting this one rounded up, so we should be good to go to give you guys a hand because, of course, we only have a few days and …"

"I know," Kate interrupted, "and then it's off to the next case."

"We caught two more," Lilliana announced, as she walked in, clearly overhearing Owen talking about their workload. "Gang fight down on the East Side. Only so much help we can give you."

"Got it," Kate acknowledged, lifting a hand at Owen. "Thanks for the thought."

"Hey, if I can get there, I will," he muttered, turning to look at Lilliana. "Two dead?"

"Two dead, two in hospital, and, as we saw, … badly sliced," she added.

And that's all Kate heard, as she walked out with Rodney.

He turned to her. "Are you up for pimps?"

"I'm up for talking to pimps. I am never up for pimps. Utilizing somebody else's body for gain sucks, as far as I'm concerned. And to do it by force? That'll never go down on my books as being fair and aboveboard."

He laughed. "It's so funny to hear you so angry on behalf of a stranger."

"Why?" she asked crossly. "What does it matter whether I know them or not? It's worse if I do know them," she admitted, twisting in her seat to look at him, as he was driving.

"Why is that?" he asked her.

"Because I'm more invested emotionally," she shared, with a haunting expression. "Strangers? No big deal. Yet family and friends screw you up every time."

"I would have just said family."

"We've seen enough betrayal to realize friends aren't always friends either."

"Ooh, ouch," he said, as he headed toward the East Side. "You're definitely on a roll this morning."

She slipped back into her seat. "Patricia's brother was so overwrought, so upset," she murmured. "They had done so much, especially over the last couple years, to get her off the streets and to get her cleaned up and to get her into a decent life, and then to see this happen?" Kate shook her head. "Was she chosen as a random victim, or was her killer deliberately choosing somebody who had worked hard, and then he pulled the carpet out from under her? It messes up my mind."

"Oh, now there is an interesting thought," Rodney noted. "You think we have any helplines or groups for people like this?"

"I'm sure there are one million of them," Kate replied. "But anybody watching probably would have seen it happen anyway, without having to contact the group to find these people." She made a lazy gesture. "I hate to say it, but I highly suspect the next victim will show us the pattern that we can't see yet because we don't have enough evidence yet."

"You're sure there'll be a next victim?" he asked, his voice low. "Because you know what that means."

"I know exactly what that means," she murmured. "Yet no other way for this guy to continue his *game*, unless it's already game over. and Simon lost, and I can't see *that* happening."

"You can't see Simon losing the game, or you can't see him getting into the game, where he could then eventually lose?"

She shook her head. "Neither. Simon plays poker, but he doesn't care about the outcome. Something like this though, he'll be tormented by the outcome," she shared. "He cares, and, as much as I don't want to"—she shrugged and shook her head—"I can certainly appreciate that part of him."

"Oh, no doubt about it," Rodney concurred. "I'm thoroughly convinced that Simon is one of the good guys. It's just harder convincing everybody else of that fact. ... Still, that's a whole different story."

They pulled up and parked off to the side, near the area that Stone worked. Kate hopped out, looked around at the street, and asked, "I suppose they're working twenty-four hours a day, aren't they?"

"Yes, although the pimp himself may not be around." Rodney looked around, then pointed to somebody. "Except, in this case, he is here."

"I don't know if that's good or bad." Kate watched an argument in progress.

With that inner sense of those who always were on the wrong side of the law, the conversation came to an abrupt halt. One of the men quickly walked away, and the other one, obviously Stone, turned to glare at her.

She laughed with a pointed look at Rodney. "Have to love their instincts, *huh*?"

"I don't know about that," Rodney countered. "Sure makes our job a lot harder."

"It does, indeed," she muttered. She walked over and introduced herself and then looked the pimp up and down. "How's your day, Stone?"

"Not …" His gaze narrowed, as he studied her for a long moment, and then a mock smile broke out. "Well, look at this. A new copper to add to my roster." Stone rubbed his hands together. "When you leave the station, come work for me."

"Never going to happen," she replied immediately. "The pay sucks and the hours? The hours are way worse, but I prefer to walk rather than spend my days on my ass."

He burst out laughing, with a sense of humor that surprised her. It seemed to really shock Rodney too—or maybe not. The turn of events was certainly not expected though, as Owen had mentioned that Stone didn't like women, but his response here to Kate was something altogether different.

Stone shifted to the side, keeping the two of them slightly apart, as if he didn't notice Rodney immediately, but then he turned to look at him. His laughter cut off immediately, as Stone pinned Rodney with a look. "I don't like you."

"Doesn't matter whether you do or not," Rodney stated calmly. "I don't know you, and, as long as I don't know you," he declared, "we ain't friends."

"Damn right, we ain't friends," Stone snorted. He turned and looked back at Kate. "You, on the other hand? I like you."

"But then you like women, don't you?" she asked calmly, knowing it was completely opposite to what she been told. "At least you like them when they're working for you."

"Damn right I do." He winked. "If you have a woman in your life, she might as well bring in the money, nothing else good about them."

"And yet you use your own women for your sexual purposes too," she shared, as a statement of knowledge.

"Of course. I own them anyway. I might as well get my needs taken care of."

She wanted to punch him for that comment, but, hey, it was the least of her worries. "I want to talk to you about Patricia Blinker."

His eyebrows shot up. "Damn, woman," he said, with a playful tone, "she's not even in my stable anymore."

"I understand that." Kate gave him a half smile. "I wondered if you decided you should get her back again now that she's looking a helluva lot better."

But immediately Stone shook his head. "Nope." He shook his head too vehemently. "That one's trouble. Her brother is the trouble I guess, more of a trouble. The only reason I sold her was to get him off my back. Goddamn family's a piece of shit. They don't know when to quit."

"Well, you can understand where he's coming from. This isn't where he wants to see his sister."

"She had opportunities to leave," Stone replied, not giving an inch. "She never took them."

"Probably because those opportunities always came with strings attached."

He gave a ghost of a smile. "What is an opportunity, if you don't have to do something for it? … Not everything in life is for free."

"And, in your case, nothing's free, is it?"

"What? … Am I supposed to feel bad about that now?" he asked in a mocking tone.

"Have you seen her since you sold her?" she asked, using the term deliberately.

"No, sure haven't. As I told her, her brother was a piece of shit, kept coming and breaking up my girls, stuffing the johns, taking pictures, and generally making life a nightmare."

Her eyebrows shot up at that, and Stone nodded. "Yeah, he was a real pain in my ass for so long. The only reason I sold her was to get him off my back," he snarled. "Besides, she lost her looks, and her income was certainly dropping."

"Maybe if you fed her and treated her better and didn't beat her up quite so often, she would have kept making you the big bucks."

"Now, you see? I tried that, and then they just give you a lip, and all you end up doing is having to plow into them to smarten them up," he explained, his voice hard. "Now, if you don't mind, I've got other things to do, like keep some of my girls occupied because, while we're here talking, they're standing around doing nothing. Waste of God's fucking space." He turned and glared at the one closest and yelled at her. "Clarice, get your ass out there and shake it."

The woman immediately turned and raced away on her stupidly high heels, clicking like a loud tinker. Kate eyed the heels and shook her head. She'd have broken her neck for sure on those suckers. Good thing she wasn't in the business, and that thought rang in her mind.

She looked back at Stone. "What about the brother?" she asked in an offhand question. "Did you ever see him again?"

He slowly nodded. "Yeah, actually I did. That was a funny thing. He hung around for a while, as if he wasn't sure that his sister would be okay. I didn't quite get it. I told him to piss off and to get out of my life, or I'd fucking sic the hoods on him."

"Interesting," she murmured. "Did he say what he wanted?"

"He told me that he was keeping an eye on me." He snorted, making it obvious what he thought of it. "His heart wasn't in it. He wanted to make sure his sister was safe. I told him that his sister was fucking safe, as long as she stayed the hell away from me. However, the minute she came back, looking for something from me, you can bet that I wouldn't give a shit about him anymore."

"And did she?"

His expression turned sly. "You're taking up valuable time here, which I don't do for nobody."

"Well, we can go down to the station and talk there for a much longer time," she suggested immediately. "Besides, why do you want to bring all the cops down on you here for?" she asked, with a laugh. "If you don't cooperate, I'll call in the narcs and make sure that they hound you constantly. It's obvious you got more drugs up your sleeves than these guys who even sell for you."

"Hey, hey, hey, hey." Stone held up his hands in protest. "You don't see me with no drugs."

"That's 'cause your girls are carrying them," she replied smoothly. "Goes along with the tricks, doesn't it? A few tricks, a few extra blows. What the hell. Blow on both ends and they're happy."

He gave her a fat grin. "See? I knew I liked you. You get it, don't you?"

"I get it, but, if you don't help me, you ain't going to be very happy about what you don't get."

He glared at Kate and then shrugged. "I don't give a shit. It's no skin off my nose, but she called me last night out of the blue."

Her eyebrows shot up at that. "What did she want?"

He gave her half a smile. "She wanted some blow. Said she was in rather *desperate need.*"

"And did she sound as if she was in need? As if she was a junkie still who wanted that fix?"

"No, but she sounded terrified, told me that something had happened, and she needed to take the edge off." He took a moment to think and continued. "Now that I under-stand—because these girls, they always tell me that shit—it was a bad john. He was really brutal, vicious. Even the young ones, when they first came on board, they need that hit to take the edge off what they're doing." He laughed one hearty laugh. "Christ, it's Mother Nature. All you have to do is lie there and spread your fucking legs." He snorted. "What the hell? But, no, they've all got the same damn whiny story about needing to take the edge off."

"So you give it to them."

"I always give it to them," he said. "That's what I do. I take care of my own."

"Right." She shook her head, turned toward Rodney, then asked Stone more questions. "So did you give her any?"

"No, I didn't give her any. I told her that she should go ask her fucking brother for some, and it's her brother's fault that she didn't have any."

"What did she say to that?"

"She started bawling. She was getting to be such a pain in the ass with all those damn tears all the time, and it was more of the same," he muttered. "Like seriously, man. It's bad enough when you have to deal with these chicks, but when you get the whiny ones, and they're out there thinking that their shit doesn't stink and that they don't have to do the same goddamn work everybody else does?" He scrunched up his nose. "Got to start seriously thinking about getting rid of them."

"What does *getting rid of them* mean to you?"

He laughed. "I don't kill them, if that's what you mean," he replied, with a smirk. "No way in hell I'm bringing that kind of heat down on me. I make a nice living here." He sneered. "And I told her to go talk to her brother, and, other than that, she was to lose my number. Although maybe, don't hold it against me, but I might have been a little rougher in my tone."

Such mockery filled his voice that Kate clenched her jaw, while staring at him, trying hard not to pop him in the nose. But aggression would never get her agenda resolved, and it would get her in hot water with her department, something she wasn't prepared to do.

He grinned at her and turned to Rodney. "Man, you see the fire in that gaze? I really like that. Anytime you want to change your career and actually go with a real man," he offered suggestively, "you give me a call."

She half laughed. "No point in calling you, if I'm looking for a real man. That would be a waste of my nickel and yours." As she turned to walk away, she pivoted and asked, "And that's all it was in that conversation?"

"Yeah, I hung up on her," Stone stated. "Like I need that shit in my life again. That brother of hers was psycho, so no way in hell I was doing anything to bring him back into my life. Besides, as I said, she lost her looks, and she wasn't bringing in the money anymore. Selling her was a good deal for me. I scored big-time on that."

"Yeah? How much did you sell her for?" she asked curiously, looking Stone straight in his face.

"Twelve grand. I would have given her over for half that." Stone laughed. "But the brother didn't even argue. He paid it, and that was it."

She winced, as Terry was so eager to save his sister that he probably didn't even realize how Patricia was a bargaining chip. Then Kate wondered about a person who would bargain for a person's life, instead of paying the damn bill, and figured the brother's way was better after all. "It's just money," she declared. "You can always make more money. What her brother really did was try to save a soul." She turned and walked away without a word, Rodney by her side.

"A soul that was already gone," Stone called out after her. Then he yelled back, "Hey, Copper!" She turned her head around, and he asked, "Why you even asking?"

She grimaced. "Because that soul may have been gone but she was somewhat present even then. She was murdered last night or in the wee morning hours," Kate added, as he paled somewhat. "So you can bet we're checking on everybody's whereabouts."

"You didn't ask me about mine." His face flushed all kinds of shades. "So you don't think I'm capable of killing her?"

"I didn't think you were." She walked back to him. "So, since you want to be asked, where the hell were you last night?"

"At home, with two of my girls. One of them's down sick." He almost stuttered as he spoke now. "Christ, was she ever sick. She's puking all over the place."

"You ever think she's pregnant?" At that, the pimp

stopped and stared at her in horror. Kate nodded. "Birth control doesn't work on everybody," Kate shared. "Take her in and get her checked, before she ends up losing it in a bad way, and then you lose her. Alternatively she'll give you whatever the hell she's got."

"Hell no, that ain't happening."

"Then let me take her in." Kate crossed her arms over her chest. "She needs care, and she'll make you and your stable sicker."

He hesitated for a moment, but it was obvious that this girl was severely ill because he immediately nodded and agreed to Kate's offer. "You take her then, fucking good riddance."

He lifted a hand, and two men immediately appeared. He told them to bring out the sick one and fast. They didn't say a word but turned around and headed right back inside, and Kate noted which door and which building. When they returned, dragging a waif of a girl, who couldn't have been even seventeen, Kate's heart damn-near broke. The girl was green around the gills, barely on her feet, and Kate grabbed her arms and immediately Rodney picked up the waif.

Kate nodded to Stone and said, "I'll take her into the hospital and see what's wrong." Then she walked away.

He asked in a half cry, "You gonna pay me for her?"

"No," Kate called back. "You'll pay me for her."

After a moment of silence came Stone's laughter again. "Damn, I knew I liked you," he repeated, with a snort. "Make sure she ain't got nothing contagious and hasn't already brought down my whole stable."

"You'll find out pretty quick all on your own," she told him, "because it'll spread like wildfire, depending on what she's got."

And, with that, they quickly bundled the poor girl into the back seat of their vehicle, with Kate beside her. Kate looked over at Rodney, worry etched all over her face.

Rodney nodded. "I know. I'm on it." And, with that, he drove like a street racer to the closest hospital.

As Kate stepped inside the emergency section of the hospital, she flashed her badge and explained what was going on. She got an ER doctor almost immediately. He took one look at the patient, shook his head, and immediately got her on a gurney and whisked her away to a room.

Kate wasn't sure if the girl was even cognizant, but they were still working on her an hour later, and nobody came out to say anything to her. Rodney had gone to pick up coffee, and, when he returned, the doctor stepped out and walked over toward Kate.

She bounced her feet. "And?"

"She's in a bad way," he explained, with a sorrowful expression. "Not only is she coming off the drug high but she's had something really ugly, and we've found an anomaly in her blood that's not quite right. We're running a bunch of tests, but it looks as if she could have a major disease."

"And not one caught from the street?"

Immediately the doctor shook his head. "Not one caught from the streets. I'm thinking potentially leukemia, something along that line. We're running tests now."

"Aw, shit," Kate muttered. "That girl can't catch a break."

"She's a hooker?"

"Let's just say that she was in a pimp's possession. I don't even know how old she is, but she looks barely even seventeen."

"No, she doesn't," the doc replied. "In fact, I would hazard a guess that she's probably closer to the fourteen mark, but she is currently menstruating, so she's past puberty."

"Got it," Kate nodded. "Is that significant?"

He nodded. "It's a heavy flow, too heavy."

"If she was with a john, could it have been a rough *encounter*?" she asked. "For lack of a better word."

He nodded. "She has had sex, forcible sex, recently," he concurred. "So quite possibly we're seeing the end result of a rough rape."

She turned to Rodney, standing beside her. "And the pimp doesn't consider it rape because he owns her," she said in a hard voice.

"We don't know much at this point," Rodney reminded her, "that it even was him. He was pretty damn confused too."

"That's true," she agreed, thinking of Stone's response. "Anyway …" She looked over at the doctor and sighed with a heavy heart. "Call social services, and we'll get started on checking her history. Someone has to be missing her, and she needs care, and she needs somebody—outside of the pimp— to give it to her."

"We're on it," the doc replied, as he turned and walked back to the patient. Then he called out, "Good thing you brought her in. She probably wouldn't have lasted another forty-eight hours out there." And, with that, he disappeared behind the curtain again.

Back at the registration desk, Kate quickly handed over her details and contact information, requesting a call for any change with the patient, also looking for any ID on the patient as well. If they came up with anything, they were to let her know. If the patient woke up, they were to let her know.

With that, she turned around and headed toward the parking lot.

⁓⁓

SIMON'S VOICE SLAMMED into the phone, even though he tried hard to modulate it. "What's wrong?" After a long moment of dead silence on the other end, he winced. "Okay, let me try that again," he said in a slightly calmer voice. "I got a message that something was wrong. And I guess, after last time, I'm feeling a little sensitive."

Kate's snort on the other end made him grin. She's the only person he knew who could communicate so much with just a sniff. Sometimes it came across as a huge whiff or a sneeze, and sometimes it was a simple curt snort, but always she got her point across. "In other words, you're fine, I hope."

"I'm fine," she replied, but her voice was low, modulated, as if she might be fine, but something *did* happen.

"You want to tell me what's going on?"

She gave him a rundown about a teenager they'd found, when talking to a pimp. The story didn't surprise Simon, but it saddened him. "So she's in the hospital right now?"

"Yes, and they're supposed to let me know when, … if … she wakes up. She wouldn't have survived another forty-eight hours if she'd stayed where she was," she murmured. "Of course that makes me feel even worse."

"Why?" he asked. "You didn't have anything to do with this."

"No, it wasn't me, but, at the same time, what a nasty-ass world we live in that this is how you treat another person. All he had to do was get her help. And yet it was too much for him."

"The only reason he gave her to you now is because she would cost him if any of the other girls got sick, which would also drop them, and he'd be out of his daily income. Most of these pimps—now I'm not trying to excuse their behavior—but you also have to understand that generally they also pay enforcers or mafia or street owners as well, so he's got bills to pay himself."

"Yeah, I don't give a fuck about that," she snapped, again bringing a big grin to Simon's face. She called a spade a spade, and God help you if you got in her way.

"I can check in at the hospital later and see how she's doing," Simon offered. "Yet you probably have them on speed dial to double-check to see where she's at."

"Somehow," she admitted, with a note of humor in her voice, "you seem to know me so well."

"I do know you"—he chuckled—"who you are at the core. You might still be fighting it, but I've definitely seen that rescue heroine on the inside."

She laughed. "You need to go take another look, buddy. Anyway I'm off. We're still trying to find information on Patricia's former life. With her stepfather released from prison, we need to figure out exactly where he is now and whether he had anything to do with her murder."

"I don't think I heard about the stepfather," Simon noted, his voice neutral.

"Ah, all part of an ongoing case," she replied in that breezy tone she used—almost as a brush-off—that he absolutely detested.

He glared at the phone, all his good humor disappearing again.

And then, in a complete twist, she added, "Missed you." And she disconnected.

His emotions were all over the place, as he fought against catching her brushing him off for further information that would also help her to deal with this case. This one action kept him firmly, squarely on the personal side of her life, but not in her inner circle. Despite his own inner turmoil, he recognized that she was fighting against the myriad emotions inside her.

And here she said, just right there, something to him that would absolutely break his heart wide open if he let it.

Missed you.

He slowly pocketed his phone and carried on to his next rehab project. His stomach growled, a reminder that he needed some food. The pretzel was a long time ago, even the second one he had had as well today. As he walked into the next rehab project, his foreman was yelling into his cell phone. Simon sighed, as he waited till his guy was off that call, then turned and acknowledged him. "Don't tell me. More crap."

"It's always more crap." The foreman glared at him. "We're living in the shitstorm these days." He was raging like a storm too.

From Simon's experience, his foreman would go on and on for some time.

"Nothing's being delivered. Everything's stuck at the docks. The containers aren't being unloaded. It'll be weeks, they say. Then they tell me that it'll be months. *But wait. Oh, hey, look at that. You might get it next week.*"

Simon knew all that and still let his foreman rage.

"They're all full of shit."

Simon hid his grin, knowing that his foreman was fully justified in being frustrated, but it was a global issue right now. No supplies to be had, and what are you going to do?

Give yourself a heart attack? Not Simon's style. By the time they had done an evaluation of today's current problems, trying to come up with a solution for suppliers who could help them in a pinch, Simon's stomach grumbled again.

His foreman laughed at him. "Jesus, I heard that over here. You're the worst one for not bringing lunch."

"Hell, I don't bring a lunch half the time," Simon muttered. "I never know where I'll be either."

"Which is why you should bring lunch," his foreman stated comfortably. "I can't do without my groceries."

As he patted his ample belly, Simon could believe it. He smiled at him. "I'll stop and pick up something if we're done."

"We're done," his foreman replied, with a flick of his hand. "Go get some food before you collapse."

"Oh, I'm not that bad off," Simon noted, with a grin.

He headed out and around to a famous little corner eatery that he absolutely loved. It was more of a fish-and-chips place than anything else, but the food was hot, and he could do with fast right now. When he walked in, it took barely minutes before he was served, which was one of the reasons he loved this place so much.

They really did a good job of keeping the customers moving. Everyone eating here was pretty well on the clock, and it was important for them to get back out into the craziness of their workday as fast as possible, and that's what this place catered to as much as anything.

With lunch done, Simon stopped and picked up a cup of coffee. At a much slower pace, he sauntered toward his next rehab. He hadn't gone very far when he heard a shout behind him. He turned to see one of the guys who had worked for him in the past running up to him. "Hey,"

Simon greeted him, as he sipped his coffee and eyed the other man. "Problems?"

"Yeah," he spat, with a nasty look, while huffing and puffing from his short run. "I haven't been paid in three weeks." And the fury in his voice was unmistakable.

Simon's eyebrows shot straight up. "What?"

"Yeah, you heard me," he said, with the same force. "I've worked for you for a long time, but it's the first time, … first *ever*, that you've stiffed me."

"I wouldn't have stiffed you," Simon stated, trying to stay calm, as anger flashed through him too. "You're talking about the Hamilton job?"

"No, the one on Main," he corrected. "I was working on that one, and then I got laid off."

"Why'd you get laid off, and when was this?" Simon asked, racking his brain as to when this happened. Normally he was kept abreast of all these issues.

At that, the other man's face flushed even darker with fury. "Two weeks ago. I was told on that Friday that it was my last day, no explanation, nothing, just that I need to get the hell out." He shook his head. "I worked for you for three years now, damn it. 'Course, I haven't seen you around a whole lot lately," he admitted.

"I have been around, been talking to the foreman almost every day."

"Yeah, well, the foreman's usually okay," he admitted, "but the new super that he's got under him? He's a piece of shit," he snapped.

"Have you been calling him that to his face?" Simon asked, with quiet humor.

The kid shook his head. "No, but, if I ever see him now, I will. He's bad news. I don't know if he's bleeding you dry yet or not, but he's got that snarky, sneaky attitude."

"Did you ever catch him doing anything?" Simon asked, his tone sharp, as he narrowed his gaze at the young man—who had worked for him for years, and there hadn't been a problem at all with him before. "Besides, if you're looking for work, I can put you on a different job, and I will look into him."

"Then put me on a different job, but I still want my pay, and I want that pay before I start again," he demanded. "I don't know who that super is trying to screw over"—he shook his head vehemently—"but nobody screws me over," he growled.

This guy was small in stature but had been known to be a good worker, so it made no sense to Simon. He held up a hand and pulled out his phone. Immediately he got ahold of Joe, the foreman on the job, because these things can creep up on you if left unattended. He had learned that one the hard way. When the call was answered, Simon dove in. "This new super you got?"

"Yeah, what about him?" Joe asked, but a wariness filled his tone.

"Sounds as if we got an issue," Simon noted, keeping his voice mild. "You know how I feel about issues."

"Yeah, I know," he said, with more wariness now. "I was hoping that things would work out better than they have," he admitted.

"What's going on with the payroll?'

"What do you mean?" Joe asked in surprise.

"So I have a guy here"—Simon turned toward the unhappy young man expectantly, and he supplied his name—"Ricky. Apparently you fired him two weeks ago, and he hasn't been paid."

"I didn't fire him," Joe declared. "I was told he was a no-show. I gave him a couple weeks to show up, but he hasn't. Honestly I hadn't even got around to taking him off the payroll yet."

"He never got paid, and he's here, adamant that the new super's the one who kicked him out of there." Simon heard Joe swearing in the background. "You told me that we're short on staff. How much of that is due to your super?"

"I don't know," he gritted out through his teeth. "I'll find out." And, with that, Joe disconnected.

Simon turned and looked over at the kid. "Let me call the accountant." And, with that, he made another phone call and checked in with the accountant.

She checked her records and replied, "I don't have any payroll slips for him." She was clearly confused, and that was bad news. "You sure he worked?"

Simon nodded. "Yes."

"Okay, fine. I'll set up a paycheck, and you'll have to track down the paperwork for me."

"Yeah, will do," he agreed, as he shut off his phone and faced Ricky. "She's doing your paycheck right now."

Simon quickly sent a text to Joe, saying that none of the pay stubs were handed in and that Simon had okayed payment for Ricky. However, it was up to Joe to come up with the paperwork to balance it out.

Simon gave half a smile as he hit Send, and the kid spoke up, flushed now, with a hint of embarrassment. "Joe won't be happy with me."

"He'll be even more unhappy when he realizes how many other guys are gone."

At that, Ricky raised an eyebrow. "We've been short a couple guys," Ricky noted.

"Are you telling me that's the super's work?" Simon asked Ricky.

"Yep, sure is. You can only work with him if he likes you, and he sure doesn't like anybody."

"You mean, nobody likes him," Simon corrected.

Ricky grinned. "True, I'll give you that one," he said, with an easy smile. "Honestly the guy's an asshole, and, if you want me to work again, as soon as that paycheck hits my bank account, I'm up for it—but not, ... *not* with Joe and not with that super."

"Why not Joe?" Simon asked, as the kid turned to walk away.

Ricky pivoted on his heels and called back over his shoulder. "Because Joe hired the super, and, even though we told Joe that his super was no-good, Joe kept him on payroll. That means Joe's judgment's lacking too, and he didn't stand up for us. So, hell no, not Joe either."

It was a fair statement, but it would cause Simon some headaches now because, however many other people wrongfully fired must be replaced, and nobody would trust Joe anymore. He gave Joe a few more minutes and then phoned his number back. "So who's the super?" Simon asked in a conversational tone.

"My fucking brother-in-law," Joe snarled. "And before you ask, ... no, I wouldn't have hired him because of that, but he's got quite a bit of history in the industry."

"I'm not sure it's good history though. Did you check into that?"

"No, I didn't," he said, with another snarl. "I'm in the process of kicking his ass out of the company," he stated, followed by a groan at the end.

"You'll also find a whole lot of other people wrongfully

fired won't show up again. Ricky will be at another job because he won't work with you anymore because you hired the super, then dismissed their complaints about him," Simon added, with a harder note. "You know how I feel about employment issues becoming something that stops the work being done."

"Yeah, I know," Joe replied. "I know. I'm trying to find a way out of this mess now."

"Is there a problem finding a way out of this mess?" Simon asked forcefully. "I'm not sure what problem there could be."

"I can't find my damn brother-in-law." Joe swore again. "He's not answering his phone, and he didn't show up for work."

"Is he a drinker?"

Joe sighed. "Yes, but I can't leave the site because we've got concrete coming in the next hour. I need him here."

"Chances are, he ain't coming."

"Yeah, I already got that message," Joe snapped. In a calmer voice, he said, "I'll have to run past his place when I get off work," he muttered. "Damn asshole."

"I didn't think you needed to be told this, but that's what happens when you try to give somebody a break," Simon spelled out.

Joe hesitated before speaking. "I screwed up this one. Are you pissed off at me enough to fire me?"

"Hell no, not for bad judgment." Simon took a deep breath because Joe needed to hear this next part. "However, I really, really won't be happy if you do it again."

"Yeah, got it. My sister ain't gonna be happy either."

"No, I'm sure she won't."

"And unfortunately, when it comes to shit like this,

there ain't no way to keep them happy."

"Are they living together?"

"They were. I talked to her this morning. She said he didn't come home last night."

At that, Simon froze and turned to look around, with a sense of doom settling at the back of his mind, so far off. "What's his address?"

"He lives up in the commercial district," Joe replied, a bit alarmed. "Why?"

"Maybe I'll take a swing past there."

"My sister's there, and apparently he didn't come home. So I don't think that'll do you any good either."

"Right." Simon considered that for a moment and then asked, "Has he got any favorite haunts?"

"Lots of them, but the pool hall is one of them," Joe said, clearly exasperated. "I wouldn't be at all surprised if he were there. Sometimes he stays there when he's drunk. And, if he can't come home, he hangs there until he sobers up."

"Which is still better than him driving home and having a car accident and killing somebody else."

"True enough. It probably wouldn't be a good idea if you're the one who finds him though."

"Why is that?"

"He's ... He can be belligerent."

"He can also be a flat-out asshole, according to Ricky."

"Yeah, ... apparently he doesn't have very much in the way of friends when it comes to this industry, but I'm only just finding that out now. My sister told me that he had a hell of a rep, but I didn't check into it because she believed him. And I believed my sister."

"Love can be blind," Simon remarked gently. "Since you can't find this asshole, give me a phone number or a street address for the pool hall, and I'll go find him myself." When Joe hesitated, Simon came on strong. "I mean it. We need to sort out wherever he is and bring this to a close. He's off my team, and we can't have this shit continue."

"No, no, I understand. I don't know where he'll be."

"What pool hall did you say he goes to?"

"The one down here." And he gave him the address. "He won't be too far off that."

"Fine, I'll wander around. I think I know the joint you mean."

"Doesn't mean he's there though," Joe noted cautiously.

"No, he probably isn't. Chances are, he's sleeping it off somewhere."

"And that would be a good thing, if he was, because he can get into some shit, that guy, like holy Hannah."

"Fine, let me go check it out and see if anybody's seen him." Simon sighed. "If we can find out what happened to him, we can at least get that sorted and dealt with, but, as far as I'm concerned, … he's not on staff anymore since thirty minutes ago. You got that, Joe?" he asked, his voice sharp for emphasis.

Joe immediately answered. "Yeah, I got that."

"I mean *never*. I don't care what kind of stew he's in or what kind of trouble, he doesn't come back. Don't cross me on this one."

"Nope, I won't. Besides, he had his chance, and he caused nothing but hell at my end too," he muttered.

"Good, and tell your sister that he had his chance and that he blew it. That's all there is to it."

"Okay."

With that, Simon disconnected, but he couldn't let it go. Pondering what may or may not have happened, he headed to the pool hall that, as he recalled, was not very far away. When he walked into the front door twenty minutes later, it was nice and cool. Of course it was dark in here too. He walked up to the bartender and the manager, one and the same in this case, asked if he'd seen … only Simon didn't have this SOB's name. He quickly texted Joe and asked and got the name back. *Luca.*

Simon faced the pool hall manager and ask, "Luca? Have you see him?"

He snorted. "Yeah, he can stay away too."

"You too, *huh?*"

"Yeah, guy's an asshole, picks a fight with everybody."

"Okay, that's good to know. Was he here last night?"

"Sure was, and he picked a fight with everybody here, as far as I know, got real cocky too. Said that he was some big superintendent on a job and that people needed to listen to him."

"Nobody'll be listening to him," Simon corrected, "because it's my company that he's fucking over, and I don't have tolerance for that."

"Good, he needs to get his ass kicked," the bar manager added, with a grunt. "He left here about eleven p.m. last night, but the guy was pretty drunk, three sheets to the wind. Hell, I didn't even think he could walk. I told him to call a cab and to not drive, and he said that he would go to a hotel here around the corner."

"So did you believe him?"

"Yeah, the laws are getting stricter around here, and I didn't want him to drive and kill somebody," the manager explained, "so I headed out to the street and kept an eye on him. He did go up to the hotel around the corner. After that? … Where he went from there, I've got no clue."

"Good enough." Simon gave him a nod, then turned back to him and asked, "If he shows up again, can I get you to call me?"

"If you'll ream this guy out, kick his ass, absolutely," the bar manager replied. "If you'll come in and pay his food bill, I might too." He rolled his eyes. "Guys like that? They're just shits right from the beginning."

"I know, and yet somehow he still has a wife and kids who care."

"They always do, and they're the ones who suffer the most."

CHAPTER 5

I T HAD BEEN a hell of a long and frustrating day. Kate and her team were so close to the wire on time with another new case due to come in soon, and yet, outside of sorting the stepfather's history and the fact that he was still in Ontario, there was no sign that he had come west in any way. He'd blubbered over the phone, still with remorse and then tears, when he heard that Patricia had died, and Kate realized that the stepfather had nothing to do with it. They had run down as much of Patricia's history as they could. Kate's team had checked in with Patricia's neighbors and her coworkers, only there wasn't much to find.

Kate waited on forensics still because, gee, wouldn't that be nice if that happened on time? Only it never did. Always too many other cases needed to be dealt with as well, and she couldn't keep asking the lab to supply her case info ahead of anybody else's. But she wanted to, damn, she wanted to, and still she knew it wasn't fair. Sometimes life gave you lemons, and sometimes it gave you nothing but shit.

Impatiently waiting for news from the hospital on the seriously ill waif, Kate phoned several times, just to hear "Call back, please. Test results aren't in yet." Kate was totally frustrated by the end of the day, running around checking alibis for Patricia's death, checking if anybody had seen anything at her apartment, checking with the street cams to see if Patricia's kidnapper had been caught on film, whether picking her up or dropping her off.

Tracking down the cab driver who drove Patricia from the hospital straight to this station, after her kidnapping ordeal, however, had proved elusive so far. The cab company had given her an address for the driver, and every time Kate went to the cabbie's house, she got no answer. She didn't want to think bad thoughts that maybe the kidnapping asshole had gone after this cabbie guy as well, but she didn't really understand what was going on. Since Patricia was not here to tell Kate, and she hadn't asked about that part, it was really pissing her off.

Kate was kicking herself that she didn't ask Patricia at their interview how she had been released. It never occurred to Kate that Patricia would have grabbed a cab to get herself home from the hospital.

At the word "hospital," Kate was reminded to check on the sick teenager she had rescued from Stone. As she walked into the hospital at the end of her day, her phone rang. She glanced down to see that the hospital was calling her.

"She's awake and ready to talk," said the woman at the other end.

"Good, I'm walking into the building now," Kate replied. "I'll be there in a few minutes."

As she walked up the stairs to where the poor teenager was, her phone rang again. Now the taxi driver was calling her back. She headed over to the landing on the stairwell to talk to him.

He had received the call for a cab ride, and he went to the Emergency parking lot of the hospital and picked up Patricia from there. She was in bad shape, he noted, and allegedly he took her straight to the police station. He didn't ask any questions, and neither did he charge her for the trip.

"Something obviously traumatic had happened to her," he shared in a careful tone, "and I didn't feel good about charging her."

Kate smiled when hearing that. After getting a few more questions answered, none of which were helpful, she let him off the hook, at least for now. With that, she walked into the hospital room where the sick teenager was.

The poor girl's head rolled over toward her, and she stared at Kate.

"Hey," Kate greeted her, as she walked closer. "How're you feeling?"

"Like shit," she said in a raspy voice, "but I'm still alive, unfortunately."

Kate nodded, not saying a whole lot, because if that's how you thought life would go, and you didn't want any part of it, waking up would not be a good thing. Kate grabbed the spare visitor's chair, brought it over, and sat down on it, close enough that she could talk to the girl in a low voice. "You don't have to go back, you know?"

Her eyes widened. "Go back?" she asked cautiously.

She nodded. "I'm the one who got you from Stone and brought you to the hospital."

The teenager's eyes widened in fear. She looked around. "Is he coming here? He is coming after me?" she cried out.

"No, he isn't. He was afraid that you would make the rest of them sick, so I offered to take you off his hands."

At that, the girl narrowed her gaze suspiciously at Kate. "What do you want with me?"

Kate sighed, and she pulled out her badge. "I guess I should have done this first."

Seeing the cop's badge, the girl shook her head. "I don't

understand."

"No, I don't imagine you do, but we were there questioning Stone about one of the girls. And that's when he told us about you being sick, and he didn't know what to do with you, and he was pissed off about it all."

"Yeah, he was pissed off. I was sick all right," she confirmed, "but I wasn't making it up. Yet he kept telling me how I was making it up."

"No, you're obviously not making it up, and, if you'd stayed where you were, you would have been dead in two days," Kate told her calmly. "That's what your doctor told me."

At that tidbit, the teenager winced, but she looked around a bit at her surroundings and shrugged. "There are worse things than being dead."

"I do know that, and I also know that, with any luck, you'll make good use of this opportunity to get free and to build a new life for yourself."

The teen pleated the sheets nervously. "Are you sure he doesn't want me back?" she asked nervously. "He's pretty ugly when he wants something."

"I'm sure he is," Kate agreed, searching the girl's face. "Do you want to go back?" She hoped the answer was a hell no but still felt that she had to ask.

The teen shook her head, almost violently. "No, I don't want to go back on the streets," she said, almost hysterical. "But ..." Then she scrunched up the sheet into fistfuls.

Kate reached over and gently placed her hand atop hers. "If you don't want to go back, you don't have to go back."

"It's not that easy. I don't have any job skills. I don't know what to do. I don't have any place to go or to live," she cried out painfully. "It's all I've known for so long."

"How long?" Kate asked.

The teen stopped and blinked, as if she hadn't had that question asked of her before. "I don't know. … As long as I can remember."

"So maybe it's time to try something different because this doesn't seem to be working out so well for you."

The teen gave a snort of laughter. "Aren't you funny," she noted. "He … teaches us to hate cops."

"Of course." She didn't allow the poor abused girl's attitude to sway her. "We're not all bad guys. In fact, most of us are pretty damn good," she admitted. "There'll always be a few we wish we didn't have to deal with ourselves, but, as a general rule, I would say, most cops are decent people."

"That's because you're one of them," the teen pointed out. "You saying that because you are one …"

"And, of course, you're always breaking the law," Kate parroted equally quickly.

"Yeah, when you're in that lifestyle, you don't have a choice," she declared, with a snort.

Kate nodded in acknowledgment and then decided to be upfront, as it was the best way to get to the bottom of this mess. "And then there's the drug issue," Kate noted.

The teen shuddered. "They … gave me something to help me."

"To help you get off the drugs or to help you get healthy?"

"I don't know." Her eyes widened at the question. "I don't know."

"And if you could do anything other than what you were doing," Kate began in a whimsical tone, "what would you want to do?"

She stared at her and shrugged. "I don't know. It's not

something I could ever ask myself. I've been with Stone for as long as I can remember."

"Does he supply your drugs?"

"Sometimes," she said timidly. "I never used to do drugs. He got me on them, kept me on them." She shuddered. "And now, if I don't do what he says, I'm stuck on them, and he'll make me pay and withhold the drugs." Her voice was so low, as if she were talking to herself. "Then things could get really ugly."

"Of course they can," Kate murmured. "On the other hand, you can also work to get off them."

She gave a burble of laughter. "That might work in your nice cozy little world, where you have paychecks and a bed to sleep in and a roof over your head and somebody to protect you from the assholes of the world," she argued. "However, in my world, that's not reality. If I fall asleep somewhere, some asshole will steal me and put me to work on the street. If I don't do what he wants, he'll beat the crap out of me," she stated, her voice bitter. "*Choice* isn't something in my world."

"It hasn't been up until now, but that doesn't mean you have to stay that way," Kate noted, her tone inflexible. "If you want to change, you can change."

The teen started to cry. "You damn do-gooders," she muttered, then sobbed harder and harder. "You make it sound as if hope is out there. There's no hope. You know that. No fucking way anybody will help me. I'm nothing but a loser."

Hearing refrains from years of abuse and torment in the teen's words and her tone, Kate patted the girl's hand. "I can see how you might think that way, given the circumstances." She took a moment to add, "However, I can tell you that there certainly is hope and that there is another way to go through life. Do you like taking drugs?"

"No," she stated in a rebuke. "They make me sick. I hate them, but I don't have any choice. Once you're hooked, you're hooked."

"And yet I'm pretty sure that you've already started getting off of them because you've been so ill lately," Kate pointed out.

The teen stared at Kate for a long moment. "I don't know how that works."

She nodded. "I don't either, but there are ways to help reduce the effect of the drugs on a day-to-day basis," Kate shared, with a comforting tone. "We'll have to look into a little more. I also know somebody who might help you."

"Yeah? What does he want?" she asked.

Such a sneer filled her expression that Kate immediately knew what this abused teen was expecting. "Not that," Kate stated.

"Honey, they all want that," the teen replied in a mock tone. "They say they don't want that, but then it turns around that's what they want. That's what they all want. Absolutely no way they don't."

Wisely Kate kept her counsel quiet. She knew Simon wasn't like that. He didn't need to deal with anybody at this level for sex. He could get whatever the hell he wanted from the world out there just because he was drop-dead gorgeous and rich, and, of course, that was a direction she didn't want to go in anyway.

Kate held up her hand. "Let's go back to one of the reasons why I ended up talking to Stone. Did you know Patricia Blinker?"

The girl nodded slowly. "Yeah, I did. Her brother came

and bought her," she said, and wonder filled her tone, as if she couldn't imagine such a thing.

"Does that sound good to you?" Kate asked curiously.

"Yeah, sure it does," she replied. "The only way Stone lets us go is if somebody pays."

"Okay, and how does that work?" Kate asked.

The teen sagged back into the bed, looking around the room listlessly. "I don't have any family," she muttered. "So ain't nobody buying me out of this hellhole."

"You don't have any family?" Kate immediately questioned. "Or none that you have had any contact with?"

"Same diff," the teen replied, as she stared at Kate. "You got to remember that there's only so much that people will put up with in this world, and taking on losers is not one of them."

"Sounds as if Stone really worked your self-esteem into the ground," Kate noted, "because you're not a loser. You're a survivor, a fighter. Otherwise you wouldn't still be alive right now," she suggested. "After all the damage that he's done, … you can work at fixing it, if you care to," she murmured, but the girl rolled her eyes at Kate. "Right, it's not that easy. It's not a slam-dunk case. It's not a *Hey, one-and-done,* but it is doable. And, if you wanted help to do it, people are out there who are willing to give you help. No strings attached."

The teen sneered openly at Kate. "You really do live in that world of make-believe, don't you?"

"Some would say yes, but, considering the work I do," she added, "maybe not. Now I have a name down here for you—Annie Duggal."

She nodded. "Yeah, that's my name."

But something in her voice had Kate eyeing her closer.

"Meaning that's the name you gave Stone? Or that's the name that he knows you as?"

After a hesitation, the teen nodded.

"So, what's your real name?"

She winced. "Then you'll contact my family, won't you?"

"It might be interesting to see what their response is."

"*No-good trash can go to hell,* most likely," she quipped. "Absolutely no way they want anything to do with me, and I don't want the humiliation of ending up asking them for help one more time."

"Right. So … you would rather go back with Stone, right?"

She glared at her.

"You really don't know how your family will react, especially with the passage of time," Kate suggested, trying to be patient. "I can talk to them and see. If they'll be ass-hats, I won't give them any contact information, and I won't have them get in touch with you."

"They wouldn't want to get in touch anyway," she declared in a monotone.

"What did you know about Patricia?" Kate asked, abruptly changing the conversation immediately, trying to see if she could get some information from Annie and keep the girl off balance. Kate wasn't sure what *Annie* was lying about but definitely a few lies were floating around, and Kate certainly wasn't prepared to judge the abused teen for that, not when life had thrown her so many ugly curveballs. Yet, at the same time, Kate also needed some idea of where to go and what to search for in Patricia's life.

The teen shrugged, then answered Kate's latest question. "Patricia was nice. Her brother kept trying to get her off the streets, kept trying to help her, and she kept trying too, but Stone was being an asshole about it. He'd loop her up on drugs, so, the next time her brother would come around, Patricia wouldn't even be awake and cognizant enough to talk to. Stone did that a couple times, just for laughs. At one point, somebody said something to Stone about her dying of an overdose, and he seemed to back off at that point in time." Annie gave a lifeless laugh. "But the threat was always there that he could do whatever the hell he wanted and that included killing us, which I know perfectly well I was slated for." As she slumped back on the bed, she stared up at the world above her.

"What do you mean, *slated for*?" Kate asked.

Annie turned to look at Kate. "I couldn't bring in the money anymore. … My looks are going. Stone said my attitude sucked. … According to him, I wasn't producing as much or as well as the others. So I would always be the one who was treated roughly. I think that's probably why I ended up sick."

"Maybe. Did you stay in bed when you got sick?"

"No, he sent me back out on the street because I hadn't done enough work for the day," she replied dispassionately, with no bitterness in her tone. It was almost as if she believed Stone.

"So obviously a lot of healing needs to happen, both physically and emotionally," Kate stated gently. "I need to get you into a safe place, once you're released from here."

"I won't be safe from him, not unless you do something official-like that gets me away from him."

"What do you think official-like means in this case?" she asked.

Annie shrugged. "I don't know. You should talk to Patricia's brother about it. He seemed to figure it out."

"I think he was such a pest that Stone was happy to get rid of him."

Annie studied Kate for a long moment and then nodded. "That sounds like Stone. He's really not a bad man. He's just got high expectations. If you don't meet them, well, let's just say, life isn't quite so nice."

The doctor came in then and did a quick check of Annie. As he stepped outside, Kate joined him to ask a few questions.

He was honest when he told her, "Annie's not out of the woods yet. She's still severely dehydrated. Whatever situation she was in, returning there will likely kill her," he stated bluntly. "Nobody was looking after her, even when she got this bad. So anything that can be done to keep her away from there is a good idea. I get it. It's not necessarily your job," he admitted, cutting off what response Kate might give. "I don't know if anybody out there gives a crap, but Annie needs a place to stay, while she recovers. It took a bit to sort out, but we think she has Lyme disease."

Kate nodded. "How long do you think she needs to be in the hospital?"

"At least another day, if not two." With that, the doctor left.

Before she had a chance to sort through what the doc had said, she received a text from Simon. **Yes.**

She looked over at Annie and said, "I'll step out for another few minutes. Be right back."

Annie shrugged and didn't say anything.

Kate also needed to get her correct name, which meant, chances were, that Annie needed to be fingerprinted too. Kate expected that to also upset the poor girl, but sometimes you had to do things in order to get the truth, especially if they refused to talk. Back in the hallway, she sent Simon a text. **Yes to what?** Her phone rang almost immediately, and she launched into him without preamble. "That's great that you can send texts like that," she noted in exasperation, "but I have no idea what you're talking about."

"But you do," he corrected her. "I'm the one who has no idea what I'm talking about."

She snorted at that, but a reluctant grin crossed her face. "I think that's … that's always a great line for you, isn't it?"

"Not so much," he admitted, "but I'm supposed to say yes to something, so I gave in without a qualm, and I'm saying yes."

"This is in regard to what?" she asked, confused.

"I don't know, but I see a woman who needs help."

"Oh, shit." Kate turned back to the hospital room to see Annie huddled under the blankets. "It's an awkward case, and it could be a lot of work."

"Yes, of course it is." Simon chuckled. "Thankfully I do know some people."

She felt some relief sweeping through her at that. "Some people?" she repeated in a cheerful tone. "You know some people."

"I do know some people," he teased, and then his tone turned frustrated. "But I can't help if don't know what the deal is."

"I told you about the teenager we brought to the hospital, right?"

"Yes, how is she?"

"She's sick. Lyme disease. Recovery will take a while, as she's exhausted, dehydrated, and has pneumonia, with that cough I hear. If she goes back out in the streets, it'll likely kill her. She also doesn't feel safe from the asshole who owned her up until now, and we're not sure what department to call to get her back on her feet. Of course funding is … it's there, but it's not there."

"Of course it's not there," Simon confirmed, with a light chuckle. "She's one of a million in need, which is the next problem. We can't solve this problem for everybody all the time. However, … let me make a couple phone calls, and I'll see if I can get her a room."

"Where would this room be?" she asked curiously.

"A center that deals with ex-junkies and, in this case, also a lot of streetwalkers, both male and female, but we keep them in separate wings."

"Of course you do," she said, with a note of humor.

"Hey, believe me. It's a necessity in this case," he added, with laughter in his tone. "It's too easy for them to get things in their life by plying their old trade. We're trying to get them past that and into something else."

"Right. That makes sense too," she admitted. "Anyway, if there's anything you can do to help, its much appreciated."

"I'll call you back soon." With that, he disconnected.

Not sure that Annie was even interested in getting some help, Kate walked back into the teen's hospital room. "I have somebody interested in helping you."

"Of course someone is." She coughed again, then collapsed back down. "He will want something for that help, won't he?"

"He doesn't want anything for that help." At least she hoped not, but Simon had never done so in the past. "He's been helping a couple centers already, so it's quite possible that he's thinking about one of those."

Annie frowned at her. "You mean, like a women's shelter?"

Kate nodded cautiously.

"Because I won't really belong there."

"If you don't belong there, I'm not sure who does," Kate declared bluntly. "You've been beaten, abused, and left to die, without the proper care. At what point in time do you think you *do* deserve some help?"

Annie flushed and stared at her, but she stayed quiet.

Kate nodded. "Do you have any idea why or who may have hurt Patricia?"

"Did something happen to Patricia?" Annie asked, puzzled.

Kate winced and then nodded. "She's been murdered."

Annie's eyes opened wide, and then, in a surprise move, she burst into tears.

Kate walked closer, sat on the edge of the bed, and waited for Annie to calm down. "I'm sorry. I didn't realize that would hit you quite so hard." Kate found some napkins off to the side and brought them over for her.

Annie blew her nose noisily, looking over at Kate, sobbing. "But she's the one who got out. She should have been safe," she wailed. "If she got caught, then there's nothing for any of us."

It took a bit to decipher what Annie was trying to say, but Kate understood it well. "So you seem to think that because she got out, she should have been safe, and the fact that she wasn't safe was because of Stone?"

She nodded. "Obviously it was him."

"Not according to Stone. According to him, he was well paid for her and didn't want Patricia's brother hanging around and making Stone's life miserable, so Stone didn't have anything to do with killing Patricia."

Annie blinked several times and then slowly nodded. "That may be, but he was really angry at the brother."

"Would he have killed Patricia to get back at the brother?"

Annie stared at Kate and then shrugged. "I don't know," she whispered.

"Okay, good enough. Now, if we take Stone out of the equation, and we assume that it was somebody else, do you know of any johns who beat up Patricia and would have come back for her or were angry at her? Do you know of anybody who might have held a grudge against her?"

Annie frowned. "Some of the johns are just brutal, but Patricia's been out of it now for a while. And that's good. I'm glad she got out of it. That's not a life for anybody. We didn't have a choice, you know?"

"I know you didn't. Not back then. But you do now. That's why I want to see you get out of here and into a better life." Kate smiled gently. "But I can't do it alone, and you have to want it."

"Yeah, people say shit like that all the time, but they don't really know what's involved."

"No, I sure don't," Kate admitted in mild exasperation. "I've never done drugs, never been hooked on something similar, can't imagine what it would be to try and kick it." Then she took a moment to add, "Yet that doesn't mean that I wouldn't be there to try and give it my all."

Annie slumped in place, as she thought about it. "Yeah, of course you would," she muttered. "I'm not even sure I know what'll be required, so how is it I'm supposed to commit to that?"

Enough spirit filled her words to make Kate smile. "You keep up that attitude, and you'll probably do just fine because it is so important that you question life and that you look at it from all perspectives. However, when somebody reaches out a hand, and you're desperately in need of that help, … you say thank you, and you reach back."

And, in truth, that's exactly how Kate felt because there would be a lot of ups and downs in Annie's life coming up, and there would be times that she wanted to go back to making it easy. "The hardest thing," Kate offered, "outside of building your self-esteem and your need to feel safe and secure, is to refuse drugs and don't get back into that same trap."

Annie just stared at Kate. "That's not all that hard to do, considering that drugs and I don't get along." She shrugged. "Stone used them as a way to control me, but they made me seriously sick. So I would be quite happy to not have to deal with either of those scenarios again."

"That's good." Kate nodded. "So that could end up being quite a saving grace for you."

"You say things as if you understand what they mean, but you don't."

"I do know that we can get Stone to hand over whatever he considers his rights to you and have you in the free and clear on this—if you're prepared to go the distance to get yourself cleaned up and off the streets. If so, then I would call it a win."

Annie eyed Kate in wonder, but she wasn't sure whether she was wondering about Kate herself being stupid or really somebody who was offering Annie a chance?

Kate leaned over and repeated, "You're getting that chance, so take it."

Tears came to Annie's eyes, without any warning. "I don't even know what that chance looks like, but …" She took a deep breath and whispered, "Yes, please."

⌘

SIMON WALKED INTO the hotel and asked for Luca, and the desk clerk looked up at him intently. "Yeah, he came in late last night. Are you a friend of his?"

"His boss," Simon replied, with a wry look. "I've come here to tell him that he is fired as of this morning because, man, I got work to be done."

"Ha." The manager snorted. "I can't imagine him holding a job for very long. He was pretty pie-eyed last night."

"Hence my problem," Simon said, with a nod. "He came with decent references, but he lied to my guy. So you see my issue."

"References can be made up on the spot." He shook his head. "Can't believe nothing that's on paper. Man, you have to talk to people."

"Yep, well then, there's another problem. He was hired by his brother-in-law because his sister put pressure on him to give her husband a job, but my guy screwed that up too. So now I'm trying to figure out exactly what I got for a headache."

"Well, Luca's up in room 204, if you want to talk to him, probably still snoring."

"Good, I'll go wake him up and see." And, with that information, Simon headed up to the room in question. He knocked on the door, but no answer came. He knocked again and still nothing. He hesitated, knowing that it could simply be that Luca was still drunk, but Simon knew something was seriously off and had a bad feeling about it. He was getting some serious disturbing vibes.

As that feeling of doom settled in deep, Simon grabbed

his cell and called the desk clerk. "I don't feel very good about this," he said. "Any chance we can open this door, or do I need to get the cops in here?"

"Cops?" the clerk repeated in alarm. "Hell no. No, no, no, no, no. He's probably just sleeping."

"I don't think he's sleeping," Simon argued, his tone harsh. "So it's either cops or you open this door, and then we'll see what we're dealing with."

"Ah, crap, I'll be up in less than five." He raced up the stairs, panting, and came to a screeching halt. "No cops. I don't even give a shit what's going on," he got out, in between huffs and puffs. "No cops. Luca had better be sleeping this drunk off." He unlocked the door and turned to face Simon. "You didn't see me do that. This door was unlocked to begin with, you hear me?"

Simon didn't say anything because, of course, Kate would have it out of him in no time, especially if what he suspected was behind this door. Taking a deep breath, he pushed it open and stepped inside. In there, on the floor, barely inside, was his superintendent. Dead, but with a message tied to his shirt. *Well, Simon. Guess you didn't expect this step, did you? Too bad you couldn't get into the game, cuz it's Game Over.*

CHAPTER 6

K ATE ARRIVED AT the hotel to see Simon on his laptop, sitting on a nasty-looking bench in the hallway. She stopped in front of him, and he looked up and nodded.

"Sorry to bother you again, but this one … needs your particular attention." She raised an eyebrow, and he understood her questioning gaze. "Another note with my name on it."

Her face shut down immediately, and she nodded. "Not quite what I expected. I'll be back out in a minute." She stepped into the hotel room, and her heart sank as she saw the dead man in front of her, but the note was of particular importance. Simon hadn't even gotten into the game apparently, and already Kate had another dead victim. How the hell did that work? She called forensics and set the team in motion, including letting Rodney know where she was and what was happening.

Then Kate stepped back out into the hotel's hallway and sat beside Simon. "The team's on the way," she said in a low voice. "You want to tell me what happened?"

He went over it, his voice strong and steady.

She nodded at everything he had to say. "And you got into the room, how?"

He gave her a wry look. "The manager won't really be happy with me because he wanted me to keep it quiet, but he let me in because I was pretty damn sure that there was a problem."

She didn't say anything, just nodded and wrote that down. "It is, of course, pretty unusual to have that happen," she murmured.

"It is, but I also knew," he pointed out.

"Yeah, that'll always add to my aggravation." She sent a quick smile in his direction. "But considering you were here after a staff member, and you were concerned about his whereabouts," she noted, with a thoughtful gaze, "that's a *whatever* at this point."

"Glad to hear that, so maybe keep the hotel clerk out of it, if you can."

She chuckled lightly. "No way we're keeping him out of it. He'll have to answer a bunch of questions, and I presume you already questioned him yourself."

"I did, but only because I was asking him about Luca's whereabouts, confirming that he had a hotel room here," Simon replied. "The clerk was not happy when I insisted on the door being unlocked."

"Well, that's good news," she quipped, with an eye roll. "I hate to think that he would open it for anybody."

"No, and I have to admit I was rather insistent," he pointed out.

"Of course you were." She nodded. "Can't say I've ever known you really not to be. So what were the circumstances that brought you here in the first place?"

He explained everything from Ricky's visit this morning to Joe's comment about his brother-in-law and then trying to track down Luca.

Kate nodded. "So we're presuming that the killer knew that this guy worked for you, which is interesting because obviously Luca hadn't worked for you for very long."

"I think about nine weeks," Simon noted, "but I can get those records for you."

"Please do," she said absentmindedly. "What's his full name?"

"Not sure about the last name, so that I have to confirm."

"Do you have his address?"

He pulled out his phone and texted Joe, and, rather than responding via text, Joe called him. "Hey, what's up that you need Luca's home address?" he asked, worry in his voice.

Simon looked over at Kate.

Kate took the phone from his hand and quickly identified herself. "This is not for public knowledge until we have notified the next of kin," she instructed him, "and, for that, I need the address for his wife."

Joe, still blubbering in the background, quickly gave it to her, and she returned the phone to Simon and got up and left him to do the explanations. She heard him say that they'd found Luca dead in a hotel room.

And then she looked over at him. "Make sure he doesn't say anything to the wife. I will be on my way as soon as forensics shows up. So tell Joe that I'm heading over there now."

He nodded. "Joe, you can't say anything to your sister yet. The detective is heading over there right now."

Joe was still sputtering in the background. She heard him wailing over the phone, saying, "Oh my God, oh my God, she'll be devastated."

Of course she would be. Everybody would be devastated at the loss of a loved one. Kate didn't understand why Luca hadn't gone home. That would likely upset his wife too.

When the forensic team arrived at the same time as the local cops did, she sent several of those beat cops to knock on doors and to sort out if anybody had seen or heard anything in regard to Luca's death. Kate was damn sure nobody had, but, hey, she had been wrong before. As she was about to walk away from the scene, Dr. Smidge, the coroner, called her into the hotel room. He stood over the body. "What's going on?" she asked him.

Smidge pointed. "This guy may have come here to sleep off his stupor, but I'm pretty sure he found something else instead."

"What do you mean?" she asked, puzzled.

"Look at his feet," Dr. Smidge stated adamantly. "His bare feet have been walked on, almost to ribbons." He took in a deep sigh. "The guy's dressed, but I'm not sure that we won't see more of this, more of these marks up and down his body."

"Aw, crap," she muttered. And then she thought of Patricia. That woman had probably been tortured like Luca too, yet why did she say she hadn't been hurt? Kate shook her head. That poor woman. Given her former life as a prostitute, was this torture less that what she received daily from her johns? How sad was that thought? She nodded at Smidge. "Chances are you will find more wounds on his body," she admitted, her voice grim. "This is top priority."

He laughed. "You always say that."

"Yeah." She grinned. "Everything that you see here on Luca's body, you should compare to Patricia's wounds, who's already in your morgue. It's the same killer in both cases."

"No, no, no," Smidge said, his gaze widening in shock. "Not one more of your special cases again."

"*My* special cases?" she asked, glaring at him.

He glared right back. "Yeah, *your* special cases. You always end up with the shitty ones. And maybe it's because you're good at it. I don't know, but I don't like serial killers."

"You think I do?" she cried out. "This will be bad news, if we don't get a handle on it right away."

"It's already bad news for these dead guys," he pointed out.

She rolled her eyes at that because of course it was, but she didn't have any knowledge or understanding of how these two people had gotten into this situation. One thing connected them both, and that unfortunately was Simon. She headed back out to the hallway, sat down beside him again. "It's a little worse than we thought."

He stiffened and slowly lifted his gaze from his laptop to her, waiting.

"We have to wait on the full autopsy, but it could potentially be a similar torture element that Patricia went through."

Simon stared at her, bewildered.

She nodded. "I don't understand it either, but I will. Believe me. I will. But right now I'll go talk to the wife, see what the deal was with Luca being here and not at home— where he should have been—and if there's been any strangers in his life recently."

"And yet who would know?" Simon asked in a confused tone. "I got the definite impression that Luca and his wife were having some issues, quite likely due to his lack of employment. She seemed removed from his life in many ways."

"That'll often do it," Kate murmured, "but that still must be checked. So, while they're busy here"—she looked around, indicating Smidge and his minions—"I'll run over there, and then I will be back. You want to head off to the rest of your day? You are free to go, but I'll need to get your statement."

"I can give it to one of the guys here," he suggested, with a careless wave. "In circumstances like this, it's probably better."

She gave him a ghost of a smile and nodded. "Glad to hear that you're so well versed in our oh-so-lovely procedures."

"Way too much exposure to them," he muttered.

She gave him a smirk and said, "I'll see you later."

"Do you mean that?" he called out, as she hit the stairs.

She glanced back at him, but a cop walked up the stairwell and entered at that time, giving her an excuse to escape without answering. Downstairs, she headed to her vehicle, looking up the address for the wife, making it as fast a trip as possible. It still took twenty-four minutes to get there, even with the GPS directing her. However, you always had to deal with the two seasons in Vancouver; one was construction, and the other was construction.

Laughing at the old joke, she headed up to the front door of Luca's home and knocked.

A woman, a little tired and worn-out looking, answered the door, and she sighed. "If you're trying to sell something, I don't have any money to buy."

And such a worried note filled her voice that Kate believed her. She held up her badge. "I'm not here to sell you anything. May I come inside?"

Fear immediately struck the woman deep into her gaze, and she held open the door and let Kate in. "What happened?" she asked. Without waiting for any answer, she panicked. "What happened?"

Kate waited for Luca's wife to take a seat in front of her, and then she replied, "Your husband was found dead in a hotel room this morning. He's been murdered."

It took a minute for the news to sink in. She bolted to her feet and yelled, "What are you talking about? He's at work. He told me that he was staying at a friend's place because he was so tired from his new job, and he was having to do an awful lot of overtime because so many people had quit because he'd found out that they were stealing, and he would have to … in order to keep the job and to do as good at it … as he was doing, *he would have to stay.* Luca's been working. He'd made a friend at work, and I knew Joe was around. … He's my brother," she babbled uncontrollably, staring at Kate, bewildered.

"You must be wrong. It won't be Luca," she argued, feeling almost immensely pleased at her conclusion. "Joe could identify this man. If it was really my husband, if you had found him, Joe would have called me. My brother would have called me."

"I already spoke to Joe," Kate replied, lifting a hand before the woman went on another emotional rant. "The ID that we found on the body is the same from his boss at the construction site. Both say that this is your husband."

"I want to see him," she declared, as she threw herself onto the couch and stared at Kate in shock. "I want to see him. It can't be him. You're wrong. You have to be wrong."

"We can arrange that," Kate noted, "but an autopsy must be performed first."

At that term, the woman seemed to finally understand exactly what was happening, and all the color faded from her face. She started to sob.

Kate waited until she calmed down and then added, "So

are you telling me that you didn't have any contact with Luca last night?"

She shook her head. "No, he called me late and told me that he was staying at this guy's house."

"And what guy was that?"

She started at her, bewildered. "I … dunno. … Joe would know, my brother. He would know. You can talk to him."

"I will be talking to Joe again," she shared. "Do have any idea who this *friend* was, so I can contact him?"

"No."

Her silent acceptance seemed to highlight how little she knew when it came to her husband.

"I thought he was staying at his friend's because he was overworked."

"The hotel," Kate noted gently, "is right around the corner from a pool hall."

At that, the woman jumped her feet, fury in her face. "It's what?"

Kate winced and nodded. "And he was there earlier in the evening."

"Of course he was. That's his weakness, pool halls. He blows all kinds of money on it," she said in a disgusted, disgruntled, and grief-ridden tone. "It's one of the reasons he had to get a different job, and I begged my brother to give it to him." She smeared her tears around her face. "He's terrible with money."

"Terrible with money or terrible with gambling?" Kate asked.

The woman flinched. "He's not a bad man. He wasn't a bad man," she said, correcting herself and yet shuddering as she did so, closing her eyes and wrapping her arms around her chest. "He's ... He was ..." She stopped, swallowed hard. "A good man. He was just ..." She winced. "The gambling bug had him," she relented and took a deep sigh, as if reliving some old wound. "It was ruining our lives. It was the only bane of our miserable lives."

"I'm sorry," Kate said. "I know that's tough. It's an addiction, and that's hard to beat."

"And he never seemed to get a handle on it. He promised me that he would never go back to that place."

Kate considered that remark, wondered how many days the kidnapper had with Luca to torture him, then focused on Luca's wife. "What are the chances that's where he'd been every day this week? Did he come home this week at all? When did you last see Luca?"

"I haven't seen him in four days now," she muttered. "Normally he would come home because he needs a change of clothes, the usual." She shrugged and then looked around absentmindedly. "We've never really had marital problems, but then I've never really pushed him, not until the gambling got so bad that our mortgage was in jeopardy." She stared at Kate in horror. "He's supposedly worked late every day this week."

"I can certainly find out if he worked late this week, if you would like."

The woman nodded mutely, and Kate quickly texted Simon, asking him, and got a response saying he'd check. "I contacted his boss, the owner of the company, and he'll check for us," she told her.

But Luca's wife looked as if she were absolutely terrified of what the answer would be.

"I'll just ask my brother," she whispered.

Kate could certainly understand why the wife was hesitant to get answers. And, if this were a classic case of an addiction gone wrong, she also could potentially figure out how Luca had been picked up, had been slated to be the killer's next victim. Pool halls were not exactly the friendliest of places, but it was pretty easy to bond over a couple games and some beer. And, if this killer knew where Luca worked, it would set him up for being an easy mark all around.

Finally his wife asked cautiously, "Can you tell me how he died?"

"I can't actually. I have to wait for the postmortem myself."

"So maybe it was just like a heart attack?" she asked hopefully.

Kate gave a decisive shake of her head. "No, that much I can confirm. It was definitely murder."

She said goodbye and walked away from the wife, with both relief and pain, because how did one leave such grief and confusion? Nobody understood why Luca had done what he'd done, and yet his wife had it in her mind that there was likely another reason—any other reason than the one staring her in the face. The realization that her husband was a gambler—although it shouldn't have come as any surprise—was obviously enough to shock her.

Kate figured the wife's anger would come pretty quickly after the grief and shock. Anger that he would do that, anger that he'd put them into that precarious financial situation again, anger that, even after telling her that he was no longer involved in gambling, he obviously still was. Anger was like a fire that had no outlet. It burned hot and bright and damaged so much, and yet, for this poor woman, now a widow, it might also give her some peace, once she finally reached the point where she understood and realized how much gambling was an addiction and that maybe Luca would have made it through this, except somebody cut Luca's life short.

Because of Luca's connection to Simon.

To think of somebody dying because of Simon's involvement was enough to terrify Kate, and it made no sense to her. Why did somebody have it out for Simon anyway? She knew she needed to sit down and have a deeper, longer, harder talk with him, but she also knew that he was racking his brain trying to figure this out too. That this killer was somebody Simon may have touched in his life in a superficial way didn't feel right because the anger revealed through this killer's MO was so extreme. Yet what could possibly be so wrong in the murderer's world that it triggered this kind of reaction?

Stumped, she left the widow's home and returned to the hotel crime scene, then back to the station, even as she sent in requests to have everything about this new victim's life completely uncovered, so they could see if there were any similarities between him and Patricia. But, in her heart, she figured that it would be a case of bad timing—as in Luca was there—and the killer either realized who he worked for or hunted him down because of his gambling addiction.

Maybe the killer knew that Luca had this weakness and that it would be the killer's way to get at Luca. Bringing him back into the gambling world would leave Luca much more open and vulnerable to this killer's level of persuasion. She'd certainly seen that BS from people before, and, as much as she hated to think of it happening over and over again, people were people, and sometimes they were absolute shits.

Now Kate had compelling evidence of a very strong personal vendetta against Simon.

As she parked at the station, she hopped out and realized that she'd put her phone on Silent and had missed a call. It was Simon. She quickly called him back, as she walked in the station.

"Hey, how bad is it?" he asked her.

"It's bad," she replied succinctly, "as in, it's big bad."

"I don't even want to know what that means." He groaned.

"What would be your worst nightmare right now?" she asked curiously.

"That it's another one of this asshole's victims," he replied immediately, "but then the note on Luca's body already made that clear. Yet I didn't even know Luca."

"But he worked for you, and maybe all this killer needed was somebody close enough to you that he could hate enough to do this to," she suggested casually. "I don't see a rational mind in all this, but I do see very rational thinking in working out this plan. However, the motive behind it? … I don't get it …yet. Still, somebody went to a great deal of effort to take somebody in your sphere and torture and kill them."

"But we don't know that, or do you?" he asked immediately.

"Luca's feet were torn to ribbons. I've asked the coroner to compare his injuries to Patricia's."

She heard Simon suck back a breath, as he realized the implication. "Jesus."

"I won't get any forensics back today, or tomorrow, although I could try and push them, yet that'll put me in hot water too."

"No, I understand," Simon acknowledged. "You know that I never wanted this to happen, right?"

"Both victims would agree with you," she replied. "And this Luca guy was supposed to be home with his wife. However, she had no in-person contact for the last four days."

"Meaning?"

"Meaning that he's been gambling at the pool hall and staying away from home these previous four days now. A weakness which our killer then likely used to connect with Luca, then exploit. Maybe the gambling and the drinking made Luca a good victim," she noted, with a long sigh.

She stopped in the lobby and pinched the bridge of her nose. "I'm back at the station. Luca's wife is pretty broken up about him. However, I think the anger about Luca staying at the hotel instead of at home is hiding a certain amount of fear. Then, when I told her that Luca had been spending a lot of time in the pool hall again, she got quite irate."

"In other words, he was supposed to have stopped, and this proves that he's been lying to her."

"Yeah, more or less," she confirmed. "Yet she didn't know anybody who would hate Luca, and, as far as she knew, he didn't really know you either."

"Did you ask her about his reputation?"

"*Yeah*," Kate said, with a note of humor. "She says that he's a great guy, and he deserves a second chance, and that's why she pushed her brother to give the job to him."

"Yeah, and her brother is already in hot water over that because he didn't clear it with me, and he hired somebody that's family, which I'm against, unless I know full well what's going on. Plus I lost a lot of good people over this because of Joe and Luca, which is causing all kinds of backups in my rehabs."

"So, in a sense, the killer did screw up your life over this."

"Yep, a mess to clean up."

She checked her watch, realizing how late it was. She picked up her pace.

"Hang on a minute. You're thinking that's what this is ultimately about, for the killer to mess up my business world?"

"I would hope there's a whole lot more behind it to motivate these murders," she replied, "and that we're not dealing with somebody operating on such a superficial level, but the essence is that this brother-in-law of your foreman, by hiring him, messed up your life because he screwed up a lot of your solid employees, and they quit on you. Now, by killing Luca, the investigation will land on you."

"I don't see that so much," Simon countered.

"Hey, I had another thought. Is there ..." She took a deep breath, "You won't like this question, but is there anything in your life that you don't want investigated. See? I'm not making myself very clear, but considering that now we have an active investigation, where we will potentially dig deeper into your life—and I know how you feel about that, but we don't really have a choice. Anyway, so my point is, was this what the killer wanted? As if he's thinking that you got away with something, and any investigation into your personal and professional life would bring it to the surface, maybe even implicate you in something else?"

"I have no idea what that could be," he said in frustration. "I can't think of anything that would fit that line of thought, but that doesn't mean that somewhere along the line someone got their feelings hurt, with no malice on my part," he shared in a resigned tone. "People take inferences and insults where none were intended."

"That's very true, but to kill certain people and to torture them, … as this killer's doing, there must be a whole lot more than … curiosity involved. Something much deeper under the surface would have this much stink."

"Maybe, or maybe not. Maybe it's a classic case of an asshole looking for an excuse to hurt people. I don't know. I'll talk to you later." And, with that, he disconnected abruptly.

He was rattled. Yet she understood his response.

Wincing, she finished the short trip to her desk and sat down, opened up her notes, and proceeded to document both conversations—with Luca's wife and with Simon. When a shadow fell across her desk, she looked up to see her sergeant, standing there, glaring. "Can I help you?" she asked Colby.

"I don't know. You tell me. How is it going?"

"It sucks," she said in a light tone. "We've got another death, quite likely the same thing as happened with Patricia. I'm waiting for forensics for that confirmation though." She shrugged. "It seems Patricia's killer went after an employee who worked at Simon's company—a construction worker on one of the rehab houses he's got underway."

"What would be a motivation for that?" Colby asked, puzzled. "Particularly considering Simon hires how many workers? He has multiple rehabs up and running, from what we know."

"Oh, good question," she noted, looking up at him. She snatched her cell phone and quickly texted Simon. **Approximately how large is your payroll? In terms of number of staff.**

He shot back a number that had her eyebrows raised.

"He says just under two hundred. Jesus." Kate stared down at the number on her cell phone screen. "I had no idea."

Her sergeant nodded, and then shook his head. "How could you not know?"

That comment was off-hand, but, given she was a detective and involved with Simon, that was unnerving too.

"So there is an awful large pool of people to draw on," he noted.

"But that's …" Then she stopped, shook her head. "I understand why you're saying that, but I guess I'm not sure that this couldn't have applied to almost anybody else as well."

"What do you mean?"

"I'm saying that, in theory, if our killer is out to hurt Simon indirectly, then anybody in Simon's world could be a victim. Could be any neighbor, could be anybody who makes regular deliveries for him, could be any of his staff. It could be anybody in his past, like a friend or acquaintance. Killing Luca was fairly impersonal." Yet she frowned.

"Luca's not somebody Simon worked with closely. So emotionally it's … not as if Simon will take that personal hit. But, yes, the anger and frustration and inconvenience of targeting and killing somebody who worked for him is there." She took a moment and then shook her head.

"Still, it's not the same as if the victim were Simon's sibling or somebody he's much closer to. Also the first victim, Patricia, … we still don't even have a connection to Simon, other than the note she delivered."

"And yet we need to find it, in order to keep this theory mobile," Sergeant Colby pointed out.

"I'm working on it. I've shown Simon her picture, and he doesn't recognize her." She winced. "I haven't come out and asked him if he might have used prostitutes on the street." The statement left her flushed. "I'm sure that'll be a great conversation."

Her boss was amused nonetheless, as his lips twitched. "On the other hand, he's been fairly open in most of your dealings, so I doubt this would be any different." He made a casual gesture. "Not that that'll help you. ... Look. You may not like this, but I'm thinking that you should get off the case."

She bolted to her feet in outrage.

Her boss immediately held up his hand. "Just listen to me."

She glared at him.

"Have a seat." He took a moment, as she sat down, stiff as a board. "You're personally involved, and we don't want anything to jeopardize the case, whether closing it or moving it forward to court. We don't want any emotional blinders on, which may bite us in the ass."

She shook her head. "That won't happen," she snapped. "If I haven't been taken off any of the other Simon-related cases up until now, it makes absolutely no sense to take me off this one. And Rodney is on this case with me. So, even if I weren't already working completely by the book and aboveboard, without reproach, he's also keeping me honest and real."

The sergeant frowned, as if struggling with her answer.

"It really won't do any good to pull me off." She repeated this to emphasize her point. "Believe me. It won't do any good. Obviously I'll continue to look into this, so you're much better off utilizing whatever form of help I can give."

He nodded slowly. "But then I want Rodney with you ... *all the time*," he stated firmly. "No running off on your own, no checking out leads solo and filling him in later, nothing to be done without him present. He goes with you, everywhere, all the time."

Then Rodney walked into the room and saw the conversation in progress. He may not have heard the words, but he got the mood all right. "Do I need to leave?"

"No, not only do you not need to leave," Sergeant Colby replied, "I want you to stick close to her."

He came forward immediately. "What happened?"

"Nothing's happened." she snapped, but her tone was biting enough to show where her head was. "He's doubting that keeping me on the case is a good idea."

At that, Rodney winced and nodded. "I have to admit that we thought that would come up anyway." She glared at him, but he didn't shy away from her intense gaze. "Sorry, but, when you're personally involved with somebody of interest in these cases, … that'll always get questioned."

"And, for the moment," the sergeant told Rodney, before she interjected herself into the conversation again, "I'm determined to keep you glued to her to make sure that she doesn't go off and do anything emotionally unwise. *And* I want to keep her legally on target, so that we have no problems closing any of this in court."

"Not a problem," Rodney said. She stared at her partner intently, and Rodney turned to Colby. "I can't imagine that she would be anything other than professional in this instance, sir, but I certainly note your concerns."

At that, her sergeant nodded at Kate. "I am aware that you can keep it under wraps. But, if that changes"—he glanced from Rodney to her and then back to Rodney—"believe me. I will pull you off the case."

"Got it," she noted.

And, with that, Colby turned and walked out.

She slumped into her chair and scrubbed her face. She looked over at Rodney, flustered but still grateful. "Thanks for that."

He nodded. "I'm not surprised, and you shouldn't be either."

"It's not that I'm surprised, but, after so many cases involving Simon, I guess it came out of the blue."

"Doing what you're doing," Rodney stated calmly, "we all see that you have a gift, and we're all quite willing to try and figure out a way to work with you." He snorted. "Even if that means I get to shadow you on the job," he teased.

She rolled her eyes at him. "You're as qualified as I am to do this job," she replied, "so, hardly job-shadowing."

He chuckled. "But I knew it would get your goat if I said that."

"You're not kidding," she muttered. "I get it. I do. Hey, it is what it is."

"So you want to fill me in on what you did after leaving the crime site?" Rodney asked her.

"I got back from speaking with the wife of the second victim," she began, "and we're still waiting for forensics. I did ask Smidge if he could move up this second case because it looks to be connected to the earlier one of mine." She heard Rodney snort. She nodded. "I definitely got the impression that Smidge wasn't happy with me, but I think it was more a case of he's not happy about the fact that there's a chance of a serial killer on the loose," she murmured.

Rodney nodded. "Let's go over what we've got so far," He pulled his chair out right away. "You're the only one who could push Smidge anyway. If one of us asked, he'd get his back up, and our cases would be last," he muttered.

She shrugged. "Generally he and I get along well."

"Which is a surprise because, as a rule, he doesn't get along with anybody."

She ignored that and didn't even have time to contemplate such a relationship because, as long as Smidge was the coroner, she would do everything she needed to do to ensure that her cases, her victims, got as close to special priority as she could get them. It's not that anybody else's cases weren't just as important, but they weren't hers.

"When I mentioned that this latest death was connected, Smidge definitely got quite upset." Then Kate snorted. "Even he noted that my cases were *special*."

"Of course. The thought of a serial killer is enough to give all of us the heebie-jeebies."

"What is it, four to make a serial killer?" He shrugged in response, and she nodded. "So what are the chances that we haven't found other victims yet?"

At that, Rodney twisted in his chair and stared at her. "Why would you even bring that up?" he asked in mock horror. "You'll jinx us."

"Because it appears to me that it's quite possible that somebody who's done what this killer has done, and, as covertly as he's done it, might have had some practice."

He sucked in his breath, as he sat here. "So when you say *practice* …"

She nodded. "*Practice*. As in maybe he killed before. Maybe he's tortured before. Maybe he's been acting out this scenario before," she suggested, getting more and more animated and excited. "We need to go through cold cases, and I …" She winced. "I am getting ahead of myself. … I don't know if we would be looking local or not." She stared at Rodney, as he gave her the same wondrous looks she often got from him. "What are the chances that this guy has tortured other people or gotten to the point where maybe torture is even a euphemism for what he's doing."

"Okay, but, if he's a sadist, and he's had, up until now, some basic relationships that have functioned on the surface, we won't have any knowledge of that."

"Right, I know," she accepted, with a sigh. "Wouldn't it be something if we had a big mass registry of every psycho out there?"

He snorted. "*Yeah*, let me know how that works for you. All those privacy laws would have a heyday with that."

"I know. Until it's their family who's been tortured and killed," she added.

"I will start a run and see if we can come up with any cases that in any way trigger something such as this." Rodney then started typing into the database.

"I'm not saying that there'll be something quite on target, except maybe with the feet torn to ribbons," she pointed out. "Just that maybe he's been utilizing some of his style, techniques, and torture patterns, in order to get to where he is today. Like maybe testing on animals before he graduated to people."

"Oh, I hear you. Can't say I like it, but I do understand what you're asking."

She laughed. "Yeah, I know, and it's sick and it sucks, but …"

"I'll get Reese in on it too," he suggested.

"If she's got time for us," Kate reminded him. "The other departments use our analyst as well."

Rodney winced. "Right. I'll check her availability. We could sure use her because she can do a much wider and deeper search than I can."

And, with that, they both returned to their desks and their respective work to hopefully make progress, before another victim showed up on their doorstep.

———

BY THE TIME he dragged his sorry ass back to his apartment, Simon was dead exhausted and mentally stressed at the thought of people dying because of him.

What kind of sick fuck out there in this world would do that? Why would the killer blame a complete stranger for some injury Simon had supposedly inflicted on the killer himself? Every time Simon got out into this world, it seemed to him that it was way more messed up than ever, and it sucked. It truly did.

As he walked inside his apartment building, he looked over at his doorman, trailing him quite closely.

"Ooh, ouch, tough day?"

Simon winced and nodded. "Yep, sure was. Not sure the night will get any better either. Calls for a liquid dinner," he muttered, as he headed toward the special elevator, designated for his penthouse suite.

His doorman raced behind him. "No, no, no, no, not a liquid dinner." He raised his hands. "You need food, a shower, and a chance to recuperate from whatever has happened."

He nodded slowly. "I haven't even managed to go grocery shopping yet."

"I'll order something in and send it up to you, sir," Harry offered immediately, smiling brightly at Simon. "Hey, sometimes we all need somebody to help us out." He took a moment and then shrugged. "You've always been good to me, and right now you need somebody to be good to you."

There wasn't a whole lot Simon could say, but it certainly warmed his heart. He nodded. "I could really do with some pasta."

"It'll be on its way shortly. You go on up and get that shower. I'll try to get it here by the time you're done."

"Ha. That would make you a miracle worker."

Harry laughed. "Hey, don't doubt it." With that, he walked back to the reception desk and picked up the phone. Simon was too tired to even care if he got dinner or not. He doubted he'd eat it, but he probably should. And Harry was right; this wasn't exactly the time for nothing but liquid sustenance. Still, every once in a while, your soul was so damn weary of life that it seemed to be the better option— even if it wasn't.

Taking his doorman's advice, Simon headed into the shower first, and, by the time he stepped out, he felt moderately better. He wrapped a towel around his waist and stepped into his bedroom to put on a comfy pair of pants and then walked out to the kitchen. He popped a beer because it was there and faster and possibly a better choice than the whiskey sitting off to the side. When his elevator dinged to announce a visitor, he walked over and allowed it to open. Harry stood there, a big smile beaming on his face, as he held out a bag.

"It's here," he crowed.

Simon nodded. "You really are a miracle worker."

"Not always, but, every once in a while, things do come together."

"Well, I appreciate it—rough day and all."

"You need to eat some food, followed by some downtime," he stated in a firm tone.

"Got it," Simon acknowledged, with a chuckle. "Thanks

for this."

Harry nodded and punched the down button on the elevator.

Simon carried the bag back into the kitchen, opened it up, and found it was from his favorite Italian restaurant. Of course Harry probably told Mama that this order was for Simon because there was enough here to feed at least six people. He shook his head, but the scent of spicy meatballs filled his nostrils, along with that rich tomato sauce, and he was soon digging in, as if he hadn't eaten in days.

As he thought about it, he hadn't had lunch. That was not predictable, once everything had gone south pretty quickly after the noon hour, but this spaghetti hit the spot quite nicely. Even as he considered the serving amount again, he wondered whether Kate had eaten at all today or whether she was in the same scenario, too damn tired to care. His fingers dialed without him even giving them permission, and, when she answered, he winced. "You sound like I feel."

"Yeah," she muttered, "a shitty day."

"I hear you. I wasn't planning to have dinner myself to-night." He sloshed down his swallow of pasta with a sip of beer. "I planned to hit the whiskey, wanted to fade the day away."

"You and me both," she said on a yawn, "but you at least have food, from the sounds of it."

"I am eating, and it's from my favorite Italian place too."

"Oh, *Mama's*," she guessed.

"Yeah, my doorman ordered it for me. I looked pathetic, I guess, and Mama sent me enough for at least eight people." He laughed as the number automatically rose in his head. "Or maybe just enough for you and me."

In mock outrage she asked, "Are you saying that I eat

enough to feed a crowd?"

"Most of time, yes, because, like me today, you don't take care of yourself."

"Hey, that's not fair. I've been doing much better."

"Yeah, that's because I'm sitting there, looking over your shoulder."

"That could be it too," she grumbled. "I'm still at the office."

"Well then, you should come here as soon as you're done and get some food. There's lots of it, and it's hot, and it's fresh."

"And that is very tempting."

"It should be tempting, and don't forget. I mean it. You need to eat."

"I know you mean it," she replied, with an audible sigh, "and I'm almost done." And then she checked her phone and groaned. "It's almost eight."

"It *is* almost eight," he confirmed, "so get on over here." And, with that, he disconnected, smiling because she hadn't said no. Leaving it that way, there was a good chance she would follow his orders and make it here. He quickly sent a message to the front desk of his apartment building, saying that, if Kate showed up, to bring her right up. It was never a case of *when* Kate showed up, send her right up. It was usually a case of *if* because it was still anybody's guess if she would make it tonight.

Simon had learned to be happy when she showed up and had tried to be philosophical when she didn't. Sometimes cases took her away. Sometimes she got too tired, and she crashed at the office. That just made him angry when he found out she'd done that. But it was a gift when she came over, and tonight he could use that gift. Both of them could use the time to just be with each other.

Nothing was joyful about seeing the killer pull that stunt on Luca today. Simon still couldn't get the image out of his mind, and he'd seen more than enough death for it not to have been as shocking as it was. But, hey, there it was. Sometimes no good answers explained the little shits in the world around them, or at least in his world.

He'd had way too much exposure to them, and now here he was, exhausted and letting this asshole get under his skin. Maybe that's what really pissed him off, the fact that he had let this killer get to him, but he didn't seem to know or understand how to get out of this mess driving him batty. Surely there was a way to stop this from happening. There should be a way for all this to go away. Yet his mind was not thinking clearly enough to see any way forward, which didn't make sense either.

He yawned again, finished off his plate, got up, popped open a bottle of wine, and poured two glasses. Sure enough, he'd barely poured the second glass, when the elevator door opened, and Kate walked in. He took one look at her face and winced. "I thought I looked bad."

She rolled her eyes at him. "*Great*, nice to see you too." Then she sniffed the air and grinned. "But you do come in handy for some things."

He laughed. "And, of course, you're hungry."

"Well, I am hungry, but I would have gone home and crashed without food." Yet she walked to the kitchen, opened up a couple of the to-go packages, and seeing what else was inside the to-go bag, she reached for a plate and immediately served herself at least as much as he had eaten, if not more.

When she sat down right there, he gazed at her plate in

wonder, grinning at her eagerness, then placed the wineglass in front of her. "Here. You can enjoy that with it."

She took a sip cautiously and then beamed at him. "That's great wine," she said. "I don't know where you got it or what it costs, and I don't really want to know because it probably doesn't come in my square boxes."

He rolled his eyes at her. "No, it definitely doesn't. It's an awesome wine, a local BC wine, and it runs about seventy-five a bottle."

She stopped with a meatball on her fork midair and stared at him in shock. "I'm not ... I'm not saying anything." She raised one brow. "It's a great wine. I'll leave it at that."

He laughed, as he pulled out a chair and sat down across from her. "It'll be a rough week, won't it?"

"I hope it doesn't last that long, but, considering we're getting nowhere, yes," she admitted flat-out. "It'll be a rough week."

That's what he liked about her so much. She was always honest, fair, and straight to the point. He nodded and stayed quiet while she ate. When she hit the bottom of her plate, she looked over at the bags, and he asked, "Do you want more?"

"Want? Yes. Should I get some more? No," she admitted. "I don't think my brain has even registered the fact that food has hit my stomach, so I think it's still telling me to keep eating against the future times of lack," she noted, with a wry tone.

He understood because sometimes, when you eat so fast, your body didn't even register that you were eating and that this pain would be over fast.

She settled back at the table with a glass of wine.

"Come on," Simon suggested. "Let's go to the couch, where it's comfortable." His favorite couch sat in front of the floor-to-ceiling windows, where they could see the city of Vancouver sprawled before them. He sat down, patted the empty space on the couch, and she crashed beside him, curling up against him.

"It's been a shitty day," she murmured.

"For both of us," he said in quiet acknowledgment.

"Why are people such assholes?" she asked casually. "I just … I can't even imagine."

"And I spent all day trying to sort out what level of assholes I could possibly know who would do this," he shared. "The trouble is, a lot of assholes are in my life, and a lot of assholes were in my past life. I just didn't think any of them were at this level."

"But then we have seen some of the people in your world before," she mumbled, as her head rested again his shoulder.

"Right. And I was hoping to never have to do that again." His hand gently stroked her shoulder and back, as he tucked her up a little closer. "We thought that that deal was done, and we could park it and move forward, and it would never be resurrected again," he muttered, desperate to keep the bitterness out of his voice. However, when her fingers linked with his, he realized that he hadn't succeeded.

"And we solved that one. And we will solve this one too."

"You get any flak from the sergeant yet?"

"Yep, sure did, and, for whatever stupid reason, it caught me off guard." She sounded angry. "I should have seen it coming." She yawned then and sighed, as she curled up tighter against him.

Simon murmured, "You cannot see everything coming. Sleep if you want."

"Well, if we'll sleep," she said, with another yawn, "we would both benefit from a bed."

"I know, but it seems such a long way away, doesn't it?" he teased.

She gave him a chuckle.

"Finish your wine, and then we'll crash."

"We have to put the food away," she added.

"No, we don't," he countered. "You're so tired that you didn't see me put the leftovers into the fridge."

"Ah," she murmured.

He looked down to see her eyes closed, her wineglass resting gently on his thigh, her head against his shoulder. He pulled the wineglass from her fingers, and her eyes opened immediately and stared at him. "Either finish it or put it on the coffee table"—he pointed to the half-turned glass—"before I end up wearing it."

Her lips twitched, as she tilted the wineglass to her mouth and drained it.

He winced at the lovely wine being guzzled, as if a glass of water, but, when she curled up against him once more, he gave a happy sigh and wrapped her up closer.

When he felt her breath flowing calm and steadily through her, he realized she was right; they should have gotten into bed. But he'd been in this position with her before. He set his empty wineglass on the coffee table beside him and shifted so that he could stand, and her eyelids fluttered open, but her gaze seemed blurry, and then she closed them tight again.

He scooped her into his arms, and she murmured something, snuggling in closer to get more comfortable. He smiled at that, wondering how long it had taken for her to find that level of comfort and security with him. She was such a special woman, and these moments were few and far between, so he really wanted to enjoy them. Yet he was also too damn tired to get there.

As he moved into the bedroom, he laid her on the bed and quickly stripped off as much of her clothing as he could without disturbing her too much. When he rolled her over, Kate completely trusted that he would do what he needed to do for her comfort. He rarely saw her like this and only when she was alone with him.

According to her it was something that she didn't do, but, at least when they were together, there was that level of trust. It did his heart good to see her this way, but it also hurt him to see her so exhausted, in so much pain, where both were never-ending in her world. He didn't understand the need or the drive to do what she did, but he understood that, for her, this was what she would always do because she felt this calling for it.

The fact that her little brother Timmy was out there somewhere in the world—now missing for so many years that he was presumed dead, so an unknown question mark in Kate's mind—was another aspect of what drove her. Simon wished he could get answers for her regarding her baby brother, but, if she hadn't found those answers herself, Simon wasn't sure that he could do anything.

Even this stupid psychic ability of his was very hit and miss and not something that he could count on. Just one more of those things that mystified him. If being a psychic was such a gift, then why couldn't he use it all the time for what he wanted? Only it didn't work that way. As he'd found to his dismay, when it needed to be called upon, sometimes it was there, and then sometimes it wasn't.

By the time he was stripped down too and had gone through his nightly ritual and was climbing into bed beside her, she opened her eyes. "I have to pee." She slid out of bed, stumbled to the bathroom, and quickly used the facilities. By the time she returned to bed, she was yawning heavily, barely conscious, and now completely naked. He flipped the covers back, and she slid in beside him. Then he pulled her into his arms, and, spoon fashion, they both crashed.

A few hours later, the dreams hit him. He thrashed in bed, before his eyelids popped open. As if a complete switch from day to night, he saw around him a weird glow.

He wasn't even sure where he was, and it took a moment to realize that he was stuck, caught up in a vision. He hesitated and then tried to sink deeper into the vision to get answers, at least some information, something that would help them to sort out the most recent nightmare killer cases that had engulfed them. And yet there was nothing.

Then he saw dice flying on a craps table, poker cards hitting a dealer's hands, horses on a race track, greyhounds running. He tried to concentrate and to get deeper into the vision to figure out what all this gambling had to do with two recent murders, and then it hit him hard; it wasn't about gambling. It was about *games*. It was all about games, and that's what this killing spree was about—*games*.

Somebody had gotten bored with some game and had decided to up the ante.

Simon woke with a start, hearing a weird voice around him. And then he noted Kate, who stood silently to the side of the bed, looking down at him warily, the covers pulled off him. She was wild-eyed. They were both nude, and he was the only one lying on the bed. "What happened?" he asked her.

"You started thrashing and kicking, getting caught up in the blanket, so I took it off you, but that didn't seem to help much."

"It was the dream," he said, as he sank back into the mattress. "That crazy-ass dream. I am sorry. Are you hurt?"

"Nah, I am good. Anything useful?" she asked in an off-hand way, but her gaze was intense, as if she understood perfectly well what she was asking.

He gave her a lopsided smile. "All I saw were all different kinds of gambling," he replied, his voice tired and coming from afar. "Well, at first, I thought it was all about gambling, as I was being shown games of chance—so a craps table, a poker table, various things such as that. And then it came to me. That vision wasn't so much about gambling as it was about *games.*"

She nodded at that. "Games. So what does that even mean to you—or to the killer?"

With a note of anger threading through his voice, Simon stated, "He's bored, and he's decided to up the ante. He has decided to create his own games, to write his own rules. And I am afraid it'll get way worse."

⚬⚬⚬

IT WAS ALL Simon's fault. It was easy to pin everything back to that beginning. How it wasn't fair, but it had happened anyway. So many things in life weren't fair, and yet no one could do absolutely anything about it. It was infuriating. At the same time, no real way to change it. Staring at the screen, the killer looked down at the keyboard, trying to figure out exactly what words to type. The killer's fingers moved automatically, and the words appeared on the screen in front.

Simon's at fault. It's Simon's fault. If Simon hadn't done what he'd done, it would be different. Life would be different. Life would be happy. There would be joy. There would be romance. There would be … love. It was all Simon's fault.

And with that, the killer went back to the notes that he'd gathered on Simon's life, trying to sort through what else needed to be done. The killer was on point, yet this emptiness was inside, this longing for what could never be, for what had long since passed, even if it had been ten years ago. And now recently, yet again, it seemed so unfair. The killer closed down the screen, got up, and walked over to the window to stare out into the darkness, knowing a teeming city was below, a city full of opportunities, a city full of possibilities, and such hope and dreams and so much more than anything and everything the killer wanted.

And yet here, among them, were no answers. The killer grabbed a bulky coat and stepped out into the night, calling out, "Be back in a few minutes." The killer took several deep breaths, straightening up and standing taller in the evening air. Outside, the killer wandered, big and unafraid, knowing that most people would avoid someone of this size alone, and that made a huge difference. And the killer walked tall, with an attitude. Of course the coat helped, as did the attitude.

The killer smiled, then lifted up the collar against his neck, trying to get distance from the growing knot of pain inside, that … nudge that told the killer to act, needed to do this all over again. The killer didn't really want to, but some people needed to be taught a lesson. So, if nobody else was willing to do it, that fell to the killer. It also fell to the killer because of Simon. Simon had changed everything. If Simon had left well enough alone, then revenge wouldn't be needed.

It's all your fault, Simon.

CHAPTER 7

THE NEXT MORNING Kate headed to the office. She drove directly from his place, grateful that she had followed his suggestion a while back to keep at least one change of clothes at his home. That way, should she stay over, she wasn't forced to wear the same clothes to the office again. And now freshly showered and changed and feeling a whole lot better, she mulled over his vision from the night before. It didn't help much in the sense that they already knew it was a game. They'd earlier been told it was a game. So absolutely nothing about that perspective was a new insight. However, the vision hinted that boredom was an element to this.

That part was different.

It boggled the mind to think that somebody would kill people because of boredom of all things. It took a special mentality to even get into this mind-set and play it willfully. And, if it was a game, how come Simon wasn't given any rules? How come he wasn't invited to play? Why was he only shown the results of whatever it was he was losing?

That's the part that got to Kate. It's not as if Simon had been invited into this game, and then she realized that Simon wasn't invited at all because Simon wasn't playing the game. Whoever this asshole was, that was *his* game. His game was the whole of it; his creation was absolute.

It was up to Simon to figure out what the game was before somebody else died. It's not as if this were a straight-up kidnapping, and he was supposed to deliver $50,000 or $500,000 someplace. This was all about a game that somebody else was playing, and the challenge was for Simon to stop it before it went too far. Of course Simon had failed because he hadn't even realized what game they were playing. Simon wasn't told the rules because it wasn't his game. It was this asshole's make-believe scenario, forcing everybody else to just react.

The game was rigged. The game was one-sided. The game was torture, then death.

As she walked into the office, Rodney looked up at her and smiled. "You look better."

She nodded. "I feel better too because, if you ask me now, I was pretty dead yesterday," she admitted.

"How's Simon doing?"

She shrugged. "Pissed off, upset, and angry that somebody would be killing because of him, in his name even." She shook her head. "How would anybody feel to know that somebody was doing this because of them and yet not tell Simon in what way he was supposedly responsible."

"But that's part of the game, isn't it?"

"Well, that's the thing. Simon was getting visions of games, games of chance, racing horses and craps tables and whatnot. He thought it was maybe *about* gambling, but then the message came for him—in whatever way, shape, or form you want to take this," she added, with an eye roll. "This wasn't about gambling as much as it was about that our killer was bored and had decided to up the ante, and, for whatever reason, he had locked on to Simon."

"That's pretty thin though," Rodney replied skeptically.

"Upping the ante? Somebody who's been playing games of chance for a long time and putting money where his mouth was has decided that tossing a dice, where you get a different answer every time, that's … that's not enough of a challenge?" he asked doubtfully.

"I know. None of it makes any sense yet. We're all reaching for clues. And who knows? *Games* could be a euphemism for *torture*, like *passed away* is a nicer way to say *died.*" She sat down at her desk and quickly logged in to her computer. "The thing is, in a stupid way, it does make a certain sense."

"How so?" he asked, turning to look at her.

"Because the game isn't for Simon to get into. The game is for this asshole. He's making it more challenging for himself, which is why I go back to the fact that this isn't his first time killing. This might be a personal vendetta against Simon, just so the killer has someone else to blame for his own serial killer addiction. This is about the killer, who's been doing this for a long time, and that part has become boring to him. So now he wants to up the ante by bringing in Simon, adding in Simon's pain, maybe putting into play Simon's torment. Hell, this killer even drew me in from the beginning, giving Patricia that note addressed to me here at the station. This killer was asking for our detectives to get on the killer's trail. Maybe that's what this is all about. Maybe he's just been doing so much for so long that he needed something to shift it so it was more exciting for him."

At that, Rodney winced. "That thrill-kill MO will be a little rough to track down then."

"Especially when we know absolutely nothing about the player. I don't even know if this guy is local," she said. "Simon himself has got quite a global presence. He knows a lot of people out there, and one of the things that is quite feasible is that our killer may be used to traveling the world, and we could be looking at cases that have absolutely nothing to do with Canada," she suggested.

"Which means, once again, it'll be almost impossible to track our killer," Rodney pointed out.

"Which is why," she added, "I think he's bored. He's been killing long enough and has never been caught, and he's blasé. It's not a challenge anymore. And we are walking around blind, with no leads."

As her other team members filed into the room, Kate began anew. "But consider this. If this killer has been doing this for a very long time, and the thrill is gone, yet he can't get out of his compunction to murder, you know what that's like. We've seen that with serial killers, with druggies. They get a certain hit from doing this, and then, over time, it's not enough of a high.

"Maybe he's been a contract killer, taking out enemies—ours and others—for years. Maybe he does it strictly for the money. Maybe he does it for favors. Maybe he does it because, hey, he can. I don't know," she admitted, getting to the same excited outbursts she so often got to, and no one tried to stop her in any way.

"But now his high from these killings is not enough of a high. So he's experimenting with what he can do to make it a bigger hit for him. So that, when he kills somebody else, knowing that we're walking around with stupidity all over our faces," she guessed, "maybe that makes him feel better. Maybe he gets a bigger high. However, he really wants Simon to get into the game, so the killer has a bit of a challenge to start giving a crap as to what he's doing on a day-to-day basis."

Lilliana sat down on her chair beside her. "I am glad you woke up on the right side of the bed."

Rodney snorted at that, but Kate ignored him.

Lilliana added, "That's a pretty fucked-up mentality."

"Yeah, sure is," Kate agreed. "And, no, I don't have any proof, but …" And then she thought about it and nodded. "It's starting to have a real feel to it."

"Whatever the hell that means," Owen said, as he walked in and sat down at his desk. "What the hell?"

"And yet she's not necessarily wrong," Sergeant Colby added, as he joined them.

She was startled by his acceptance of her suppositions; he had obviously heard her excited hypothesis.

"We have seen a couple cases like this before—not here, not locally," Colby corrected himself. "But globally, there have been a few other cases where people have been almost bored doing whatever they're doing, and they've tried to up the ante for more of a challenge. Obviously we've got a sick individual here, somebody who is completely desensitized to his effect on people. Otherwise why do you first kidnap your victims, making them walk into rivers, blindfolded, if it isn't because the killer's bored."

"He's an asshole."

"Definitely a bottom-feeder."

"All true because he wants some fun, because he needs something in his life to give him that high again. Then, when you think about his releasing Patricia, promising that he'll leave her alone if she does what he wants, but killing her anyway? That's the part that really cements that boredom element for me. He isn't here about the killing as much as he's here about *Give me something in life to make me feel better*, and then turns around and takes away a life all over again," Colby shared, with a nod. "Whether we like it or not, we seem to have somebody who's running with his newest theory, testing an experiment."

Lilliana shook her head. "Sick fuck," she muttered.

"Maybe, but he's our sick fuck now," Colby stated, with a look in Kate's direction. "And we want him in our interview room, preferably damn fast."

"And yet," Kate noted cautiously, "this quite likely is somebody with a lot of experience killing people and not getting caught. So the best chance of getting him is if he makes a mistake, which, with that level of experience, won't happen very much," she pointed out. "Also, looking into the Simon angle in both these murders, that could literally mean our killer knows about Simon's psychic ability."

"So how the hell will we catch this guy?" Rodney asked, looking around at the team.

"I don't know," Kate answered, "short of forensics giving us something to go on. So I'll go talk to Smidge in a little while. ... I did ask him to put a rush on it."

Owen rolled his eyes at that. Lilliana, on the other hand, shook her head and added, "Good for you, if it works. I tried to do that in the past and got it slammed in my face."

"I'm not trying to step on anybody's toes, but I do want answers," she stated, her tone hard. "So, if he can give them to me, then I'm willing to play whatever game the killer's got going on."

"No game," Colby said, holding up a hand. "Better not use that word near our coroner, given your killer is so stuck on that one. Smidge's a good person, but he's also dealing with more than our cases. Therefore, it's not about our getting priority—yet obviously you want priority for your cases. If you can get it, I won't argue with that because, of course, it helps us. However, we have a very active department, and unfortunately the city has a crime level that refuses to stop. So Smidge will be overwhelmed and under pressure, just like the rest of us, or maybe more so than most of us."

She nodded. "But if being nice gets me a little more of a response"—she shrugged and smiled sweetly at Owen—"you can damn-well believe I'll use it." And, with that, she got up to walk out.

When Colby whistled, she turned to him. He grinned at her and asked, "Aren't you forgetting something?"

She frowned and then turned to look at Rodney. "That would be the other shoe I was waiting for. I'll be heading to the morgue. You coming?"

"Apparently." Rodney bolted to his feet, with a big grin. "Sounds as if it's you and me against the world."

She rolled her eyes. "If you burst out into song, I'll drop you off at the first corner."

He laughed. "What's wrong with good songs?"

"Nothing," she stated. "What's wrong is your singing."

When the rest of the group heard their joking, they burst into laughter.

Kate grinned at Rodney. "Let's go, partner."

⚬⚬⚬

SIMON'S FOREMAN JOE was in a very subdued mood when Simon arrived on-site this morning. Simon looked over at him and asked, "How is your sister doing?"

Joe shook his head. "She alternates between devastated and angry and then pissed off at me for giving him the damn job," he complained, with a headshake.

"We don't know that his death is connected to the job,"

Simon noted cautiously, although he knew it was.

"Doesn't matter. She seems to think that if she hadn't pushed him to get a real job, then everything would be … fine." He frowned. "She's delusional, but she's my sister, and she's grieving. I am sorry for her, but Luca was a fucking loser—yet he was her loser."

Simon understood completely. "I'm sorry, man. That makes it hard. … What about our staffing issues?"

He nodded. "Apparently you talking to Ricky yesterday may have helped. I had a couple guys reach out and ask if their positions have been filled and whether my brother-in-law was still around. I told both guys that Luca's gone, that he won't be back, and then I apologized for all the shit that went on and then some. I thought he would do a better job than he did, and clearing the air has been easy without him. I've now got six of the men back," he stated, with a satisfied sigh. "That will help us quite a bit." He had a genuine smile on his face. "And some of them, I'm damn glad to have back too. Some of the replacements were fucking awful."

"I hear you," Simon replied, "and you're right. I'm glad to have them back too. Anyway, let's take another look at what we'll need for adjustments. Any news on the shipments coming in?"

"No, none," he said somberly. "Plus some graffiti is on one of the walls." He pointed off to the side.

"Yeah? What?"

"Just bullshit stuff."

"Is it important right now?"

"No, it will get covered up when we get through to the next stage," Joe advised. "It's on the inside of one of the raw walls, and it'll be covered over."

"It happened overnight?" Simon asked.

"It did. Again, no idea who."

"Do we have cameras up?"

"We don't on this site because we've got security on a regular basis. Remember when we had equipment that went missing, and we opted for in-person security?"

"Right, I do remember that." Simon stopped and looked around. "And yet security didn't catch anybody spray-painting?"

"He interrupted them, so that they took off."

"Right, another one of our perpetual headaches."

"Exactly."

Simon nodded. "Let me take a look at the graffiti."

"It's really nothing to worry about," Joe said, as he walked over with him. "It's the typical BS stuff."

"Yeah, what's this one about?"

"Something about freedom and games."

At that, Simon stiffened and repeated, "Games?"

"Yeah. Come over here. I'll show you," Joe stated, getting ahead of him. "And, no, the security guard didn't see him, other than to yell at him and to chase him off. He didn't get a good description of him. I did talk to him about it this morning. The guard says it was some tall, fairly thick guy, but the guard is guessing because of the speed the guy took off running."

As they walked around the corner, Simon immediately saw the graffiti on the wall. He stared at it for a long moment, trying to figure out what this was.

"So you can see that it's random words everywhere, not really saying anything, and then you see *games* written over here. I think that's supposed to be *games*," Joe corrected, as he pointed off to the side, where the word was written on a slanted angle.

"What is that?" Simon pointed at another corner, frowning.

"I don't know."

Simon stared at the series of parallel vertical lines and then realized that it was the tally mark for four. If it had had that fifth cross stroke to make a tally of five, it would have been easier to read it for what it was. He stared at it, but Simon had absolutely no reason for any of it to apply to him personally. He studied it closely, then looked around at their surroundings. "It doesn't seem to make a whole lot of sense."

"No, and maybe because the guy got chased off, and this isn't finished. I don't know," Joe replied, with a wave of his hand. "But it's minor vandalism, and we can get this covered up when the building's finished anyway, but it still sucks."

"Yeah, it really does suck," Simon agreed. As he shifted his angle of view, he moved off a distance, so he could look at the graffiti from a slightly different perspective, and then it hit him. He sucked back his breath as he stared at it, pulled out his phone, and took a picture of it.

"What is it?" Joe asked curiously.

Simon shook his head. "Not sure, just something weird from this angle."

Joe joined him and stared at the wall in question. "Oh, look at that." Joe's voice had a strangled note to it. "Is that your name?"

"A variation of my name," Simon stated mildly, effectively hiding his own distress. "That still doesn't mean they intended to put my name up there."

"No, but it is freaky to see *Simon Says*, as in …"

"Yeah, I know what it means," Simon snapped. "It means, I need to phone somebody."

"Oh, I don't think the cops will give a shit about this."

"You could be wrong about that," Simon said, waving Joe off.

When his foreman's phone rang, he headed off to the side to talk.

Meanwhile Simon took a picture and sent it off to Kate, who promptly called him.

"What the fuck's that?"

"Graffiti on one of the walls of one of my rehab projects, where our dead guy Luca worked," Simon explained. "There's a scribble of *Simon* on top, with *says* below."

"So *Simon Says*," she noted, "like the children's game? But what's the point of that?"

"Who knows, but see those four vertical lines? All it needs is a fifth line slanted through them to make it a five."

She sucked in her breath. "But we only have two bodies so far."

"Exactly," he murmured. "And that's what I'm afraid of. Whoever this killer is, he's already attributed two other deaths to this game, and we don't even know about them."

CHAPTER 8

K ATE WALKED INTO the morgue, her shoes clicking on the hard floor. Smidge looked up from his desk and glared at her, and she glared right back, earning her a half smile.

"Everybody's afraid of me. You know that, right?" He practically growled at her.

"That's okay. They're afraid of me too."

He burst out laughing at that, and she caught Rodney's look of surprise in her direction, but she was pretty sure that she was correct because people treated her differently than others, and that was okay too. She understood Smidge, and he was damn good at his job, and that's what she cared about more than anything else.

Kate stood calmly, staring him down. "What have you got for me?"

"Who says I got anything for you?" the coroner snapped. "I tell you one thing, and, if you'd return the favor, that would be good too."

"Meaning?"

"Meaning that, if I don't have anything for you, then you don't have anything for me."

It took her about ten seconds to understand what he meant, and then she burst out laughing. "*Right.* I'd be more than happy to not bring you any more work, yet not sure that's quite so easy."

"No," he muttered. "Seems we've got a never-ending stream of assholes out there."

"So?" She nudged him back to the finished sheet-covered tables.

Smidge sighed loudly. "Yes, I've done him," he confirmed in a curt voice. "And, yes, there are similarities. However, nothing specific, except that it's obvious Luca's been tortured, stabbed, and whatever was going on with his feet of course. There are cuts all over his body." The coroner walked over to the coolers and quickly opened up a drawer, bringing out the related white-covered shrouded body for her.

"So time of death?" she asked.

He gave her the hours of the previous early morning at about 4:00 a.m. to 10:00 in the morning. "I don't think he was killed in the hotel room, not based on what we're seeing with his body. I think he was dumped back at the room."

"But that doesn't make sense," she noted, looking at him. "That ups tremendously the dangers of the killer getting caught."

Smidge nodded. "Maybe he wants to get caught. Anyway wasn't a whole lot of blood at the hotel room crime scene. He could have been dumped before death, but he for sure wasn't tortured in that hotel room."

She nodded, as she thought about it. "It sounds gruesome, but any chance the blood was taken away? Sucked out or whatever? Exsanguination or at least partially?"

He stared at the victim and seemed to be considering it. "It's possible. Yet I didn't see any evidence of that at the scene—but neither was I looking for it. They didn't do a complete job of exsanguination because his veins were still full. It would help to find the other crime scene where he was tortured."

She tilted her head at the body. "Would any of these wounds have bled a lot?"

"Yes." Smidge pointed to the one stab wound. "This injury would have filled his body cavity very quickly with blood, and it would have spilled outward as well, everywhere. His artery was nicked, which is why I think he was dead when dumped in that hotel room—or on death's door."

"Okay." Kate let out a disgruntled sigh. "He bled out somewhere else and was obviously in no condition at that point in time to get back to the hotel on his own. Not sure how much blood is in the human body or how much you need to function," she continued, thinking out loud, "but I'll take a guess and say he didn't have enough."

"No, he sure didn't. Death was not instantaneous, and he would have bled quite a while, and, in a way," he added, "I think that was deliberate by the killer."

She winced. "Quite likely, considering the torture this guy's doing. On the other hand, Patricia Blinker, who was tormented and then supposedly would be safe, after delivering her torturer's message, was then stabbed to death anyway. The killer did that murder efficiently."

At that, Smidge nodded. "I don't get into the psychology of the whys and the motivations by which anybody might be killing these people, but probably Patricia was a loose end, an afterthought. Dead people don't talk."

"And yet"—she smiled at Smidge, pointing to the body next to him—"apparently, you speak the language of the dead pretty well." He gave her a beaming smile, and she realized how few compliments he likely got.

"That I do," Smidge confirmed, "but can't say it's what I

want to do."

"Nope, got that too," she agreed. "However, we have two victims so far, and the only connection to them that we've found to date is Simon."

Smidge frowned at Kate. "Simon?"

She nodded. "Simon St. Laurent."

His eyebrows shot up. "Oh, that's an interesting twist."

"Why is that?"

"He's your partner, isn't he?"

"Well …" She stopped, flustered.

Rodney joined in this conversation now, a grin bursting free. "It's a relatively new association, but yes."

"That sounds … awkward," Smidge noted, smiling too.

"Yeah, it is," she muttered, not liking the direction of the conversation. "We don't know the connection between Simon and the killer either."

"No, never do at first." Smidge nodded. "These killers start executing their plans, and that leaves you playing catch up."

"Yep, exactly." She looked down at the victim and gave a headshake. "Somebody befriended this Luca guy at a pool hall. Then decided, either before or after, that he would be a perfect victim for this killer's cause. It didn't matter who he was. Luca just fit the profile, and that was it." She shrugged.

"It's all it ever takes," Smidge replied. "You can't feel guilty about it." She looked over at him, startled. "You think I don't see that you're wondering if it's got something to do with you, whether Luca was targeted because of you?" Smidge tilted his head. "These assholes? They'll target whoever. It probably ups their joy to know that you are involved. Maybe it makes it a little bit more of a challenge," he suggested, "but don't go getting sucked into that *you're to blame* mentality."

Rodney reached out and clipped Kate gently on the shoulder. "I hadn't considered that, but Smidge's got a point."

"Let's hope we're at the end of whatever plans the killer's got going." She sighed. "I still don't quite understand how somebody gets this proficient without practice."

Smidge shook his head. "He doesn't. You don't know which ones were the practice."

She studied his face for a moment, and something occurred to her. Some previous murders came before these deaths. Even a clue could help. "Have you seen anything like this before?"

"Sure." Smidge gave her a faint nod. "So far we don't have a whole lot that's terribly distinctive. We've got heavily utilized feet, as if the victim walked barefoot over rough terrain for an extended period, or maybe even a belt was used to whip the feet. Don't know. We've got some torture, and we've got some stabbings." He frowned. "I see stabbings on a regular basis. The feet, however? That's a whole new element."

"Right. I'm hoping it's a new element and that you don't have twelve other murders similar to this in your history." She eyed Smidge intently.

He shook his head. "Not that comes to mind—but, now that you've mentioned it, I will consider that."

"Good, because I'm pretty sure that this killer is a whole lot different than a first-timer. We also have some graffiti over at one of Simon's job sites." Kate turned to face Rodney, realizing that she hadn't kept him in the loop. She held out her cell phone, revealing the last text and the related photo that she had gotten from Simon.

Rodney checked out the photograph and frowned. "So you and Simon think, from this graffiti, that the killer's confessing to four murders, and so far we've only got two bodies?"

She nodded. "That's what makes the most sense to me, yes," She turned to Smidge, holding out her phone for him to see the graffiti too. "So we could potentially be looking for two more victims."

He nodded. "I'll keep that in mind, but remember. I only handle this morgue."

She winced and nodded. "And, of course, that adds to the challenge."

"I'll take a look though, through my old files," he promised, muttering to himself, his focus heading off to a corner where his computer was. "I'll let you know if I find anything."

She grinned at him. "Much appreciated."

"And it'd be much appreciated if you don't bring me quite so much work," He raised an eyebrow pointedly. "Especially SKs."

Serial Killers. She nodded. "Got it."

As they walked out, Rodney asked, "He really doesn't think that you can do anything about curtailing our murder cases before they even happen, does he?"

"No, I think he wants us to solve this as fast as we can, so that this particular killer doesn't get more victims."

"As if we're not trying to do that already," he grumbled in exasperation, looking back at the morgue.

"And Smidge knows that. It's one more push from another professional to say, *Hey, are you doing your job? I'm doing mine. Let's speed this up.*"

Rodney snorted as he got into the vehicle beside her.

"What now?"

"We'll go take a look at that graffiti and document it for the case. Even though it may or may not have anything to do with it."

He nodded. "Anything to do with Simon is important."

It took them twenty minutes to get to the location of the graffiti. As she walked up to the wall and stared at it, a man spoke from behind her.

"Hey, hey, hey, who are you, and what are you doing here?"

She turned to see a larger man, running toward her. She held up her badge, and he stopped in his tracks.

"Oh." He raised a hand in a peace gesture.

She smiled and nodded. "Are you security or foreman?"

"I'm the foreman," he stated.

"Good, I wanted to talk to you anyway," she muttered. "About your brother-in-law."

At that, Joe paled and nodded. "Yeah, I'm still in shock over that one."

"Doesn't sound as if he got along with anybody."

Joe snorted. "We lost at least eight crew members due to him, eight crew we couldn't afford to lose. Even now we're desperately trying to rehire them all, and it'll cost us. Some of them are even renegotiating their pay, all because of Luca." Joe let out a deep sigh. "And I don't mean to say nasty things about the dead, but he was arrogant, thought he should be boss. I think he was eyeing my job," Joe added, with an eye roll. "I've worked with Simon for ten years, but my brother-in-law was of the opinion that he could walk off the street and do a better job."

"Did he?"

He paused for a moment. "The trouble was, Luca didn't

even do his job. He came in, raised shit, insulted everybody, told them they were doing crap work, made people redo perfectly good work." Joe's face flushed in anger. "When you have a good team. like ours, you trust them. And, if you don't trust your crew, you better not keep them." Joe blew out a heavy breath.

"I've worked with this crew for a long time, and I have not had any occasion to have them redo anything, not in many a year, not since they were trained to do things the way that Simon wants them. And I can tell you that Simon isn't an easy taskmaster either. He expects the job to get done and expects it to be done on time, and we had a good working relationship with these guys. Then I hired my brother-in-law," he admitted on a sorrowful note. "Now everybody's pissed off at me, and my sister is a mess." He shook his head. "You do a good turn for the wrong type of person, and it ends up completely ruining everything as you know it. It really sucks."

"What about the day that he died?"

He stared at her and nodded. "He never left his shift. I thought he would go home to my sister. Yet apparently he was found in a hotel. Nothing more I can tell you about it."

She nodded. "His feet were trashed, as if he'd been out walking barefoot for hours and hours on rough surfaces."

"That doesn't make any sense either because Luca didn't do physical exertion. So not his style."

"Maybe not his style, but sounds as if he got in with a bad crowd potentially."

"No *potentially* about it," Joe declared, with a snort. "That's part of who and what he was. A bad crowd was everything to him." Joe shrugged. "Luca went from catastrophe to catastrophe. I'm supposed to be grieving and sorry and all that, but the damage he did here and potentially to my job is still a little close to heart." Joe groaned. "And my sister may never recover. So not really sure how much sympathy I can work up for Luca. But I would have preferred my sister left him instead of this."

"Of course. I do understand your candor."

"Good." Joe seemed relieved, and then he frowned at her, studying her closely. "You're Kate, aren't you?"

"That's what my badge says," she replied, with a note of humor.

He flushed and nodded. "As in *Simon's* Kate."

She winced at that, and Rodney snickered. She corrected Joe. "If you're asking if I know Simon and if we're dating, the answer's yes. … Can't say I particularly like being called *his* though."

The older man flushed and immediately stammered out an apology.

She waved it off. "It's fine," she stated, stifling his advances to apologize again. "Don't worry about it."

But obviously she'd upset Joe somewhat, and she hadn't meant to, but just something about being called another man's possession got to her. "Can you tell me anything about your brother-in-law's associations, friends, enemies, weaknesses?"

"Anything to do with gambling," he replied, "but honestly he was a hell of a pool player, and I think that's where his biggest weakness was."

"Which fits with the area where we found him," she agreed.

He nodded at that. "I've dragged him out more than a few times from various places myself. … They've been married ten years, and I think I've chased him home at least ten times. When he hits a certain spot in life, he goes back to what he knows, and what he knows is that godforsaken pool hall. Luca grew up in that era. Never really had a chance to get out of it, I guess."

She pondered that.

Joe continued. "I remember all the excuses my sister has given me all these years too, yet Luca had every chance to pull out of it."

Kate decided to let Luca off the hook a bit. "And yet gambling and drinking are both addictions, and, like all addictions, it's hard to leave them behind. It could have been drugs, which may have been worse," she added.

"It *was* drugs for a while." Joe faced her. "But I did warn him that I'd personally pay for the divorce and make sure he ended up on the streets if he didn't get off those."

She didn't say anything, just nodded. She'd certainly heard similar stories from other people at other times in life.

"He wasn't a bad guy, he was just"—Joe winced—"weak. I think that's probably the best way to describe him."

"And it sounds as if he had a bit of an ego, someone who thought he could do everything."

Joe snorted. "Oh my God, he was arrogant. Take my job for instance. He was always telling me how he could do a much better job. He just needed a chance, and he'd prove to the world what he could do. But it was always that he needed *a chance.* He was always the victim of not *getting a chance.* He didn't want to hear that I had worked with Simon for ten years or that I had started many, many years ago in the industry to learn all these trades. You don't become a foreman without having worked your way up and really knowing your shit," he explained. "That's not how construction works. Not one of these guys will respect you if you can't do the same job or do it better than they're doing. That's the facts of life, and Luca didn't want to hear it. He could do better, totally green off the streets, no experience, because of who he was," Joe shared, with a snort of disgust. "I failed to see what he was doing here, and that was a mistake on my part. I took my eyes off him for a minute, and he cost me so much."

"Any other friends, relatives, enemies? Anybody in particular?"

He stared at her and winced. "The friends in their marriage were my sister's. I don't think he had any, except for whoever was at his favorite pool halls. He certainly didn't stick to any one pool hall because sometimes he got banned from one of them. If he was having a bad night and decided to make life miserable for somebody," Joe shared, "often they would kick him out and give him a thirty-day ban. However, Luca spent good money at those places, so they always let him back in again. It's the nature of the business."

She could imagine. "Okay, that's good enough. If you think of anything else, give me call." She pulled out a card and handed it to him. "All info could be helpful. Now, we'll take a look at this graffiti and see if it's got any connection."

He led her to it and asked, "Why would it have any connection to Luca's death?"

She shook her head. "Only in that it's got Simon's name on it and your brother-in-law worked for Simon."

His eyes widened in horror. "Hey, Simon didn't do this," he declared. "He couldn't. That's not his thing at all. You have to know that."

She gave him a ghost of a smile. "I do know that, but we look at all the evidence regardless, as we try to figure out who's behind this. So it doesn't matter whether Simon did or he didn't. What's important is that we find out who did it in the end."

Relieved, Joe took several steps back. "Okay, I'll leave you to it then." But he sounded uncertain as he walked away.

She nodded and waited until he was gone, then turned to Rodney, who had been busy taking photos. "What do you think?"

"I think his brother-in-law Luca was probably an easy target. Big ego, which somebody could so easily see that he was desperate to be loved and appreciated and seen for the big man that he thought he was versus who everybody else thought he was. Therefore, flattery would have gone pretty easily to his head. And unfortunately with fatal results."

"That's what I was thinking too. Particularly for anybody looking to haunt Simon's world, they would have seen a weak employee, dissatisfied, somebody who's willing to talk. Whether Luca gave our killer anything of interest is a different story, but who knows."

Rodney nodded. "No, I hear you, but this graffiti isn't definitive either."

"Sure isn't," she agreed, "but I don't know about those lines." She pointed out the ones that appeared to be tally marks, as if counting victims, and Rodney stared at them for a long moment.

"But to find two victims that we've supposedly missed won't be easy, particularly when we don't have anything other than this killer's simple stabbing patterns to go by."

"That and the torture," she noted.

"And that too, yet even that's not huge because we don't have a location."

She pondered that and looked around to the site behind them. "We never got a location from Patricia either, did we?"

"No, not at all, only a rough time frame."

Kate nodded. "Let's take a look on the maps. Where does that rough time frame of driving take us? Because the killer and his victims had to be somewhere close enough to do whatever torture he had planned but not necessarily put him out in any way."

"Put him out?"

"Yeah. Inconvenience our killer. I don't know for sure, of course," she added, "but I seem to think that this guy's all about *easy*."

"And yet if he hauled the body back …"

"Yeah, how did he haul the body back? Granted, the brother-in-law was not a big man," she noted. "Hell, it's a hotel, so even a suitcase would do it."

Rodney frowned at her. "Or a laundry cart."

She nodded. "That works too. He's really not that big. Isn't he about five-one? The sister wasn't big either."

"No, but I'd have pegged Luca at about five-three," Rodney suggested.

"That fits too."

"So then he really fit the profile—somebody the killer could easily manhandle, overpower, and con, plus Luca worked for Simon."

"Exactly. So let's look at the map and also go back to the hotel and see if a bloody laundry cart is found. Or maybe one is missing. Check cameras—if they have any, which I somehow doubt."

SIMON ANSWERED HIS phone to hear his foreman on the other end, saying the cops were here. "Oh, good," Simon replied, his mind distracted by the figures on the laptop he reviewed, while sitting at the coffee shop.

Joe hesitated and then added, "I think it was your girl-friend."

"Should have been. She's the one I called."

"Oh man, okay. I wasn't sure if I was supposed to say anything or not. That's always a dicey scenario."

He smiled. "You tell her anything that she wants to know. She's a cop and a good one, and, if anybody can solve your brother-in-law's murder, it'll be her."

"I'm glad to hear that," Joe said, relief washing through his voice, all with enough emphasis to make Simon smile. "Because I wasn't sure."

"No, it's all good. Are they still there?"

"No, I think they walked away a little bit ago. They took a bunch of photos, made some measurements, took note of the surrounding locations. I don't know what all they were doing." He snorted. "I wanted to stay close, but obviously I wasn't welcome."

"No, you wouldn't have been welcome," Simon concurred. "*I* wouldn't have been welcome. She would have thrown me out of there too."

"Really?" Joe asked.

"Yep, when it comes to being a cop, she's very professional."

"I guess that's a good thing," he said doubtfully, "but it's your place. You'd think that she'd give you whatever information you'd want to have."

"She might if I asked," he stated gently. "But the less I have to do with the workings of the investigation, especially when it involves my properties and my employees, definitely the better."

"Oh, I hadn't thought about that," Joe admitted.

"That's … That is very true."

He waited to see if Joe was after anything else. When it appeared Joe was done, Simon told him, "Okay, I have to get back to work now."

"Yep, yep, sorry, boss."

And Joe disconnected, leaving Simon wondering whether Joe was nervous about something or just checking to see if Simon was okay with the cops being there, the answer eluded him. It wouldn't be an issue either way because it's not as if Simon had any say in the matter. Still, it was all good. He sent a text to Kate. **Thanks for checking out the graffiti.**

She sent a thumbs-up back. Of course. What else did he expect? He was lucky that she'd even responded, knowing the number of times that she ignored him throughout any given day. He half laughed at that too because it wasn't necessarily a bad thing that she ignored him sometimes. She got too busy, and that allowed him, when he got too busy, to also not feel bad when he ignored her.

As he got up, his phone buzzed. He looked to see a text message, coming from a number he didn't know. And the message was cryptic.

Two delivered because you can't seem to find the ones that I left as gifts.

He stared at the words in horror, quickly screenshotted it, and sent it to Kate. He added a text message, saying, **This came in.**

She phoned him immediately. "Do you know that number?"

"I don't. I'm sitting at a coffee shop, and I just talked to Joe, my foreman. He told me that you had been there, and I disconnected from him on the phone and got up to leave, when this text came in."

"We're working on the number now," she said. "Pretty sure it'll be a burner phone or something equally impossible to trace. So I can't say it'll give us any joy, but having just been sent, there's a good chance that the sender's phone is still on."

"I hope so." Simon waited, and he heard her talking in the background. "Is that Rodney with you?"

"Yes."

Her response was a bit laid-back, but something in her tone he didn't get. "Is that a problem?"

She groaned. "No, it's not a problem, but it's the boss's idea that Rodney shadow me."

It took Simon a moment and then he said, "To keep it all aboveboard, I presume."

"Yeah, you got it because the sergeant wanted me off the case."

"Ouch," Simon muttered, knowing that she would utterly hate that.

"Yeah, you're right," she replied. "That's about how I feel about it, especially when he knows that I would specifically want to be involved in this."

"But can't compromise the case if it goes to court," he filled in for her.

"Exactly," she agreed.

"If anything else happens, let me know."

"Hang on a minute."

"What?" he asked, about ready to end the call.

"Any idea about the two who were left as gifts that you didn't know about?"

"No, not a clue." He gave a deep sigh. "But believe me. It'll be what dominates my thoughts for the next while."

"Good, any insights you get or anything you think of, you let me know pronto." And, with that, she disconnected.

CHAPTER 9

RODNEY STARED INTENTLY at Kate, as she ended her call, then updated her. "Reese's working on the trace right now. No laundry carts missing. Plus Lilliana is in the office, and she'll work on this too, as everybody needs to find these other two victims," he shared, his voice low. Kate nodded at her partner, while he continued. "And that'll mean spending a lot of time checking out cases that could be the two in question but maybe aren't."

"And yet we have no choice."

"Exactly."

"So …" Kate pondered it.

"Now what?" he asked, looking at her curiously.

"I'm still trying to figure out where could our killer have taken his victims? Somewhere close enough to do this thing and yet not be seen."

"One of the parks," Rodney offered immediately.

"Yeah, which one?" She stared at him. "What's close enough to where both victims live or work to get us an idea of where the killer would be taking them for the torture part of his game?"

At that, Rodney opened up his phone and pulled up the maps. "I've got two here."

As he pointed out their locations on the online map, she shook her head. "That one's not really rough enough, is it?"

She frowned.

"It's hard to say."

"From the evidence so far, you need water, rocks, gravel … to chew up Luca's feet, but Patricia's injuries? I think she was tormented further. Bring up the GPS and get us to the first park. Then, after we've checked out the first, we'll go to the second one."

It took them twenty minutes to get to the first park. As soon as she walked in it, she shook her head. "This isn't the place."

Rodney asked, "Why not?"

"Too many people. I suspect, even at nighttime, too many people would be here." She pointed out the vantage point and open space. "Look at it. The parking lot's full, with people having picnics, people all over the place, and above all else, … it's soft ground."

Rodney frowned, adding, "Maybe, but a lot of places around the park aren't that nice, haven't got that cared-for look." She pondered his remark, as they took a walk farther in the park. However, by the end of their circuit, Rodney came around to agree with her. "Yeah, it doesn't have the right look or feel."

"And yet something is forcing our killer to do this, some motivation," Kate noted. "Like the abused often become the abusers. So the question is, what's this killer's particular motivation, and does the place matter to him or to the victims?" She added, "Also, even here, we have more of a man-made pond, with a nice little walkway around it, very manicured. Just not a place to torture someone."

"Agreed," Rodney said. "I think you're right, as much as I wanted this park to be the one."

Twenty minutes later they pulled up at the second location. Kate immediately pointed out, "Oh, now this appeals." The terrain was already on the rougher edge here.

Her partner snorted. "Should I be worried that you can look at a place from inside the car and say this appeals to a serial killer?"

"Maybe. You really have to get into their heads, if you want to solve the case."

He stared at her, as if she had gone out of her mind. "I have been working in this department for a while, but your mind is somewhat messy."

She winced.

Rodney explained, "I'm not trying to get you to change your technique. I have to remind myself that you do look at this from the serial killer's point of view. I'm not trying to be snarky either," he added. "Yet it is a strange feeling to know that you walked into our department—where we thought that your nose was up in the air, that you were too good for us. And then, when you proved yourself to be too good for us," he noted, with a wry look, "it made all of us look at our game and try to pick it up to your level."

"I never thought I was too good." She shook her head. "I knew that I was new, and any acceptance appeared to be impossible, at least initially. And I get all the reasons why, so I put my head down and got to work."

They exited the car and walked the front section of the park. It had lots of well-maintained green areas, but she could already see edges of woods off to the side that looked a whole lot more promising. She pointed out one direction. "I'll go this way. You go that way."

He nodded, and they quickly split up. She headed toward the water's edge, remembering what Patricia had said in her interview. As Kate neared the water's edge, she saw a bunch of ducks, wildlife, some geese, but no people. She walked a little bit closer to the edge—and because it was a lake and a small one at that—the surface of the water was calm, still.

It had been several days since Patricia's death, so Kate wasn't exactly sure if anything would be left to find. It didn't, however, take very long to see odd tracks—hesitant, as if somebody wasn't sure where they were walking, and behind them a second set of much more solid tracks. Kate noted more of these two sets of footprints, tracks in and tracks back out. She nodded, and then she saw the blood droplets. She followed them down and around, until she came back around, close to the parking lot. And there was Rodney, heading toward her. "Anything?" she asked him.

He shook his head. "No. You?"

"I found a blood trail." She turned to show him where.

He raced behind her to see her find. "This is definitely blood," Rodney noted. As they walked toward the lake, tracing the bloody tracks, he stated, "It starts here after the rocks. The victims bleed pretty freely, and then their torturer gets them into a vehicle and leaves." Rodney nodded. "Fits our theory."

"Sure, but what we really need," Kate said, "is DNA proof that this is Patricia's blood."

"Or Luca's."

She nodded. "Or one of the other two victims, portrayed by the four lines in that graffiti." She hesitated. "Do we take back some samples, or do we bring in forensics?"

"Forensics," he replied instantly. "I do like your instincts."

She laughed. "You say that, and then shit hits the fan."

"I'll be right there in hot water with you," Rodney admitted, with a smile. With that agreed on, they phoned forensics and brought out a team. They waited off to the side, walking through the area.

Only by chance did she stop and look down. "Look at this." More blood but it looked different.

Rodney nodded. "We should check this as well. We do have two more potential victims that we know nothing about."

She nodded and carefully tracked this new blood trail, which droplets were older and half under cover, and again followed their trail back to the parking lot. As they stood here, discussing this find, she got a text message from forensics on the other blood trail.

Come here. We found something.

She showed the text to Rodney, and they raced back to where forensics were.

As she neared Michael, the team lead, she asked, "What did you find?"

He looked at her, his face grim. "Another body."

<hr>

SIMON WORKED THROUGH the rest of the day, disturbed by weird but vague inklings, probably of the psychic nature, but trying to keep a handle on it.

As he walked into his apartment building, his doorman raised his eyebrows and said, "Looks to be another tough day."

"You're not kidding. Some seem to go that way."

He nodded. "Sorry about that, man. Appears as if it is all that way lately."

"Yep, to me too, but what can you do?" He smiled as he headed to his private elevator. He turned to his doorman and added, "If Kate shows up, send her straight up."

The doorman gave him a big grin. "Will do. I do like that woman."

"Me too." Simon chuckled, as he headed up to his penthouse.

After a quick shower Simon opened a beer and crashed on the couch, wondering what the hell was going on in his world. He smiled when he got a phone call from Kate. "I hope your day was better than mine," he greeted her.

"We found a body," she stated, her tone grim. "We think it's connected."

"Shit." He bolted to his feet, snatched the beer off the coffee table, and took a long swig. "Why do you think it's connected?"

She went through what they found at the park, and he stared at his phone in amazement. "You narrowed it down to a park and then found blood?" he asked in wonder.

"Yes, and, of course, that makes me suspicious that maybe we were intended to find it."

He pondered that and nodded. "I guess that makes sense. Still, there is a hell of a lot of ground out there to have even found this much."

"The question is why this park and who is the victim?"

"Does it for sure connect?"

"No, we don't know that definitely," she admitted. "We're still checking on it. What I can tell you is the body was tortured and not a whole lot is left to the feet, but they look more or less flayed, and it's a woman, … a young woman."

CHAPTER 10

IT WAS A little after midnight before Kate dragged her butt home. As she walked up the apartment building steps, she stopped and frowned. She had come to Simon's place, without even realizing it. She swore at that and realized it was way too late to visit him.

As she turned around to leave again, tired and exhausted, wishing that her stupid instincts hadn't been to come here, as if some homing pigeon, the front doors opened, and the doorman stepped outside. She knew him quite well by now but almost immediately had forgotten his name.

He called out, "Madam Kate, he's waiting for you." When she stared at him, he added, "He only got in a little bit ago and told me that, if you came, to send you right up."

She hesitated, then nodded. "I figured it was too late, and I'm so damn tired," she murmured, as she walked past him.

"Tough day?" he asked in a commiserating tone.

She nodded. "Some days are tougher than others."

"That's what Simon said too."

She nodded in agreement, as she headed to Simon's elevator. She hit the button to take her up to Simon's penthouse to find him standing there, waiting for her. He opened his arms. She walked in them and buried her face against his chest. He didn't say anything and scooped her up in his arms and carried her through to the bed.

She immediately hopped off the bed. "I'm gross and dirty and sweaty," she said, wriggling away from him.

"In that case, a shower," he murmured.

She nodded. He walked behind her into the bathroom and quickly turned on the water. By the time he turned around, she stood there, exhausted, weaving on her feet, and completely nude. She stepped under the water and, with half a smile, added, "I am exhausted, but I'm not dead, … if you want join me."

He snorted, "That's an invitation, kind of," he teased, "but I'll take you up on it."

With that, he quickly dropped his sleep pants, while she stood there with a grin on her face, as he joined her. Sex in the shower was not what everybody thought it should be, but options like this right now were damn good. When he had her clean and completely exhausted, she shut off the water, grabbed the nearby towel, tossed him another towel, and then stumbled to the counter, where she brushed her teeth and made her way to bed.

As she crashed on the bed, she murmured, "I wasn't going to drop in, when I realized how late it was, and I'm sorry. I shouldn't have come by."

He placed a finger against her lips and whispered, "You can always come by. I like that you come here automatically, instead of thinking about it."

"Maybe you do," she murmured. "Not sure it's the best thing though." And, with that, she closed her eyes and slept.

When she woke several hours later, Simon had shifted in bed, standing up and then lying down, standing up and then lying down. His actions quickly cleared the confusion in her head, as she watched him warily. When he sat back down again the next time, she placed a firm hand on his shoulder and said, "Time to sleep, Simon."

He immediately crashed his head on the pillow and went into a deep sleep. She kept a wary eye on him for a little bit longer, but he didn't appear to be planning on doing any more calisthenics, so she crashed beside him.

The next thing she could put her finger on was the smell of coffee, as she woke to see a fresh cup sitting on the night table beside her. She sniffed the coffee and rolled over, instinctively reaching for it.

"You could open your eyes first," Simon suggested.

She opened her eyes to see him standing there, a smile on his face, watching her. "I could," she agreed, her voice throaty and raspy. "Doesn't mean I want to."

He immediately frowned. "Are you getting sick?"

She shook her head. "No, I was out at the park late last night," she murmured.

He nodded. "You didn't fill me in on it."

"No, not sure even now that I should," she noted. "Just be warned that we have some more developments, and we'll need you in the station to ask more questions."

"Will the questions bother me?" he asked.

She eyed him and then shrugged. "I don't know why they would," she replied, a note of challenge in her voice. "They are definitely necessary for us to fill in the blanks on our end."

He nodded. "We'd better make it official and not question it over breakfast, right?"

She nodded. "Considering Rodney has to shadow me every step, yes. It would be better if we wait."

"Fine," he muttered ruefully. He checked his schedule, as she sipped coffee. "How about we start there then?"

"That works," she said agreeably. "I'll still need a bit to get my head on straight," she muttered, as she glanced at her watch. Seeing it was almost 8:00 a.m., she bolted out of bed. "Good God."

He smiled. "I know. As far as you're concerned, that's late, but, if you don't mind, … I'll drive you down there."

"I have my car here," she murmured, and then threw back her coffee and groaned. "I need to get going."

With that, she dressed in the same clothes from yesterday, and he reminded her, "You need to bring more clothes by."

"I guess." She shrugged and then looked down at her sweaty, dirty T-shirt from yesterday. "Do I have anything here?" He walked over to open a closet full of T-shirts. She frowned. "Where'd these come from?"

"I picked them up on sale. I figured that there would be enough times that you didn't have clothes here, so … seemed to be a good idea at the time."

She quickly picked one up and noted that it was her size and threw it on over her head, while giving him an odd look.

He frowned. "It's against some rule of yours, right?"

"I'm not used to people buying stuff for me—definitely not clothing."

"Got it," he replied, with an understanding look. "I also didn't want you to go to work exhausted and still in blood-soaked clothing."

She winced as she looked down at her clothes from yesterday on the floor. "Right, still the jeans have their share of blood too." At that, he walked to the second closet and opened it up, and she stared at him. "Seriously?"

He shrugged. "It's nothing to me, but it makes a huge difference to you. You prefer looking clean and all business."

Groaning, she considered wearing her old bloodied jeans or new jeans and promptly stepped out of the old ones. He picked them up immediately, tossed them into the hamper, along with the dirty T-shirt. "We'll have them cleaned, before you get back."

She didn't say anything, being low on time, plus not too sure how to feel about his new clothing purchases for her. Still, she managed a brisk *Thank you* and then raced away, leaving him with a smile on his face.

She made it about four feet down the hallway toward the kitchen and the elevator, and then groaned and turned back. "I do mean that." She returned to him and gave him a deep tongue-lashing kiss, before stepping into the elevator and dropping down to the reception level. There she raced out and headed to work.

To even think of being late would be quite acceptable for many people, considering how late she was out last night. However, knowing that she needed to get reports in and to get Simon in for questioning and hadn't even told him anything, that was ... a *pleasure* she wasn't looking forward to.

As she walked in, Rodney hugged a cup of coffee, looking like death warmed over.

She winced. "Do I look as bad as you?"

He glared at her and asked, "No, how come?"

She shrugged. "I got a good night's sleep."

"Yeah, how's that even possible?" he muttered.

She smiled. "I went to Simon's."

"Ah, in that case you probably got a hot shower, food, and ..." He stared at her suspiciously. "And it kind of looks as if you keep clothes at his place too. Not what I expected."

She didn't say anything because she didn't want him to

know that Simon had supplied the clothing, so she shrugged. "Seemed to be the thing to do, don't you think? The number of times we don't even get a decent night's sleep …"

"I know," he muttered. "I managed clean clothes, but I didn't get any breakfast." She stared at him. He gave her an evil grin. "Gather you didn't either."

"No, I didn't." At that, her stomach started to whine. "I got coffee in bed, if that counts." Rodney rolled his eyes at her. "So," she added, "we'll pick up something later."

"I'm not sure about later," he muttered. "I'm pretty dead."

"Well, if you want, go grab something for both of us. Simon's coming in for questioning soon."

"Is he?"

"We need to know if this newest dead body is related to him. We need to figure out his association with this new victim."

"We don't have an ID though," he pointed out.

"No, but is there any connection with Simon to the park? Also he got a text message. I think I forgot to mention that too." He glared at her, and she nodded. "Which is also why I'm bringing him in for questioning, instead of even mentioning anything to him. So, yeah, I know that I'm walking a fine line here, but it's also not the easiest pathway to walk."

"I'll give you that," Rodney noted. "I'll go downstairs and grab some bagels." And, with that, he got up and disappeared.

He hadn't been gone two minutes when Audrey contacted her. "Simon's out front."

"Right, thanks." Kate headed out to the lobby and greeted him.

He smiled and handed her a bag. "You didn't get breakfast."

She winced and looked down at it ruefully. "You're right. I didn't. Can't say I was thinking about breakfast myself."

"Of course not. You were way too eager to come in and question me," he said gently, yet with an eye roll.

She sighed. "It's that whole *fine line* thing again."

"It absolutely is, and that's why I'm here," Simon replied. "I don't mind. Let's solve this problem, and we can all get back to our normal lives, preferably without anybody else dying in my vicinity," he muttered.

She led him into an interview room.

"That's still warm." He motioned to the bag that he had brought. "Breakfast burritos."

She nodded. "Thank you. I'm sure Rodney will be absolutely thrilled to hear about my breakfast."

"Why?" he asked, looking at her in confusion.

"He went down to get bagels," she replied, with a half smile.

"Well, if it's any consolation, two burritos are in there, so you could share."

She bit back a chuckle. "I could."

He laughed. "Let me put it this way. They are for both of you."

"Ah, there's the trick."

At that, Rodney opened the door, took one look, and said, "He was earlier than I thought." A note of resignation filled his voice.

She nodded. "But he came bearing gifts." She pointed to the bag.

Rodney frowned and asked, "Is that food?"

"Breakfast burritos apparently," Kate told him.

"Well, hot damn. That works. No way I could get us bagels this morning. The lineup down there is way too long."

"Then I guess we're doing good here."

He smiled at Simon, "Thanks, man."

"You're welcome. Better eat them up though, before we start interviewing, in case it looks like a bribe."

They both rolled their eyes, dug into the bag, and quickly scarfed down the burritos. She smiled as hers went down. "That was really good, thank you." She turned to Rodney and asked, "You ready for this?"

"No," he muttered shortly, "but it's what we have to do." He told Simon, "Sorry, bud."

Simon shrugged. "It is what it is. Let's deal with it."

And, with that, Rodney turned on the recorder and started the questioning. The interview was now in progress.

SIMON WAS ALWAYS fascinated when everybody reverted to professional mode versus informal. It confused him to see how easily Kate slipped from one attitude to the other, without any reservation. She did it subconsciously sometimes. However, when she did it deliberately, there was almost this switch of a light in her facial expression, and she went completely pro on him. He could sense that, if it were anybody but him right now, they would probably be completely intimidated. Yet he was just comfortable enough that, although the switch was enough to make him sit back and study her intently, he knew that it was still her and that this wasn't a setup.

He could imagine what she was like in someone else's interview though. She must be an absolute demon. And maybe that's why she did so well in her chosen field because everybody was petrified of her. As soon as the interview started, the questions sent him reeling.

"Do you have any connection to Clement Park?"

He stared at Kate. "I'm not even sure what park that is," he noted in confusion. "Where is it?" She gave him the location, and he contemplated it. "I'm not sure I've ever been there. Maybe a while ago, I am not sure."

"When you say a while ago? Ten years plus? Longer?"

"It's possible I was there when I was much young—" And then he stopped.

Her eyebrow raised, she studied him. "So that sounds like something."

"I don't know if it's something," he replied gently, "but the park was named after Mary Clement."

She stared at him in surprise. "Who is … was Mary Clement?"

"She was a victim of domestic violence, who sent me in the direction of helping other victims," he stated.

"Did you know her?"

He gazed off in the distance. "I can't say I knew her. For that matter, she's dead." He turned to look at Kate. "I knew her daughter."

"Interesting," Kate murmured. "In what capacity?" He gave her a crooked smile, and she nodded. "You were lovers."

"We were for a short time. But Elizabeth Clement was a mess, after seeing what her father did to her mother. I was there in her life for a few weeks maybe, maybe not even that long, as her mother died from her most recent injuries inflicted by her father. Elizabeth had been looking for a fresh start. I ended up giving her enough money to go to an aunt's down south," he noted.

"Have you had any contact with her since?"

"No, I haven't." He frowned, a thought crossing his face. "I got a text to say she had arrived safely and to thank me, and that was about it. … I hadn't heard that name in a very long time." He asked Kate, "Do you think the choice of park is on purpose?"

She nodded. "I think, in this murder case, everything was done on purpose, yes. It's not something that we can rule out, and now that you have a connection to people the park was named after, I would say it's deliberate."

He nodded, thinking back to all the times and to all the people who he might have helped, as well as other philanthropists. "A lot of people in my world, or a lot of people in the fringe of my world, I've helped money-wise, supporting quite a few battered spouses." He hesitated and then relented because Kate would know one way or another. "At least hundreds, or could be one thousand domestic abuse survivors by now."

Rodney winced. "*Great*. Was there somebody you wanted to help or didn't help that maybe our killer's got this vendetta against you?"

"Or," Kate studied Simon intently, "somebody you helped get away from their abuser, and that somebody might be pretty pissed off that you helped them."

He stared at her. "Now you're talking about violent husbands."

"Potentially, yes." She shrugged. "Did this daughter, Mary's daughter, have anybody she was trying to get away from?"

"Her father," he stated immediately. "He did go to jail, but I do not know if he is still in jail. He lost his wife—due to his own actions—but he lost his daughter because I helped her," Simon declared. "Ultimately it was his own actions as well because she didn't want anything to do with him after her mother died."

Kate wrote down a few notes as he continued his story.

"The father's name was … I think it was Chester, Chaz, … Chet? Something like that. The last name was Clement of course, so you can find out where he's at right now."

Rodney immediately sent off a text. "Any other family or just the daughter?" he asked.

"Oh, good question." Simon frowned, deep in thought. "I seem to remember there might have been a younger brother." He winced. "God, I would hate to think the younger brother was heading in this domestic violence pathway because he lost his family too."

"And yet often victims perpetrate their father's crimes too," Rodney noted in sorrow. "So it's a possibility that we'll look into. I don't suppose you know any more about the family?"

"No, I don't, and honestly I don't even know where Elizabeth might be now. She first wanted a plane ticket to Chicago, then to go on from there."

"Was that to deliberately keep you out of it?"

"I think so," he replied. "As much as she wanted to trust me, I don't think she trusted any man."

"Also understandable," Rodney agreed. "So we will track her down and see if she has been contacted in any way."

"Christ, I hope she's not one of the victims," Simon noted suddenly. Kate grimaced, while he shrugged. "If this is connected to the Clement family, and Clement Park is literally honoring their name, then it makes sense that the family itself could be in danger." He shook his head. "But that doesn't make any sense, not when considering no *game's* involved."

"We are also possibly missing other victims," Kate shared. "That's a working theory." And then she took a deep breath and added, "We don't have an ID on our Clement Park victim yet."

He nodded, numb, as he realized that this wouldn't be over anytime soon. It was horrible to consider it could have been Elizabeth.

"And we have to also consider," Rodney reminded Simon, "that it has nothing to do with you."

"I sure hope it has nothing to do with me because, damn, I really didn't think that I had done anything that would trigger all this."

"And yet we also know that you don't have to do very much to provoke others," she mentioned. "For people who have a vendetta against you, it doesn't take much to prod them into doing something about it. Your lavish existence is one thing to put you on the spot all on its own."

"Meaning that I'm easy to hate," he stated, a note of amusement in his voice.

She laughed. "Anybody who helps somebody to get away from their abusers, we have to look at. Are there other people you helped?"

"Hundreds for sure," he said. "I donate a portion of whatever poker money I win. I haven't even gone out and played poker lately. I've been a little preoccupied," he added, with an eye roll.

Rodney grinned.

"Sorry to cramp your style," Kate replied immediately.

"No, you're not." Simon smirked. "You probably don't even like poker."

"Well, it depends. If you're sending the money to a women's shelter, then I am all for it," she declared.

"Oh, good, look at that," Simon shared with Rodney, who was busy grinning at the two of them. "Sounds as if I have a license to gamble away my life, if it's for a good cause."

"I presume you know how to stop when you're in trouble," Kate suggested to Simon.

"I'm very good at what I do." He sent a smile in her direction. And then he tapped his head. "Some of it's instincts, some luck, and some? Sometimes I don't even know what I am doing, but I seem to win."

"And that," Rodney interrupted, "brings me to something that I want to bring up." He looked over at Simon.

But Simon interrupted him and said, "No connections, no inkling, no insights. Believe me. It's been on my mind."

"And yet," Kate said, standing, and then nodded at the recorder.

She was leaving the room, and the interview was being terminated—to be continued when she came back.

With the recorder off, she looked over at Simon. "Last night, during the night, you kept getting up, standing, walking to the door, turning around, coming back to bed, lying down, sitting up, and then you'd repeat it. About the fifth time, I convinced you to lie back down again and go to sleep."

He stared at her in shock. "What?"

She nodded. "I didn't mention your vision this morning because honestly I didn't have a chance. I ran out of the apartment because I suck at getting to work early apparently."

"You did work all night," Rodney pointed out, as he

looked over at Simon and asked, "Do psychic things like that happen to you when you sleep?"

He nodded. "Unfortunately, yes, and sometimes way too often. I don't always know what they mean," he admitted, pondering it. He looked back at Kate. "Any idea how many times?"

"Five, six, maybe seven," she replied. "Somewhere around that point in time, I figured you needed to sleep, so I convinced you to go back to sleep again. And honestly that's all I did," she pointed out, "was put a hand on your shoulder, told you in a firm voice that it was bedtime, and sent you back to bed."

He nodded. "The other night, I caught myself getting up and wandering around the bedroom."

"So, out of curiosity, did you ever do these kinds of things as games?" Rodney asked. "Did you have anybody else you worked with, lived with, or someone who knew about it?"

"My grandmother was a psychic. But nobody about *games*. She would say that games of this level would be very dangerous." He gave Kate a wry look. "And I can't say that I always took it seriously."

"So the question is," Kate began, "was anybody else gift-ed like you back then? Someone who treated this like a game?"

"Christ," he muttered, as he stared at her. "You're … going back a very long time."

"Anything that would connect to this Clement woman?"

He shook his head immediately. "I don't think so. Again I don't know." He pondered that.

"Something to consider though."

He frowned at them both. "We need an ID on that body

in the park."

"We're working on it," Kate acknowledged. "And it sounds bad, but I'm hoping it's one of our two missing victims that seem predicted in the graffiti at your Main Street rehab."

He didn't say anything, then sighed. "I hope it is too." He hesitated but then asked, "And the text, anything on that?"

She looked over at Rodney, and he shook his head. "Not yet. Burner phone, probably been disposed of. We'll be lucky if we ever find it."

Simon nodded. "It's definitely targeted at me though," he muttered. "I wish to God I could figure out why."

"You and me both," Kate agreed, with half a smile. "But we will get to the bottom of it. I'll let you know if we come up with anything else."

With that, he stood. "So I can go about my day now?"

She nodded. "We're assuming that this is all targeted because of you, but what we can't lose sight of is that it could be targeted *at* you."

It took him a moment to understand what she'd meant, and then he gave her a pained look. "I would much rather he came after me, than torturing innocent victims. Patricia didn't deserve any of that, and neither did Luca, for all his faults."

At that, Rodney pounced. "Did you know her? Patricia?"

Simon shook his head. "No, but I do believe she may have gone through one of the shelters that I helped."

"Ah, that would explain it." Kate turned to Rodney. "We were trying to figure out whether you had known her or not."

Simon gave her a look. "Meaning, whether I was ever a

client?" he asked in a dry tone.

"I would ask that," she explained, "because it's my job, but I wouldn't have expected a yes answer."

"And you wouldn't have gotten a yes answer," he said drily.

"So somebody could know that you're helping these victims," Rodney noted. "And it's a victim that the killer probably didn't want helped."

"Or that he thought he could help better," Kate corrected, looking at Simon. "And he didn't appreciate that Simon was supporting whatever was keeping this person away from him."

"Still doesn't explain the *game* part of his message though," Simon added, his voice a bit tamed and in a monotone. "I don't know if that's his own twist on this or whether something completely different. I just don't know."

"Were there ever any rescues that you were involved in?" Rodney asked.

Simon nodded. "Yeah, a couple. I tend to not think of them as rescues but, of course, that's what they were."

"What do you mean by that?" Kate asked, looking over at Rodney.

"Sometimes when it's an ugly domestic scenario," Rodney explained, "they'll mount a rescue to get a woman out of a tough spot, and she disappears into the network." He turned to face Simon.

Simon nodded. "And, yeah, I guess I have been involved in a bunch of those, ... but not recently. I would say, probably eight years, ten years ago maybe. It's been a long time because I separated myself, as it can get really ugly sometimes."

"Can you tell me what a standard rescue would look

like?" Kate asked.

"There is no standard rescue," Simon noted, with a wry look. "We get a heads-up that somebody has been abused, heading to a restaurant with the husband or to be at a specific location. Then it's a matter of causing a distraction so that the woman can get away without being dragged into a big confrontation. We supply the vehicle and a driver, and then we take her to a safe house." Simon shrugged. "We've only ever had one of those cases go bad, and I think the only one where the woman was persuaded by the husband to go back. *He was going to change his ways*," Simon mimicked, with an eye roll.

"Any idea what happened to either of them?"

Simon sighed. "She got injured, and her husband ended up shooting her. When the cops arrived, … he turned the gun on himself."

Kate frowned at Rodney, and he shrugged.

Simon continued. "We don't handle most of those. They're quite usually reported as domestic violence cases, where the local cops respond," Simon explained. "However, we do know of several cases, where these other kinds of rescues have happened. It's all aboveboard."

"What do the husbands usually do?" Kate asked Simon.

"Sometimes they're pissed right off. Sometimes they call out *Good riddance*. Sometimes they are panicked, until they realize that she's not coming back. Usually he receives some notification that they are alive but are done with the abuse, and, if he continues to harass them, then it will become a criminal matter," Simon added. "Every case is different, but, if we don't help these women escape, when they are too scared to do so by themselves, who will? It usually requires a much stronger man than their abuser to help these women,"

Simon noted.

"Oh, I'm definitely not against accepting your help," Kate replied. "Obviously we don't want you going outside of the law. However, if you're rescuing women in vulnerable positions, then I won't say anything about it."

Rodney smiled and nodded. "I've been involved officially in a couple of those, and, in most cases, it turns out that the woman couldn't get away by herself. Often they just need help for that initial step." Rodney gave a wave of his hand. "Sometimes the women can turn pretty violent themselves. So it's not just women who need rescues."

Kate nodded. "And yet the couple of battered men we met in one of our previous cases, obviously they didn't know about having help."

"It's much harder for men to report the abuse and to accept any help," Simon noted in a quiet tone. "There's a huge stigma that they should handle this themselves, and they don't generally go looking for help."

Rodney agreed. "What are the chances of a list of every rescue you've been involved in?"

Simon winced. "I didn't even know the names half the time," he shared. "In a rescue, you want to get them out of there, out of the situation. We're not worried about crossing the *T*s and dotting the *I*s. I could ask the shelter that I donate a lot of money to," he suggested, "if they know of any particular scenarios. I am sure they can help you out."

Kate nodded. "We don't even know for sure that Patricia is related to one of these shelters—or this latest woman in the park—but, if either are related, it's one more puzzle piece that will help lock this down."

"No," he disagreed, looking at her. "You're hoping it is. This guy's gone to a lot of trouble, and he has done it so thoroughly. He's picked a park, named after somebody who was a victim of abuse. He's picked somebody who had saved herself from a very tough lifestyle. The killer picked … somebody who *works for me*."

"But also a weak person," she pointed out. "So maybe, in the killer's eyes, Luca was weak. Maybe the killer can't handle someone big, someone burly, right?"

"It's possible," Rodney agreed, with a shrug, "but then drugs would do that."

"Right." Kate nodded because that was a given. "Did they use drugs to subdue Patricia in her case?"

"I'm not sure about it, but we can check with Smidge." Then Rodney added, "According to her pimp though, she was begging that he give her some, just before her murder."

"Right," Kate murmured. "The tox screens won't be back on our latest victim anyway."

"No."

As Simon turned to leave, she called out, "Thanks for breakfast."

"Anytime, sweetheart." And, with that, he was gone.

CHAPTER 11

K ATE WAS STILL living down the *sweetheart* moniker, as she walked back to her desk, Rodney teasing her mercilessly. "On the other hand, he brought breakfast," she pointed out, "and you were the beneficiary of that, so you better be nice."

"That's true, *sweetheart*."

She rolled her eyes. "Oh, that'll get old very quickly."

As soon as she sat down, her phone rang. It was Smidge. "Hey, Dr. Smidge. What's up?"

"I have an ID on your last victim."

"Wow, that was fast. The one at Clement Park?"

"Yeah." His voice was hard, gruff. "I knew the victim, and, as soon as she arrived, I was sure of who it was."

"You have a name for me?" she asked.

"Elizabeth Clement. … You need to come down and see me." And, with that, he hung up.

She turned in shock to Rodney. "It is the daughter."

Rodney winced. "Simon won't like that."

"No, but it sure brings in an angle that we didn't have before," Kate said. "I don't know how long that woman had been buried there, which, considering the shape of the body, it's hard to say."

"But it wasn't years," Rodney pointed out. "Besides, Smidge can give us a timeline."

"So she probably came back, after ten years or so of hiding, maybe saying goodbye to her mom or something," Kate suggested, as she got up. "Smidge wants to see me."

"I'm coming." Rodney stood. "How the hell did he get to that body so fast?"

"He said he knew her and so potentially knew something that would help identify her." And it didn't take them long to get the answers.

Smidge looked up when they walked in and nodded. "I knew her mother," he stated, "and she had a very defined jaw. When I saw the skull, I have to admit that it was the first thing that came to mind. … We have Mary's DNA on file, so it wasn't hard to check. I just had to pull some favors to get the results. Anyway, believe me. I'm not terribly happy to find out that I was correct."

"No, of course not." She hesitated. "Cause of death?"

He glared at her. "Same as the others."

"Ah, shit." Kate groaned. "So a woman who's gone through hell as a child, escapes her tormenter, ends up tortured and she is murdered to boot."

Smidge nodded. "Yeah. Her feet were really badly lacerated. They've bled a lot, and she's been stabbed several times." The coroner shook his head. "We're doing a tox screen to see if she was aware at all during this time. Also, I found strangulation marks on her neck, but … I suspect that he used that to knock her out and then to bring her back around again."

Kate paled at the idea but nodded. "Not an uncommon scenario either."

"Correct," Smidge acknowledged, "but it shows a level of hate that I wouldn't want to think of in this case."

"No, of course not. Elizabeth already went through hell

growing up with an abusive father."

"Did you find the father?" Smidge asked, turning to her.

"Still in jail. He killed a fellow inmate," Rodney supplied. "He's not getting out anytime soon."

"Good, I hope he dies in there," Smidge stated. "He did a helluva number on Mary."

Kate heard the sadness in Smidge's tone as he spoke. "What do you know about the family?" she asked gently.

"I knew them fairly well, as we were somewhat neighbors at the time. He was an asshole, but we had no idea Mary was being hurt like that. Elizabeth's brother used to laugh and joke about bullying and physical abuse, and we didn't really think anything of it, as he was a kid back then too, so ..."

"I never hear very much mentioned about the brother," Kate stated cautiously.

Smidge nodded. "Not sure if he's even alive. He was heading down a pretty rough pathway too."

"In what way?"

"Drugs, alcohol, stealing, pretty sure he has a record," Smidge suggested. "Wouldn't be at all surprised if he wasn't in jail with his dad."

"Did he get along with his dad?"

"I don't know that anybody got along with *Dad*," Dr. Smidge replied. "Dad was an asshole. We didn't get along with him, I can tell you that. If his son did, it was only out of self-preservation."

"Or because they're two of a kind," she pointed out.

"Or because they're two of the same kind, yes," he agreed. "Also doesn't bear thinking about to consider that Elizabeth might have been murdered by a family member."

"Do you know anything else about the case?" Kate prodded.

Smidge shook his head. "No, can't say I do. We were only their neighbors for a while, before I ended up moving, So I don't even have much on the latest details."

"Right." Kate gave a quick nod. "Okay, we'll deal with what we've got for the moment and carry on."

At that, she started to walk out, when Smidge called her back. "We might not have known her mother all that well, but ever since Mary died, there always remained that element of guilt that *What if we did see, what if we could have done something?*" He frowned. "Now that I see what happened to the daughter, also dead and murdered, and the guilt … intensifies."

"Of course," Kate acknowledged. "We didn't even know about her death, and that is particularly distressing."

Smidge nodded. "That's right."

"Can you give me a time of death?"

He shook his head. "Honestly I'll go with approximately three weeks ago, but I can't be any closer. There was a lot of bug activity and has been a lot of rain," he said in exasperation. "I'm sorry. That's as close as I've got."

"That's fine," Kate noted gently, and, with that, she walked out.

Outside, Rodney at her side, she asked him, "What do you think? Is that the first killing for our guy?"

"It would make sense," Rodney replied. "And considering that the other two have happened rather quickly, he probably got impatient with nobody finding Elizabeth and decided to up the ante. Which would be part of the *game* he keeps mentioning over and over."

She nodded. "I still don't understand this game thing though."

"You might not, but, for whatever reason, it's how he's

trying to play this."

"And that seems to be more about whatever the word *game* means to him," she mentioned, looking at her partner. "I feel as if it's right there, right inside my head, but I can't figure it out."

"And that's okay," Rodney replied. "I admire that brain of yours, so give it a chance, and it'll come up with it again."

⚬⚬⚬

SIMON ANSWERED KATE'S phone call, still half distracted from the calculations on his mind.

"Elizabeth Clement," she stated immediately.

He frowned. "What about her?"

She hesitated, then replied, "That's the body we found in Clement Park."

"Ah, hell," he murmured, as he sat back and pinched his brow. "That can't be right."

"Just what everybody was attempting to stop. Her father is, however, still in jail, having killed an inmate, so he's not getting out anytime soon."

"Well, that's one bit of good news," he noted in frustration. "I had no idea she was even in town."

"And according to the forensics, she's been dead at least three weeks."

He mentally cast back three weeks, but they were already dealing with other ugly murder cases at that point in time too. "She didn't contact me. I know that for sure," he declared.

"Would she have? Is there any reason for her to call you?" she asked curiously.

"I'm part of her ugly past. I would have imagined that she moved on and didn't want anything to do with me or any reminder of that part of her life that she left behind."

"And this was what, ten years ago?"

He hesitated. "Could be as long as twelve. I don't remember. Going by the father's conviction, he hadn't gone to trial at that point in time, so I don't know how long it was," Simon admitted, his mind reeling.

"I'm sorry," Kate murmured, as is if catching the weight of his mood.

"Yeah, me too," he admitted. "You help people, hoping that it'll make a difference. Still you wonder if you can do anything that lasts or if this is just fate coming around to bite them in the ass, saying, *Hey, you were supposed to be a victim a long time ago.*"

Kate sighed. "There's a movie about that, people cheating death. If that's true, we're all so screwed."

He didn't even know what to say to that because she was right. It would mean that you could never change your fate. "I won't believe it's true," he finally said. "I can't. Otherwise I can't help anybody because the thought process is that they'll just die anyway. That's no comfort."

"Exactly. And yet unfortunately …"

He winced because her hesitation meant that he would not like what she had to say. "Go on."

"It looks as if she was killed by the same perpetrator who got Patricia and Luca."

"Fuck," he uttered in a low voice.

"Her feet were cut to ribbons, and she was stabbed. Then he didn't even bury her, just made a small attempt to cover her up with leaves. I don't know why she wasn't found earlier. Probably the killer was bothered by that too. So the perpetrator decided it was taking too long, and that's why he went after Patricia. And then delivered the text to you because obviously you weren't getting the message."

"What message?" he cried out, stunned. "Where in any of this was there a message that I was supposed to understand?"

"I'm not sure anything was in here," she replied. "You aren't to blame. Remember that."

"And yet I feel as if I am," he shared. "I'm not even getting any visions."

"So maybe …" She hesitated. "I know you can't direct it. I get that, but maybe instead look at who you may have rescued and who is pissed off that you might have rescued them."

"We already discussed that in the interview," he noted.

"Yes, but I'm wondering if we could direct your psyche to consider that."

"I don't know. I don't think my psyche considers anything at this point in time," he muttered.

"I'm sorry," she whispered. "Obviously I wish I had better news."

"It's not your fault," he said, with a groan. "Not much I can do though to find this asshole, and that leaves nobody with really any decent answers."

She added, "Which is pissing me off too."

He smiled at that because pissed-off Kate was Kate with determination and motivation. "As long as you stay pissed off, we will all be together in a whole better place."

She snorted at that. "If you're trying to say that me pissed off gets better results, you could be right. I still need something to go on."

His smile fell away. "Look. Let me see if I can attempt to do something with this *gift*. It doesn't really work that way, but, at the same time, it kind of works."

"I know," she agreed. "I remember the little boy. The one you helped save soon after we met."

His breath gusted out at that. "But we don't have any live victims, right?"

"I do not know that," she admitted. "For all I know, he's got one captive right now."

"Ah, hell, not what I even want to think about."

"Honestly he's three for three in this. If this is a game, we are beyond losing. We're getting creamed."

And that's how she ended the call, leaving him staring at his phone.

CHAPTER 12

BACK IN THE office, Kate slumped in her chair, brought up her typed notes, and quickly updated them manually.

Lilliana walked over, dropped a hip down on the corner of Kate's desk, and asked, with a clipped nod, "How's the battle going?"

Kate shook her head. "Definitely still a battle," she muttered. "We have a new victim, possibly ground zero, but we don't know that for sure. If the killer already had two other victims who weren't found yet, then it makes sense that this could be victim number one." Kate explained about the body found in Clement Park and how another one possibly could still be out there.

Lilliana pondered that. "Definitely possible, isn't it?" she muttered. "Obviously though, the killer thought, for some reason, that particular park location would be something that Simon would pick up on."

"That's one of the odd things about it," Kate confirmed, looking up at her teammate. "I did talk to Simon, and he knew about the park. He had even donated some money for the park too. Although I'm not exactly sure whether that has any bearing on this. I don't know if he put up a bench or something as a memorial to the mom, but the daughter's body wasn't found anywhere close to a bench."

"That would be an interesting thing to find out," Lilliana noted, looking at Kate. "Simon really does spend a lot of money on stuff like that, doesn't he?"

She shrugged. "I honestly don't know what he spends money on. I haven't asked. I've been trying to keep that out of our relationship."

Lilliana laughed. "Good luck with that," she noted, with a wry tone. "Money is and will always be part of everybody's relationship."

"It is a big deal. I get that," Kate admitted, "but the longer I can keep it from being part of our relationship, the better. I'm still quite uncomfortable with the relationship as it is. The fact that he has mega money compared to me is not an easy thing to adjust to."

"But he's not billionaire status," Lilliana pointed out. "He's just … I don't know what he is," she said, with a self-deprecating laugh. "For all I know, he *is* billionaire status."

Kate immediately shook her head. "I don't think so," she murmured. "He doesn't act it."

Lilliana twisted her lips. "Do you even know what that would look like?"

"No, of course not," Kate replied, with half a smile. "So you're right. It was a stupid answer."

Lilliana cackled. "No such thing as a stupid answer. It's one that came from your heart and shows that's not where your thinking goes, and that's a good thing. I think Simon's had enough gold diggers in his life."

"That's the truth," Kate murmured. "Anyway, in terms of this case, I'm not sure exactly how to find another victim. If the body hasn't shown up yet, it's not as if I can turn around and wave a magic wand and have it appear out of the blue."

"Wouldn't that be nice," Lilliana muttered. "Although *out of the blue* you just found one. Otherwise we're all stuck waiting for things to show up, unless you have a way of jogging Simon's memory for other locations that he might have had something to do with."

"And yet, if this park has to do with this Mary Clement—which would make sense, considering her daughter is now in the morgue downstairs," Kate said, with a wince, "we should be centering around everything else to do with that family."

"Which you already have to a certain extent or have you not?"

"Sure, but it feels as if more is out there to find."

"Well, there you have it," Lilliana declared, as she stood up. "Knock yourself out."

Kate watched her teammate saunter back to her desk, wondering at the ease with which Lilliana compartmentalized these cases. Maybe it was just her length of experience. She'd been on this team, Kate thought, at least twelve years, or maybe even a little bit longer than that. Kate couldn't imagine getting to the point where crime seemed to make sense, or maybe it never made sense, and you just came to terms with it somehow. She half smiled as she sent Simon a quick text, asking if he was heavily involved in any of the parks around the same area. Rather than answering her, she wasn't at all surprised when her phone rang.

When she answered, he said, a note of humor in his voice, "Are you seriously thinking that every park I might have had something to do with could be involved?"

"This one, in a way, makes sense," she noted, "because, of course, it centers around the Clement family," she murmured. "And we must focus on the Clement family, as far as this case goes," she added, "but I don't want to be so blind as to not double-check that another case may be similar, may be related, or, in any other way, may be connected. So we can't lose sight of that as well."

He pondered that. "It's clever that you would even come to that, but I have to give it some thought. I'm not sure I would have come up with Clement Park in the first place. Uncovering that lead goes to you."

"Which has definitely been a bit of a challenge," Kate noted, "because, if you didn't think of it, how is it that the killer knows to think of it?"

Silence. "And that's another good point," Simon admitted briskly. "And I'm not sure that I want in any way to contemplate what that means."

She understood how he felt, but it wouldn't help her case if Simon didn't spend some quiet time thinking about just that. "For the sake of the people who have already passed due to this asshole, and any others he may be planning on sending to the afterlife in a short time frame," Kate began, "or anybody who he's got captive right now, perhaps you could spend a few minutes and see if you can come up with anything."

She heard the note of humor in his voice when he replied, "So hang on a minute, Detective. Are you asking me to actively use my *gift* to help you?"

"I'm not asking you," she corrected, "and certainly not about any *gifts*, but whatever tools you have in your toolbox," she stated, "I would expect you to use to the best of your ability." And with that, she said, "And I have to go." And she quickly disconnected.

She heard Lilliana laughing in the background.

"That's an interesting way to handle it," Lilliana muttered.

As Rodney walked in, she remembered what Smidge had mentioned. She turned to the rest of the team and said, "By the way …"

Immediately heads came up, and the team focused on her. She explained what Smidge had shared about his association with the Clement family and all the drama that came with it. "Smidge doesn't know what happened to Elizabeth's bad-seed brother. So any help you can give on that matter is appreciated."

Owen spoke up. "I can give you an hour. I'll see what I can dredge up."

Kate nodded. "Thanks, Owen. Also, Smidge feels particularly affected by Elizabeth's death, and the message is that we need to solve it as soon as we can," she stated, a wry note in her voice.

At that Rodney asked her, "Does he really think we're doing nothing?"

"I don't believe that. I think he's afraid that we might let things slide, especially with other cases coming in," she suggested. "Obviously we won't, but, from his perspective, he deals with the aftermath, and we're supposed to deal with stopping it from coming as far as him."

"Wouldn't it be nice to think that that was actually an option," Rodney muttered, looking over at her with a headshake. "Obviously we're doing everything we can, and, if he had anything to offer, it would certainly help. But that suggestion, *Hey, you need to solve this*, isn't helpful."

She agreed, but no point in arguing with Smidge because he was in a class all by himself. Nobody wanted to cross him. Everybody wanted him on their side. Sometimes it worked, and sometimes it didn't. She was, so far, blessed to have a decent relationship with him, and she didn't want to do anything to jeopardize that, and yet nobody wanted this killer more than her particularly, insofar as other people might be concerned that it could affect her ability to do the job, but this case was also connected to Simon, and she wanted him out of her investigation as much as possible.

Also not an easy fix.

With everybody now filled in, she headed back to her research database, and then Reese, their wizard analyst, popped up. "I might have a few other cases that you should look at."

Kate stared at her. "Connected?"

With a frown, Reese walked closer and passed out copies of the same materials to everybody on the team. "Now I'm not sure that these are 100 percent connected, and I need to do another deep dive into this," she noted, "but there are enough similarities that I would suggest it's possibly worth a second look."

"Absolutely it's worth a second look," Kate agreed, already skimming the copy in her hands. "What we don't know is if the killer's modus operandi would have changed over time, as this killer developed a system or if he found something that worked right off the bat and never changed it."

"I would say he found something that worked right off the bat, and nothing changed it," Reese suggested, as she tapped the papers in her hand. "Give those a read. I'll keep working on what else I can come up with." And, with that, Reese quickly left.

THE FACT THAT it was Elizabeth bothered Simon. She was a

voice from his past, a blip on his radar, a small blink in his memory banks, and yet she'd had a pretty powerful impact on him back then, and it was one of the reasons why he continued to help women's shelters even this day. Those abused women never seemed to catch a break, and Elizabeth was a prime example. She should have been safe. She should have been long gone from this life and from Vancouver, and yet here she was, killed in a local park, named after her mother.

And even if she wasn't killed in the park, she was dumped there, to be another Clement memory on that same passage to death by abuse and torture. And a bench was there that he had built for her mother, partly as a way to say goodbye to her and her family and that whole stage of Simon's life. He'd been determined to move on and to move up and out of that scenario back then and had managed to do it. The money didn't matter to him except for what he could do with it—whereby he made something good that allowed him the freedom to do some of what he wanted and some of what other people wanted too.

He provided scholarships for those in need. He provided medical treatments for those who needed it as well, but not, … not publicly. He let his name be known to a few inner circles, just to contact him if they knew somebody who needed something. Almost everybody was willing to keep an eye open for somebody in need, particularly when it came to kids.

As far as Simon was concerned, any child who needed surgery should get it. Canada had a great medical system for the masses. However, with some problems, not everybody could get exactly what they needed. Then sometimes Simon helped out.

He pondered all that as he walked home, completely preoccupied to the point that he walked past his doorman and didn't even see him.

When the doorman asked in a concerned tone, "Hey, you okay?"

Simon turned, acknowledged him, and nodded. "Yeah, but I'm not to be disturbed for the next"—he checked his watch, looking at it briefly—"two hours."

"Good enough."

Simon stepped into the restricted private elevator and quickly made his way up to his penthouse. As he walked inside his home, he took off his jacket, tossed it over the hook that he kept right at the entryway, and then moved toward his couch, loosening his shirt and rolling up his sleeves.

Kate was right. Simon hadn't done any deep dive into trying to figure out what was going on here, mostly because he didn't want to, and yet fear was not something that he would have ever allowed to rule him. However, some of this stuff was pretty damn freaky and depressing to consider. Yet he knew that, if something were in the deep recesses of his mind, the only way to get to it right now, when it wasn't voluntarily coming, was for him to dig it out.

He wasn't sure that he had any ability to force this, and he was pretty sure that his grandmother would say, *Force was never the answer.* He needed to let go and to surrender to the process, and only then would he get answers that would make any sense. He was willing to give it a try.

And, with that decided, he sat on his couch, closed his eyelids, and slowly dropped into a meditative state. He gently relaxed his way down and out from the day's stresses and troubles, trying to let it all go, so that he could do something—anything that would help make for a little bit easier process.

As he sank deeper and deeper, he felt his mind shifting back and forth to the day-to-day stuff, and he kept calming his mind, until he got to the point where he saw the thoughts come, observed them, and let them go on again. It had taken him a long time to get to this point, but, now that he was here, he could sense that inner peace, and his body gravitated toward it.

As he shifted and relaxed a little more, he started to surrender to the energy, mentally calling out for answers. As he sat here quietly, letting names and dates and faces drift through, but not clear enough or slow enough for him to capture.

He stayed quiet for several more moments, letting everything float around him, while deep enough under that there was essentially no past or future time element involved. He heard his grandmother's voice whispering in his mind, *Now stay in the present moment, stay here, and listen to what comes.*

Her voice shifted something inside him, almost making it harder to stay wherever he intended to be, but almost immediately he heard another whisper, something off, as if a person sat right beside him, a whisper of cloth against cloth, a bit of ... He tilted his head to the side, as he tried not to analyze and just allowed the information to flow and yet, at the same time, tried to recognize whatever he heard.

Then came a half cough, almost a whimper.

Instead of crying out, he tried to relax a little bit more into the sensation, and, when he heard a bit of a snuffle, he whispered, "It's okay."

Almost a start came within him, as if he had reached out to this other person, and that person had received whatever message Simon had sent.

He immediately sent out another reassuring message, almost a warm hug, and yet he knew that it could be a lie, that he could possibly be giving her false reassurances, when he couldn't even begin to figure out where she was. And yet he knew it was a she. Somewhere a woman was suffering, and he didn't even know who it was, where she was, why she was there. Still, here he was, trying to hand off those same assurances.

When he heard a quivering voice, whispering in his ear, asking, "Who are you?" he froze and then whispered back.

"A psychic, looking for you."

A sob broke free from the other woman. "Then help me, dear God, please help me," she cried out.

"Where are you?"

"I don't know. I don't know," she wailed. "I don't have any idea."

He waited until she was calmer, then asked, "What happened?"

"I was walking home from work," she began, "and this man came up behind me. I stepped out of the way. He passed, and then he turned around to face me, reached out as if to smack me on the shoulder, and then I don't remember more," she murmured.

"Your name," he urged, feeling the connection slip away.

"Samantha," she whispered. "Samantha Cole." And then her voice was gone.

He snapped awake, stared out at the incredible Vancouver skyline in front of him. All he could grab on to from his vision was *Samantha Cole*. He reached for his phone and called Kate. When she answered, her voice distracted, she asked, "Is this urgent?"

He hesitated, then said, "I don't know if it's urgent or not, but it might help."

"What is it?" she asked, her voice immediately perking up.

"I tried to connect, to somebody, to anything. You know I'm not very good at willfully trying to reach out."

"Did you reach someone?" The question was phrased too neatly.

"Yes. I'm not sure that I connected to anybody in this situation."

"Ouch, I guess you can't control the people you connect to."

"I'm not sure that I can control any of it," he admitted, with a note of humor. "Remember that part?"

"Oh, I do," she murmured. "Who was it?"

"Her name's Samantha Cole, and she's a prisoner somewhere. A man came up behind her, walked past her, turned around, clapped her on the shoulder, as friends do, and she doesn't remember any more."

"So a pressure syringe," Kate noted, with a sigh.

"Possibly."

"Do you know her name at all?" she asked him.

"No, I have no idea who she is." He heard Kate clicking on her keyboard.

"Interesting. I have a Samantha Cole registered as missing but not here locally," she read in a clipped tone. "She's up in the Chilliwack area, not quite a couple hours' drive from here. It came through as an alert, in case she'd come into the city."

"Well, she's in the city. I don't know if she was here willingly or not." And then he stopped. "Okay, I don't know what city. I don't ... I don't even know if she's in the city.

So scratch that. I assumed she was in the city but that could have been completely erroneous on my part."

"Good to know," Kate replied in a dry tone.

"All I can tell you is, I connected with her, and she didn't tell me anything other than she was a prisoner and to please help."

"*Great*," Kate mumbled, half under her breath.

He winced. "So, in other words, I'm not helping. I'm hindering because now ..." And then he broke off.

"Because now I have a Samantha Cole on our radar."

"And she may or may not have anything to do with the current murders."

"Right. So the next time you try this, why don't you try connecting to the asshole who is playing games. That would be helpful."

"But would it? Or would it allow him ... Samantha talked to me, and, if that happens in this particular killer's case, I don't know if that's good or bad."

"If it helps you identify who he is, if it happens to be somebody you recognize, a tone of voice, something," Kate replied, her tone sharpening, "it would be great. Obviously we still want to keep you safe, so I don't want you setting him off in any way. Yet, if you connect with him, and he knows that you're connecting with him, that'll set him off. Won't it?"

"That would be my take on it, yes," Simon agreed in a dry tone. "Hence my problem."

"On the other hand, I would rather deal with him pissed off, especially if it means we can connect to him, and we can learn anything. Plus a pissed-off killer can make mistakes," she explained, speaking all too quickly, and then she groaned. "And I know how hard it must have been for you to try this, and I appreciate it."

"Do you really?" he asked. "Because right now we have yet another missing person."

"Sure, but I'm not part of the Missing Persons' department. Remember?"

He winced. "Right. Didn't even think of that, but I can't *not* help her."

"Can you help her though?" she asked instantly. "Can you figure out where she is?"

"I don't know." His own frustration boiled over. "Maybe not, but I guess I'll give it a try. Now that I know that this woman is out there, hoping that I'm looking for her," he repeated in exasperation, "I feel as if I have to do more. Otherwise she's sitting there and waiting forever."

"Did you tell her that you were a psychic?" she asked.

"Yeah, I didn't know what to say because I wasn't expecting her to be receptive."

"I guess that's never happened before, has it?" she asked. "Usually you connect to them but they do not connect back to you."

"It happened, like the little boy I managed to give instructions to, but it's so much easier with children. They're so ... so much more open, so much more available, and not full of doubts and disbelief. This woman I think is desperate, and even now she's probably wondering if she's off her rocker and starting to lose her marbles because of our prior conversation."

"I wouldn't doubt it," Kate agreed, with a note of humor. "I'm still not sure if I'm not having hallucinations when it comes to you and your messages."

"*Thank you*," he stated, his voice turning sharp.

"Hey, hey, I didn't mean it in a negative way," she muttered. "I get it. This is pretty sensitive stuff for you, and, of course, … I hadn't expected you to connect with anybody else."

"And yet it's always a possibility," he pointed out. "I can't direct my connects."

"Have you tried that direct connection?"

"No, I haven't," he said crossly. Because of course he hadn't; he had gone in there hoping to maybe connect in some way. He just hadn't directed how he would make that connection. "Dammit," he muttered.

"Yep, I know. I hear you. Let me see if I can pull the file on this Samantha Cole and see if we've got anything."

"Is she listed as a missing person?"

"Yes, that's all I've got her as. Just a minute." He heard more clicks, and then she came back and added, "She has been missing two weeks approximately, short what? Two days I guess," she mumbled, as she clicked through the file. "Was last seen walking home from work."

"That's what Samantha told me, how she was walking home from work, so whoever else saw her walking home from work quite likely saw what happened to her—or is the person who kidnapped her."

"Why would the person who kidnapped her register her as a missing person?" she asked. "Doesn't that defeat the purpose of keeping your prisoner secret?"

"Unless he wants us to know he has Samantha," Simon suggested. "However, if she was last seen walking home from work …"

"Could have been her boss seeing her, as she left for the day," Kate offered, "but I will follow up." And, with that, she disconnected.

CHAPTER 13

T HE OTHERS IN the team waited for her to end the call. "Apparently Simon helped us but connected to this missing woman instead."

"Well, hell," Owen replied, "that's pretty awful."

"Awful in what way?" Kate asked, a bit sidetracked.

"Awful for this young woman, who we didn't even know was in trouble."

"Yet she's a missing person," Kate pointed out.

"Sure," Lilliana agreed, "but that's not our department, and it's not something that we would normally cross into, outside of being on the lookout for. It's not a case that we would be running down, unless we had absolutely nothing else on our plate," she noted, with an eye roll. "What are the chances of that ever happening?"

"Right, so what do we do with this?" Kate asked. "And, if you tell me nothing, that's great, but then you'll also have to explain it to Simon too because now that he realized that she's in trouble, he of course has to help her."

"Which means he's expecting us to help her as well," Owen acknowledged, with a nod.

"Of course he is," Rodney said, "because we're expecting him to help, and he's expecting us to help."

"Crap," Owen muttered. "Did he have anything, any location, anything?"

"No, and I did suggest that maybe he try again," Kate shared, looking over at the others and seeing their group winces. "Of course that didn't go down so well."

"But, of course, he might still try to connect with the ones we want him to connect with," Rodney noted.

"All I can tell you is, this is what he told me, and I don't really understand all *this* … or what I'm supposed to do with it."

At that Sergeant Colby walked in, as he looked from one to the other. "What's up? What did I miss?" Kate took a deep breath and explained. His eyebrows shot up. "Well, shit," Colby muttered, under his breath. "So now we have a reliable source who says this victim's kidnapped?"

"Yeah? You'll tell the media how Simon's a reliable source, or you'll tell your boss that Simon's reliable?" Kate asked on an odd note.

He pondered that before speaking. "Because it's Simon, he would get a little more weight than many other sources." Colby ignored Kate's eye roll. "However, you're right. Simon is hardly a reliable witness, not one I can put out to the media." Colby faced Kate and asked, "Any chance of his trying to reconnect?"

"I've already suggested it. Can't say that the suggestion went over very well," she replied cautiously. "He's also tired and upset and frustrated because he wants to help this Samantha woman but doesn't know how and is further frustrated that we have her on our books, but technically we didn't even know that she was in a difficult spot."

"That's the problem with missing persons though, isn't it?" Colby pointed out. "They can willfully walk away, and, even though she was last seen at work, according to you, or leaving work, it still doesn't mean she didn't meet up with her boyfriend and decide that running away to Paris was her next best option in life."

"I know, but explaining that to Simon won't be easy."

"I can talk to him if you want," Colby offered.

She stared at him and then slowly nodded. "If you'd like to, you're more than welcome to. Also, Reese brought in some possible connected cases, so we need to take a good look at those."

Colby glanced around the room. "Instead of everybody running off on this, let's set up the meeting room and focus on these other possible cases and break them down. Let's make sure that everybody's on track. And, Kate, call Reese back here to sit in on this meeting. If any one of these cases is connected, we need to be on it."

She nodded and stood. With Rodney at her side, they quickly set up the meeting room, and everybody sat down with their copies, and Kate quickly scanned through them and began, "Okay, four cases are here."

"Interesting," Colby remarked. "Four deaths noted in that graffiti art angle, correct?"

"Yes," Kate replied.

Colby looked over at her, his gaze sharp. "Spit it out."

"It doesn't mean that our killer doesn't have other cases. It's just that he was attributing those four in the Main Street graffiti art to Simon."

At that, everybody blinked. "Hang on a minute." Colby frowned.

"I know. I know," Kate admitted. "It doesn't make any sense. Yet our killer's the one in this *game*. However, I guess I'm wondering if this *game* isn't something that he's been developing over the years, rather than his MO."

"So you think he's not changing his methods, only he's

changing the *game, his game plan,* or whatever that means, right?" Colby asked.

"It's a working theory," she said quickly.

Rodney sat back and looked at her, with a mixture of wonder and disgust. "Your mind's a scary place."

She snorted. "That's all right. So's yours."

He grinned at her. "I won't argue with that. But, if our killer has been playing this game with other people, how will we know?"

"Other than his MO, we may never know," Kate pointed out. "With this killer, the game itself could have changed or the game is a result of whatever he's been doing before this."

They went through the methods of the killings on the four cases. "All women," Lilliana noted. "We already have a male victim in this set of murders."

Kate nodded. "Agreed."

They quickly set up a big whiteboard with all the cases, so they could look at them. Reese came in a little bit later with the photos of the victims and put them on the board too. "As far as I can see, these are still unsolved, and some of them go back eight years."

"Eight years is a long time too," Kate noted, with a mild monotone.

"It is, and yet it isn't."

It didn't take them long to realize that most of the women had all gone missing within a few years of each other. Then nothing for four, almost five years. One had gone missing within the last two years. Kate looked over at Reese.

"And that *was* one of the reasons why I wondered if they were all connected," Reese admitted, nodding in agreement. "Because he slept for however long and for whatever reason, but now he's back active again. And I don't know what would have brought him back into active status again."

"Simon," Kate declared.

At that, Reese's gaze widened. "So you're thinking that Simon ... somehow brought the killer back into circulation?"

"That's what I'm thinking." She turned to look at the others. "What do the rest of you see?"

"And yet why?" Colby asked. "Maybe it's what triggered him back again but what would have caused that trigger?"

Kate shrugged. "Do we have any connection between any of these victims and our current victims?" she asked Reese.

"I'm working on that." Reese frowned, as she stared at the women's faces on the board in front of them. "Honestly, there's a similarity in the facial features between these four and Patricia and Elizabeth. However, we've got that male victim, Luca, as well now. And that could be for a couple different reasons," she muttered.

"No, I agree," Kate confirmed. "So we've got a period where we have three victims, and then we have ... the hibernation, where he went to sleep, and, for whatever reason, he stopped doing what he was doing. Now he's back, and this time he set his sights on Simon. So I would first want to make sure there was absolutely no connection between these four possible victims and Simon, and that there is no connection between these four possible victims and Samantha."

At that, everybody turned toward her, and she shrugged. "I can't get past the fact that, once again, Simon is the connection. I don't know that the missing Samantha Cole has anything to do with our three current murder cases. No, long-term kidnapping doesn't fit the current MO. Do we know how long our killer kept the others? … Mostly two to four days, right? So this Samantha woman has been missing for"—Kate checked her notes—"approximately two weeks."

"No," Colby corrected at her side. "She was *reported* missing, but we don't know how long she's been kidnapped."

Kate stared at him, and, recognizing the distinction, she nodded. "That's a good point too," she muttered, "because maybe she is the next victim. Although why keep her this long?"

Rodney asked, "Why would he have kept the brother-in-law who worked at the construction site less than the others? Why pick him at all?"

"I don't think our killer had any respect for Luca," Kate offered. "I think he thought Luca was a loser and wasn't anywhere near as much fun as the killer had hoped—whether *fun* was part of his reasoning or not. I think … our killer felt more disgust and wanted to get rid of Luca."

"That works too," Colby concurred, still at her side. "So, everybody, we need to track everything we can on these four possibly related cases. Let's see if we can find any connection between any of these cases and our current three. And I don't care how slim a connection either. It could even simply be that a women's shelter was involved."

"And, if we take that back a generation, we could be looking at all kinds of stuff," Kate suggested, "maybe their mothers were even connected."

At that, the others grimaced. "I guess that would fit our latest murder, wouldn't it?"

"It would because of Mary Clement. And, yes, Simon did help her, and a bench is in the park with her name on it," Kate replied. "And, yes, Simon did pay for it." They all stopped and stared, and she nodded. "So whether that was a trigger, I don't know." Kate raised both hands in frustration. "We don't have enough to understand the psychology of this killer."

"Maybe you want to run that past our psychologist," Colby noted, looking squarely at Kate. She stared at him and immediately shook her head. He frowned. "We do have a new one, you know?"

"Yeah, sure," she grumbled, glaring at Colby. "Haven't really worked with this one, and honestly I can't say I really want to."

"It's not a request," Colby declared, his voice firm.

Her shoulders slumped, and she nodded. "Fine," she muttered, "but I don't expect she'll help."

"It's a he, so keep your sexism to yourself."

She snorted at that. "Says you, but I'll try." And then she looked over at Rodney hopefully. Rodney immediately shook his head. "Yeah, no. I am not taking that on. You are riding solo for this jaunt."

"Oh, but you're supposed to job-shadow me anyway," she countered, with a big fat grin. "So I'm dragging you along with me. You can be my ... what you called it earlier, ... my shield."

"Why would you need a shield?" Rodney asked. "It's almost as if you're scared of him."

"Yeah, I remember the last one I had to talk to," she grumbled, under her breath. "I've avoided every other one since." At that, Colby stared at her, and she shrugged. "Hey, scary people and all that."

"Not so scary," he pointed out, "but very helpful. Find the psychology and motive of this guy behind doing this shit and get a profile worked up."

"If they're connected, which is what we need to know, preferably first," she considered out loud, "otherwise we're just making stabs in the dark."

"Yeah, taking stabs in the dark is kind of what we do," Colby stated. "Hopefully you're taking educated, logical stabs in the dark. Right now, the only connection in any of these current damn cases is Simon." He faced Kate. "Maybe it's time to bring him in."

"He's been in several times. I've made sure that Rodney was in on all of them."

"Anything?" Colby asked.

"No, nothing," she replied, showing her palms. "Nothing other than the fact that somebody is targeting him or using him somehow to play this game."

"It's that *game* usage that I don't like," Colby noted in a disgruntled tone.

"Right, you and me both," Kate acknowledged. "And the fact is, we do theoretically still have a fourth victim that we haven't found yet, according to that Main Street graffiti art."

"If we're listening to the graffiti," Colby pointed out.

"And yet how can we not because, once again, the only connection between the three recent torture-murders is Simon and the graffiti was on one of his buildings."

Colby closed his eyes for a moment, pinched the bridge of his nose, and nodded. "So you expect there'll be another victim?"

She tapped one of the four photos on the whiteboard, among the other possibly associated victims who were killed earlier. "I'm thinking it's her."

"Why?" asked Colby.

The other team members gathered around to look at the

woman's face. She looked as if she were twenty, twenty-five, with long brown hair, but remarkably average.

"Just because …" Kate began, yet frowned. "I don't know why. I need more than *just because*, but it feels like a *just because*."

"Christ, you're sounding more like Simon every day," Owen remarked from behind her. She rounded on him, glaring, and he raised both hands in mock surrender. "You just said it. We need more than a *just because*."

"I know. I know, but this one fits. She breaks away from these other three possible because her death was way later. It's as if these other three were victims all at once. Then *whatever* happened, and the killer went to sleep. So this fourth woman is *current*. This one's in our wheelhouse. It's in our neighborhood. It's exactly the same MO, even closer than the original ones. I'm not saying that he refined his process at all because this is definitely the work of a deranged mind," she explained, with an eye roll, "versus somebody who's sane. But I'm wondering if we can connect this one in particular to Simon. If so, that would give us something to go on."

"So, call him," Colby said, "preferably right now." And he crossed his arms and leaned against the door jamb.

Kate took her phone and snapped a picture of the photo on the board, sent it to Simon, and then sent him a text. **Do you know this person on the left? It was one of the case files we are trying to connect.**

When her phone rang almost instantly, she winced and put it on Speaker, saying, "Simon, I'm in a meeting, and you're on Speakerphone."

"I don't know her," he stated. "I know *of* her."

"Okay, and what do you know of her?"

"She, her mother, and her sister were at one of the women's shelters that I know of," he stated.

"*Great*," she murmured. "And would they have known you or of you?"

"Only if they saw me there at some point in time, but it's not a place that lets in males, if you know what I mean."

"So how would they have seen you?" Rodney asked in the background.

"When I dropped off the cash," he explained, "and I usually do cash drops after a poker night. I'll walk by and knock on the door. We have a little knock system, and the manager checks the peephole, sees me there, opens the door. I'll hand her a wad of cash, and I walk away."

The others all looked at each other.

"So …" Kate prompted, and then she fell silent.

"Exactly," Simon said, with a sigh. "If somebody had seen me, then that's what they would have seen."

"How did you know about this woman in the picture?"

"Because I'm the one who sent her to the women's shelter," Simon said, with exasperation in his voice. "Same as I sent Annie, your young drug-addicted prostitute, to the same shelter. I sent her directly to this one, actually," he added.

At that, Kate stiffened. "When did you do that?"

"Yesterday," he murmured. "I didn't tell you about it. One, it's better if you don't have anything to do with this stuff. Two, if you needed to contact her, I could have gotten her in touch with you at some point in time. However, Annie wasn't at all sure that her pimp wouldn't come back after her."

"And yet this is a women's shelter."

"Yes, and I was planning on finding Annie a place in a rehab center after this."

She smiled at that. "But she's in this shelter …"

"Yes, she needed some time to rehabilitate, and I couldn't really figure out where else to put her," Simon admitted. "Society doesn't have places for people like her—in between drug use and getting sober, or getting whatever you want to call it." He took a deep breath. "She's off the drugs because of her actual medical condition, but she'll still need to fight the addiction. Thus she must go into rehab, and that's not so easy to do."

"Okay, so temporarily you found her a home at this shelter, and you're paying the cost, I presume."

"I am," he confirmed.

"And this other woman you may know of, how would you have seen her?"

"I saw them at the hospital, after the mother and the sister were badly beaten," he related, with sorrow in his voice. "The father was given jail time, but he had friends who thought that his behavior was totally normal and that his wife should get her ass home where she belonged. So she didn't feel safe, and I arranged for her to disappear. One of the stops in that disappearing act was the same shelter."

"Jesus," Kate replied. "Do you know what happened to her after that?"

"No, I step back, so that one link in that chain doesn't know what the next link does." He hesitated and then added, "I did provide money so that they could be funneled through the system and start fresh somewhere else."

"And how much money would that be?" Colby asked. "This is Sergeant Colby, by the way. Hi, Simon."

"Sir," Simon greeted him. "I believe I gave them $15,000 to move the three women someplace safe."

"Have you had any contact with any of them since?"

Colby asked.

"No, I have not."

"And yet you recognized her?"

"Yes, I recognized her," he declared calmly. "It's not a hard thing to do. I remember most of the people I help. So, in that instance, yes, of course I remember her. Do I remember the details? Only in the sense that she was coming from domestic violence. Something I have no patience or tolerance for." And he fell silent.

Kate looked around at the rest of the team. "Any other questions for Simon?" They all gave a headshake. "Okay, Simon, do you remember the mother's name, the sister's name?"

"I'll have to think about that one. I don't even know her name, at least at the moment," he replied. "Only her picture is triggering my memories."

"Okay, if you can get me that information, that would be helpful, so we can confirm it with our own database."

"Will do." And, with that, Simon rang off.

Kate looked over at the others. "Presumably we have the family's information somewhere."

"We didn't have any ID," Reese replied. "She's a Jane Doe."

"Really? Why is that?" Kate asked.

"Because, in this particular murder, she's missing all her fingers."

"On that note, people," Colby ordered, "get back to work. Kate, get to the psychologist's office."

Kate growled, as she trudged to the shrink's office. She twisted the doorknob to enter his anteroom and found the door locked. She heaved a sigh of relief and quickly turned on her heels, happy to avoid the shrink once more.

SOMETIMES THE STENCH of humanity gone evil was more than Simon could handle.

The fact that he'd connected with Samantha in a two-way psychic communication had him worried. He ran his hands through his hair, staring around. He was in the middle of one of his rehabs. Thankfully nobody was close to him; otherwise they would have gotten quite an interesting tidbit of conversation on how he worked with the police now.

The fact that he was even working with the police blew him away. So *not* who he was, and yet exactly who he was now in so many ways. A law-abiding citizen. *In so many ways.* That rolled off his tongue so thick. That a little bit of gray area existed for him was something that he would deal with down the road—if it ever came up in terms of his relationship with Kate.

As he walked steadily away from his rehab project, still rattled, he really wanted this asshole to come after him and not for the killer to end up continuously targeting young women. And before he realized it, he found himself standing in front of freshly painted graffiti.

He stared at it for a moment, wondering at such a mindset as this.

As soon as he was done, he headed home, dropped himself into a meditative state, and reached out to Samantha. This time he knew various tricks about trying to follow a pathway that had already been forged, but, when he called out to Samantha several times, Simon got absolutely no answer. He tried to drop himself lower, easing his breathing back, trying to change the level of his actual meditation and breaths, but it wasn't working. All he kept getting was this blank wall.

He stared off at the distance, hoping it didn't mean what his mind was automatically jumping to because that would mean that Samantha was dead—and this poor woman, who had so much hope that he was out there, looking for her, was already gone.

He shook his head at that, got up, made himself some coffee, took a quick shower. When he came out, he poured a cup and then sat back down, closed his eyes and called out in his mind, *Samantha, talk to me.*

Almost immediately this faint quiver of a voice whispered, *Is that you?*

Relief like he couldn't believe washed through him, slamming against his heart and chest, and he whispered, *Yes. It's me.*

She started to sob. *Did you find me? Why haven't you found me yet?* she cried out.

Because we can't find out where you are. Did you know the man?

No.

Did you see him?

No.

What kind of place are you in?

It's dark, like a bedroom. I'm chained to a wall. There's a bathroom. I can get that far but nowhere else.

Does he feed you?

Yes, he comes in, drops food, and leaves it behind.

Has he hurt you?

She started to cry at that.

He hesitated, then added, *I need to know.*

Yes, she whispered. *He does.*

Has he raped you?

No, no, she said softly. Then she added, *Not yet.*

The chances of him raping her at this point weren't great. Chances were, this was somebody other than a sexual sadist, or it was somebody working his way up to it. *Can you see around the room? Can you see a shape of a window? Can you see anything?*

No, she replied, *there's no light. There are no windows.*

So you're high up in an attic?

She sighed. *Maybe,* she replied in a lament. *When he comes in, he drops the tray on the floor and backs out again. He never loosens my chain or takes it off or releases it in any way.*

Does he talk to you? Does he say that somebody'll pay? Does he say who's responsible for this? Does he say what he wants you for?

No, he doesn't say anything.

Has he ever laughed? Received a phone call? Have you ever heard anything?

Nothing, she whispered. *Absolutely nothing.* He groaned, and she started to cry again. *Please, please, find me.* And, with that, she was gone.

As Simon came out of his meditative state, he reached for his coffee, his hand trembling. He wasn't sure how often he had connected with a person he could communicate with in such a way, but it was working this time. So everything else in his life and in his abilities were changing. Almost immediately his grandmother's voice wafted through his mind, telling him that his gifts would shift and change, until they cemented themselves into a certain set of talents. Until then, he couldn't count on anything, and yet he could gather a lot of good information, if he sifted through it.

"Sift through it," he muttered.

What do you sift through when nothing's here? What do you sift through when there's just a voice, a person on the other end, a person he had connected to who couldn't help him? At that, he bolted to his feet. He closed his eyes, facing the downtown Vancouver core, sending out a message, asking his mind, his energy, which direction to go to find Samantha, to find where this message from Samantha came from.

Almost immediately his grandmother's voice snapped into his brain again, with another tidbit that he had forgotten over the years.

There is no time. There is no distance. Sometimes you can even reach into the past and speak to people who have come and gone already. You cannot count on anything, not until your talents lock in. And, even then, depending on what goes on in your life, circumstances could set them all off again.

Simon swore, but, as he stared out at the late-afternoon sun, it seemed to him that maybe, just maybe, he was staring in the right direction. He closed his eyes and slowly rotated, using his senses to tell him which direction Samantha was in, knowing it was one of those foolish little things that nobody would trust and that nobody would believe. Yet he had no choice but to at least try.

As soon as he got to the same mental point where his instincts prodded him to stop, he opened his eyes, and he was facing the same direction. With a heavy sigh, he stared out at the miles and miles of city before him. It was possible that Samantha was here locally. It's also possible that, if he continued in this direction, he'd reach Chilliwack, not even a two-hour drive away.

He picked up his coffee, sipped it, wondering what he was supposed to do. Then he realized that it didn't matter what he was supposed to do. He really only had one option. He couldn't deal with anything to do with Kate's case because no information was coming his way. But Samantha was out there. Samantha, a prisoner of some psycho asshole, who was keeping her locked up, possibly in an attic.

Frustrated, infuriated, he checked his watch, noted it was almost 5:00 p.m. now. If he went out, he could then, in theory, continue to test this little bit of directional information he'd sussed out. If he couldn't help Samantha or Kate in one way, maybe he could help in another.

CHAPTER 14

KATE DRAGGED HERSELF inside her apartment and made it to her shower before the exhaustion hit her. She'd stopped at her martial arts training for an impromptu session, burning off some building frustration over her case.

Even her master nodded. "You need this tonight."

"I do," she murmured.

What had followed was such an intense session that she knew she'd be sore for days to come. She'd expected to see Simon after this, but, when he wasn't at his apartment, she'd come straight home. Maybe he needed distance; it couldn't be much fun with the police all over him because of this case. Not to mention stirring up bad memories.

When she stepped out from her shower, she opened the fridge and stared at what looked to be a very sad bluish mold on top of her block of cheese, some stale bread, and a jar of peanut butter. She slammed the fridge shut and leaned her forehead against it, realizing how little interaction she had with her own space anymore. She wasn't here long enough to have groceries that could maintain freshness, so she rarely shopped, and, when she was out—mostly because Simon was with her—her meals were spent with him, more often than without.

Frowning at that, she sent him a text message. **Where were you?** She got a response.

Downtown.

She straightened and stared at her phone and hesitantly called him. When he answered, she asked, "Whereabouts downtown and why?"

He snorted. "Hi, Kate. How are you? How was your day? Hope it was fine. Mine was good. Thanks for asking."

She winced. "Yeah, I know. I suck at all these rules to relationships," she muttered, then audibly sighed. "Thanks for making me feel bad."

He laughed. "Now, if I thought it would make you feel bad, I wouldn't say it."

She groaned. "So you want to tell me where you are, and why you are there?" He hesitated, and she spun around, looking wildly around her apartment. "Did you come up with something?" she asked in a low voice.

"No, not really, nothing that I could put a finger on to give you," he admitted. "As I don't have anything to offer in terms of these other damn victims, I was wondering about Samantha."

"Can you find her?" Kate asked in delight.

"No," he replied immediately, squashing her joy. "I had an inkling that I should be going in a certain direction and that it's possible she was in that direction."

"Hang on a minute. You mean, you got a direction as to where Samantha could be, and you're following that up?"

"That's a good way to put it, yes," Simon said.

"Thank God for that. Even that much is a help."

"Not really," he countered, "because I'm standing downtown, close to the Pacific Center Mall, and absolutely nothing is here."

"Maybe it's on the other side of the harbor."

"Maybe, but I came over here from this side of the river."

"Ah, then I don't know what to say."

"Neither do I," he admitted.

She heard the frustration in his voice. "I'm sorry. I know what it's like not to have answers."

He gave a small laugh. "Now that is very true. You certainly do. I thought that, if I could find something useful, then I wouldn't always be horrified to sleep at night in my comfortable bed, while this poor woman was being held prisoner in some godforsaken attic."

"Why an attic?"

"Because there are no windows, no light," he replied. "When the guy comes in, she can hear him coming upstairs. Otherwise I'd have thought *basement*."

"What if it's an apartment? With a bedroom loft?"

"I hadn't thought of that," he said, as he turned and looked up at a bunch of the apartments, where he'd been directed to. "I'm standing here, staring up at all these apartments, thinking there wouldn't be an attic."

"True, but, if he didn't want her to sense light, which would keep her very disoriented, then all he had to do was block off any windows."

"You have a scary train of thought sometimes."

"Yeah, I'm pretty sure that's what Rodney told me just today."

Simon laughed. "It does make you a good investigator though."

"Says you," she muttered. "Right now I'm sore and tired."

"Hard day?" he asked sympathetically.

"Yeah, and then I went and worked my ass off in the dojo."

"Ah, that would have been a hard one too. You don't recover as fast when you're beat down like this."

"No, and yet I needed it."

"A penance?" he asked, his voice sharp.

She stared down on her phone and frowned. "Dammit, I didn't even think of that. Why do you have to bring shit like that up all the time?"

"I don't," he murmured. "I'm not trying to bring up a discussion where you don't want to go, but it instinctively came out of my mouth."

"Why would that come out of your mouth?"

"Because you feel guilty that Samantha is out there, held captive, and that somebody may be out there, if not a captive, being targeted, and that some asshole is killing people connected to me because of me. You want to solve it even more because it's who you are. You want to solve it in the worst way possible, and you can't make any headway, so you feel guilty."

She glared at her apartment, her eyes wide, and didn't say anything.

"So as I said," Simon repeated, "I'm sorry for bringing it up, but you have no reason to feel guilty."

"Really? And how do you feel about it?" she snapped. "Are you telling me that you don't feel guilty?"

"That's different," he stated immediately.

She snorted.

Silence. "Right, fine, okay. It's not different," he admitted sadly, "which is why I'm out here, walking the damn streets, trying to get some compass reading off my stupid abilities, whatever they are, and have it make sense. Yet my rational mind knows it doesn't make sense."

She smiled, feeling better at having tweaked his goat too,

and she sighed. "We're a hell of a pair, aren't we, Simon?"

"That we are," he agreed. "I'm walking around the corner up here, and, if I can't get any reading, I'm coming back."

"Okay, while you do that, I'll crash. I need some sleep."

"Did you eat?" he asked, his tone sharp, and she heard his footsteps, as his boots clicked on the pavement, as he turned the corner.

As she went to answer him, she heard a hard *oomph*, and then a crash and a bang, as his phone maybe hit the ground.

"Simon," she roared. "Simon." But there was only silence on his end of the call.

CHAPTER 15

"SIMON!" KATE SCREAMED into the phone. "Simon, can you hear me?"

But she was already throwing her boots back on and grabbing her jacket and her keys. She kept the call live, as she raced to her car and headed downtown. She tried to remember the few landmarks he'd given her earlier in their conversation, but it wasn't much. Matter of fact, it wasn't enough in any way or form. She hesitated calling in 9-1-1 because she didn't have a location to give them. And yet nothing else came to mind. She quickly parked in the general location and started running.

She called into the phone, "Simon, Simon." Finally a female spoke near the phone. "Simon?" That was not Simon.

"This is Simon's phone," the woman said on the other end.

"Who is this?" Kate barked.

The other woman hesitated. "I'm Lisa. Lisa Sands."

"I'm Kate, Detective Kate Morgan," she barked, with authority. "Where is Simon?"

"I found him, Detective, and he's been attacked."

"Is he alive?" she asked, her voice choking.

"Yes, he's sitting here, looking dazed."

"Where exactly are you? I'm on foot, heading somewhere close around you."

Lisa gave Kate the street corner, and, checking her whereabouts, Kate brought it up on Google, even as she ordered Lisa, "Stay on the phone. Don't hang up on me."

"I won't. I won't," Lisa vowed. "He doesn't look very good."

"I'm almost there." And, sure enough, Kate was only a couple corners away. When she burst into the alley, she saw Simon, sitting up against the brick wall, blood running down the side of his head, but he gave her a lopsided grin.

"Hey, sweetheart. I knew you'd find me."

She groaned, as she crouched in front of him. "Jesus, are you okay?"

"Do I look it?" he asked.

"No, you don't. You look fucking awful."

She manually checked the wound, and it was definitely a deep split in his scalp. "You need stitches," she muttered.

He shook his head. "Nope, not going to the hospital."

"Why is that?" she asked, sensing something more, as if he weren't quite there.

"People die in hospitals," he replied, his voice slurring.

She swore, pulled out her phone, and called for an ambulance. She looked up at the woman standing to the side, looking terrified. "Are you Lisa?"

The older woman had a dusting of gray in her hair, pulled back into a severe bun. "Yes, I live around the corner. I was coming back from shopping, when I saw him, collapsed right there."

"Do you know him?"

She nodded. "Yes," she said, with affection, and tears filled her eyes. "I run a women's shelter around the corner here. Simon comes here on an irregular basis."

Kate looked over at her and nodded. "You're one of the

shelters he helps support?"

Lisa's eyes widened, and she looked around nervously, but she nodded.

"That's good," Kate stated. "I was looking to talk to you anyway."

"Why is that?" Lisa asked, puzzled.

But already in the distance an ambulance blared.

"Where's your door?" Kate asked Lisa. "I'll come after this to talk to you."

Lisa hesitated.

Kate pulled out her badge to show her. "You don't need to be afraid of anything,"

Relieved, Lisa gave Kate instructions on how to get there, just as the ambulance pulled into the alleyway. She had Simon checked over and loaded up and on his way to the hospital within minutes, completely ignoring his protests. As she straightened, she called out to Simon, "I'll be down there in a little bit." But she didn't even think he had heard her. If he did, he wasn't cognizant of it. She groaned as she looked back at Lisa, surprised to see her still here. "Do you have any idea what happened?"

Lisa shook her head frantically, her hands stuffed deep into her pockets, even though it was a warm September day. Lisa looked as if life had almost been a bit too much for her. "No, I saw him slumped up against the wall. Honestly I would have hurried past," she admitted in an apologetic tone, "but I recognized him."

"I'm glad you did." Kate dropped her head in her hands. "I don't know whether he was coming to give you something or looking for something around here.," she said, knowing perfectly well why Simon had been here. "He didn't talk to you, did he, before I got here?"

She looked at her in bewilderment. "He kept saying, *Call Kate. Call Kate.*"

"Yeah, and did he say anything else?"

"Yes, he mentioned Samantha. Something about *Samantha's here.*"

Kate froze. She turned slowly and looked around the area. "Do you know a Samantha?" she asked Lisa.

Lisa pondered it. "I've probably had some women through the shelter called Samantha," she replied, "but I don't have anybody there now."

"Anybody? Or not anybody by that name?"

"Not anybody by that name," she clarified.

"And did you have anything to do with Mary Clement many years ago?"

Lisa's eyes widened. "Oh my, that's a name from way back."

"What about her daughter, Elizabeth?"

"Yes, yes, of course. Simon helped to arrange that too." Lisa smiled in the direction the ambulance went. "It's important for us, for those of us who have seen the harsher side of men, to also realize that not all men are the same. Thus Simon … restores our faith each and every time we see him," she murmured.

"Do you run the women's shelter?"

She nodded. "I do, and it gives me a place to call home. I barely escaped marriage with my life," she shared, "and that was many, … many years ago. Thirty years." She shook her head. "A lot of young women seem to put it behind them and move on, but I never could. All I ever saw were the fists and the knives and the fear that that man put me through," she stated, her voice breaking even now.

"I'm so sorry." Kate gently stroked Lisa's shoulder.

"Come on. Let's get you home, and I have a few other questions."

"I don't understand what any of this has to do with Simon's assault," Lisa admitted. "Will he be okay? Don't you want to go to the hospital?"

"Oh, I do want to go to the hospital, and I will go to the hospital," she said, with a smile. "But let me come to the women's shelter to see where it is, and then I can ask you a few questions." Moving ahead, she looked back at Lisa and asked, "Is Annie still there?" Lisa's eyes widened, and Kate shrugged. "I'm the one who got her away from the pimp and to the hospital, then contacted Simon about her."

"Oh," Lisa breathed, her face wreathing in smiles. "So you're one of the good guys."

"I'd like to think so," Kate replied, "but I can understand how you might doubt it."

"Most women aren't abusive," Lisa stated, "but definitely a few are. So a few you have to watch out for."

"I'm not one of them."

As they continued to walk, Lisa led Kate to a small back-alley door. She pulled out keys, and, checking both ways, she let them inside.

"How many women do you have here right now?" Kate asked, as they stood inside the dark, gloomy interior.

"I have six, about half our normal."

"So it's a slow period."

"I hope so," Lisa replied, with a nod. "I have never had an empty house in twenty years, and sometimes we've had upwards of twenty-four women here—well over capacity. While I do get some funding, ... I don't get anywhere near enough."

"I'm sorry," Kate said, as she stared around the dingy

room. "Does Simon ever come in?"

Lisa shrugged. "We had a plumbing problem once. He came in and fixed it for us. Then I had some doors that I couldn't close. The hinges were pinched or some such thing. Anyway he popped the hinges and the doors off, put new hinges on, and fixed them. I can do a lot of things, but some I'm really not good at," she said, with a sigh. "So, every once in a while, I have to bring in repairmen, but having men around makes the women extremely nervous."

"Even Simon?"

"Oh, yes, of course. Not all of them know Simon," she explained. "Sometimes, when they've come from a recent scenario, they're terrified of anyone but trust women more."

"I'm so sorry." Kate looked around the kitchen. A large table sat off to one side, easily with room to sit eight, maybe ten people. One woman in the kitchen did some prep work. Kate smiled at her, and the other woman smiled quite freely back.

"This is Helen," Lisa introduced her. "Helen's been with me almost as long as I've been here."

"Hello, Helen," Kate said, as she pulled out her badge for the other woman. "Simon was assaulted around the corner."

The other woman's face paled. "Oh my. *Simon*-Simon?" She turned to Lisa. "Not our Simon."

Lisa nodded. "I'm the one who found him," she whispered. "It was awful."

"He's at the hospital now," Kate added. "I wanted to ask Lisa some questions, and, of course, if you were here at the time, did you also have anything to do with Mary Clement or her daughter Elizabeth?"

Helen's eyes widened. "Wow, I sure haven't heard those

names in a long time."

"It's a bit of an issue for me right now," Kate explained, "because Elizabeth's body has been found at Clement Park."

"Oh no." Both women gasped in horror.

Kate nodded. "So we're backtracking, wondering if she would have had anything to do with any of you or this shelter or Simon or anything? We're grasping at straws," she admitted, with half a smile. "So we'd be grateful for any information that could help point us in the right direction."

The women looked stunned that even this conversation had come up, and Kate could understand that. It wasn't one of the easiest conversations to have, especially when it related to women who had come through the shelter, beaten and abused, and survived all that to come to this brutal end.

And then Kate asked, "What about Patricia, did you … do you remember her?"

"Oh, Patricia Blinker," Lisa said. "Simon mentioned something about her."

"Yes, she was murdered as well," Kate stated, with a nod.

The two women reached out for each other and hugged tightly, as both their stark faces stared at Kate in shock.

Kate added, "I don't think women from here are being targeted, but obviously, as two have come through here, we have to consider it. We don't think that you're in any more danger than normal, but obviously please take a lot of precautions."

"Oh yes," Helen replied, "we take a lot of precautions. As soon as any of the husbands find out that we have wives here"—she shook her head—"we've had them come to the doors and break windows. It can be very ugly. We did get one in here one day, and he … beat up several women. It was just … awful."

"What happened?"

Helen smiled proudly. "I broke a fry pan over his head."

"Ouch." Kate looked at her in admiration. "I'm glad you stayed calm at least."

"Oh, it's been a long time for me," Helen stated, with quiet fury. "I don't let any man in my life anymore. Unlike a lot of people who have been victims, I'm not a victim now. I changed that program. For men it's a game, and I won't play it any longer," she muttered, her voice hard.

Even the mention of the word *game* made Kate wince because it reminded her too much of this other male and the perpetrator they currently had under investigation. "I don't imagine anybody here has any good experiences."

"No, we sure don't," Helen agreed, as she led Lisa over to a kitchen table. "Now you sit down here, hon. Let me put on the teakettle." And, with that, she walked to the other side of the kitchen and started to brew tea. She looked over at Kate intently. "Would you have a cup?"

Kate hesitated, but then nodded. "I would, thank you. I'm heading down to the hospital to see Simon as soon as I'm done asking questions here," she explained, "but it's been a shock to see him like that."

"You're friends?" Helen asked.

Kate smiled. "Yes, I will say we're a bit more than friends."

Lisa, the Good Samaritan, smiled at Kate in delight. "*Ohhhh*! You are *that* Kate."

"I am, indeed," Kate muttered, "and, yes, I'm the one he meant for you to contact—although how you were supposed to do that, I don't know."

Lisa shook her head, then bounded to her feet, walked over to where the phone was, and brought over a card. "Is this you?"

Kate looked at it and smiled. "Yes, that is me."

"Simon told us that, if we ever had any serious problems, to call you, that, even if it wasn't your department, you'd make sure that something happened to help us."

"True enough." Kate nodded. "I'm a detective, and we do handle the most serious cases, so unfortunately murder happens to be what fills my plate more often than not."

"Well, in that case," Helen replied from the sideboard, "I hope we don't need to call you."

"Exactly, but considering how many women die due to domestic violence each year, I would certainly understand if I were called." Kate shrugged.

At that came silence in the room. Helen bustled around and made tea, while Kate tried to rack her brain for any other questions she had. "Do you remember anybody in the Clement case, any names, anybody who was concerned, anybody the Clement women were concerned about, or who were concerned about them?"

"Her son. I don't remember his name," Helen said, turning to look at Lisa.

"No, I don't remember his name either, but I guess he'd been beaten by his father too. However, when they're adults, we can't take adult males here," Lisa said apologetically. "They have to go to a men's shelter."

"Right. That makes sense," Kate remarked.

"Exactly. If he'd still been a child, … that would have been a different story, but he was at least nineteen or twenty. Good-sized lad too, as I recall," Lisa noted, looking over at Helen.

Helen nodded. "I think so. It seems such a long time ago though. … But how sad that Elizabeth's dead," Helen murmured. "That girl was bound and determined to get her life together."

"So was Patricia," Lisa pointed out.

At that, once again silence fell, this time a little more awkward. When Kate was given a cup of tea, she sipped it gently, trying to figure out what else to say. And then she came to. "Is there anybody else who helps you with repairs here, like Simon does, anybody else you interact with on a regular basis, anybody who would know when Simon came and left?"

The women looked at her and then slowly shook their heads. "We don't deal with any males here," Lisa said. "Obviously, if we have to bring in a contractor, we ensure that they don't have any exposure to the women. Nobody knows it's a women's shelter. We keep it very much that way on purpose," Lisa declared, with a reservation in her tone. "Even if we did have some repairman in here, he would think only the two of us were living here, so the answer really is no."

"So you do your own bookkeeping, your own cooking, get food delivered?"

Lisa nodded. "Sure, to help hide our shelter here and to keep costs down. In fact, not too long ago, we had to let Julianne go. She helped us out so much, but the money was just not there anymore. Yet she still helped us out voluntarily, until she landed a full-time job.

"But back to your question about food deliveries," Lisa said. "We don't use the same people. We just act as if we're a household, and anybody who delivers here wouldn't know the difference."

Puzzled, Kate asked, "But why Simon?" She got a blank look from both of the women. "If both Patricia and Elizabeth had been through your shelter, I'm wondering whether the attack on Simon was random or also connected to their deaths.

"Oh dear." Lisa stared at Kate in horror. "He's done so much for us. I'd hate for him to get hurt because of us."

"I understand how you feel. I also know he helps because he cares," Kate replied. "Anything he does is because his heart's in it."

"That's true. Simon is one of the few people who does care." Helen sat down with her own earthenware cup in her big beefy hands and shared, "Lisa needs to go lie down."

Kate looked over at Lisa, who smiled and said, "I'm fine. I've been dealing with some flu, so I've certainly not been as good as I could be."

"You've also got cancer," Helen shared, looking back at Lisa with a sad look on her face. "She's recovering from her chemotherapy."

"Oh my." Kate regarded the woman sadly. "I'm sorry. It doesn't seem fair that you should suffer with that as well."

"Yes," Lisa agreed, "but the other side of that is waking up every day and being grateful for not still being in that situation and knowing that the women here are grateful for not being in their prior situations," she murmured. "And that Kate Morgan can make all the difference in the world."

SIMON WOKE IN the hospital with a pounding headache. He stared at the curtain around his bed and groaned. Almost instantly the curtain whisked to the side, and Kate poked her head around. She frowned at him, and he glared at her.

"I'm glad to see things are normal," she murmured, as she stepped closer, reaching out for his hand.

He immediately grabbed hers and brought the back of her hand to his lips and kissed it gently. "And once again you came to my rescue."

"Isn't it the other way around?" she asked, with a smile. "Aren't you the one who always comes to my rescue?"

"No," he replied, "but I did when it counted, so that matters."

"Of course it matters," she murmured. "It all matters."

He rolled his head gently to the side, wincing at the pain screaming through him.

"I don't suppose you saw anything, did you? I saw Lisa, standing over you protectively. She answered your phone when you fell. She came around the corner and saw you pretty quickly." Kate studied Simon's face, as she talked to him. "So she picked up your phone, when I was still screaming your name into it, while I was already driving down here. By the time I got directions from her, I was on the scene pretty fast."

"Of course you were," Simon declared. "I wouldn't expect anything different."

"Did you see anything?"

"No. Somebody came up behind me and slammed me on the side of the head."

"I'm sorry," she whispered.

"I gather no evidence was at the scene."

"No, there isn't. I have Rodney going over cameras in the area, but none cover that alleyway or block, for that matter."

"I was stepping around the corner of the alleyway, so I could talk to you." Simon sent a wry look in her direction. "So I'm damn sure there won't be any footage."

"No, I wouldn't be at all surprised, but we will do our

due diligence."

"He can go home now too," the doctor said, from behind her.

She frowned at a grinning Simon and asked the doc, "Seriously? He was almost out cold when I found him, his words were slurred, and then he collapsed."

"Yeah, he needs to stay home and check with his doctor. He's got a concussion, but his vitals are solid. We've stitched up his forehead, and he's been lucid and talking, demanding for somebody to call this Kate person."

"That would be me." She held up her badge.

He looked at it and nodded. "Good, then, in that case, I can leave you in good hands," he said, looking over at Simon. "You have any problems, any issues, blurry vision, dizziness, pain, or you have any loss of consciousness, you get right back in here. Do you hear me?"

Simon immediately agreed. "As long as I can go home now." He slowly sat up on the side of the bed and looked over at Kate. "I might not be able to walk very far though."

"That's all right. We have a wheelchair for you," the doctor replied, with a chuckle. "However, if you can't walk at all, then I might need to keep you."

"No, I can definitely walk a little bit," Simon declared, as he stood and took several confident steps forward. "But if she doesn't have a car here, I won't be walking home."

She snorted at that. "We would grab a cab anyway." She took his hand, as he leaned on her. "Come on. Let's go. Harry's waiting for you."

"Good. Maybe phone ahead and make sure that some food is there for me. I'm starving."

"That's a good sign," the doctor noted, with a laugh.

Kate led Simon to the front reception, where they took

care of the paperwork, and then out to her car. She let him in the front seat of her car and slowly drove him back home. As she parked, she asked him, "Do you think you can walk up to the front lobby?"

"Absolutely," he confidently stated. Yet, even as they got up the front steps, he slumped slightly. But, damn it, he would make it on his own …

Harry raced to the front door, obviously seeing him, and opened the door wide, asking, "What happened to him?" Harry immediately swooped in to support Simon.

Simon threw an arm over his neck. "I sure hope you ordered food."

"I did. I ordered Chinese. I hope that's okay."

"It's perfect," Simon said, but he staggered.

Kate raced ahead, got the private elevator open, and, with Harry's help, got Simon upstairs to his place, where she immediately had Harry help Simon to his bedroom.

Harry noted, "Kate, you are very good in this situation. Simon's not used to needing help. Then again he spends most of his time alone."

Kate nodded. "Thank you very much, Harry. I'll look after him from here."

Simon heard them as they walked to the elevator.

"What happened?" Harry asked Kate.

"He was attacked downtown, hit over the head, and left on the corner. He was talking to me at the time," she added, "so I had to find him very quickly and get him to the hospital."

Simon smiled at Kate's impatience with the questions and the worry about being away from him for even those few minutes.

"If you need anything, if he needs to go back to the hospital, you let me know," Harry offered.

"Will do."

When she walked into Simon's bedroom, almost tiptoeing in, he smiled at her. "I'm fine."

"Yeah, you look it," she murmured.

"I know," he admitted, "but now that I'm horizontal and not trying to walk, I feel much better." He slurred a bit as he added, "I'll work at getting out of these clothes, how about you serve food and bring it in here, *huh?*" Simon waggled his eyebrows.

She laughed. "Only you would be concerned about eating food in bed in that tone of voice, as if it would lead to something so much better."

"You mean, it won't?" he asked, with a crestfallen look.

"It won't," she declared, sending an eye roll in his direction. "Absolutely no way, José. Not today."

He groaned. "Fine, but tomorrow morning's a whole new option."

"We'll see, but I make no promises."

CHAPTER 16

K ATE WOKE THE next morning, groggy and sore. During the previous evening, she woke up every couple hours to check on Simon, and he'd groused at her almost every time too. Realizing that she was waking him up to check on him and how that was probably doing more harm than good, she'd fallen back asleep and slept for at least four hours. Now she was just tired.

She rolled over to see him snoozing quite comfortably. She crept out of bed, had a quick shower and dressed, then put on a pot of coffee. As she sat in the living room, waiting for the coffee, she wondered about postponing going into work, not wanting to leave Simon on his own. Pouring her first cup of coffee, she looked up to see Simon shaved and dressed, leaning against the door jamb, looking at her with a smile on his face. She walked over immediately, and he folded her in his arms and held her close.

He leaned over and kissed her gently on the temple. "Sure hope you made enough coffee for two."

"I did, but I'm finishing the second cup." He had such a woebegone look on his face that she burst out laughing. "No, I just made a pot, and I did make enough for two."

He grinned. "I knew you wouldn't let me down."

Together they sat watching the early morning view, as Vancouver woke up around them. Eventually she broke the peaceful silence. "I do have to go to work, but I don't want to leave you alone."

"I'm fine." He gave a wave of his hand. "I don't know who's on shift downstairs, if Harry was on late last night," he mentioned, "but I do have people here who can give me a hand, if I run into trouble."

"Only if you call me or send me a text every hour," she demanded. "Otherwise I'll send somebody here for a welfare check."

"You would too, wouldn't you?" he asked in mock outrage.

She nodded. "I absolutely would. I will check in, any chance I get," she murmured, "but I do have to get to work. Particularly as I'm not so sure if this is all connected."

"If what's all connected?" he asked, looking at her. "You know what that area of town is like. My attackers could have been anybody."

"And yet you were right around the corner from the women's shelter."

"I was," he agreed. "It occurred to me that they might have some information too."

"And apparently you mentioned that Samantha was there."

He stared at her in shock. "What?"

"According to Lisa, you told her several times to contact Kate and to tell Kate that Samantha is here."

"I have no recollection of that at all."

"Which is too damn bad," she announced, glaring at him, "because that would have been good to know. We really need a break."

"You're right. Maybe I'll go back there today."

She was in the act of grabbing her keys and wallet, when

she spun around and snarled, "What?"

He glared at her. "Of course I'll go back and take a look. Obviously I have to thank Lisa for helping me and you. I was bringing them some cash anyway." He took a deep breath and added cautiously, "Plus, we have to make arrangements for Annie to get into a rehab facility."

Kate noted that Simon was making some mental calculations because his brows were glued together.

"I think I have a line on one for her, but it'll require some paperwork. I also want to return to where I was attacked."

"Of course you do," she muttered, "even though you should spend the day at home, recovering."

He frowned. "I'll see how I feel at noon," he announced. "I might go back to bed and have another nap, until then."

"*Fine*, but, if you do go down there, let me know," she ordered, with a closer look at him, "so I won't worry."

"You'll worry anyway." He chuckled. "Even if it's only because you don't want anybody to know that you care."

"*Ha*. I think it's pretty damn obvious by now that I do care."

"It is," he agreed, with a fat smile in her direction. "Yet still a way to go."

"If you say so, but I'm not even discussing it right now." As she walked out, she blew him a kiss and quickly descended to the main floor. She told the doorman—Edgar, not Harry—about Simon's much-improved condition, and, should Simon need any help, Edgar should be ready to assist Simon. She'd met Edgar a couple times as well, and he nodded.

"Harry left a message here, so we're all rooting for him."

"He's doing much better this morning," she noted, with

a smile. "Still, keep an eye out on Simon for me, will ya?" And, with that, she quickly ran out the door and down the stairs and around to her car.

As she walked into the office twenty minutes later, the others were in an impromptu meeting. Colby saw her, raising one eyebrow.

"Simon was attacked outside the women's shelter last night," she shared. "By the time I got him to the hospital and questioned Lisa Sands, who owns the shelter and who found him in the alleyway, I then went and checked with her at her shelter. Lisa and Helen, her assistant, have been at the women's shelter for the last twenty-plus years. I quizzed them on both Elizabeth and Mary Clement, not to mention Patricia."

Owen asked, "Why didn't you call us?"

"By the time I got to Simon in the hospital, nobody had seen anything in that blind alley, including Lisa and Simon. He'd ducked into the alleyway to talk to me, so I heard the attack over the phone. I was going to write up the police report this morning but haven't got there yet. I did ask Rodney to check street cameras in the area, but apparently there are none at that corner."

Rodney walked in then and confirmed her statement.

With that, she yawned and added, "I'm not sure whether you guys are trying to talk to me or not, but I need more coffee."

With that, she headed to the coffee station and grabbed the second of many cups for that day.

WITH KATE GONE to work, Simon could admit to feeling a little worse for wear. He curled up on the couch, but his mind wouldn't stop. Maybe because he was so focused on Kate? Maybe because he thought that he should be better but wasn't? He didn't know, but it was frustrating. He was hungry, but last night's leftovers looked very unappealing. Yet a fresh pretzel from downstairs on the street? That would be good. He pondered the sensibility of going out and attempting to walk around and assimilating back into the normal world just yet. He figured that was probably not the smartest of ideas, at least for the moment. He'd wait a little bit longer, maybe tomorrow.

Then his phone rang. Edgar from downstairs. "Just checking if you need anything, sir. I heard what happened."

"Yeah, can't say I'm feeling all that great," he muttered. "But if you wanted to do something nice …"

"Absolutely, what do you need?"

"I'm craving one of those fresh pretzels from down at the corner stall."

Edgar started to laugh. "I know just the one. You're a sucker for those anyway, aren't you?"

"I absolutely am," he muttered. "Hey, when you're not feeling good, nothing like a bit of comfort food," he noted lightly. "I do have leftover Chinese, but that doesn't appeal."

"Cold Chinese food never appeals," Edgar agreed. "I'll be up there in a minute." With that, he disconnected.

Simon smiled, rummaged through his jacket pockets to find a tip to give Edgar and to pay for the treat—which, in his world right about now, seemed to be much more of a necessity.

As he went through his pockets, he felt a wave of energy. Instantly it dropped him to his knees. He stared around, but he was in a room other than his own. He was still holding his own jacket. He frowned, trying to make sense of the sudden shift. As his jacket fell from his fingers, he immediately snapped back to his bedroom.

Shaken, he looked around and muttered, "Good God."

He wasn't sure what would happen if he tried it again, but also, with Edgar coming to him pretty quickly, Simon wasn't sure he wanted to take a chance either. Yet he immediately grabbed his jacket again and was transported instantly to a small dark room. He called out, "Samantha?"

But it wasn't the room as much as an odd sensation that had him immediately going quiet. He watched a woman—and he didn't know whether it was Samantha or not—frozen in fear. The action was happening, like in a still-motion movie set. Something old, something creepy was going on. The back of someone slowly climbing the stairs, while, in his hand, he had a belt that he was whacking against his fist, a closed fist.

Although every step was slow and determined, it wasn't a race up the stairs. It was calculated, moving slowly toward something that he evidently looked forward to. Simon winced, knowing exactly what that end result would be. He didn't know who was involved, whether it was a current scene being played right now or some old situation, or if it was somebody who he could help or somebody now well past help.

Simon jerked back to his own surroundings because he heard someone coming.

Paying Edgar, Simon quickly took the treat and walked slowly back to the couch, where he sat down, still a little disoriented, and stared down at the pretzel. "What the hell was that?" he muttered.

He could try it again, but he needed a little bit more sustenance, not to mention a little bit more clarity in his head before he did. He couldn't place where he'd been, couldn't place anything about it, just that vision of a man walking up the stairs with a belt in his hands. And that was terrifying enough, but also knowing that the person in the room upstairs was terrified and knew what was coming added to the terror. Yet Simon was not able to help. That was always the hardest.

What he couldn't do yet was place a timeline on it. Was this something that had already happened recently, would happen shortly, or, indeed, had happened a very long time ago. That was one of the big challenges that Simon faced when he did this psychic work.

And he couldn't really talk to anybody about this. Hence his grandmother's own loneliness during her psychic period too. She had been very gifted, and yet she had worked at it, possibly because she had nothing else in her life, except for those all-too-few years with Simon. She'd sacrificed everything else in order to have this gift. None of it even made any sense to Simon, and that was his fallback response anytime he thought about it.

He figured that, as long as these messages, these visions, didn't make sense, then he could ignore them. Except when Kate needed whatever he could give, did he realize this pull to do something with his gift. The trouble was, doing something didn't always give him the answers that he was looking for. He slowly ate his hot pretzel, sipping the fresh-made coffee.

As soon as he started to feel better, he kept looking back at his jacket, wondering. And not able to ignore it, he got up and picked it up again. Only this time, whatever was there had reduced down to a fraction of what he had seen before. It was distant, faint, as if he'd used up whatever energy had been there.

He pondered that, as he put down his jacket once more, wondering how to get that vision back again, or was it gone forever in the ethers? If it was gone forever this time, did that mean that every time this happened he had a one-shot chance at it?

Again, more questions and really no answers. He grabbed his laptop, answered a bunch of emails, told his foreman he wouldn't be in today, checked in with Lisa Sands via email, and, when his phone rang not too much later, he wasn't surprised to see it was Lisa. "Hey, how are you?"

She snorted. "What do you mean, how am I? I'm fine. How are you?" she asked. "You're the one who ended up being attacked."

"Isn't that the truth. Did you see anything?" he asked curiously.

"No, sure didn't. I wish I did. I saw you as I came back to the shelter. I presumed you were coming to us, but I … I didn't know."

"No, and I don't remember either," he admitted ruefully.

She hesitated, then asked, "Is there any chance you had a lot of money on you?" she asked in a timid tone.

He heard the hope in her voice and yet also maybe a sense of disgust that she felt compelled to ask. He half smiled. "No, that's not why I had been coming in the first place. I rarely carry that much cash on me, unless I intend to dispose of it fairly quickly," he shared, with a note of humor.

"And we've been very grateful for every penny that's come our way," she stated.

"I know that, and I'll be by with a little bit more in a few days. However, I'm not traveling too far right now, given the state that I am in."

"I don't think you should be traveling at all. I'm worried that it wasn't random and that somebody was after you."

He didn't say anything to that, not sure how much Kate had told Lisa about the current cases they were working on.

Then Lisa added, in a different tone, "Your Kate is an interesting person."

The use of the possessive pronoun surprised him. "She's a very talented woman," he replied. "And she comes from her heart."

"Yes, of course," Lisa agreed immediately. "I didn't mean to imply anything other than that."

"Oh, I'm not worried about that. Kate has helped me a lot, and, every once in a while, I've been able to help her. So I presume that's why I was coming to talk to you," he suggested, with a note of confusion in his tone, "but I really can't remember what happened then."

"And that's quite possibly what you were coming here for. I did tell Kate everything I knew about Mary and Elizabeth and, of course, Patricia," she said, her voice deepening in pain. "To think about these poor women, what they already suffered, and then to turn around and be dealt more of same? It's ... so wrong."

"It is," Simon agreed, "and it's one of the reasons why everybody fights so hard to find out who did this and make sure that they pay."

"But making them pay isn't always the answer," Lisa noted. "Usually people who do this stuff either don't care or are so embroiled in their own pain that they can't see any other way out."

"And yet why would somebody, who's in pain them-selves, do this?" he asked out loud.

"I don't know," Lisa admitted, "but, over the years, we've certainly seen more than enough circumstances that made us wonder how any of us survive this craziness called life."

"That sounds as if you've had a pretty tough couple days."

"I think it was seeing you on the ground," Lisa replied, "that reminded me of so many things that I had hoped were forgotten." Then she gave a light laugh. "Oh, listen to me, how maudlin I can get. Anyway, when you're feeling better, we'd love to see you." And, with that, she disconnected.

He knew that the *We'd-love-to-see-you* part was most likely *Would love to have you stop by and deliver some money again.* It was hard enough to get donations for a women's shelter, and he knew that a couple times both she and Helen would work odd jobs to supplement whatever was needed to run the shelter, and that made him angry too because, when women were in need, there should be a system in place to help them.

And there was, and yet there wasn't. It was always a case of government grants, subsidies, and then you had budget cuts and all kinds of other excuses and reasons for why they didn't get anything from one time to the next. He thought that they got salaries, but again he wasn't too sure how that worked, and he didn't really want to pry. He'd often thought that maybe he should set up something but, so far, had left it at the level that he helped when he could.

At that, he frowned and realized that he had been a little bit more sporadic than normal lately. They were probably hurting. Vowing to get down there with some cash in the next little bit, he looked again at his jacket and then got up and tried one more time to connect to the vision, but nothing came.

Nodding to himself, Simon grabbed a journal and started writing. If he could track some of these events, he might find patterns in his visions.

There had been a distant quality to his latest vision, a sense of a time long past, and, if *long past*, then how would he ever find anybody to validate what he had seen?

The woman in his vision sat in front of her mirror, her hands trembling as she stared at her reflection.

⁓

SHE SHOULDN'T GO out tonight; she really shouldn't. And yet she already felt herself reaching for her big coat. When somebody called her from the back room, she froze, put the coat back on the hook, and turned and walked into the kitchen. "What's the matter?"

Yet here she felt needed, felt wanted, felt in control. And it was all about being in control. It was hard for her to understand just how out of control her life had been, and, having grabbed a taste of it a while back, it had fed something inside herself, and it had been enough.

It had been enough for a while, well, until she'd seen Elizabeth. And that had just opened the wound all over again, and now nothing seemed good enough, nothing was enough, she couldn't get full again. The hole would never heal, it would never close, and she needed it to close. She knew what it would take. It would take Simon; it would take Simon to close it. And then, only then, would she be free.

At least she *hoped* she'd be free.

CHAPTER 17

KATE CHECKED HER phone for the tenth time, and this time saw a message from Simon.

Call me.

She got up and walked out into the hallway, away from the noise of the bullpen that had resounded at a much higher level all of a sudden, and called him. As soon as he answered, she asked, "Are you okay?"

"I'm fine," he said.

She hesitated, not really sure what was with the odd tone in his voice. "Well, you don't sound okay," she stated bluntly.

He snorted. "I can always trust you to keep me on track."

She grumbled a little at that. "Is something wrong?"

"No," he replied, half-heartedly. Then added, "I had a weird vision."

"Oh? When you say a *weird* vision, I'm really not sure what to expect because, to me, all the visions are weird."

"Sometimes they are weirder than expected," he noted, with a half laugh. "Anyway, when I picked up my jacket that I was wearing last night, I immediately zoomed into something." And he quickly explained.

Kate leaned against the wall, pondering the information. "But you don't know whether it was a new or old event."

"No, … I don't, and that's where my frustration is."

Sure enough, she heard it in his voice. "I'm sorry. That's got to be the worst part for you."

"No, the worst part is not being able to help. I get this insight into something terrible about to happen, that I'm connecting with the victim, who already knows what's coming for her."

"Her?" she asked sharply.

"Yes," he muttered. "It was a woman."

"Okay, so we have a woman, potentially a captive, not sure, but upstairs, unable to get away, otherwise surely she would, and some guy walking up the stairs slowly, deliberately, with a whip. A belt."

He took a deep breath and let it go. "When I went back to my jacket and tried to reconnect, the vision was fainter. Then, when I tried it the third time, … the vision was gone."

"Okay, so there's a … what? A memory to this, a time limit for this to be available to you to connect to?"

"I don't know," he admitted in misery. "Again, this is new. I've never really worked to have a vision repeat for me before, so your guess is as good as mine."

She smiled. "And that makes you even more frustrated,"

"It'd be nice if you weren't quite so happy about it all."

"Hey, any information you get can help my cases. I know that's a far cry from what I was saying before." She chuckled. "But, as they have proven to be valuable," she added, "I'm definitely willing to take a look at whatever might come up."

"*Gee, thanks,*" he said in a sarcastic tone.

She winced. "I get it. I get it. I probably haven't been the most open and amiable, and I'm certainly not looking at any of this as being a problem, but I do understand your frustrations. Is there any chance that you could pick up anything about the house that was in your vision, maybe something from the stairs? Were they old, carpeted, bare wood?"

While Simon pondered that, she waited, knowing that he had great recall, but some details would always get lost in translation.

Simon began, "I would say that they were old, not very well kept, seemed to be scarred wood but not a nice hardwood, just beaten up over the years."

"Which is quite possible, depending on what care anybody might have taken for it," she murmured.

"It's still not helpful though," he stated.

"Everything is helpful. What would make it really helpful is if it was connected, and we had a way to know that. It could be yet another side case, like Samantha's."

"You don't think Samantha's connected, do you?" Simon's voice gained in volume at the thought.

"I'm not saying it's *not* connected," she said immediately. "I don't know yet, and I don't have any way to prove it, and that would help a lot if I could. But again a man going up the stairs."

"It feels as if I'm always tossing you tidbits, and then, when you ask me the first question about it, I can't tell you anything."

"And that's apparently the way it is these days," she confirmed. "If anything else happens or comes to you, then let me know. If you come up with anything other than old beaten-up wooden stairs, also let me know. This may or may not be important, but every tidbit helps us to put it into place. And if you hear anything connected to my current cases ..."

"Right, I will also let you know." And, this time, a note of humor was in his tone.

She smiled. "How is the head?" she asked abruptly.

"It's fine," he snapped.

She grinned. "Sounds like it."

"It is, honest."

"*Uh-huh*. It's not that I don't believe you …"

"Yeah, sure you don't." Then he groaned. "Not even sure I thanked you for coming and rescuing me."

"No, but you would have when you thought about it," she said in a cheerful tone. "Besides, it'll still be a while before we're even on that score."

"You know I don't care about that, right?"

"I know you don't, but it's nice to know that I won't always be the one in your debt," she added, with a laugh. "Anyway … I have to get back to work. I'll talk to you in a bit." She disconnected and headed back into the office.

As soon as she stepped in, there was silence. She looked around and frowned.

"Well," Rodney guessed, "presumably that was lover boy."

She rolled her eyes at the phrase. "What are you, still in high school?"

He gave her a flash of a big smirk and nodded. "Sometimes, yeah."

She sighed. "Yes, it was Simon. I was checking on his condition, after last night's attack. And, of course, he got some weird-ass vision today."

Immediately everybody snapped to attention, and she shook her head. "I don't even know what to make of it. I don't know that you guys will either."

"You can always give us a chance," Rodney suggested,

with a note of humor. "Tell us what's going on and what he came up with."

She explained the stairs, the belt, and the rest to her team, and they all sat there and stared at her. She nodded. "Which is why he's frustrated, and I'm a little frustrated after that call too because we get tidbits but nothing that can help." Kate nodded, as Rodney opened his mouth. "And we're stuck, trying to come up with answers for everybody out there looking for us to solve this. So good old-fashioned police work has to always be first, and, when we do get something that's valuable from Simon, then we'll apply it."

Rodney nodded. "In the meantime, he's connecting to somebody, and we don't know who."

Kate frowned. "I didn't ask him if it was Samantha."

"That would be good to know," Lilliana added.

"It would be good to know because I'd hate to think that we have yet another victim out there," she said, with a wince.

Everybody nodded.

Lilianna spoke up. "Still, we know what this is like for our world out there. And right now, in any given place, at least one if not one dozen women are held captive daily."

Rodney added, "Whether it's the sex-trade workers or something else altogether, it's the way the world around us operates. It sucks, and we know that, and we're doing what we can to fix it. If Simon can figure out if it's the same person in this latest vision, that would help."

Kate pulled out her phone and quickly sent him a text. "I've done that much, so we'll see if and when he gets back to me." Her phone buzzed almost immediately. She looked down at it and frowned. "He can't tell for sure." At that, everybody groaned, and she nodded. "Which is why we don't depend on these things," she muttered. "He does what he can do, and, when he has something to share, he'll pass it along."

She sat down to check on the reports from the black-and-whites assigned to look for any information regarding Simon's attack. When she didn't see one, she quickly picked up her phone and called one of the cops assigned to it.

He answered her on the first ring. "We're back out again, but nobody saw anything. It's so damn frustrating. Somebody gets assaulted in daylight, and, whether it's the truth or not, nobody's willing to admit to anything."

"Nobody wants to get involved is what it is," Kate noted. "I guess it's understandable, if you live in that corner. Anyway, keep at it and let me know if you come up with anything."

After that, she double-checked the city cameras for the surrounding area, looking to see if anything was happening near that corner. A few blocks away, she accidentally caught sight of Lisa, walking back home again, so that certainly confirmed Lisa's earlier statement. It frustrated Kate that no street cams covered that particular corner, where Simon had been dropped.

Of course not, that would be way too simple.

Groaning in frustration, she searched her inbox, looking for any reports from Smidge. When she found nothing, she hesitated but then called the coroner's office to check.

"I don't have anything new," Smidge grumbled. "Do you?"

"No, not enough. Simon, that friend of mine," she added in an abashed tone, "who's also kind of involved in this case, was attacked last night, dropped where he stood, while he was talking to me on the phone."

"Is he okay?" Smidge asked, his tone sharp.

"He is. He's home, and we're trying to keep an eye on him, making sure that it's nothing major."

"Head wounds are bad," the coroner noted, with a sigh. "I hope he's staying home, where he can recover. It's too easy for a head wound to become something much more serious, even when you thought it was nothing."

"*Great*, now you make me feel bad, and I want to go look after him."

"So you should," he snapped. "At least if you give a crap." And, with that, he disconnected.

She pinched the bridge of her nose and sat here for a long moment, wondering how everybody got to hand out judgment and advice at the same time. Yet it got her worried to the point that she wondered if she should pack it in for the day. Then she remembered the recent vision that Simon had had and realized he wouldn't appreciate her doing anything but focusing on the case. As that's what she did best, it was what she needed to focus on.

Feeling a gentle pat on her shoulder, Kate lifted her head to see Lilliana, staring at her in concern.

Kate smiled. "I'm fine, just dealing with all those well-meaning people who have advice to give, telling me that I should go and be with him, because head wounds can be tricky." Kate rolled her eyes. "Head wounds can be tricky. Still not sure what anybody thinks I'll do about it."

Lilliana gave her a commiserating look. "Everybody's full of advice and judgments," she agreed, "and it's hard to keep our own at bay, particularly doing the work we do. We see the worst in humanity, so it's easy to automatically pick up that same tainted view and apply it to everything around us. We have to see the worst in everyone in order to come up with theories and figure out what our lovely criminals are up to, but then you need to let it go. I'm not sure who you were talking to."

Kate's lips twitched. "Smidge."

Lilliana's eyes widened in horror, and she shuddered. "The fact that he even talks to you is amazing," she muttered. "No wonder you're still recovering from that call."

Kate burst out laughing. "It's not that bad."

"Yeah, Smidge is right. Head wounds need to be watched. We know that, but Simon appears to be doing okay."

Kate immediately nodded. "I think he's doing fine. In a way, he's doing better than we are."

"Why is that?" Owen asked, as he came back with a huge mug of coffee. On the cup were the words *Monday sucks, but then so does every day.*

Kate winced. "That's a very depressing cup."

"I know, and I really like it." He flashed her a bright grin and headed to his desk.

She sighed. "Is that what our role's down to, that every day just plain sucks?"

"Sometimes," he admitted, still with a grin. "What else will you do? Live and learn, keep up the good fight. It is what it is."

She ignored him and turned back to Lilliana. "Do we have anything to go on?"

"Which case?" Lilliana asked in a wry tone. "We've got Samantha, though none of us have a case file for, a known missing person, apparently locked up someplace with no light, with a guy who keeps bringing her food but doesn't rape her. So not likely to be Samantha that Simon connected with earlier today, when watching the guy with a belt go up some stairs."

"But Simon asked Samantha if her kidnapper hurt her, and she said yes, just no details, other than *not rape yet*. Maybe he's been beating Samantha," Kate suggested.

They all contemplated that for a moment.

Lilliana broke the silence. "Okay, so, if these current murders are connected to the cold cases from eight years ago—meaning we have a serial killer who woke up from his nap—what would trigger a rebirth of this behavior?"

Kate nodded. "That's what I don't understand. If our serial killer was in jail and is free now, that might do it. The killer is no longer confined, not under guard, and can now continue his killing spree. That's from the killer's viewpoint. However, we could have a family member of a victim seeking revenge on the killer. Maybe mom or dad see the killer walking around free and clear, or completely unfazed by the pain his murders caused, or unaware and even not giving a shit about what happened to these people left behind."

"Did you talk to the shrink?" Lilliana asked Kate.

Kate slumped lower into her chair and glared at her. Kate was about to answer when the door opened and Sergeant Colby walked in. "I heard that last question." He turned to pin Kate with a hard gaze.

"No, I haven't seen him yet," she replied irritably.

"Go. Now."

She glared at him, and he motioned toward the door. She jumped to her feet, snatched a notepad, and walked away, heading toward the shrink's office—the last place she wanted to go. She always felt that, no matter what she said, somebody would judge her for it.

Even worse, where she would now judge the shrink.

HAVING TALKED TO Kate, Simon was somewhat better balanced over his latest vision. He grabbed his notebook and checked what he had written. Then his foreman had called with a problem, and, by the time Simon solved that one, another problem arose and yet one more after that. It didn't take long for his entire morning to be eaten away with troubleshooting, but that's also how his days often went.

As he worked at his business day, he finally sat down with a cup of iced coffee and his notebook and started a to-do list. Only now, he felt himself nodding off. By the time he jerked awake again, he realized that he had drifted into a solid forty-minute nap.

He got up and stretched, feeling remarkably better. As he reached for his notepad, he froze because the notes written on it weren't what he expected to see.

He had been sleeping. Simon was sure he had been sleeping. Yet something on his notepad hadn't been there before. Instinctively he turned to look around, but he was still alone. He had to wonder if he had written the message. It was scrawled in really crappy handwriting, so was it his? Or was it something completely different? He studied the mess, trying to make sense out of the word and finally came up with *Samantha*.

He groaned, as he sat down again. "Samantha, I get it. I just don't know what I'm supposed to do about it."

If she had reached out to get through to him while he was asleep, had she been sending other messages that he wasn't receiving because of his injury? What messages could he possibly receive, when as injured as he had been?

Knowing it wouldn't do any good, he answered right back, via the same damn notepad, feeling like an absolute idiot. *Samantha, I'm here.* As soon as his pen lifted from the notepad, a voice slammed into his head. *Help me. Help me. Help me, help me, help me.*

He covered both his ears, as he tried to stop the litany of never-ending screams in his head. And finally when they slowed to a din, he collapsed in his chair, shaking, his whole body in shock from what had just happened. He could almost hear his grandmother say, *Well, what did you expect? You opened a door, and, as soon as you do that, people always want to come in.*

Sometimes it was damn irritating to have his grand-mother's voice be this litany in his head, and yet other times it was reassuring, somehow letting him know that what was happening was what was always happening, and it was normal, even if he didn't like it. He took several slow deep breaths, not sure how to help this Samantha person because he didn't even know who she was or where she was.

He called back out to the room around him. "Tell me where you are, give me something so that I can find you."

Instead the voice screamed—one long, loud, and drawn-out scream. *Find me.*

CHAPTER 18

A T THE END of the day, Kate still couldn't believe they were no further ahead. They had checked into Samantha's family, looking for any answers, but basically everybody confirmed that Samantha had left work on foot, going home, and nobody heard from her again. Samantha's mother swore up and down that no way her daughter would have disappeared like that, without something being wrong, and her mother was grateful that at least somebody was listening to them now, but why the hell hadn't anybody given a shit before?

Kate tried to explain about Samantha being of an age, where she could easily leave on her own, but, of course, her mother wasn't interested in hearing about it. And Kate, if it were her daughter missing, she wouldn't have either. But they could do only so much, when they didn't have anything to go on, other than a woman had disappeared. Outside of Simon, they could still be looking at the fact that this woman could be visiting friends and decided not to tell anybody, or she had taken a walk off a bridge, and her body had yet to surface.

The latter possibility still came to Kate's mind and brought shudders to her soul after of her recent cases, where she'd been dealing with suicides—and yet not suicides—in one of the most twisted cases she'd ever seen. Of course she didn't have the experience of everybody else here on this journey, but it was definitely at the top of theirs too.

Kate went up to the front steps of Simon's building to see Harry racing toward her to open the door.

She held up the takeout bags that she had collected on her way home. "Have you heard from him at all?"

Harry laughed. "I heard from Edgar that Simon did have a fancy for a pretzel this morning. So, as soon as I came on shift, I checked up on him, and he said he was fine. That was some hours ago."

She cracked a big grin and nodded. "He does like his food, doesn't he?"

"He does, indeed, and that's a good sign."

"Can't argue with you there." She walked to the private elevator and hit the button for Simon's penthouse.

Harry asked, "You want me to tell him that you're coming?"

She shook her head. "No, it's a surprise this time."

He nodded, and she wasn't sure whether he would say something or not. It was hard to let go of a lot of training, even though she was here on a regular basis. For all she knew, the doormen were instructed to tell her that they wouldn't tell Simon, but that was the first thing they'd do the minute she disappeared from sight. She couldn't blame them. Whatever happened, happened, and she'd deal with it.

As it was, when she arrived, Simon looked up from the kitchen table and smiled.

"I guess with this elevator, you get plenty of warning when somebody is coming anyway, don't you?"

He shrugged. "I don't know about *plenty* of warning, but having the only penthouse does mean that, if the elevator is coming, it's coming for me." He gave her a big smile.

"Besides, you're always welcome."

"Well, I did tell Harry not to alert you that I was on my way, not so much because I wanted to surprise you," she admitted, "but more because I was afraid you'd be napping."

"*Napping*," he repeated. "You make that sound as if I'm a two-year-old."

She lifted an eyebrow. "Did you not have a nap today?"

He stared at her and asked, "How did you know?"

She shrugged. "I'd texted you a couple times, and I didn't get a response. When you did respond, it was maybe an hour, an hour and a half later."

He shook his head. "Yes, I did get a nap," he stated crossly. "And, apparently while I was sleeping"—he picked up his notepad and tossed it in front of her on the table—"I wrote this."

She read it and then slowly nodded. "So, she's reaching out for you?"

He nodded. "She's reaching out for me, while I was at my most vulnerable, and she made contact."

"And you responded?"

"I don't know that she heard my response," he said, and then he told her the rest.

Shaken, she sat down and looked over at him in concern. "That's a little on the disturbing side. Are you okay?"

"A little disturbing?" he repeated, with an eye roll. "I would have used a much stronger word than that."

She wasn't sure what to say, but to think of somebody screaming in his head had to be disturbing. "You appear to be fairly adjusted to it," she noted cautiously, looking at him for any sign that it was upsetting him.

"Oh, I was upset at the time," he muttered. "But ..." Then he shrugged. "What am I supposed to do about it?"

"I don't know. … This is your deal, not my deal," she told him, raising her hands in surrender. "I have no advice to give."

"And yet you are most often the one who tells me exactly what to do."

She frowned. "Hardly," she muttered. "Unless it's telling you to take a hike."

He burst out laughing at that. "How was your day?"

She pondered how to answer and then shrugged. "Frustrating, irritating. We checked up on people's stories. We found Elizabeth's brother in jail, just like Smidge suggested, so he's in the clear. We're looking for answers from a multitude of different directions, and, sure, there are answers but not good answers. I called Samantha's parents, who were alternately happy someone was looking for their daughter and angry it took this long."

"Of course," Simon agreed, "and, for you, you can only solve things if and when something breaks. That hasn't happened yet."

"We do what we can do with the information at hand," she explained, "and, what most people don't understand is, … too often we need other murders, other nastiness to happen, before we can get a clear shot at solving this. If we have no witnesses, nobody shows up in any cameras, and all we have is a body? Sometimes we have no forensics to deal with. In fact, I am still waiting for Smidge to get me whatever he can for answers, so there isn't really much I can do. That drives me crazy."

He smiled and nodded. "Of course. And I really didn't expect you to have any answers, at least not yet," he replied, "and I sure as hell don't have anything to offer, … so we're at a stalemate."

"Which is not where either one of us want to be," she said gently. "I get that you're trying to help, and I appreciate that you did make an attempt to reach out. I also realize that it probably isn't fair to even ask it of you, but I'm going to anyway."

He studied her and shook his head. "This really has you stumped, *huh*?"

"I'm not happy about it. Believe me. If I had anything else that I could do that would answer or solve some of this, I'd be there in a heartbeat, but, barring any other options, what am I supposed to do?"

"I won't argue with you on that." He sank deeper into the chair across from her. He sniffed the air and asked, "Did you bring food?" He bolted to his feet.

She nodded. "I had this idea that you might want food, but I hear you sent somebody out on a mission to pick up a pretzel."

"Sure, and that pretzel was a very long time ago," he stated, looking at her in joy. "What did you pick up?" She shrugged as he walked over, opened the bag, and the aroma of souvlaki filled the kitchen. "Oh, good choice," As he quickly took out the packages of food, she laughed. "I thought I was the one driven by food."

"You are," Simon agreed, "but I'm learning."

And, with that, he quickly served up two plates, and they sat in a comfortable spot in the kitchen and ate. As soon as she was done, she looked over at him and asked, "What about that direction thing you were working on? To even think about somebody out there waiting to be rescued, it's heartbreaking," she murmured.

He nodded. "It's more than heartbreaking. I'm just … out of ideas. That's why I did what I did. I am willing to go out again, but I need to feel better first. Samantha keeps reaching out. I keep reaching back, but it's not getting us anywhere."

"And yet, downtown at that corner where you were attacked, you told me that *Samantha's here.*"

He nodded slowly. "I remember you saying that, but I don't remember saying it or why I thought it."

She nodded. "How are you feeling?"

He slowly put down his empty plate and in a wary voice asked, "What is it you want me to do?"

She hesitated, then shrugged. "I might as well ask. I don't know what else to do." She was in a tough spot. "Samantha's not exactly on my caseload." She took a moment to add, "We usually don't handle missing persons, and I don't have a body, but ..."

"But?" he asked cautiously.

She studied him. "I thought maybe we could take a trip to the same area and see if you picked up on her energy again."

He slowly nodded. "That's a good idea. Particularly if we go together."

"Yet it's also quite possibly a terrible idea because I don't want you to go if you're not up to it."

"You will be there to protect me?" he asked again, his smile splitting his face wide.

"I'll be there, and obviously I'll do my best. However, I might not be able to protect you from the boogeyman—who knocked you flat on your ass without any warning—because I don't even see those guys coming."

He stared at her for a long time and then cracked a smile. "Just the thought of you standing guard, waiting for a boogeyman to come jump out of nowhere to attack me, and be on guard for me? I will tell you that it does warm the cockles of my heart."

"Cockles of your heart? What the hell does that even mean?"

"I'm not sure," he admitted cheerfully, as he glanced at his watch, looked outside, and asked, "Why don't we go now?"

His change in demeanor was so abrupt that she frowned at him. "Is there a reason to go now?" she asked.

He stared at her, and an oddly disquiet look filled his gaze.

She immediately hopped to her feet. "Let's go."

But he was slow to rise, and, when he got to his feet, she was not sure that he would hold up on his own. "Unless you can't travel."

"I can travel," he said. "I don't know how far I can walk, if something happens."

She chewed on her bottom lip, as she contemplated the thought of a downed Simon out there. "That's really not making me feel very confident," she muttered.

"Not supposed to," he noted, equally unsure. "But, yeah, something out there's calling me. So let's go."

He walked to the elevator, and she cried out, "Wait, wait, wait. What do you mean, *something's calling to you?*"

But he was already in some weird zone. She watched his features shift and change, but he was determined to get out that door. She groaned and followed him. "I'd really feel better if you did this at home."

"I need to go," he declared.

She felt that urgency in his tone deep in her soul. "Fine," she muttered, "but I'm driving."

She quickly led him to her car, trying hard to make it

look as if he was completely normal, as they got through the reception area. As they headed out of the parking in her vehicle, she glanced at him. "Where am I going?"

"To the women's shelter," he replied, his voice in a flat monotone.

Kate noted that Simon wasn't sure anything was wrong at the women's shelter, but still something was off about that area. … She didn't say anything but drove quickly in that direction. When they got there, he looked around and pointed out the parking lot off to the side. The sign said *paid parking*.

"Pull in there."

They pulled into the parking lot. She hopped out, grabbed a ticket, shoved it onto the dashboard of her vehicle, and turned to look at him, one of her eyebrows raised.

She fell behind him, as they headed down the street to where he'd been attacked. When they got there, he looked around and asked, "Is this where I was attacked?" A puzzled note filled his voice.

She smiled up at him. "Yes, this is where we found you."

"I don't feel like it was here though."

"Well, it was."

He stood here, closed his eyes, and probably mentally asked where he needed to go. Almost instantly his feet started moving in a specific direction. As he kept going, Kate raced to keep up. Apparently right now, he needed to be someplace, and someplace fast. She didn't say anything, just followed along, her gaze constantly searching the area.

⚬⚬⚬

SIMON COULDN'T FOCUS on Kate; he was too busy focusing on the message in his brain. He wished to God he knew if that message was something that he should be following because there was always a chance that somebody was yanking his chain, as his grandmother would have said.

When his feet came to a stop, he looked around. They were standing at a slightly different corner, almost on top of the women's shelter. Then the urgency stopped. Confused, he searched the area.

"Maybe close your eyes again, and see what's coming up," Kate suggested.

He immediately did so, happy that she was not judging him. His feet turned in another direction and headed back the way they came. Again she didn't say anything. She just walked beside him. He wasn't sure what was going on or in what way this had anything to do with him, but he seemed almost powerless to change it.

They walked for another few minutes, and then he came to a dead stop and whispered, "Here."

She turned and eyed the area carefully. "Okay," she murmured. "Here what?"

He opened his eyes and looked around, bewildered. "I don't know, Kate, but here's important."

"Who's saying it's important?" she asked cautiously. "Is it Samantha, or is it somebody else?"

"I don't know," he admitted. "All I can tell you is that *here is important*." He heard his own frustration, knowing that wouldn't help. Still it was hard to back off enough to let *whatever this was* be something all on its own—to not analyze, to not judge, to just let the information flow—and then he smiled sadly.

"She was kidnapped. From here." He turned to look at Kate. "Samantha Cole was kidnapped from this spot."

CHAPTER 19

HAVING TAKEN SIMON back home again, Kate now bolted to her office, determined to see if anything showed on the street cameras. She had to go back to the day that the woman had been reported as missing. She opened up the appropriate website, quickly double-checked, and, when she finally got access to the cameras at that intersection, she backed it up several weeks, hoping to find something. She managed to get to the correct date, and, as she stared at the screen, watching what was going on, she saw a young woman walking down the street, casually yet tired, as in the end of the day had come, and she had been more than ready for it.

As Kate continued to watch, the woman yawned, covered it up with her hand, looked around, and was about to cross the street, when a vehicle drove past. It then turned around on a one-way street, tucked in off to the side, the wrong way of all things, making it extremely obvious that he was there, hopped out, and walked up behind her, seemingly calling out to her. She turned around to see him, and he reached out a hand, as if he were an old friend. Almost instantly she collapsed into his arms.

So a hypodermic syringe was used.

Her kidnapper half-walked her, half-carried her to his vehicle, dropped her into the back seat, completely uncaring as to whether she sat or collapsed, quickly raced around to his driver's side, hopped into the vehicle, and took off.

When the door opened to the bullpen, she looked up to see Rodney coming in.

He nodded. "There's something about you," he muttered, "but I knew that I needed to come into the office. I wasn't sure why."

She raised her eyebrows. "You could have called."

"Yeah, probably should have too, or you could have called," he quipped, with half a grin. "What did you find?"

She winced. "Simon."

"Okay, what did Simon find?" he asked for clarity.

"I'm not exactly sure, but he says he found where Samantha was kidnapped from."

"Okay, good enough, and where was that? Anything we can use?"

She nodded. "Even better, I found it on the street cams."

He stared at her in shock and then bolted to stand beside her monitors. "What the hell," he mumbled, as he watched the kidnapping take place. "And, just like that, she's gone."

"And that's the problem. It's that easy from the looks of it," Kate remarked, "but, outside of this evidence, … we don't have any idea on facial features or even if it's male or female."

He played it back again and then nodded. "Unfortunately you're right, but I would assume it's a male."

"Sure," Kate agreed. "It's easy to make that assumption, but I'd feel better if I saw that for myself."

He didn't say anything but played it back a couple more times and then sat in the nearest chair. "Well, damn," he muttered. "Shit, that is huge though."

"It is, and confirms the fact that we have a kidnapping

case to go on," she pointed out. "Glad to confirm that it's not Simon's imagination."

Rodney's lips twitched at that, but he nodded. "Where did this person take her and why? Plus, I hate to ask, but do you think it's connected to the other vision Simon had of somebody climbing stairs?"

"It's possible," Kate noted. "I won't say it isn't. Samantha did tell Simon that her kidnapper was hurting her. We don't know in what way, but she denied being raped."

"Still we don't know if that stands true *now* though," he pointed out. "Those were the first messages from her, and that situation could have changed any damn time in the last few days. God help her if it has," he murmured.

"But I don't know that this person is connected in any way to our current murder cases."

"Right." He slumped in his chair. "That confuses the issue entirely."

"I feel as if we've gotten derailed from our Clement murder," Kate shared, "except for the fact that, once again, Simon's in the middle of it."

"He is in the middle of it. Whether we like it or not, he's still trying to do what he does best, which is answer these messages."

"It's helping us, but he's not coming back with a link," Kate said, "for want of a better word."

"No, you're right. Absolutely nothing here clarifies how these cases are connected, much less who our killer-slash-kidnapper may be."

They sat and pondered the street cam video, and she played it again and then again. "In each case, the kidnapper's face is never revealed, making sure that his features wouldn't be seen."

"That would be my take on it."

"He also used a syringe, which unfortunately people can get almost anywhere," she pointed out. "So we can't even determine that the kidnapper's male."

"Right." Rodney groaned. "Even the way he half-carries, half-shuffles Samantha to the vehicle could be to hide the fact that he's kidnapping her, instead saying she was ill. Also there's no visible license plate. But our tech guys should pull the make and model of the vehicle from this video."

She agreed with him on all points, but, for her, it wasn't enough. "All that is true." She rubbed her eyes.

Rodney noted, "Seems you need to get some sleep."

"Sure," she muttered, "but saying that doesn't mean it'll happen."

"Maybe not," he agreed, "but sitting here, rattling our brains, with no lead to follow, won't help either."

He had a point. She groaned, as she got up and walked around and paced. "There has to be a way to track that vehicle."

"Did you check the other video cameras to see if we have anything that gives us a direction of the vehicle, after she's been picked up? Let me look." He shifted to sit in her vacated chair. "We might follow this to another location and pick it up somewhere along the line."

She nodded. "You do that. I'll grab coffee."

"Grab me one too," he said absentmindedly.

She headed over to the coffeepot and put on a pot, given the hour and their task at hand. By the time she had that done, she headed back to find Rodney, with a fat grin on his face. "Did you find it?" she asked, stopping at her desk, still holding two coffee mugs.

He nodded. "Picked up the vehicle several blocks away,

and now, at least, I have a license plate."

"Can we track where it went?"

"I'm on it. That's where I'm at right now."

As he sat here, she watched from behind him, as he followed the vehicle, giving them a merry dance. "It's almost as if they were expecting the vehicle to be followed," she murmured.

"I would assume that, if they're into kidnapping, they must be fully aware that this will get them in a lot of trouble, if caught. So, sure, they're trying to evade capture, and that means evading arrest without being seen," he replied.

"Assholes," she said, with a groan. "It would be nice if the criminals would screw up every once in a while and give us a break."

Rodney burst out laughing. "Where'd the fun be in that?" He started to swear a few minutes later. She eyed him warily, and he finally spoke. "I lost him." He backtracked the video. "I don't understand how or why, but look."

She watched the driver's evasive maneuvers. "You don't think anybody was picking up on their location, do you?"

"I don't think so," Rodney said. "We don't have any reports about it."

"Or do we?" she muttered, as she stepped over to his computer, brought it up online, and quickly did a search to see if she noted anything in the traffic cams or in the reports.

"I think the kidnapper may have backtracked around again," he muttered.

"What do you mean?" She stopped her search to look over at him.

He shrugged. "That's what I'm trying to figure out, but that does appear to be what he's doing."

She got up, walked over, and took another look. "But

where's he going?"

"I don't know."

And, just then, the vehicle disappeared into a parkade and was gone. "But that's a downtown parkade," she pointed out.

"I know, and chances are, we'll find that vehicle sitting there since the date of her kidnapping," Rodney complained.

"Crap," she muttered. "Then chances are, we'll find out that it's stolen."

"That would be my take," he muttered, "but we need to find out for sure anyway."

When Kate's monitor buzzed, Rodney crowed, "There it is. The license plate did come through."

She saw it, nodded. "What do you think the chances are that it's stolen?"

"I'd say 100 percent, but we'll find out." He quickly ran it through another database to see if it had popped up anywhere on a police report, and he nodded. "There's no mention of it being stolen but considering it's a long-term lease lot and the car owner is in Europe, maybe they have no idea what happened to their vehicle?"

"So why her? What about Samantha triggered this?" Kate muttered. "What made her a target?"

"Are you still thinking that she's connected to our three DBs?"

"I don't know whether she's connected or not," she admitted, with a shrug. "We can't assume either way."

"Well, let's get a black-and-white to check out the kidnapping vehicle," he muttered. He made the phone calls, while they waited. When the callback came a couple hours later, they were still sitting here, going over the evidence that they had collected so far.

As Rodney answered the phone, he looked over at her, while asking the techs, "Yes, did you find the vehicle? … You did. Interesting." He grinned. "Apparently it's a long-term lease," he told Kate, as soon as the information was relayed to him.

She nodded. "That makes a sick kind of sense too. We need to get forensics on that vehicle."

"Let's go check it out and confirm it's the right one," he muttered.

She was already grabbing her jacket. "You really think it's the wrong one?"

"It's not that I think it's the wrong one or the right one," he clarified. "I just want to make sure before we involve forensics."

She added, "You know perfectly well that we'll get there and have to turn around and call them. If we do, then you make that call."

"Are you sure?" Rodney asked.

"It's the same license plate," Kate noted, "and, yes, I am that confident."

They got there at the same time forensics did. As they neared the vehicle, she called out, "Check the trunk first." The forensics team turned to her, now very wary. She shrugged. "We're pretty sure this vehicle was used in a kidnapping," she explained. "I don't know whether it was used again or anything was left inside, potentially another body." One of the team walked to the back of the vehicle, opened the trunk, and even Kate saw it was empty. "Thank God for that."

He called back to her, "But blood is in here. I'm not sure whose, but we will find out." And, with that, forensics got to work.

She looked over at Rodney. "Why the hell would there be blood?"

"I don't know." Rodney stared at the activity going on around him. "I wasn't expecting blood."

"Neither was I," she muttered.

They had worried that this vehicle had, indeed, become Samantha's grave and that they had found her too late. As they sat, their arms crossed, waiting to see if anything else came out of this forensics detail, Rodney turned to Kate. "And you still don't think this is connected."

"I *do* think it's connected," she corrected. "I just don't know how. We don't know anybody else, anything else, that connects this case—except for Simon. Meanwhile, because he's sending us looking for Samantha, that really doesn't mean it's connected to Elizabeth's murder, or Luca's."

"Or Patricia's."

"I know." Kate moaned. "That one hurts a lot. I can't help thinking that I shouldn't have sent her home that night."

"And yet she had already checked out of the hospital because she wanted to go home. She would not have wanted any interference from you."

"What about assistance?" Kate asked in a low tone. "What about a suggestion that she not go home alone?"

"I'm pretty sure that she knew all that anyway."

"The one thing that I keep coming back to is that she went looking for drugs. What if she had gone for drugs prior to this as well? What if somebody had seen her? What if somebody knew her?"

"Who are you thinking?"

She shrugged. "I guess … I want to double-check her brother's alibi." Rodney swore. She shook her head. "I'm reaching for straws, but what if he was mad enough that she was sliding backward again?"

"What then? So he took her out and made her walk barefoot on sharp rocks as a punishment?" he asked incredulously.

"Maybe not," she relented. "Maybe that was somebody else. But what if the brother found out that Patricia had gone on a drug binge, and he killed her in a fury? Maybe he'd read some of the related newspaper articles. Maybe he'd decided to cover it up afterward. I don't know. I just ... Why wouldn't somebody care?"

"Meaning that so few people cared about Patricia, then why does this person care enough to kill her?" Rodney frowned.

"It's not that so few people cared about Patricia," Kate clarified, "because we know that the people who cared were the ones who mattered, and they got her off the streets, got her cleaned up, and gave her a new life, but somebody snuffed out that life. *Why* is the part I am struggling so hard to get. Why was she chosen? If it wasn't because of her history, then why, why pick her?"

"Who knows," Rodney muttered in a weary tone. "Maybe because she had brown hair."

"And sometimes it's just that stupid, isn't it?" Kate turned to face him.

He nodded. "Sometimes you're just in the wrong place at the wrong time, and you look like an easy victim. In this case, ... maybe because Patricia was connected to that women's shelter. Maybe they've really got this hate on there."

"Which is why I've been running through everybody we have on the books who has been through that place."

"When you say, *on the books*, what do you mean?" Rodney asked.

"I know. I highly suspect they help a lot of people who aren't *on the books*," she admitted. "A better answer than that I can't really give you. It seems to me that people out there, helping others, they'll be a whole lot less concerned about making sure that paperwork is connected to them and in order."

"And yet it makes a difference to their grant money."

"Sure. But, if you've got a husband ready to beat the crap out of his wife, will you immediately help her or will you worry about paperwork to secure the grant money?"

"Both," he stated immediately. "It's what keeps them going."

"And yet they're not doing very well," Kate stated, remembering her recent conversation with Lisa Sands. "I don't want to say that they're starving because obviously they're a step above that, but the place was in woeful shape when I saw it."

"Crap," Rodney muttered. "That's our tax dollars *not* at work."

"It is to an extent, and there'll always be a certain amount of government funding for these places, but it does make you wonder how much of it is enough to do what they need it to do, and how much of it is not even close."

"I imagine a lot of it isn't even close," Rodney guessed. "If that shelter gets thirty people in a month, is that a lot or is that a few?"

Kate frowned. "Lisa mentioned twenty-something as being a lot, but is that based on fluctuating funding or the rooms available? I didn't really have that talk with her."

"Sounds as if you might need to. I can go, if you want."

She shook her head. "I think the fewer male appearances in that shelter, the better. Lisa won't like it. And Helen? … She will be so pissed."

"How about cop interferences?" he asked, his voice hardening.

She smiled at him. "Not trying to keep you out of the loop here. Just letting you know that these women have been battered time and time again by the men in their lives. Therefore, I want to minimize their pain, if I can."

He nodded and settled back. "That's fine, but I don't want to leave you inside for too long, just in case."

She gave him a smirk. "In case of what?"

"You don't know *what*." He took a deep breath, as if trying to arrange his thoughts. "A lot of strange people are out there. Let's not have somebody attack you because we didn't consider that it could be somebody from the shelter."

Kate frowned. "And that goes back to the fact that we don't know for sure that our perp is male or female, doesn't it?"

He nodded. "Knowing and even making that small distinction … would help too."

Just then forensics called them over. "Nothing's here but lots of trace evidence," he stated in a businesslike tone. "No weapons. A small amount of blood. I wouldn't say that anybody dead was moved from here, but we will do our full run on it, especially if you've got a kidnapping connected to this vehicle."

"We do," she stated in a forceful tone. "The vehicle was caught on camera."

The lead forensics tech nodded. "You guys don't need to stay. Go home. Get some sleep. Then you're ready to catch the bad guys another day."

As his spiel had a half-loopy rhyme to it, she rolled her eyes at him and then shrugged. "That's pretty corny."

"Hey, it's best I can do at this hour."

She checked her watch and noted it was 1:00 a.m. "Sorry, guess we should have towed it in."

He shrugged. "As we have a kidnapping right now, let's deal with what we've got, and we'll take it back to the lot later."

"Good enough." Kate waved goodbye and looked back over at Rodney. "Bedtime."

"Sounds good to me." He yawned. "I'll see you back here in the morning."

"Here?" she asked, with an eyebrow raised.

"No, not here." He laughed. "I'll see you in the morning." And, with that, he took off.

She slowly stepped out from the car park, looked around, wondering what would make this place a nice alternative to anything else somebody could have thought up. She walked to the manned parkade ticket booth and asked, "Do you guys keep somebody on staff twenty-four hours a day?"

He shook his head. "Nope, but when the cops came, they sent me in here to keep an eye on things."

She nodded. "And that vehicle is a long-term lease, you said?"

"I didn't say it," he corrected. "Nobody officially asked me about it, but it is long-term, yes."

"Okay, so that must have been your boss we talked to earlier."

He nodded. "If that was on the phone, yes," he stated in a bored voice. "He's the one who called me in to keep an eye on you."

"Yeah, as if we'll steal something."

"I don't think it's that as much as the fact that there's always been a certain number of problems around this place, and we do try to keep it contained," he noted. "However, there are problems, and then there are problems."

"When you say, *problems*, exactly what do you mean by that?"

"Break-ins, couple of thefts, uninvited guests, that sort of thing."

"And yet you're not here twenty-four hours a day?"

"No, but we did set up a new security system." He gave a quick shrug. "Although it's only been functional for a couple weeks."

"Of course it has been. Can you tell if this vehicle has left the lot in the last few weeks?"

He went to his records, and, after a few minutes on the computer, he shook his head. "I don't have any record of it leaving the lot, except for around three weeks ago." He gave her the date. Which coincided perfectly with Samantha's disappearance.

She pulled up a picture of Samantha on her phone and held it up to him. "You ever see this woman?"

He looked at it and shook his head. "No, sure haven't. Why? What's going on?"

"She was kidnapped in that vehicle three weeks ago, the night you mentioned," she stated. "Nobody's seen her since."

"Ah, shit." The color drained from his face. "I really don't like hearing that."

He might not like hearing that, but she had a whole lot more to go. "Do you see any people around here on a regular basis, anybody who makes you question why they're here?"

He shook his head. "And, if there was, we would question them. We would immediately head over and talk to them to find out what they were doing. No loitering's allowed. It's not that we have a homeless problem in this particular area, but you always have to watch out for people looking to break into cars. That's never a good thing either."

"Of course not," she muttered.

Not sure what else to ask, she finally asked him if any regulars were here that he had trouble with—or anybody the opposite, almost too ingratiating.

He frowned at her and slowly shook his head. "No, but obviously from now on, I'll be wondering," he muttered, as he looked around. He shook his head, as his gaze went in the direction where all the forensic vehicles were. "Really don't like hearing about a kidnapping. That sucks."

"If you see anybody acting suspiciously or you hear anything off, let me know, will you?" She handed him a card and then turned and walked away.

SIMON OPENED THE door to Kate. She looked tired, worn out, and it was the early hours in the morning. "What the hell?" He rushed her inside. "You look exhausted."

"Yeah, well, that's what happens when you go wandering around, checking out areas. We found the vehicle used to kidnap Samantha." He stopped in his tracks. She shook her head. "There was no sign of her and no blood, outside of a little bit in the trunk of the kidnap vehicle."

He closed his eyes in relief and then opened them. "So you have the vehicle. ... Then that means you have the owner."

"It was parked in a long-term car park. The owner is in Europe. By the looks of it, has been for a couple months now, doing some internship."

"Jesus, so somebody might have known that."

"Somebody could have known that, or somebody could have also just taken a vehicle that they potentially hadn't seen moved in a while. Whether that means weeks or months, or whether they know the owner of the vehicle, I don't know. It's an opportunity, but it's not an answer."

Simon nodded slowly, as he put on the teakettle and then turned to her. "Did you eat?"

She shook her head. "I raced out of here, after I left you, headed to the office, and within a few hours we had the vehicle. Now that's good news."

"What about video cameras?"

"I found on the feed where Samantha was kidnapped, just a few corners away from the women's shelter." He frowned at that, and she nodded. "I know, but I don't think Samantha had anything to do with that place." And then she stopped, when a strange expression crossed his face. "Did she?"

"I have no idea." Simon raised his hands in frustration. "I don't personally have anything to do with her." He busied himself making tea and then turned to look at Kate. "I had groceries brought in. Do you want some toast and eggs?"

She nodded. "That would be great, and then I'll crash for a few hours, before I meet Rodney at the office." She yawned just then.

"Maybe you want to sleep before eating?" When she looked at him bleary-eyed, he nodded. "Taking the decision away from you." He nudged her onto her feet. "Let's get you to bed. You can have some food in the morning."

With her tucked into bed, sleep was a long way off for him. He checked his watch, but it was way too early to contact Lisa. He went through all his files, but he had absolutely nothing on Samantha Cole or any record of anybody working at that car park or any of the businesses around the women's shelter. And he worked with multiple women's shelters, and they were all hidden in the city. It never occurred to him that anybody would be hitting a women's shelter because of his assistance.

Exhausted, he decided to crash and get a few hours sleep, before Kate got up and hit the road again. As he went to lie down, he got back up again, feeling an odd disassociation. He closed his eyes, sat back down, and immediately stood up again and walked out of the bedroom.

And then a voice behind him said, "Stop."

He froze.

"Now take five more steps in front of you."

He immediately took five more steps, and yet he came up against a wall before he completed the fifth. He slammed his nose against it and cried out, wincing, only to realize he'd been walking with his eyes closed. In the background he heard laughter, harsh caustic laughter. He froze as he realized that he had connected to the asshole or to the victim who was doing the walking.

He tried to connect again to see where they were, but all he got was the same bedroom. As he tried to drift himself further back in time, he was back out in the woods. He could almost smell the pine around him. It was the strangest of feelings. He sat back down on his bed, buried his face in his hands, while he tried to figure out if he could pull anything good from this.

Kate gently stroked his arm and whispered, "What's the matter?"

He twisted to look at her and replied, "The asshole has

somebody out walking again." Her gaze went from sleepy to sharp in seconds. He always loved that about her mind. Something was so awe-inspiring, seeing somebody so aware and so intent, so focused. So many people would say that they lived in the present, but really they were always reminiscing about the past or dreaming about the future. But, in Kate's case, she was right here; she was present in every conversation, and right now she was locked on to every word he said.

"Tell me everything," she replied, as she shifted upright.

He closed his eyes and explained about sitting and then standing and afterward hearing about the order to walk five paces.

She nodded slowly. "Okay. Could you sense anything about a location? Could you sense anything about the voice?"

"He was having way too much fun, for one," Simon noted. "As far as the location, all I got was a really strong sense of pine."

"So you were outside. Did it rustle under your feet? Could you feel anything?"

"No, that was weird. Almost as if I snapped out of it before I could sense what was under my feet." He lifted a foot and stared. "Jesus Christ," he cried out.

She shifted and turned on a light. His feet were completely black. She bolted off the bed and slammed up against the far wall, her hand across her mouth.

He shook his head. "I have no idea." He got up slowly and gingerly walked into the bathroom, and sure enough he could wash it off. His shaky hand reached up to pull his hair off his face, as he stared in the mirror. "Grammie, you didn't tell me about this part," he whispered. He stared back down at his feet, but they were clean now. If not for the dirty washcloth in front of him, he would have thought for sure he had imagined the whole thing. As he stepped back into the bedroom, he realized Kate would never forget this.

"Please tell me that you were out walking when that voice told you to walk."

He frowned. "No, I *was here,* in the bedroom."

She nodded. "And earlier, any chance your feet were dirty from before?"

"I have no idea, … but I don't think so."

"It has to be because that, … that doesn't make any sense, Simon."

"Maybe not," he agreed, "but stuff does manifest, even if we don't want it to."

"Hell, I don't want it to," she declared. "That fucking terrifies me."

He nodded, and feeling more alone than he ever had in his life, he slowly walked back to the bed and laid down, very close to the edge. He closed his eyes and in a weary tone said, "Just sleep. We'll deal with it in the morning."

And he rolled over, pulled the blanket up to his shoulders and closed his eyes.

CHAPTER 20

KATE HAD EVERY right to be terrified, but, as she stared at Simon's still body on the bed, she realized that he wasn't feeling any better. She groaned, walked over to his side of the bed, sat down, and wrapped herself around him. "I'm sorry. This shit never seems to calm down."

He didn't say anything, but he seemed to relax a little bit under her arm. She kissed him on the neck and whispered, "I'm sorry. I wasn't saying *you* fucking terrify me," she murmured. "I was saying this whole psychic stuff terrifies me."

He shifted enough so that he could roll onto his back and look at her, and she saw the hurt, the pain, in his eyes. She made a muffled sound and buried her face against his neck, hugging him hard.

Slowly, finally, he wrapped his arms around her and held her tight.

She sighed. "You don't have any control over that … but, Jesus."

"I know that it's not what you signed up for," he stated in an oddly formal voice.

She reared back and glared down at him. "Don't fucking say that. None of us sign up for any of this shit. Just because I didn't sign up for it … doesn't mean I'll walk away. Terrified or not, I'm not a quitter, and I will be here."

And she glared down at him, wanting to see a change. When his gaze warmed, and he snatched her back into his arms, she felt tears and wasn't sure if they were hers or his. Her heart full, she tilted her head back and kissed his chin, then his jawbone, cheeks, finally his nose.

Before she knew it, she was flipped onto her back and pinned in place. His dark gaze locked on hers, as he stared into her eyes. She opened her mouth to speak, when he lowered his head, sealing her words forever inside. But the heat flared from a slow burn to a fiery conflagration within seconds—almost as if the need for the acceptance found in this feeling between them, could burn away the fear of what could lie ahead. Yet that incident would forever be burned into their hearts and souls. And the fire burned brightly as they stripped to the skin, leaving nothing between them.

The complete transparency was needed—at least in this very intimate act, before frantic hands and heated kisses covered every inch of skin. Soft murmurs and gentle sighs accompanied the sinuous movements, as he finally slid between her thighs and drove home. Smooth and heated skin against skin, they sank into the joy of having each other. The joy of coming together to forget and to forgive. To, for the moment, step past what happened and move on. In the best way possible.

They held each other close, both of them finally collapsing, exhausted for hours, until Kate woke a little later, still held in his arms. She shifted ever-so-slightly, and his eyes opened.

"Is it morning already?" he asked, his voice gritty.

She nodded. "It must be"—she groaned—"because light's coming through the window."

"Close the blinds please, and we'll go back to sleep."

She gave a half laugh. "Not a bad idea but I have to go to work. Rodney will be in soon, and he won't like it one bit to deal with Smidge alone."

Simon groaned and opened his arms wide. She shifted, got up, and peered out at the city. "Oh, it's morning all right. Got to be at least eight-thirty."

Behind her, she heard Simon call out, "You're right. It's eight-twenty."

"*Great*," she muttered, "late for the office again."

"I hardly think an eight o'clock start time counts when you've been up half the night."

"Maybe not," she agreed, "but I sure won't make it by nine either. I need coffee, and I need food." She dressed quickly and walked into the kitchen, where she put on coffee, deciding to forego the eggs. She was sorting through what options she had for toast, when Simon quickly moved her aside and proceeded to fry up eggs for each of them. Shortly she had a plate of eggs on toast. She dug in with a fierceness that surprised her—and him too, from the look on his face, as he watched her with a searching gaze.

She shrugged. "I burned through a lot of calories last night, whether I wanted to or not. It was a very strange evening."

"Yeah, me too," he added pointedly.

"I'll just forget about that aspect," she shared.

"Yeah, you do that, if you can," he replied. "I don't know if it's even possible for me to forget that."

"Maybe it was a vision," she suggested. "I woke up thinking something along that line."

"Maybe," he muttered.

But she saw he wasn't convinced. "Too bad your gram isn't around to ask."

"Yeah, I was thinking the same thing." Simon dropped his head in his hands. "It's not as if I heard about anything such as *that*."

"No, but various psychic incidences have been proven, right or wrong, truth and logic notwithstanding," she mentioned, stuffing her mouth again. "You do hear some pretty strange scenarios, where things, such as this, do manifest."

"If you say so," Simon muttered. "Can't say I'm convinced."

"No, I'm not sure *convinced* is the word for it," she added, "but whatever, it happened."

He nodded. "I would suggest we maybe do a short tour, a cruise out of the harbor, when you have a couple days off, whenever we solve this case."

"One of your gambling cruises?" She eyed him with amusement.

"Oh, I might gamble a little bit," he said, with a tug of his lips.

"Maybe I'll come too," she suggested, "as long as you don't expect me to gamble."

"Not necessary," he agreed. "They will have some live shows, mind you. Then we can have dinner, sit out on the balcony, and act like normal people."

"*Normal people*," she repeated, rolling the word around in her mouth. "What the hell does that even mean?"

"God only knows," Simon noted. "I sure as hell don't."

She gave a burst of laughter, jumped to her feet, cleaned up her plate, then gave him a hug from behind and kissed him on the cheek. "I'll call you later."

And, with that, she was gone.

WHEN THE KIDNAPPER wanted to use the car again, the coppers had found it. Staring at the forensics goons running around the car park, it was apparent that they'd been here all night. Drove the kidnapper nuts to think that they'd gotten that close. Not only nuts but pissed right off.

Did Simon or somebody else find the vehicle? To even think that Simon had gotten this close was terrifying. The kidnapper turned back and walked away, avoiding the gathered crowd.

Walking along the downtown streets, the kidnapper wondered what to do. Up until now, it had been pretty easy to borrow that vehicle. But with forensics all over it, not so safe now to grab another vehicle from the same lot or even other lots nearby, though those were not quite so convenient or easy for procuring a vehicle. Could steal one off the street. That might work.

Should take Samantha out for a walk somewhere and leave her or make her walk off a cliff. That might be an answer too. Pondering that for a long moment brought on a grin. That would sure stump Simon, wouldn't it? Then who was the woman seen leaving the car park? Talking to the ticket agent had confirmed it was a detective, named Kate. *A cop.*

After the first kill, the kidnapper had thought for sure he would be good, but it hadn't been too long before the need had risen again, that need to assuage the feelings inside, that drive to find justice, that drive to make the world a better place. And for many, many years, everything had calmed down, where the kidnapper had been happy, until *that* had happened. *That.* And everything had changed all over again.

As soon as that need returned, the kidnapper had known what to do.

He'd hoped that maybe, maybe, this would be the end of it. There'd been five the first time—those four young women and that old broad, Mary. He was working on number four now, had her already stashed away. He needed a fifth, even a sixth. Maybe that's what he needed. Maybe that's how this would end. The kidnapper pondered it, wandering to the back door. Stopping here, looking around at the world, it seemed so cruel and heartless that anybody who tried to redeem themselves didn't make it—because they weren't strong enough, because the world had battered them down. But then you met all these people who were given so many chances, and all they did was turn back to the same damn shit that they had been given a hand up out of.

Those were the ones he picked.

He hated the others but these people? Ruining their second chances? … He really hated them.

SIMON KNOCKED ON the back-alley door, and, when Lisa opened it, he smiled at her. "Hey, how're you doing?"

She shrugged but didn't open the door any wider. He reached over with a roll of bills, and her face lit up. "The car park around here, do you know anybody who uses it?"

She looked at him blankly. "I don't even know how to drive."

"No, I didn't mean you," he stated simply. "I just wondered if you knew anybody who worked there or kept their car there."

She shook her head. "That's so far from the world I live in, I can't even afford car insurance. No matter even the pain of putting gas into the tank …"

"And you don't drive?" he asked curiously.

"No, Helen does, and she's done all the driving … since forever." Lisa smiled.

"Do you keep a vehicle?"

"Yeah, we've got that old beater in a garage nearby," she replied, with a casual flick of her hand. "It's getting harder and harder to keep it on the road. Helen's always worried about something else breaking down on it, but, so far, it's held us in good stead, and hopefully everything else will stay in good stead too. Thank you for this." She held up the cash. Then her gaze sharpened. "How are you feeling?"

"I'm better, much better actually, no lasting damage."

"Oh, good," she said in relief. "You're a good man, Simon. We really appreciate the help."

"I know, and don't worry. The world needs people like you too."

"Yeah, unfortunately they're not very good at showing it though."

"I know." And, with that, he turned to walk away.

She called back, "Thank you."

He nodded, lifted a hand, and headed to his meeting with one of his foremen, Joe. As he walked into the coffee shop, Joe stood off to the side, with a newspaper in his hand.

Joe looked up, saw Simon, and in a booming tone, asked, "Hey, boss. How're you feeling?"

"I'm okay," Simon replied.

At that, Joe took one look at the stitches on Simon's forehead and whistled. "Holy shit, what did you do that you got stitches? Are you okay?"

"Got hit over the head, attacked a few blocks from here the other night. That's why I didn't show up for work yesterday, but I'm fine today."

Joe was amazed. "You don't have to come into work. We

can do all this over the phone."

"Yep, we could. However, it's much better if I stay on the job," Simon stated.

Joe nodded. "Let's do a quick rundown."

And, each with a coffee in their hands, they headed down to see the first of the rehab projects. "It's not a whole lot different from it was a few days ago," Joe noted, "but, with my brother-in-law gone, we did get six workers back."

"Good to know." Simon was damn happy to hear that. "I'm sorry that your brother-in-law caused all the headaches."

"Me too. My sister hasn't stopped crying. Now that she's got all the funeral preparations to make, I'm hoping that, when those are done, she'll find some closure. I mean, I get it. Luca wasn't exactly the guy I wanted for her, but she loved him, and, maybe in his own way, he loved her."

And, with that, they got down to the jobs at hand.

An hour later, Simon walked to the next rehab project. He stopped at one of the big buildings along the way, this one on his list to consider buying down the road—one of the grande dames of Vancouver on the East Side, definitely needed a few million dollars to fix her up.

Labor costs had soared. Supplies were almost impossible to get. Everything was a mess after the global pandemic, and, of course, everybody was still trying to get back on top. But the cost of goods had quadrupled in the construction industry, and he felt that pinch. Even now that things were flowing, it was hard to keep his cost overruns on the small side.

He went from building project to building project, noting a couple buildings in his journal that could be potential projects down the road. He didn't buy projects to make money necessarily, but some buildings needed the assistance of somebody like him. Those special buildings needed to be understood, cared for, reprised back to their former beauty, and repurposed in some cases.

It was such a hard world out there, where everybody just took, and nobody gave back. Properties were the same thing. People often stripped a property down, until it had absolutely no material value left. Then they ditched it or put it up for sale or ignored it, and it became derelict, unloved.

If it was something that Simon could save, he did. If it was something he could modernize and rehab into apartments or low-income housing within commercial districts on the bottom rung—which helped Simon to recover his costs, so he could do it over and over again—he did.

He had a good eye for most of these buildings, and he certainly had a good eye on budgets, and he made money. It seemed to have been one of the few gifts he had or at least one of the few gifts that he appreciated. It made life a lot easier when he didn't have to worry about every nickel and dime, but some of these buildings would require more than ten to fifteen million to make them usable again. And then he must have a serious conversation with himself as to whether it was love for an old building or just the need for a project or maybe even the need to save a building.

As he wandered through his workday, he stopped, picked up a coffee, and sent a text to Kate, asking how she was. He didn't get an answer.

A niggle in the back of his mind caught his attention— this odd feeling of being followed. He checked behind his shoulder several times but never caught sight of anybody. As he stopped again—just a few blocks from the women's shelter, literally on the corner where he had been attacked—

it unnerved him.

Swearing, he looked around, at the traffic, at lots of pedestrians, hurrying past, ignoring him, as they went about their day.

He couldn't imagine what would have happened if Lisa hadn't been here at the time of his assault. Then he remembered that he'd been talking to Kate at the same time. Simon knew that, given hell or high water, Kate would have found him. Maybe not in time, but she would have kept looking. And that was one of the things about Kate that Simon had to appreciate.

She was loyal, and, even if she was stumped, scared, or terrified, she wasn't the kind to walk away and leave it. She was a terrier, making sure that she got to the bottom of what was going on and that nothing got past her.

He turned his attention to his surroundings again, noting this was where Samantha had been kidnapped. An energy pattern was here that he'd picked up, and, now that he had also been attacked here, that same energy pattern was almost calling to him.

Closing his eyes, he leaned up against the wall, sipping his coffee. When the instinct hit him, he opened his eyes and turned to the side, catching a shadow on the next block, up under an awning. Instincts, because it sure as hell wasn't common sense, made his feet head in the same direction. When he got to where he thought the shadow was, it had moved, telling Simon it was exactly what he thought it was.

Only by the time he reached him, the man was gone.

* * *

AND HERE WAS Simon again. Damn it. So much for the blow to the head. Surely that should have kept him out of everybody's way. *Should have.* So Simon would need a special circumstance. *After all, I'd waited ten years for this, ten years for that punishment which Simon deserved.*

He could be done with all this right now. At least, he could choose to be done with all this. It didn't have to be the end, but, if he wanted it to be the end, he could deem it so. And that was a choice, and that was a point in the road, a fork that he was rather desperate to reach. So many good things could happen in his life, with so many more people he could help, but finding people who actually wanted to be helped was the hardship. He had absolutely no use for all those people who had absolutely no guts, no willpower to stick to the path. They had enough to make a change, but then they always went back to their old lives. They slid back into drugs, slid back into alcohol, slid back into relationships with abusive men.

It drove him wild when he saw it, and yet so little he could do about it. Except for a few, a few connected to Simon, that he'd chosen with exquisite care. Now, if only he could get Simon off on his own.

He had seen him up ahead earlier today, and he had smiled quickly as he stepped in behind him, following him as he had done many times previously. And yet Simon never knew, had no idea that *he* was there, and that's just the way he liked it. Because one of these days, he would make Simon walk; he would make Simon walk that walk, and *he* would have his own fun.

Almost immediately, the smile fell away as he thought about his last victim. That hadn't been any fun. His victim had cried like a baby the whole time. Where the hell were the guts in the man? Even the tortured women had done better. Whimpering, whining, desperately trying to make peace with their tormentor, willing to do anything to get out of it. He snickered at that.

The last thing he wanted was sex, at least with these whores. Even the guy had been willing to do anything at the end, but he'd been blubbering so badly all *he* wanted to do was stab him. And he may have had a little overkill on that one, but, hey, it was to be expected when you had such a weak-ass slimeball.

The weaker they were, the more you wanted to beat them, then slice them up.

CHAPTER 21

K ATE WAS BURIED in street camera reviews to see if she could find anybody who was a part of the car park those many weeks ago. She was still flicking through the feeds, finding nothing, but doggedly was on her second attempt.

Rodney looked over at her. "No luck, *huh?*"

She shrugged and shook her head. "Doesn't look like it. I was so hopeful."

He nodded. "We need a lead."

"And yet," she added, "we need a lead on Elizabeth and Patricia. What we are getting right now is not even remotely close to one of them."

"Did forensics get back to you?"

She shook her head and for the umpteenth time checked her email. "No, still nothing yet. I think that's one of the biggest frustrations in our job," she murmured, looking over at him. "Having to wait to get exactly what it is we need."

"Getting what we need is still a bit of luck too," he pointed out.

She didn't say anything at first but nodded. "How is it that these people pick places where they don't have cameras?" she asked, with a frustrated groan.

"It's a good chance that's exactly why these places were picked," Rodney pointed out. "Think about it. If you're looking to do this, and you're looking for a particular victim, you want to make sure that everything is easy."

"And if it isn't easy," she added, "you must have a back-up plan."

"Exactly."

She hesitated and then told him about Simon's nighttime vision, omitting the part that really worried her.

Rodney stared at her in shock. "Well, shit, that means our killer has another victim right now."

"I know that. And, of course, we have no idea who she is or why. Unless it's Samantha."

"I hate to say it," Rodney began, "but even finding this person might not give us the answers that we need to stop him from taking another one."

"How many does he need to take?"

He winced and murmured, "We've seen that happen more than a few times, where we need the next victim to find the killer."

"More than a few times," she agreed. "And it doesn't make it any easier. What are we supposed to do when there's nothing to go on?"

"We do what we're doing now," he stated, his voice firm. "We stay focused on the evidence, and when and if we find what we need to find, then we can move forward. However, until then, absolutely nothing we can do except stay on track."

She didn't like that answer, but he was right. She nodded at him and continued to work through the feed. When Simon called her, she answered almost absentmindedly. "Hey, how was your morning?"

"Considering somebody was following me today," he snapped, "I've had better days."

She stopped, staring down at the phone. "Somebody's following you?"

"Yeah." And he quickly explained.

She wrote down a few notes about it. "You didn't recognize him?"

"No, I didn't recognize him, and, no, he didn't admit to following me, but he took off, scared."

"Yeah, I wonder why," she said, with a note of humor. "You are a scary dude."

"Like hell," he replied, but no rancor was in his voice. "Everybody thinks I'm a teddy bear."

She burst out laughing at that. "Yeah, not so much," she murmured. "Okay, what corner and when was this?" she asked, as she quickly shifted. With that info, she disconnected from the phone call and explained to Rodney, as she brought up the traffic cams.

"That was today?" Rodney asked.

"Now," she said, "as in *just* now."

"Interesting," he murmured, as he shifted his chair to come up beside her.

She quickly went through the video cameras on the road, found the corner in question, and smiled when she managed to find cameras, not that they were helpful just yet but that they were there.

As she reviewed the video and tried to find the right time frame, Rodney pointed a finger. "There's Simon."

Indeed, there was Simon, and he was coming up on the side of the road completely nonchalant. She watched as he leaned against the wall.

"What's he doing?" Rodney asked.

"I would say offhand that he's disturbed by something. Doesn't really know what but something."

As they continued to watch, Simon suddenly shifted in his casual view of the area around him to focus on a place a couple blocks out. And then, with determined strides, almost as if he were targeting something, he headed toward a specific place. Before he arrived, a man slipped out of a doorway and disappeared around the corner. When he got to the doorway, he stopped and looked around in confusion.

"That's the guy obviously." As soon as the incident was over, the other man booked it.

"So that's the one that Simon says has been following him," she murmured.

"But was he? That's the question."

"Where was he earlier and where did he go from here?" she added.

As they backtracked the video for the twenty minutes prior to that point, she nodded. "It does appear he is following Simon, although not everyone loves Simon all the time, including me."

Rodney snorted at that and hit her lightly on the shoulder. "But why? That's a load of crock." He smiled. "You're very much in love with him. You may not like what he does or some of the skills that he has, … but there's no doubt about how you feel."

She pondered that as she backtracked, lost this guy a couple times, before picking him up downtown. "I can't see when he arrived at this location," she complained.

"Let's go find where he went after his meeting with Simon. That may give us a better understanding."

She quickly fast-forwarded to where they were, when the stalker had taken off from Simon, and followed the stalker another block or two, when he disappeared around the corner, surely within the blind spot, and the cameras lost him. She searched the other blocks looking for him but found no sign of him. She sat back, pondering that. "We lost him," she muttered.

Rodney asked, "What area is it?"

She backed up slightly, so she could see a street name and swore. "Of course it's right around where the women's shelter is," she muttered.

He looked over at her. "Did we ever consider that the women's shelter might be involved in this?"

"I hope *that's* not the case. A lot of women have been through there who have needed help."

"And presumably they got that help," Rodney noted, "but we also must question as to whether that help, more or less, came with some strings."

She stared at him. "I don't understand."

"No, I don't either," he admitted, with a wave of his hand. "We also don't know whether this is related to Samantha or something else."

"I can't help but think that they're connected," Kate mentioned again. "It's possible that Simon can connect to more than one case at a time, and he may have more in common with this Samantha case than any others, but the bottom line is …" With a sudden awareness of a possibility that she hadn't looked at—up until now and honestly didn't want to look at—she switched over to the cameras closest to the women's shelter. She needed to get that cam checked as soon as she could.

Only that cam didn't show the rear door that was regularly used. Stumped, she sat back.

Rodney looked over at her. "What are you thinking?"

"It's around the corner from the women's shelter," she pointed out. "I had this sudden thought that maybe this guy had a connection to there as well."

Rodney winced and nodded. "Of course Simon can't offer us any help on that either, can he?"

"No, only that, in his most recent vision, this person is being told to walk and then not walk, as Patricia had mentioned too."

Rodney added, "But we also don't know that it's connected to Samantha."

"No," she admitted in frustration. "It's possible Simon's connected to two different cases. He's never had it happen before, but this is all so new to him anyway that there's no way to know for sure."

Rodney pondered that for a long moment. "Of course Simon couldn't figure out where he was or anything in that last vision of his."

"No, just that his feet hurt like crap," she modified. "And that the woman ..." She stopped, frowned. "He didn't technically say the victim was a woman. I have to remember that. Otherwise it could just be my interpretation. I'm not sure if Simon actually knew."

"Right, also a valuable point to remember."

"Exactly." Kate sighed. "So much is going on that we can't be sure."

Rodney nodded and didn't say anything for a long moment. "So what's next?"

"Forensics would be a big help, even if just to say nothing is here. That in itself is information," she muttered. "Then I can stop checking my email every two seconds to see if they've contacted us."

He flashed her a smile.

"We also know that we're in for a shit deal very, very quickly," she added, "in that ... the timing will be off, and we'll get another huge case on our plate, and I won't have the time to spare. Plus I don't want to face Patricia's brother," she admitted.

"But you need to. One way or another. He has to be considered a suspect or be taken off the list. He's a wild card, but is there any proof he's involved?" Rodney asked Kate.

"Damn," she muttered, but he was right. She picked up the phone and quickly phoned Patricia's brother. When he answered, such hope filled his voice that she winced, and that was, in a way, too much for her; they were actually putting him on the suspect list. "No, I don't have answers for you. I have more questions." He swore at that, and she kinda got the sentiment. "I understand. We're just as frustrated, and that doesn't help, and I'm so sorry."

"What is it you want to ask about?" he prompted her, his tone brisk.

"We know that Patricia was asking to get some drugs to handle her kidnapping ordeal," Kate began.

"And I didn't know about that," he stated, a certain level of bitterness in his voice. "But, damn, that sucks."

"Can you tell me anything about her friends, boyfriends at the time?"

"Her latest was an asshole. He found out about her previous occupation, and I guess you could say that he held it against her. Considering that it wasn't all that long that she'd been off the streets, so maybe it's understandable," he said, a weariness to his voice. "He made a couple nasty comments about *used goods* and things that really hurt her, so I'm not sure what that would have done to her."

"Yet, when I asked about boyfriends before, ... you didn't tell me about him."

"That's because they were already broken up, and he

didn't want anything else to do with her. That's the only thing I can think of anyway."

"Okay, good enough," she noted. "At least that answers that question."

"I guess that's all you can do is keep asking questions and poking and prodding into people's pain," he said, with a level of bitterness that, although she could understand, it still was hard when it was directed at her.

"Yes, exactly," she declared, with a clipped tone.

She spoke with him for another few minutes. When she rang off, she looked over at Rodney, and, as she updated her notes, she explained what had come up.

"He should have told us about that boyfriend in the first place," Rodney said in a disgruntled tone. "It gives us somebody else to look at."

"I do have a name and contact information, so I'll just call him outright." While it was still relatively calm in the office, with Rodney here beside her, she called this Francois Colbert guy. When he answered, his tone was distant, as if he were busy. She quickly identified herself, and a surprised cough came on the other end.

"What the hell are you calling me for?"

"Patricia Blinkers."

"Ah." Then he snorted. "That's old news. We didn't have anything to do with each other, once I broke up the relationship."

"And the breakup was caused by what?"

"Because of the fact that she's a fucking whore," he grunted. "It's one thing if it was ten years in her past, and she had fully recovered and was leading a nice, solid life." He blew out a disgusted sigh. "Yet I sure as hell wasn't up for somebody still such a mess from drugs and her lifestyle."

"Interesting," she murmured.

"Why? What's interesting about it? Most guys don't want to go out with a woman they don't want to take home to Mom. I was looking for a long-term relationship, not a short-term one." He took a moment to add, "And that's definitely not somebody I could take home to my mother. Judge me all you want. I really don't give a shit. I had nothing to do with her death."

"But you did hear about it."

"Sure, her brother called me, told me what an asshole I was."

She winced at that. "Of course. He is hurting though, so maybe his reaction is understandable, given the circumstances."

"Maybe. As long as he leaves me the fuck alone, I don't really care." Then some rustling was heard in the background, and he came back. "Look. I'm at work, so if you don't have any other questions, I need to get back to business." And, with that, he quickly signed off the call.

As she disconnected, she looked over at Rodney.

Rodney nodded. "He's got a point," he mentioned. "Most guys wouldn't be bringing a woman like that home, not unless they're seriously in love with them. Which, in this case, obviously this guy wasn't. He can't be blamed for that."

"Just goes to show how hard it is to get out of that lifestyle. It's one thing to make a change, but it's another thing to maintain that change," Kate noted, shaking her head, "because Francois's rejection is quite possibly what did send Patricia back to the drugs. She would have a very low self-esteem anyway, and, with that insult added to her injuries, that would completely annihilate any self-esteem Patricia had worked at improving. She probably also didn't want tell her brother about it, knowing what his reaction would be."

"And yet her brother … is probably no different, if the circumstances were about his girlfriend," Rodney pointed out.

Kate nodded, although wincing too. "Not a great thought."

Pondering the information she had so far, she asked Rodney, "Can you print me off an image of the guy who followed Simon? I'll go out and take a look at that area, maybe even stop in at the women's shelter and ask them some questions too."

"If you'll be at the women's shelter, I won't be allowed inside," he acknowledged, "but I'll come with you down-town because I also take my assignment to look after you quite seriously."

"And yet it shouldn't even be an issue," she murmured.

"Maybe not, but now that Simon is being followed, and with the victims still out there being tortured somewhere, that ups the ante too."

"But what would the purpose be?" she muttered. "I don't understand. Why would somebody follow Simon?"

"To see where he's going," Rodney said simply. As they printed off the photos that they needed, they headed out to Kate's car. Rodney asked her, "Why else do you follow somebody?"

"To see who you interact with," she suggested, "to see what you're doing with your day, to see who you meet, things like that."

"Which means that this guy is definitely of interest, and we need to track him down," Rodney stated. "Let's go walk the streets and see what we can come up with."

She laughed. "Sure, you'll make a great streetwalker."

He rolled his eyes at the lame joke. "Thank you. If I ever needed a new career, I'll know where to go."

"Not ... not so much," she teased, with half a smile. "Unless you've got a little bit more bedazzle to that walk of yours, I don't think you'll make much of an income."

In her car, she quickly headed to the women's shelter and parked a few blocks away in the same car park where the vehicle with the blood in the trunk had been found.

As Rodney got out, he asked her, "Was that deliberate?"

"Absolutely it was deliberate. We are very quickly running out of time."

Starting with the attendant at the parking garage, and a different person this time, she identified herself and held up the picture of Simon's stalker, asking the parking lot attendant if he had ever seen this guy. He frowned. "It's a crappy picture," he said apologetically.

She gave him a wry look. "Agreed, but please take a good look."

He took another look, twisting the picture a couple times, and then shrugged. "I don't think I recognize him or have seen him."

She nodded, "Any others on staff here right now?"

He shook his head. "Nope, I'm alone."

"Good enough." After taking his name and number for her records, and Rodney in tow behind her, she headed to the main street.

"I guess we have to double-check each witness statement constantly," he noted.

"Yes, and it's amazing how often we find things that way," she murmured. "I get it. Obviously our car park guy doesn't want to get involved, and, if it's his job on the line, ... he definitely doesn't want get involved, but by taking his name, it makes him a whole lot more worried about giving me the wrong information."

Rodney chuckled. "Very true. Very true."

She continued toward the women's shelter.

"Do you really expect them to know anything?"

"Nope," she admitted cheerfully, "but due diligence and all that."

He nodded and kept pace with her.

When they got to the shelter, she looked at him apologetically. He sighed and nodded. And she stepped forward, with Rodney out of sight, and knocked on the door.

When Lisa opened the hatch, she groaned when she saw her. "You know that having the cops around so many times in a row is not very good for us, right?" she muttered, but she opened the door and let Kate in.

"It might not be very good for you," Kate replied, "but a police presence is also not bad."

Lisa shrugged. "We would just as soon not have a police presence and not have trouble."

"Got it," Kate muttered and entered the doorway, now that Lisa wasn't blocking her entrance. Kate walked ahead, and a few women sat in the living room. They stared at her worriedly and then at Lisa.

Kate smiled. "I'm a friend. You have nothing to worry about from me."

Some of the women seemed to relax, but others stared at her nervously.

Kate turned to Lisa. "You have a place where we can talk?"

"Sure." She motioned to the second door on the right and led them to a small office. "This is where all the lovely financial dealings happen," she said, halfway joking. "Now if only some dealings were to actually happen," she muttered.

"Things that bad?" Kate asked.

"Simon was here this morning, so that'll hold us in good stead for a while, but this business is frustrating. We put out so much money in care and sometimes ... it's all for naught."

Knowing Lisa was referring to Patricia, and maybe even Elizabeth, Kate nodded. "But you and I can still only do the best we can do. I'm in the same business," she stated. "I do everything I can for the people, and still sometimes it's for naught."

Lisa eyed Kate and slowly nodded. "I hadn't thought about it that way."

"You do everything you can to take criminals off the street, and then a jury puts them right back out there," she said, with a headshake. "Go figure. And yet still it's not for us to argue about. Doesn't make it any easier of a lump to swallow, but ..." She waited for the other woman.

Finally Lisa spoke. "Okay, so what is it that you need to ask? I've got to get lunch ready for the women."

"Do you cater to them?" Kate asked.

"Not really, but knowing that somebody is here and that somebody cares"—Lisa shook her head—"it makes a big difference in their mental and emotional attitudes. Absolutely nothing is more important than their mental health after they have endured that, so we do what we can."

Kate certainly admired anybody who could do this work day in and out. Kate knew that a lot of women couldn't do what Kate did, yet she found it easy to work murders day in and day out. She held out the picture of the person who kidnapped Samantha and asked, "Have you seen this person?"

Lisa took the photo and turned it slightly. "You really do need to get better photos."

"We do, but we can only do what we can do."

"Not sure what that even means, but I'll take your word for it." As Lisa pondered the photo, she noted, "Something's familiar about it, but I'm not really sure." She shook her head, as she handed it back. "Sorry."

"Take another look," Kate urged her. "You probably don't want anything to do with this, but, if it keeps somebody else from becoming a victim, … let's do what we can."

"Oh, I don't have a problem doing what I can," Lisa said in frustration. "I don't recognize her … or him—or is it a her?"

"We haven't even identified that much yet." Kate sighed, as she accepted the photo back. "I guess it must be hard for you to see all these women come and go, and … nothing ever changes, *huh?*"

"Yet it's not so much that it's hard but that nothing ever changes," Lisa corrected. "The same thing's always happening, and we do our best, but there are definitely no answers. We try hard to make something happen so that we can stop the cycle, but it doesn't seem to ever stop," she murmured. "Which makes it even more depressing."

"I suspect that you deal with depression on a regular basis anyway, don't you?" Kate asked Lisa.

Lisa looked up at her, with a ghost of a smile. "Yeah, you could say that," she admitted, yet still with a smile. "A lot of people would urge me to go get help, but generally the help provided by doctors are drugs, and that I really don't want and neither can I afford." She shook her head. "Don't go telling me about the free health care and all that stuff, because the bottom line is, … I still don't want to be taking drugs and dulling the results of what I do."

"What do you mean?" Kate asked curiously.

"When you take the drugs, it helps you to realize that life's okay, but I don't ever want to get to the point where this"—she pointed out to the shelter—"is okay. It should never be okay to take in abused and damaged women. It shouldn't even be necessary, and I've always been concerned that, if I ever took any prescriptions, it would backfire, and I would become almost dulled to the effects around me."

"Oh." Kate nodded.

Lisa shrugged. "I know, a novel idea," she said, "but I don't want to blunt all this away. I want to change it and want it so that men do not abuse women, but I also want the women to have a better appreciation of the opportunity that they do have, and that they stay clean, stay dry, stay away from abusive men." Lisa took a deep breath. "There are no guarantees, no promises here, absolutely nothing other than more of the same, and I'm afraid that, if I ever were to take drugs for depression, it would make all this okay, and it'll never be okay."

Kate stayed a little longer, visiting with Lisa. She was an interesting person, with a unique take on life, and Kate appreciated all that Lisa was doing for the suffering women here. As she got up to leave, Kate asked, "Is Helen around?"

"No, she's off shopping," Lisa noted, with a causal gesture. "The amount of work and visitors we have dictates our grocery needs on a day-to-day basis, so we tend to do a lot of our actual shopping daily. We buy much in bulk because it's so much cheaper, but, if we have two versus eighteen guests, the grocery requirements are quite crazy."

"Of course." Kate patted Lisa's hand. Then Kate dug deep into her own pockets and handed Lisa the couple hundred dollars that she had in her wallet. "This is to help you buy a few more groceries."

Lisa's face lit up. "You are an angel."

"Oh, I'm not an angel," she corrected, "but I do appreciate the work you're doing, and I'm grateful that I'm not in a situation where I need your services."

Lisa immediately nodded. "Right? I always felt paying it forward was the best answer to keep yourself out of trouble."

***

SIMON GOT UP from eating his lunch, felt the world spin around uncertainly, and swore because he thought his head was getting better. However, a couple times today, he hadn't felt quite as good as he thought he should. He made it to his car and crashed onto the seat, wondering if he should sit here and rest for a few minutes. He leaned his head back and closed his eyes.

When the door opened beside him, he roused only to feel something hit his shoulder, and he frowned, trying to understand what was happening, when the alarm bells went off. Only they were a little too slow. Then he realized, with every ounce of his being, it had been a whole lot too late.

When he woke, he was on a cot, inside a tent. He groaned, feeling his head burning again with the same pain he'd been dealing with earlier.

A calm person beside him said, "Don't even try to struggle."

He opened his eyes again, after crashing and trying to reawaken. He tried to twist and look at the voice but there was no give in his bonds.

"You can't see me."

The muffled tone indicated he was trying to hide who he

was.

"I don't even get to know who is doing this?" Simon asked in a quiet voice, gathering his strength for whatever was to come.

"No, you really don't need to."

The voice was thicker than Simon would have expected. "Why is that?" he asked.

"In one way, you won't be around long enough to care, and, in another," he said, with an obvious sneer, "I'm trying to decide how long I want to keep you here. There's a certain advantage to having *you* at my whim."

"How do you figure?" Simon asked, startled to even consider that somebody gave a crap about that.

"Well, for one, you're not the high and mighty Simon, doling out money, as if you're some benevolent overseer."

Simon stretched slightly against the bonds holding him, his mind caught on the other guy's words. "So you know who I am, but I'm not allowed to know who you are? How fair is that?"

"Ah, but that's the world we live in," he replied. "Nothing's fair in life. Nothing's fair about helping the people who you think need help, only to have them turn around and do something completely opposite to that help."

Simon pondered that, his mind racing, trying to figure out who could possibly be here. "You're the one who's hurting all these women."

"Women?" he asked in a mocking tone. "Some women, definitely a male or two in there."

"Two?" Simon asked hesitantly.

"Well, one for sure, but he was such a mouse that I'm not sure he deserved to be called a male."

Simon clearly heard disgust in his kidnapper's tone when

speaking of Luca. "You want to tell me what your beef is with me," Simon asked. "I'm sure we can work it out."

The guy laughed. "I'm sure you *think* you can work it out, but … I'm not so sure I even give a shit."

"Which is an interesting conundrum then," Simon noted, "because I don't know what I'm supposed to have done wrong."

"I've pondered that for a while, wondering why I do this. … I started because of something that you did, and I blamed you for it, and I made other people pay, but, since then, I've been blaming you all that much more, and I'm not sure it's fair."

Simon frowned, not sure that he liked where this line of discussion was even going. "If it's not fair, why am I still a captive?"

"Because, if you know who I am, you would for sure involve that lovely little girlfriend of yours," the guy said in a mocking tone. "And you'd try to stop me, and I'm pretty well done with people trying to stop me."

He strained to hear whether his kidnapper was male or female, but the voice was disguised, just enough that it could have been either sex, and that in itself was frustrating. "So what is it that you blame me for originally?" he asked, trying to understand. "It would be nice to know what I have done wrong."

"It sure would," he agreed, with a note of humor. "But, as I've come to realize, I might have used you as a scapegoat to do what I wanted to do in the first place."

"To hurt people?" Simon asked. "Because that's what you're doing."

"Oh, I absolutely am hurting people, and I'll be the first to admit it now, and … it's probably not very good of me to be doing it."

"No, it's not good," Simon stated. "Hurting people is rarely a good thing, so I have to wonder why you're doing it, who you are planning or hoping to hurt through all this."

"That isn't quite so easy to sort out either," he said, with a half laugh. "It all stems back to Elizabeth."

He jolted at that. "Elizabeth? Seriously?"

"Yeah, seriously."

"What about Elizabeth?" he asked cautiously. Knowing that at least now they were dealing with the person who had been involved in Mary Clement's murder. "Did you have anything to do with Mary's death?"

"Oh, I might have helped her die of her injuries from that asshole. I should have taken him out then too, but he did the job himself."

"I don't think so," Simon clarified. "I thought he was in jail still."

"Maybe, maybe not, doesn't matter," the guy said. "If he's in jail, I can't get at him anyway, and I have to trust that somebody else in jail will take care of him."

"So you want revenge for what happened to Elizabeth?" he asked in confusion.

The guy gave another mocking laugh. "You really don't get it, do you?"

Holding his own temper in check, Simon asked, "How am I supposed to get it if nobody explains? You've been attacking people, torturing them, hurting them terribly, all for what?"

"All because I wanted to," the guy explained. "Maybe they deserved it. Maybe they didn't. I'm not sure I care anymore. You start off with such high lofty ideals, and then you give them up pretty fast."

"You don't have to," Simon disagreed immediately.

His kidnapper laughed again. "Not having to is a whole lot different than not wanting to, but then I wouldn't expect you to understand. You're the one full of all these lofty ideals. You help at various women's shelters. You drop off money to help people buy groceries, giving pennies on the dollar. All those things makes you feel as if you are Lord Bountiful."

"What did Elizabeth ever do to you?"

"She betrayed me," he spat in a harsh voice.

"Elizabeth?" Simon asked in bewilderment. "She was the sweetest, loveliest girl. I cannot believe it."

"She was, yes, but she was also my girl."

Simon stiffened at that. "When?" he asked.

"At the same time that I found out she was going out with *you*."

Simon closed his eyes. "So that is what this is all about?" He groaned. "You think I two-timed you with her?"

"Well, she two-timed me with you," the guy said, a raspy laugh coming to hide that he still suffered from the heartache.

"I'm sorry. I didn't know."

"I wondered about that. I thought about it long and hard, wondering whether it was something that she would have told you or was quite happy to keep it all to herself."

He didn't want to bad-mouth her. When he had been with Elizabeth, she'd been very confused, tormented, overwrought, and needed whatever comfort anybody could give her. Simon certainly didn't begrudge her another lover, if that's what she had wanted or needed or thought she needed at the time—or even was incapable of understanding what she was doing.

He wasn't giving Elizabeth a free pass, but, at the same time, emotionally she hadn't been in a good place. He'd known it, and he'd been okay with her walking away to get her life together because that's what you did when you cared about people. At least he assumed that's what everybody did. Apparently it's only something he did. He didn't know what to say for a long moment, and, while he waited, hoping the other guy would say something, there came a happy sigh.

"I'm hoping this will be it."

"No, it won't be," Simon declared. "If you were doing this out of revenge or a sense of justice or whatever craziness that you've been convincing yourself of"—he took in a deep breath and let out a harsh sigh—"there is no *enough* because there was no need to torture people, no need to send Patricia to the police station with a message and then turn around and kill her."

"I couldn't exactly let her carry on, … not on her own. Chances were very good that she'd get weak again and that she would end up doing something or recognizing something, and I couldn't have that."

At the wording, Simon tried hard not to show any sense of excitement, but that was the first inclination that something was going on here that connected them. "What about Samantha Cole?"

"Do you know her too?" Then without waiting for an answer, his tormentor continued, "Well, Samantha is still my guest. I have to decide what to do with her." Another heavy sigh came. "That's the problem. You do this, and you try to make people get better, help them out, but then they pull some shit that you can't live with. So you have to change it. You have to do something to make it better. Yet there is no making it better," the guy explained, with a sneer. "Because these people … just don't want to get better. It's too easy to be an asshole and to be part of this stupidity for the rest of their lives."

"And yet, for you, there is a chance of getting better?" he asked, looking for insight into what was making this guy tick.

"I wasn't out to get better. However, something starts this, and then you have to deal with it, even if it's not what you want to do."

"Do you though?" Simon asked. "If this isn't what you want to do, then you could have walked away from all this."

"Sure, I could have. *Could have* is an easy answer, but it's really not the answer, is it? These people have been given so much help."

At that wording, Simon froze, understanding this guy's frustration. "And they didn't appreciate it, *huh*?"

"Damn right they didn't," he said, again with that sneer. "So it was pretty easy to go from one issue to the next, but, in truth, … it's really not all that connected. I just connected it."

"Because you like this, you like the power, then the control that you have over somebody's life. You like the fear that you create. Why? Because were you also at the back end of somebody else's manipulation at some time in the past?"

The kidnapper gave a broken laugh. "I can hear you trying to psychoanalyze me. Don't bother. Really nothing to it. My life was an open book, until all the shit hit the fan, about the memories of what happened originally and what triggered it all."

"Well, that's the part that I don't understand. What's the trigger in all this?" he asked. "Elizabeth, I get that, and apparently because I helped her leave."

"Yeah, sure did. She was the best thing I could have ever possibly had, and I was rather desperate to keep it. But nope, no, that wasn't what she wanted, not after talking to you, and … you put her on this path. *I can help you get out of here. I can help you start your life again*, and all that BS. She told me how you would help her get away. And then she came back to town, and she didn't call me. I saw her by accident. And when I say *by accident*, I mean by a car accident. I was returning from errands, and she was outside, almost as if looking for the women's shelter that she had spent some time in. Maybe she was looking for me? I don't know. But I hopped out and raced toward her."

"And? What did you do then?" Simon asked, still confused and wondering why Elizabeth had returned.

"She was surprised to see me. I thought maybe she was happy to see me, but, after I brought her here, I found out that she had been just the opposite," he shared. "I thought maybe she had come looking for me, ready to pick up where we'd left off, and I had been so angry before and so lost and so hurt that I was ready to forgive her in a heartbeat—only to find out that she wasn't here for me at all. She wasn't here for anything other than to settle her own memories, and she said *to find herself a little bit more and to say goodbye. Goodbye*," he cried out.

"Dear God, how was any of this a goodbye?" he asked in an incredulous tone. "It wasn't a goodbye for me. It shouldn't have been a goodbye for her. She didn't understand how devastated I was. I tried to explain it to her, tried to get her to understand, but then she kept telling me about you, and I didn't even really know all you did. I didn't know that you had been behind her leaving and that you were the one responsible for my loss," he said, with a broken cry.

"I'm sorry, but she didn't tell me about you. I didn't know anybody else was in her life."

"There was though. There was definitely somebody in her life. Me."

The kidnapper became angry, his voice harder, and yet something was tinny about it, as if using a voice disguise device. Which could only mean that there was a chance that Simon might understand and memorize or recognize his kidnapper's voice, if that were the case.

He waited, looking for an opportunity to push a little bit more, so he asked, "What happened when you talked to her? Was she …"

"She was astonished that I even cared, astonished that I still remembered," he replied, with half a laugh. "But then I let her know exactly how I felt and that I was hoping she was coming back for me, and she made it very clear that not only was she *not* coming back for me but that the two of us had been a mistake." His voice broke up at that. "*A mistake. A mistake? How? How could you take something so beautiful and call it a mistake?*"

Simon winced, hearing the fury and the pain in the kidnapper's voice. "I am so sorry. I'm sure she didn't mean to be insulting about it."

"Oh, I don't know whether she meant to or not. It doesn't really matter because she was … *very insulting*. It was damn hard to listen to everything that she said and to realize how little regard she had for me. How fair is that? I loved her. Even right to the end, … I loved her."

"And yet you couldn't let her live?" Simon asked.

"No, no, you see? I wanted her to live, but, by the end, I hated her. I loved her, but I also hated her. She kept crying and begging, telling me that she did love me and that she was sorry, but I knew it was all lies. I saw through it, saw she would lie and make up stories, anything to get away from me, to get away," he spat, that same bitterness coming back into his tone. "After all I'd done for her."

"What exactly did you do?" Simon asked.

"I'm the one who finally put her mother out of her misery. Elizabeth should have thanked me for that but that awful woman, … she snapped. After everything I did to help them out, everything I did all those years ago, and there was no gratitude. I didn't need it as long as Elizabeth was with me, but, once I realized that not only wasn't she with me but she actually hated me, well … what was I supposed to do? Take that and lie down, roll over, and let her kick me again? No," he sneered. "Not my style. I was kicked to the curb many a time, broken, beaten, abused to the point that I didn't even know which way was up, and nobody would ever listen. I couldn't ever really tell anybody. But it's always that way, always that way," he wailed, his voice rising in anguish. "She didn't have to treat me that way. She didn't have to say that."

"What did Elizabeth say?" Simon asked, desperately trying to figure a way out of this.

Simon had sent out several mental messages to Kate, but, if she was busy, … he knew that there was no way she would even hear, and he didn't have the ability to send out a message strong enough to knock her on her ass so that she'd pay attention. He didn't even know if that was possible, but, with everything else that had been going on in his world lately, he wasn't sure that it was impossible either.

His head pounded again, and, as the guy's voice rose, Simon felt the boom increasing. "What did you give me?" Simon asked in a panicked voice.

"I considered the same drug I'd used before, but I figured you would be a whole lot more trouble than you were before. So I gave you something different, ketamine, but I wasn't sure on the dose. How's your head?"

"It's killing me."

The kidnapper snickered. "Well, that won't last too-too long, but good that you should be feeling it."

"So you're doing this to hurt me because I helped Elizabeth, is that it?"

"When you put it that way, it sounds pretty ridiculous."

It did to Simon too, but he didn't dare say anything about it. At this point in time nothing here made sense. "What is it you want me to do about it now?" Simon asked.

"Nothing you can really do, is there? She's gone."

Simon winced. "So that's all that you care about is making sure that I die because of whatever it is that I did?"

"What do you mean, *whatever it is that you did?*" he yelled. "I told you what you did."

"Yes, but I didn't even know about Elizabeth dating you. You're blaming me for something that I didn't even know was going on."

There was silence, then he said, "Well, that should matter. … I guess it should matter, but honestly it doesn't matter. I really don't give a crap."

"Ah, so this isn't so much about what I did, just making sure someone pays for your pain, is that it? Then you just keep doing this to other people for no reason."

"This is getting boring." His kidnapper paced, as Simon heard the scraping on the floor. "It was pretty fun in the initial stages, watching everybody scream, blindfolded, as they moved along to my instructions, making a game of it, but honestly, that does get a little wearying."

"So why would you do it still?" Simon asked. "Why would you torment people to that extent? Except for the fact that you could."

"That's it exactly," he said. "I could, so why wouldn't I?"

"Why you wouldn't is because you should understand what it was like to be a victim. As a fellow victim, you should understand what these people went through, and you should do your best to help them and not hurt them further."

"That would be great, if I was a lily pure idiot, like you," he snapped, "which I'm not."

This guy had some vendetta against Simon, as senseless as it was. "So all of this is because I helped Elizabeth escape, right?"

"Yes, that's what started it."

"And from there you went off on your own creative motivations."

He laughed. "I guess that's one way to put it."

"No point in not telling me everything you have to share, as nobody will ever really know all of what you've done if you don't. Don't you want people to know?"

"No, I don't. I'm not some glory hound. I'm not somebody who wants the media all over me. That's for losers."

"Ah, and you're not a loser."

"I am not a fucking loser," he snapped. "You fucking better remember that."

"No, I think I got that quite clearly. So tell me. Was Elizabeth the first one or the only one?"

There was silence, and then he laughed. "No, she wasn't. When she left, I lost it, and I took it out on a few people who maybe didn't deserve it," he admitted.

At that, Simon winced. "Who did you take it out on?"

"Why? What difference does it make?" he asked.

"Because, if I get to the other side, and some heaven is over there, and all those victims are there, it might not be a bad thing to let them all know what happened. I understand when people die in vicious circumstances that they don't always end up understanding what happened."

"Oh, so you'll go over there and explain it to them." He laughed at that. "Oh my God, that's so rich. That's hilarious."

"Well, one day you'll be over there, and they'll talk to you themselves and find out what the hell you were doing and why. However, in the meantime, maybe I can bring them some peace."

That silence following his comment made Simon wonder if he had said something that completely surprised his kidnapper.

"Do you really think they're over there waiting?"

"Oh, I know so. I'm sure, in your worst nightmares, you do too."

"I don't get nightmares." He sighed. "Not now. It's another reason for doing what I'm doing. It kinda puts me back in control."

"Right, so that the people who abused you before know that they'll never do it again because you're too strong now."

"Something like that."

"Anything you can do to gain control of your life is understandable to me."

"Right? That's what I thought, but not everybody looks at it that way."

"That's because, if your taking control is hurting somebody else, … well, nobody likes that."

"They shouldn't fucking care," he muttered, "because it's none of their business."

"So you don't think it's Patricia's brother's business that he should find out what happened to his beloved sister?"

Then came another point of dead silence. Then his kidnapper asked, "Do you really think he cared?"

"Yes, I do. I really think he cared."

"*Huh*, interesting." he muttered. "But it's too late, Patricia's dead."

"You killed her too."

"I did. I killed her too."

"Why?" Simon asked, his voice so soft, wondering how to get the killer to open up, just to get the answers that, even if he died, Simon desperately wanted to hear.

"What difference does it make?" the kidnapper asked.

"Because then I would know. I get it. You don't owe me anything, but I'm curious, considering these poor people died because of me, although how you can blame me for all of them, I don't know."

"They didn't all die because of you, but you started it, and, once it started, there was really no other answer."

He shook his head at that. "That sounds like a cop-out."

After a long moment, the kidnapper's voice turned ugly. "Are you calling me a liar?"

"No, I'm not calling you a liar. I'm saying that your *reasoning* is a cop-out. If you like killing people, and you like what the result is for yourself, then that's on you, not on me."

Silence. "Hadn't considered it that way," the kidnapper admitted thoughtfully.

"You should think about it. Whatever you did originally, you may have done because you were so angry at me, at Elizabeth, at her mother, but whatever you did since that original kill? ... That's on you, and it's on whatever it is that you decided you needed out of this. And from what I'm hearing, it's all about control, all about mastery and being the one in control. You want to be the one who makes others do what you want. For whatever reason, you wanted to make them dance to your tune, make them scared—as if you were always the victor, as if you were always to be feared." He asked, "Am I wrong?"

"No, you're not wrong."

"So then this was *your* game, even though you tried to make it sound as if it was *my* game."

"Why shouldn't it be your game?"

"If a true game, then it takes at least two players. You never let me into the game, so it wasn't a competition. It was whatever you were going through that you felt you needed somebody to understand, or not even understand so much as you felt you needed somebody to acknowledge your pain and your own needs."

"Is that so wrong?"

"It's only wrong because you hurt somebody, and you're continuing to hurt people," Simon stated. "Everybody needs to have their own emotions validated. Everybody needs to have their lives validated in some way, but, when you do it at the cost of hurting others, … it makes you no different than these abused women. Just another victim. Once again a victim yourself."

At that, the blow came out of nowhere and struck him on the side of the head, knocking him out.

CHAPTER 22

K ATE'S PHONE RANG, even as she slowly climbed the front steps to the station. It was Lisa Sands. "Hey, Lisa."

Lisa hesitated and then spoke. "Look. I don't … I don't know. I don't see how it possibly could be. … Could you … Could you come here and talk to me?"

Kate winced because it was already so late and then said, "Of course. You really can't tell me over the phone?"

"No, no, I can't. I'm not even sure if I'm safe. Please, I'll meet you at the shelter." And, with that, Lisa disconnected.

Safe? Why wouldn't Lisa feel safe? Where the hell was Lisa calling Kate from, if not from Lisa's own home? Frustrated, but heading out, she contacted Rodney. When she got no answer, she a left him a message, saying she was heading back down to the women's shelter. She then sent Simon yet another message.

She'd been trying to contact him for the last couple hours and got absolutely no response. For whatever reason, he either wasn't answering or—and this part really drove her nuts—he couldn't answer. And if he couldn't answer, why? What was going on that he couldn't pick up a phone and respond? Grimacing, she got back into her vehicle.

Then came this horrible pressure, this weird sense of something wrong, and yet, unable to sort it out, she ignored it all as she drove to the women's shelter, wondering how a location like this could possibly be at the center of everything dealing with her current cases. How? And yet, because of the actual people involved, or the reasons behind the people involved, she had to consider the shelter. As she parked once again in the paid parking lot, she realized how convenient it was to the women's shelter. She walked over and knocked on the door.

Lisa opened it and quickly ushered Kate in. Lisa immediately took her straight through to the office.

"What's going on?" Kate asked in a low tone, and then she looked back around at the shelter in general. "Do you still have a full house?"

Lisa nodded. "I do, indeed."

"And Helen, is she still out shopping? I realized how convenient the car park is from here, although it would cost a lot of money to keep your car there."

"Oh, it would, and we absolutely cannot afford that." And then she hesitated. "And that's why I wanted to talk to you."

"Why is that?" Kate asked, looking at her in confusion. "What's going on? Why didn't you just talk to me over the phone?"

"I can't." She hesitated, looked around, then got up and quickly closed the door to the office.

Curiouser and curiouser, Kate thought.

Lisa sat down, but instead of getting right to it, she fidgeted, her hands clasping, unclasping, clasping and unclasping.

Finally Kate got up and walked closer, crouched right in front of her and said, "You need to tell me."

Tears filled her eyes. "It's that picture you showed

me. ... I didn't place it, and even now I'm not sure. You have to understand that I am not sure."

"Okay, I presume you think you recognized the person in the photo."

"I'm afraid I recognized the person," she repeated. "I don't want to be right though. I really don't want to be right, but every time I think about it, ... my stomach sinks, and I feel as if I'll puke."

Kate stared at her and tried to be patient. "I need to know who it is."

"But I could be wrong, and what if I'm wrong? What if I'm wrong? It'll change everything. It'll ruin everything."

Kate slowly wrapped her arms around the older woman and held her, while Lisa trembled in place. "I'm sorry this is causing you so much trauma," Kate said. "However, you have to remember that whoever is doing this is also hurting a lot of innocent people."

"I know. I know. ... Yet I don't understand. I don't understand how it could be this person. I don't want to tell you because I must be wrong. You can't tell who the person is in the photo, but I can't get it out of my mind. Because it fits. God help me, it fits."

"And yet you called me because you know you aren't wrong."

"I called you because I'm afraid I'm not wrong. ... There's a difference. You have to be very careful with your investigation because I can't, ... I can't be, ... I can't have you saying the wrong thing."

"Meaning that you're trying to protect your women here?"

"I'm trying to protect everything here," she declared, looking at Kate. "The shelter is everything to me. I may get tired. I may get frustrated, but I've spent so long fighting for these women that it breaks my heart if I'm correct."

"And yet you haven't told me who yet."

"Because, if I tell you, and if I'm wrong, it changes everything."

"What if you tell me, and you're right?"

Lisa immediately burst into tears. "Then it changes everything."

"In which case, there really are no options. Everything will change, one way or the other."

With Lisa sobbing, Kate settled back on her heels, wondering what to say and how to say what would unlock this information. She looked around and asked, "When will Helen be back?"

And that increased the sobbing further.

Kate stopped and stared at Lisa, and then it hit Kate. She knew. "Hang on a minute."

Lisa opened her eyes and looked at Kate in fear and yet, at the same time, maybe with hope.

"You really think she did it?" Kate asked, staring at Lisa in shock. *Was it possible?* Kate cast her mind back to the pictures she had and the bits of information that they had, where they hadn't been able to lock down whether they were looking for a man or a woman. "You're afraid that it's Helen, aren't you?"

Lisa burst into fresh sobs but nodded.

"Jesus Christ." Kate bolted to her feet. She pulled out her phone, only to find a message from Rodney. She tried to call him back and again couldn't get through. Frustrated, she phoned Simon and also couldn't get through. "Do you know why?" she asked Lisa, turning to look at her.

"No, I don't know why," she said on a light wail, "but I

know that she had a relationship, only it was really just a one-off way back when, one that went nowhere. I mean, Elizabeth left. I couldn't have that here at the shelter," Lisa explained, "not with all the vulnerable women we take in. But Helen had a one-way relationship with Elizabeth, one where Helen was really hoping Elizabeth would come back."

"Only Simon helped Elizabeth leave."

Lisa looked up at the detective and nodded. "Simon did. I didn't think anything of it, until I heard recently that Elizabeth had come back, for whatever reason, and, oh, how I wish she hadn't come back." Lisa still had tears flowing from her eyes. "I don't know what Elizabeth needed for closure or for whatever her reason was to return here, … but I wished she hadn't come back."

"Did you see her?"

Lisa shook her head. "No, I didn't see her. I didn't know anything about it, until Helen mentioned it. However, Helen was different afterward."

"What was she like when Elizabeth left the first time?"

"She was angry, pissed off, and I told Helen how Elizabeth needed time, that she needed space, that it was a good thing for her to be on her own right now, and that we couldn't always choose relationships that we wanted because we needed to do the right thing and let people heal, how Elizabeth needed to heal, needed to grow. Her mom had died, and that was a pretty ugly scenario, and Elizabeth was … lost. I don't think that she would have stayed with Helen, even in the beginning, but I don't know that."

Kate nodded and pulled out her phone and pulled up the photos of the four earlier victims. "What do those faces mean to you?" Kate asked Lisa, showing her the photos.

Lisa stared at Kate's phone. "One of them was somebody

Elizabeth was really good friends with, and one of them was somebody she hated."

"So again, the connection is the women's shelter."

"Yes," Lisa confirmed. "They both stayed here, not for long obviously. I didn't know either of them were dead though."

"They were cold cases from a long time ago," Kate explained, "about the same time that Elizabeth left."

Lisa's eyes filled with tears. "Helen needs help," she said quickly. "She needs professional help."

"She needs more than help, if she's the one who's been killing people," Kate stated, turning to look at the older woman. "What about this Samantha, do you know her?"

"I don't," she said immediately. "But I do know that Helen has helped a few people privately. Sometimes we know somebody who doesn't want to come into the shelter because they're too scared, and I generally let Helen handle them. So it's quite possible that she does know Samantha."

Kate snapped, "I need you to come to the station, and I'll bring a team in." She stopped, considered all the other women here and added, "We need to move these women to another shelter. We need them to be safe."

"Oh my God, oh my God, oh my God," Lisa wailed. "No, you're supposed to tell me that I'm wrong."

"I hope to God that you are wrong," Kate declared, "but, at the same time, I'm not sure. I'm trying to get ahold of Simon as it is."

At that, Lisa gasped. "Helen was going to contact him about some remodeling here. I told her not to bother, and she laughed and said Simon could always tell her no, but she needed to ask him about adding a couple more bedrooms. She thought it would be a fairly simple job."

"When was that?" Kate asked, staring at Lisa in horror. Her stomach wrenched, as she realized just a couple hours ago is how long she'd been trying to contact Simon. "What are the chances that Helen's the one who attacked Simon?"

At that, Lisa winced. "I don't know," she whispered. "Dear God, I hope not. He's always been so good to us."

"Yeah, you're not kidding." Kate stared at the woman, who might have been complicit in covering up Helen's misdeeds. "Where would she take a victim? Where does she have another location or a spot that she feels comfortable, where she might have taken these women?"

Lisa kept shaking her head. "It couldn't be her. It couldn't be her."

"I'm not saying it is, and I'm not saying it isn't, but where would Helen take somebody?"

"I don't know," Lisa cried out.

"Does she have a favorite park? Does she have a favorite location? Where does she go for holidays? What places does she talk about a lot?"

"She ... goes camping," Lisa remembered. "She has a place not far from here, and she likes it because she can drive right up to the spot, and ... it's a place she's used for years."

"Where is it?" Kate asked for directions.

Lisa named the park and then whispered, "She has a quiet space here too. A place she likes to go and destress."

Kate slowly turned to look at her, her phone in her hand, typing a text to Rodney in progress. "When you say a quiet space, what do you mean?"

Lisa stood and led the way through the house to the back and a staircase. She motioned up. "It's up here."

Kate moved slowly up the narrow staircase to the second floor, then opened a door to another staircase.

"It's at the top of the house," Lisa called up to Kate.

Kate stared at her in shock. "When were you up here last?" She moved to the next staircase, hating yet already knowing what was up there.

"Never. It's her space," Lisa admitted. "I have enough trouble with the stairs as it is."

"And do you hear anything that might be going on up there at any time?

"No. The house is soundproofed. Helen did a lot of it herself. She said she needed to rail and to cry out in her frustration and pain." Lisa had a defeated look in her eyes. "She had a horrible childhood. Sexually abused, tortured. Her father was a sadist and made her life hell. Sometimes she finds it hard even now. So I had no problem giving her this space. She does so much for everyone else that I knew she needed it."

But... the abused had become the abuser... at least that was the track Kate had locked onto.

Kate was already halfway up the stairs. She turned to Lisa and said, "I'll be right back." And, with that, she entered the small dark room and stopped. "Anyone here," she asked in a low voice, as she brought out the flashlight on her phone. A weird light reflected off the black walls. Until it landed on a small woman, tied up on a small mattress, and the fear in her eyes broke Kate's heart.

Kate approached slowly, even as she pulled her badge from her pocket. "Samantha, I presume?"

The other woman nodded frantically and burst into tears.

❧

"SIMON, IT'S NICE and easy. You take a step when I tell you

to take a step, and, if you don't take a step, I get to hit you some more. It's a game I learned as a child. You'll see how fun it is soon."

Simon was barely conscious. He heard the instructions in the back of his mind, and the voice was coming from afar, but blood dripped down his eye, and his hands were tied behind his back. Although the drugs had somewhat eased back, he was groggy and struggling to stay cognizant. Then he was given a prod, and it had an electric jolt to it. He bolted forward, and his kidnapper laughed. Only the voice was different now. He stopped and tilted his head to the side.

"Take five steps."

He took five confident steps, realizing that he had absolutely no idea where he was and what he was doing and that the only way to get ahead of this was to find a way to get control himself.

"Now take another five steps."

"You didn't say, *Simon says*."

His kidnapper laughed and laughed. "Ooh, you think you're smart, but you're right. I didn't. So point to you."

He shook his head at that because it really was a game, a children's game, Simon Says, and somehow that meant something to his kidnapper. *Oh no.* Simon sensed the answer out of nowhere. His kidnapper had been abused as a child, taught this "game" and was now the abuser, using this same "game." How sick was that?

Then another revelation came. In a groggy voice, he mentioned, "I wonder what Lisa would think if she saw you now."

And that was it. Then came some rustling.

Simon remembered something about the way Helen

inflected her words, her tone of voice, and he said, "You're Helen."

This was received with such shock that she ripped the blindfold off his face. There she was, standing in front of him, furious. *Helen.*

He nodded.

"How did you know?" she asked.

He calmly regarded her, looking at the woman and the caricature of a human being she had become. Always tall and rawboned, she'd been quiet and had stayed in the background at the shelter. He'd always spoken to her gently, as if instinctively understanding that she was delicate, or—as he saw now—broken in some way.

She glared at him. "It doesn't matter. It doesn't fucking matter. You won't do anything about it."

"No?" he asked, smiling at her. "Do you really think that nobody'll know?"

"Why, because you guessed?" she scoffed. "You didn't even let me play my game."

"It's hard to play a game when you're the only one who is setting the rules of the game," he noted. "If both of us were blindfolded and another person were here, maybe it would be fair, but I'm not sure about that either. Not that it matters because this will be over soon."

"Yeah, it will be," she sneered, as she prodded him again with the cattle prod.

He smiled at her through the excruciating pain, knowing that she was out of control and that it wouldn't take much to push her into the abyss of madness. "I'm so sorry," he said again. "I didn't realize why or what was going on in Elizabeth's life. I knew that she didn't want anything to do with me afterward, and I thought it was because … she wanted to start fresh."

"Sure, but starting fresh didn't have to mean leaving me," she sneered. "That was all about you."

"No, but you tell yourself whatever you need to sleep at night," Simon corrected, "because really that's what this is all about. You killed somebody you absolutely adored, and you're angry at yourself. What kind of love is that?" he asked, a sneer of his own starting on his face. "Yet your childhood abuse was somehow deemed to be love and games, right?"

She glared at him and prodded him again.

But he held strong, the pain barely manageable. "Your motivation has nothing to do with love. It has everything to do with the unleashing this abusive part of your personality. You just wanted to get payback from all the people who hurt you in your life."

"They should pay," she hissed.

"Maybe, but that doesn't mean that you had to kill all these people. What did my employee have to do with any of this?"

She laughed. "God, he was such a simpleton. You weren't getting the message, so … I figured, if I took one of your employees, then you would get a better message."

He shook his head. "That doesn't make any sense either because you didn't take one of my employees for the sake of any message," he argued. "You took one of my employees for fun, for pleasure, knowing that somebody else would suffer at your hands, and therefore ultimately getting back at me yet again, or at least you hoped so. You didn't forgive me for any of this. You didn't forgive Elizabeth for any of this. You didn't forgive anything. You're still so angry and so hurt that it's all rolled into one event in your mind. You chose Luca to try to hurt me, but I barely knew him. So, as a pawn in your game, it wasn't very effective against me, was it?"

"Why shouldn't they pay?" she screeched, her face twisting in fury. "Why shouldn't you all pay?"

He smiled at her. "It's not how the world works, Helen," he said, his voice gentle. "A lot of people out there face all kinds of hardships on a regular basis, but they don't turn around and murder the people they love. Maybe Elizabeth would have stayed with you when she came back, if you hadn't hurt her so badly. Maybe if you hadn't killed Elizabeth's mother …"

At that Helen's face twisted again, and she nodded. "That was a mistake. Elizabeth really didn't like me after that."

He stared at her. "Did you expect her to?"

She shrugged. "I thought that she should have seen that I had helped her, that I was helping us, so we could be together. Her mother said we were a sin, an abomination." Helen's face twisted again, as she glared at him. "Yet she got all the notoriety because of all this media attention, because she got a park named after her. What Mary went through wasn't anything compared to what I went through," Helen hissed. "Why the hell did everybody suddenly idolize that woman? A woman who hated that Elizabeth loved me. What we had was beautiful. It wasn't a sin."

"What about Elizabeth?"

"She didn't go through anything, not any real abuse, not like what so many of the women have gone through."

"And Patricia? Why did you choose to kill her? And how did you keep everybody from knowing that you were a woman?"

"That's easy. Look at my size. Look at me. … Everything about me was man-sized, and, when I'm dressed like a man, a lot of people think I'm a man." Helen laughed. "It's convenient, and I fostered it because it made life a whole lot easier and a lot safer."

He contemplated that and nodded. "I can see that," he agreed gently. "In your world where men abuse and beat up women, your pretense of being male and pulling it off successfully would give you the upper hand again and affirmed your belief. The thing is, have you only killed these three people, or have you been doing it all along?"

Helen shrugged. "No, I killed four around the same time as her mother, and then I've already killed three this time, but Samantha is next, number four." An odd excitement filled her tone, and her face flushed. "You'll be the fifth, and then I should be good."

"But what will you do for thrills after this? What will you do to make others pay when you're angry or when somebody laughs at you or they, like Patricia, decide to go back to drugs again? How will you make them pay?"

She shrugged. "I don't know. I guess it depends whether I care at that point. I'm tired."

And he saw the weariness in her face. "Well, snuffing out a life with complete disregard has to be hard," he noted. "You've taken away their hopes, their dreams, all their plans, everything that they had wanted for themselves. You snuffed it out as if it meant nothing. That has to be exhausting."

She glared at him. "You can't make me feel guilty."

"No, I don't think anything will make you feel guilty. I think you're too far gone for that. I think you don't care about anything anymore, except maybe about Lisa? What will this do to her when she finds out?"

"She won't find out," Helen said in horror. "That … That can't happen. No way. I've done everything to make her life easier. I do everything at the shelter to help these women, among budget cuts, abuse, even the women in our home stealing from us." Helen stared at him in horror. "Do you know what it's like to get up in the morning and to find out that they've grabbed all the food in the kitchen and they've run, not a thank-you for the help you've given them, nothing?"

"And maybe they thought that was their only option," he suggested.

"Sure, and then Lisa gets up, and she can't even have a cup of coffee. She spends absolutely every minute of her day at that shelter, making it happen, and everybody has so little regard for her."

"Like you?" he asked immediately. He kept working at the ties behind his back. Yet too many more pokes with that cattle prod, and he would drop. He kept sending messages to Kate. He knew that she couldn't receive them, and he sure as hell couldn't send a location because he had no idea where he was.

I'm free.

He stiffened. *Samantha?*

Yes. Kate found me.

His heart swelled with joy, even as he looked into the eyes of the broken being in front of him. *Good. I'm so happy for you.*

Kate said to tell you that she's coming. And she also said, Don't you dare die on her. *She's on her way. Damn it.* Samantha's voice lightened. *The* damn it *part is hers. I'm on the way to the hospital.* After a moment's silence she whispered, *"Thank you. Please ... be safe."*

And the voice faded away.

He looked around and asked, "Does Lisa even know that

you come here to enact your favorite pastime, so that, when all this revenge is out of your psyche and you're calm, you can go back and deal with those women again, the women you ultimately hated because they got out of the situation and you couldn't? ...Samantha, the woman you've been keeping captive in the shelter?

He took a wild guess at the location, but it made sense now.

Helen stared at him in shock.

Simon nodded. "She's free. Everyone will know what you did. Yet maybe not understanding why you hated those women," he added, nodding gently, wishing this could have ended any other way. "Those women have done everything right to get away. They made it to a women's shelter, where there's supposed to be help for them, and what did you do? You've been making life miserable for them, probably tormenting some of them in your spare time about how it's all their fault, things like that." He noticed how tall and straight Helen stood now that she felt in control, in command. So different from the shell of a hunched-over woman from the shelter. She was very tall, large, and he saw the muscles under her thin jacket. "You like walking around as a man, don't you? Makes you feel safe? In control?"

"Of course, being a woman alone, outside, and unprotected? ... Men will attack you. They don't care. Unless you're bigger than they are. Meaner too. ... That's why I go out, and Lisa stays at the house, where she's safe." Helen's smile hardened. "I have to admit that I think more like a man these days. If it weren't for Lisa, I'd seriously consider taking on that role more and more. Seems to fit me better."

"Besides, that way you can find the aggression inside, the justification to do what you did to the others. You wandered the streets, hating the world, but feeling as if you belong when others see you as male. Not as a woman, a frail female to be victimized. Then, when the frustration and anger builds enough, until you can't stand it anymore," Simon noted, "then you'll kill again."

"You don't know that," Helen cried out. "I treat those women decent. I give them all the help they need. Do you have any idea what it's like, knowing that most of them won't make it, knowing that most of them will go back to their slimy husbands or pimps," she sneered. "They don't have the backbone to do what they need to do."

"Ah, like you do though, right? You have the backbone to take on all these cases of abuse and do what needs to be done, just like me. Apparently I'm one of the worst of the worst, even though I help out at the shelter all the time."

"Yes, oh, Lord, and all the shit you do? You get to stop in, drop off money, and walk away." She was yelling at him now.

And he heard the absolute fury of it all, how she was stuck there, that she couldn't do anything but help these women who didn't appreciate anything she did, whereas he got to drop off money and leave.

Simon nodded. "I hadn't considered it from that point of view, but you're right. It is definitely a challenge some-times, but I also know that the women don't want to see me there. A man is the last thing they need in their world."

Helen cackled. "I'm doing everybody a favor by taking you out." And then she added, "Finally."

"No, you've been holding this as your exit strategy or whatever you want to call it. You've been looking to take me out for years."

"So? So what if I have?" Helen shoved her face in his.

"The fact that Elizabeth preferred you to me?"

"She didn't prefer me to you," he said, with a laugh. "She may have said that at the end to hurt you, but that was never the case. She didn't want anything to do with me. It's one of the reasons why I let her go because you can't keep what isn't meant to stay," he explained gently.

"Sure I can, then I still have them."

"But if they don't want to be there, they're not happy, and, when they aren't there by choice, there's no joy," he explained. "Just like there won't be any joy for you at the end of this."

"No way anybody knows where you are," Helen snapped. "Nobody will find you. Not her and not you."

"Do you really think Kate won't be all over you for this?" he asked, with a smile. "She'll not only find you, she'll find me. And, whether I'm alive or dead, it won't change the fact that she'll hunt you down, and she'll make sure you're put away for life."

As he said that last word, he jumped her. He heard vehicles in the distance, but he was too busy fighting for his life and getting his arm wrapped around Helen's neck, as she was a huge woman, with more muscle than he expected. He was hampered by his bonds. But he knocked the cattle prod from her as he slipped his arms around her neck, shifting behind her body, and pulling her backward off her feet.

In the distance he heard Kate yelling, "Simon, stop."

But he wouldn't stop, he didn't dare stop. Suddenly Kate was there, an arm wrapped around him. "It's okay. It's all right. We got her."

"Well," Simon said, "I'm glad to hear that because I really need to collap ..." And, with that, he closed his eyes and dropped beside Helen.

CHAPTER 23

K ATE STILL WANDERED the hospital halls, waiting for Simon to wake up, already exhausted and knowing this would be the stuff of nightmares for a very long time to come.

Rodney walked up and handed her a cup of coffee. "Has the doctor been in to see him?" he asked her.

"He's in there now," she said.

"Simon will be fine, you know?"

She nodded. "He is. He'll be fine. If nothing else, I just need to see the proof of that myself, and it better be soon."

"You got there before he was killed, and that is pretty freaking huge too."

She nodded. "Once I had a location, it all fit. And I knew he was there. I just had to get there before Helen had her way with him."

"And not in the manner in which that phrase is usually meant."

She rolled her eyes at that. "And hopefully Simon got her to talk because I don't think Helen's too interested in talking to us."

"I'm sure she isn't," Rodney agreed.

Kate gave him a hard glance. "That woman will need a shrink's analysis, and no way in hell anybody'll let Helen go forever."

"We've got her, so you can relax."

She smiled. "Yeah, I hear you," she said, with a pat on his arm. "I can relax, or at least I will relax when we get that far."

He nodded, then the doctor came out and asked, "Detective Morgan?"

She nodded and stepped forward. "How is he?"

"He's been given a pretty hefty dose of ketamine, so it took a bit more to knock him out. I don't know whether he has a stronger stamina or she administered the dose a second time," the doc explained, "but he'll be fine. We're flushing his system right now, and he'll need to stay here, under observation." He smiled at her. "It looks as if you need to go home and get some sleep. Otherwise you'll end up in a bed here beside him."

She smiled at the doctor. "Yeah, that's not happening," she said, with a gentle smile. "But now that I know he'll be okay, can I go see him?"

He raised his eyebrows. "If I say no, will I have an uproar on my hands?" He looked at Rodney for confirmation, and he shrugged. "So, yes, but this is generally family only."

"Well, you can say that," she noted, "or you can let me in, whatever you want do. However, I do have a badge, and I do need to talk to my victim."

He rolled his eyes at that. "Yeah, I'm not stupid enough to stand between the two of you." He pulled the curtain aside and let her in.

She raced in to see a still-groggy Simon, but his eyes were open, and she stared down into his piercing silvery gray eyes, feeling the heat of warm tears in hers. He reached up a hand, and she grabbed it and brought it to her mouth and kissed it gently.

"Jesus Christ," he said, "did you have to cut it so close?"

Tears in her eyes, she nodded. "Yep, it sure seems like I did, doesn't it?"

"But you got there in the end. I told Helen that … you would."

"Did you, indeed?" she asked, with a smile.

"Yeah, I told her that you wouldn't rest until you'd found who'd done this, and, whether you found me dead or alive, Helen had no idea what she was up against because you would never let her see daylight again."

"Nope. Did you hear anything about what it was about?"

He nodded. "Sure did."

As he explained it, she stared down at him in shock. "So really, love unrequited is the bottom line? It's still all about love."

He squeezed her fingers. "And that's why you came after me so fast because you love me. I always knew it." She snorted at that, and his lips twitched. "We'll talk about it tomorrow."

"Or we won't," she muttered. "Either way, you need to sleep."

"Yep, I sure do." Within seconds, he was into a deep snore. She sat beside him, with Rodney at her side, as she explained what little bit Simon had shared, and Rodney shook his head.

"Good Christ, all those deaths."

"Yep, all those deaths."

"And the game?"

"Turns out she was abused and became the abuser. So the Simon Says game was how her family had abused her. So this was just more for herself, getting the revenge she needed. That's why the *game* part didn't make sense to us. This was all about Helen trying to find a way to justify killing people. And it gave her back some control over all the things that had been done to her during her lifetime."

"Do we have her complete history?"

"No, but it won't take too much to bring it up," she noted, with a sigh. "I suspect it'll be the same as what we've already seen on a regular basis. An abusive relationship starting at home in Helen's childhood, quite possibly some of the worst we've ever seen. She linked up with Lisa, as a way to find her soul again, fell in love with Elizabeth, one of the women in the shelter, but was jilted, left behind, and Helen realized that really there was no going forward, ever. To Helen, it would always be a repeat of the same BS."

"Pretty sad and depressing," Rodney noted.

"We'll figure out her whole sordid life story, but it'll be something along those threads," Kate declared.

"It sucks," he murmured. "So much potential and so much pain."

"Yeah, I know," she agreed.

Rodney stood. "Go home. Go home and get some rest. I can stay here if you want."

She looked up at him and smiled. "I'll sit here for a while, just to remind me that Simon is alive and that it will be okay."

He patted her on the back. "You have fun, writing up the reports."

"Hey, I thought we were partners on this one?"

He laughed. "I'm supposed to be playing guardian angel." He shrugged. "Reports? They're all yours." She groaned at that. "But I might be nice and give you a hand."

She smiled. "That's what teamwork's all about."

He stopped at the doorway, smiled and said, "Yeah, and we're damn good at it." And, with that, he was gone.

CHAPTER 24

K ATE WALKED INTO the office the next morning to a round of cheers. She shook her head. "No cheers," she said. "Simon pretty well saved his own sorry ass."

Lilliana laughed. "How's he doing?"

"Well, I saw him this morning." Kate smiled. "He's doing fine, already throwing a fit about having to stay at the hospital, but they'll keep him there for the day, and good luck trying to keep him past that," she stated, with an eye roll.

The sergeant walked in just then. "Seriously, it was all about a love gone wrong?"

She nodded. "Yeah, and we'll have to do a bunch of paperwork and interview Helen, but I talked to Simon earlier this morning, and it was all about Elizabeth Clement apparently."

"How so?"

"Helen fell in love with Elizabeth. They had one night together. Elizabeth was confused, disoriented, and struggling to deal with the loss of her mother, which apparently Helen admitted to Simon that she'd killed Mary as a way to isolate Elizabeth—figuring that she'd be better off to start fresh with Helen somewhere else, not to mention Elizabeth's mother was against their intimate relationship. Instead, of course, her mother's death was so appalling to Elizabeth that she took off and disappeared for years. When she came back some three, four weeks ago, she didn't plan on seeing Helen. It was a case of finding closure and saying goodbye to her mom, visiting the grave. That's what set off Helen this time. As mentioned, she killed five people the first time—those four women on our whiteboard, plus Mary Clement."

"*Great*," Colby said with a headshake. "What a fucked-up world we live in."

"We do, indeed," Kate replied, with a sorrowful look.

"But the good news is, this time the good guys won."

"Although not in time," she noted, "and that'll be some pretty rough phone calls to make to families."

He nodded. "But you've done a great job, Kate. So get the reports done, get some interviews done, and then take a few days off." And, with that, he was gone again.

Lilliana nodded. "Another case will hit us hard and pretty quick," she reminded Kate. "So, if Colby says take a few days, take a few days. Besides, I'm sure Simon will need somebody to look after him for the next day or so."

Kate rolled her eyes at Lilliana's big grin. "Well, Simon might try that, but chances are, he'll be up and raring to go and not listening to anybody."

"But if there is anybody he will listen to, it will be you. So do whatever you need to do and then push off and get a life for a couple days." Lilliana added, "And remember. The whole reason why people go off the rails is because the whole unrequited love thing sucks, and we want to make sure that you and Simon are solid."

Kate laughed at that. "I'd say we're solid, but who knows."

"Exactly. So don't make the same mistakes. Take some time, and enjoy being together."

And that's what she did. It took a little longer than she'd planned to get everything written for the reports and for the last interviews. So, by the time she was done and headed down to the hospital, she heard Simon arguing with the staff about letting him go.

The head nurse saw Kate as she came in, and, with a wash of relief, she muttered, "Well, thank God for that. He's yours. You do with him what you will."

"Can I take him home?" Kate asked.

"Please do," the nurse replied. "It will help us keep our staff here." She turned to Simon, glaring. "You are a terrible patient."

Simon glared right back. But, when he saw Kate, his face wreathed up in smiles, and he opened his arms. She walked over, gave him a hug, and said, "Now get your ass dressed, so I can get you home." He stared at her in delight, and she nodded. "But I had to promise my firstborn to keep you in bed for the next twenty-four hours."

Immediately a wicked grin lit the depths of his eyes, and she rolled her eyes at him, even feeling the heat washing over her face. She murmured, "Yes, I get it. Now, can we go, please?"

And, with that, she headed off to do the discharge paperwork and very quickly had Simon back home again. As she got him into bed and curled up beside him, he asked, "Is it really over?"

"It's really over. Helen will go for a psychiatric assessment to see if she's capable of standing trial, but I'm not too sure how that outcome will progress. Obviously she was cognizant enough to plan all this over the years," she noted, "and I'm sure there are a few threads to tie up still, but, for the most part yeah, it's over with."

"Damn good thing." He yawned, as he pulled her into his arms. "We can talk again, but right now," he muttered, "I need to sleep. Wake me in a little while." And then he opened his eyes and added, "You can wake me in the best way possible, whenever you can."

She chuckled. "Your health first."

"And you know that being in your arms is the best thing for me." Then he yawned and proceeded to sleep.

She lay here for the longest time, wondering at the shift in her own life and how love made such a damn difference. And yet, when it went wrong, it could make such a horrible difference as well. And then she looked over at Simon and decided that he'd had a long-enough nap, so Kate gave him a soul-searing kiss, which brought him awake immediately.

His arms wrapped around her tight. "Okay, that was perfect." He whispered against her lips, "Now on to the rest of our life."

And, with that, he lowered his head and kissed her again.

This concludes Book 6 of Kate Morgan:
Simon Says… Walk.
Read about Kate Morgan: Simon Says… Forgive, Book 7

Simon Says… Forgive: Kate Morgan (Book #7)

Some cases stay with you longer than others. This is one of them for Detective Kate Morgan. That poor child was the worst part. Plus it's one thing to desecrate a church, but it's quite another to commit murder in one—particularly in this manner. Confused, but knowing she must understand the psychology of this killer before she can understand where his next killing ground will take place, Kate buries herself in the case.

Simon is trying to be there to support Kate, but his own world shifts when he's asked to step in to analyze issues in a poker buddy's company, only to have the guy commit suicide soon afterward. Or did he? Between his buddy's issues and the horrific nightmares Simon's dealing with—surrounding Kate and her latest investigation—Simon's life is slowing unravelling too.

Finding the killer is paramount. … Finding him before he annihilates another family? Well, that's a much harder

job. Kate has no choice. … She must stop him before he kills
yet again …

Find Book 7 here!
To find out more visit Dale Mayer's website.
https://geni.us/DMSSSForgive

Sneak Peek from Simon Says... Forgive

Second Week of October

KATE WALKED INTO the office one week later. Sergeant Colby barked at her, "Meeting in five minutes in the conference room."

She nodded, grabbed a coffee, and headed into the conference room. "What's going on?"

"We have three ritualistic murders that we caught today," he stated, with a somber tone.

Her eyes widened. "Three, now, all at once?"

"Three," he emphasized. "Three bodies, one scene, all last night. Bodies were found at six a.m. this morning inside a church."

"Inside a church?" she repeated, her gaze widening.

"Yes, exactly," he confirmed.

"Do we know who the victims are?"

"They're all members of a polygamous group with a self-professed leader," Colby related, with a disgusted tone to his voice.

"So a cult," she said.

"I don't think they consider themselves a cult," he murmured, "although you and I probably would. A large group of them used to be in California. They moved up to BC a good ten, twelve years ago. They've been relatively harmless.

We've never had any issues with them, until now."

"Do we know whether the issue is with them or with somebody else they have issues with?"

He gave her a proud nod. "And that is a very good question, Detective, and you will get a chance to find out for yourself soon."

"In what way?"

"Well, first off, these three bodies have been put on crosses." Colby brought up the images that had been prepped for the meeting.

She winced when she saw two bodies, spread-eagled and nailed, crucified style, to a cross. "Jesus Christ," she muttered, staring at it. "How is it people have time for this shit?"

"It's not even about time. It's all about motivation, and these are the first two." He took a moment, and then he said a bit crossly, "And this next one will get you." And there, in front, was a child. "The only thing I can say about the child is that he appears to have died first and was crucified afterward."

Kate's heart sank, as she stared at the young boy spread-eagled on a cross. He was still in his Mickey Mouse pajamas. Under her breath she whispered, "Fuck. These people are animals."

"As I said, he was killed first, crucified later. Unfortunately for the parents, … I don't think they were given that mercy."

"What church were they found in?" Owen asked.

She looked over at him and nodded. "Yeah, and what location?"

"Inside the Catholic church of the Kerrisdale neighborhood in the city of Vancouver."

"Interesting," she murmured.

"Yeah, also what's interesting was the carving on their bodies."

And, with that, the next image flashed on the screen. *Forgive* was written on the chest of each of the three victims.

Kate sat back, shook her head, and recapped, "Three people dead, left in a church, and a message to forgive," she murmured. "Christ, this one doesn't sound like fun."

Rodney looked over at her, and his lips quirked. "They aren't supposed to be. Remember that."

She rolled her eyes, nodded, and said, "Let's get to work, partner."

Find Book 7 here!

To find out more visit Dale Mayer's website.

https://geni.us/DMSSSForgive

Author's Note

Thank you for reading Simon Says… Walk: Kate Morgan, Book 6! If you enjoyed the book, please take a moment and leave a short review.

Dear reader,

I love to hear from readers, and you can contact me at my website: www.dalemayer.com or at my Facebook author page. To be informed of new releases and special offers, sign up for my newsletter or follow me on BookBub. And if you are interested in joining Dale Mayer's Reader Group, here is the Facebook sign up page.
http://geni.us/DaleMayerFBGroup

Cheers,
Dale Mayer

About the Author

Dale Mayer is a *USA Today* best-selling author, best known for her SEALs military romances, her Psychic Visions series, and her Lovely Lethal Garden cozy series. Her contemporary romances are raw and full of passion and emotion (Broken But … Mending, Hathaway House series). Her thrillers will keep you guessing (Kate Morgan, By Death series), and her romantic comedies will keep you giggling (*It's a Dog's Life*, a stand-alone novella; and the Broken Protocols series, starring Charming Marvin, the cat).

Dale honors the stories that come to her—and some of them are crazy, break all the rules and cross multiple genres!

To go with her fiction, she also writes nonfiction in many different fields, with books available on résumé writing, companion gardening, and the US mortgage system. All her books are available in print and ebook format.

Connect with Dale Mayer Online

Dale's Website – www.dalemayer.com
Twitter – @DaleMayer
Facebook Page – geni.us/DaleMayerFBFanPage
Facebook Group – geni.us/DaleMayerFBGroup
BookBub – geni.us/DaleMayerBookbub
Instagram – geni.us/DaleMayerInstagram
Goodreads – geni.us/DaleMayerGoodreads
Newsletter – geni.us/DaleNews

Also by Dale Mayer

Published Adult Books:

Shadow Recon

Magnus, Book 1

Rogan, Book 2

Egan, Book 3

Bullard's Battle

Ryland's Reach, Book 1

Cain's Cross, Book 2

Eton's Escape, Book 3

Garret's Gambit, Book 4

Kano's Keep, Book 5

Fallon's Flaw, Book 6

Quinn's Quest, Book 7

Bullard's Beauty, Book 8

Bullard's Best, Book 9

Bullard's Battle, Books 1–2

Bullard's Battle, Books 3–4

Bullard's Battle, Books 5–6

Bullard's Battle, Books 7–8

Terkel's Team

Damon's Deal, Book 1

Wade's War, Book 2

Gage's Goal, Book 3

Calum's Contact, Book 4

Rick's Road, Book 5

Scott's Summit, Book 6

Brody's Beast, Book 7

Terkel's Twist, Book 8

Terkel's Triumph, Book 9

Terkel's Guardian

Radar, Book 1

Kate Morgan

Simon Says… Hide, Book 1

Simon Says… Jump, Book 2

Simon Says… Ride, Book 3

Simon Says… Scream, Book 4

Simon Says… Run, Book 5

Simon Says… Walk, Book 6

Simon Says… Forgive, Book 7

Hathaway House

Aaron, Book 1

Brock, Book 2

Cole, Book 3

Denton, Book 4

Elliot, Book 5

Finn, Book 6

Gregory, Book 7

Heath, Book 8

Iain, Book 9

Jaden, Book 10

Kyron, Book 15

Jenner, Book 16

Rhys, Book 17

Landon, Book 18

Harper, Book 19

Kascius, Book 20

The K9 Files, Books 1–2

The K9 Files, Books 3–4

The K9 Files, Books 5–6

The K9 Files, Books 7–8

The K9 Files, Books 9–10

The K9 Files, Books 11–12

Lovely Lethal Gardens

Arsenic in the Azaleas, Book 1

Bones in the Begonias, Book 2

Corpse in the Carnations, Book 3

Daggers in the Dahlias, Book 4

Evidence in the Echinacea, Book 5

Footprints in the Ferns, Book 6

Gun in the Gardenias, Book 7

Handcuffs in the Heather, Book 8

Ice Pick in the Ivy, Book 9

Jewels in the Juniper, Book 10

Killer in the Kiwis, Book 11

Lifeless in the Lilies, Book 12

Murder in the Marigolds, Book 13

Nabbed in the Nasturtiums, Book 14

Offed in the Orchids, Book 15

Poison in the Pansies, Book 16

Quarry in the Quince, Book 17

Revenge in the Roses, Book 18

Silenced in the Sunflowers, Book 19

Toes up in the Tulips, Book 20

Uzi in the Urn, Book 21

Lovely Lethal Gardens, Books 1–2

Lovely Lethal Gardens, Books 3–4

Lovely Lethal Gardens, Books 5–6

Lovely Lethal Gardens, Books 7–8

Lovely Lethal Gardens, Books 9–10

Psychic Visions Series

Tuesday's Child

Hide 'n Go Seek

Maddy's Floor

Garden of Sorrow

Knock Knock…

Rare Find

Eyes to the Soul

Now You See Her

Shattered

Into the Abyss

Seeds of Malice

Eye of the Falcon

Itsy-Bitsy Spider

Unmasked

Deep Beneath

From the Ashes

Stroke of Death

Ice Maiden

Snap, Crackle…

What If…

Talking Bones

String of Tears

Inked Forever

Psychic Visions Books 1–3

Psychic Visions Books 4–6

Psychic Visions Books 7–9

By Death Series

Touched by Death

Haunted by Death

Chilled by Death

By Death Books 1–3

Broken Protocols – Romantic Comedy Series

Cat's Meow

Cat's Pajamas

Cat's Cradle

Cat's Claus

Broken Protocols 1-4

Broken and… Mending

Skin

Scars

Scales (of Justice)

Broken but… Mending 1-3

Glory

Genesis

Tori

Celeste

Glory Trilogy

Biker Blues

Morgan: Biker Blues, Volume 1

Cash: Biker Blues, Volume 2

SEALs of Honor

Mason: SEALs of Honor, Book 1

Hawk: SEALs of Honor, Book 2

Dane: SEALs of Honor, Book 3

Swede: SEALs of Honor, Book 4

Shadow: SEALs of Honor, Book 5

Cooper: SEALs of Honor, Book 6

Markus: SEALs of Honor, Book 7

Evan: SEALs of Honor, Book 8

Mason's Wish: SEALs of Honor, Book 9

Chase: SEALs of Honor, Book 10

Brett: SEALs of Honor, Book 11

Devlin: SEALs of Honor, Book 12

Easton: SEALs of Honor, Book 13

Ryder: SEALs of Honor, Book 14

Macklin: SEALs of Honor, Book 15

Corey: SEALs of Honor, Book 16

Warrick: SEALs of Honor, Book 17

Tanner: SEALs of Honor, Book 18

Heroes for Hire

Heroes for Hire, Books 19–21

Heroes for Hire, Books 22–24

SEALs of Steel

Badger: SEALs of Steel, Book 1

Erick: SEALs of Steel, Book 2

Cade: SEALs of Steel, Book 3

Talon: SEALs of Steel, Book 4

Laszlo: SEALs of Steel, Book 5

Geir: SEALs of Steel, Book 6

Jager: SEALs of Steel, Book 7

The Final Reveal: SEALs of Steel, Book 8

SEALs of Steel, Books 1–4

SEALs of Steel, Books 5–8

SEALs of Steel, Books 1–8

The Mavericks

Kerrick, Book 1

Griffin, Book 2

Jax, Book 3

Beau, Book 4

Asher, Book 5

Ryker, Book 6

Miles, Book 7

Nico, Book 8

Keane, Book 9

Lennox, Book 10

Gavin, Book 11

Shane, Book 12

Diesel, Book 13

Jerricho, Book 14

Killian, Book 15

Hatch, Book 16

Corbin, Book 17

Aiden, Book 18

The Mavericks, Books 1–2

The Mavericks, Books 3–4

The Mavericks, Books 5–6

The Mavericks, Books 7–8

The Mavericks, Books 9–10

The Mavericks, Books 11–12

Standalone Novellas

It's a Dog's Life

Riana's Revenge

Second Chances

Published Young Adult Books:

Family Blood Ties Series

Vampire in Denial

Vampire in Distress

Vampire in Design

Vampire in Deceit

Vampire in Defiance

Vampire in Conflict

Vampire in Chaos

Vampire in Crisis

Vampire in Control

Vampire in Charge

Family Blood Ties Set 1–3

Family Blood Ties Set 1–5

Family Blood Ties Set 4–6

Family Blood Ties Set 7–9

Sian's Solution, A Family Blood Ties Series Prequel
Novelette

Design series

Dangerous Designs

Deadly Designs

Darkest Designs

Design Series Trilogy

Standalone

In Cassie's Corner

Gem Stone (a Gemma Stone Mystery)

Time Thieves

Published Non-Fiction Books:

Career Essentials

Career Essentials: The Résumé

Career Essentials: The Cover Letter

Career Essentials: The Interview

Career Essentials: 3 in 1

www.ingramcontent.com/pod-product-compliance
Lightning Source LLC
Chambersburg PA
CBHW061054210726
48294CB00001B/150